## LETTICE COOPER

was born of Yorkshire parents in Eccles, Lancashire in 1897, the eldest child of Leonard Cooper, a constructional engineer, and Agnes Helena Fraser. The family lived near Leeds, Yorkshire, and, from the age of seven, Lettice Cooper wrote and told stories. She was educated by a governess and then at a Southbourne boarding school, before studying Classics at Oxford. On graduation she returned home to the family engineering firm.

In 1925 Lettice Cooper published her first novel, *The Lighted Room*, one of ten novels written whilst she was in Yorkshire. The last of these, *National Provincial* (1938), captured the imagination of many, including Lady Rhondda, who invited her to join the staff of *Time and Tide*. Lettice Cooper went to live with her sister in Bayswater, London, and spent a year as Associate Editor of the magazine. War intervened and she took a post in the Public Relations Division of the Ministry of Food and worked also for Civil Defence. At the end of the War she and her sister moved to West Hampstead and the appearance of *Black Bethlehem* in 1947 marked her return to writing. That year Lettice Cooper became fiction reviewer for the *Yorkshire Post*, a position she held for a decade. During the same period she began to visit Florence yearly and continued to do so until the 1970s.

A lifelong socialist, Lettice Cooper's writing career has spanned more than sixty years. She has published twenty novels, in addition to children's books and non-fiction, including biographies of Dickens and Robert Louis Stevenson. In 1972 she was one of the five founding members of the Writer's Action Group, who successfully established Public Lending Right. From 1976–8 she was President of the English Centre of PEN. She was awarded the Order of the British Empire in 1978. Her most recent novel, *Unusual Behaviour*, was published in 1986. Lettice Cooper continues to live in West Hampstead.

Virago also publishes *The New House* (1937).

VIRAGO
MODERN
CLASSIC

NUMBER
264

# LETTICE COOPER

# FENNY

WITH A NEW INTRODUCTION BY

FRANCIS KING

DEDICATED TO

## MARY CHRISTINE BRETTELL

*"Telly"*

Published by VIRAGO PRESS Limited 1987
41 William IV Street, London WC2N 4DB

First published in Great Britain by Victor Gollancz Ltd 1953
Copyright 1953 by Lettice Cooper
Introduction Copyright © Francis King 1987

*British Library Cataloguing in Publication Data*

Cooper, Lettice
    Fenny.—(Virago modern classics).
    I. Title
    823'.912[F]      PR6005.04977

    ISBN 0-86068-881-X

Printed in Great Britain by
Cox & Wyman Ltd. of Reading, Berkshire

# INTRODUCTION

Born of Yorkshire parents in Lancashire in 1897, Lettice Cooper has had a writing career that has confidently spanned more than sixty years. What at once emerges from any retrospect not merely of her novels but of her two detective stories, her biographies of Robert Louis Stevenson and Dickens, and her fourteen books for children, is a consistency of style, of moral outlook and, above all, of quality. The works of her eighth and ninth decades are in no appreciable way different from those of her fourth and fifth.

Long before it had become fashionable to say that the Two Nations in Great Britain were not the rich and the poor but the North and the South, Lettice Cooper had used this division as a recurrent theme—contrasting the stolid, reliable, emotionally reticent people among whom she had grown up and worked for a while in the family business (her father was a constructional engineer), with the more demonstrative, flighty and exuberant Londoners among whom she went to make her career as a novelist, reviewer and, briefly, associate editor of Lady Rhondda's *Time and Tide*. (The implication of the title—"Time and Tide wait for no man"—was of course far more defiantly controversial in the Thirties than today.)

In *Fenny* Lettice Cooper extended this theme of the division between North and South, no longer applying it to her native Lancashire and her adopted London but to England and Italy. In this, she was following the lead of a number of novelists before her, most notably E. M. Forster. But whereas in *Where Angels Fear to Tread* Forster constantly juxtaposes the emotional deadness of his "Sawston" with the emotional vivacity of his "Monteriano", Lettice Cooper's Italians differ from his in all too rarely feeling the emotions to which they lay such extravagant claim—at one moment eliciting from Fenny the comment "How boring it is sometimes when there is such a gap between how people feel and how they say they feel!" But if Lettice Cooper cannot be regarded as being any more in love with her Lucrezia or her Erinia—each a selfishly manipulative Italian woman—than her Fenny is, there cannot be any doubt that, like her Fenny, she is in love with Florence in particular and with Italy in general.

To be in love with Florence today is not, despite its abiding beauty, all that easy. But in the immediate aftermath of the war, when both Lettice Cooper and I, then unknown to each other, spent extended periods there, not to fall in love with the city was impossible. Lettice Cooper used to go to stay with Lionel Fielden—a former BBC employee, friend of E. M. Forster and J. R. Ackerley, who had been seconded to set up All India Radio—in the beautiful villa that, on his premature retirement, he had bought at Antella, a few miles outside Florence. As soon as, some thirty ago, I first began to read Lettice Cooper's description of the "Villa Meridiana", at which Fenny, then a young, unsophisticated, ardent North Country girl, arrives to work as governess, I at once exclaimed to myself "But this is Lionel's villa!" I, too, like Fenny and her creator, had stood at one of its upstairs windows to gaze down at "the serene lines of the Tuscan hills folded in like a stage set to enclose the formal garden". I, too, had walked beside the tiered vines, running between the corn "like stripes on a print". Darkly, beguilingly and loftily handsome, Fielden might easily have been mistaken for some Old Harrovian cricket-playing maharajah. His capricious and moody character was totally unlike Lettice Cooper's straight and staunch one. One guesses that, as so often in personal relationships, it was the differences between them that, paradoxically, cemented their friendship so indissolubly.

For me one of the major pleasures of a rereading of *Fenny* has been its evocation of that Florence now destroyed by crowds, pollution and noise. Unharassed by hordes of tourists, Fenny and her friends wander the golden city and the countryside around it; dine in small, cheap *trattorie*; consume ice-creams at Doney; watch an English company performing *Twelfth Night* in the Boboli Gardens. Nowadays almost everyone travels abroad from such an early age that Fenny's excitement as she waits, "a starter poised for a race", to leave the train that has brought her to the city from which even a world war will not prise her away, might be mistaken by the young for that of a girl not of this century but of the last. "In the clear light and the warm sun, some heaviness … dropped from her spirit." She has left behind her "the northern industrial town where beauty was incidental and happiness a by-product". All at once, what have only been names in books and on maps—the Duomo, the Signoria, the

Arno—assume magical substance for her. Surprised by joy, she eagerly reaches out to it. That, in the years ahead, she should suffer so many disappointments and yet never become embittered, never lose her faith in life, never (most important of all) lose her faith in herself, is what makes her such an admirable and appealing character.

Fenny's real name is Ellen Fenwick. That she should be known to her charges as Fenny and should continue to be known as that to them long after they have passed from her care, indicates the cruelly ambiguous nature of her status. Were she a member of either of the families for which she works in succession, she would be Ellen. Were she an independent outsider, she would be Miss or Signorina Fenwick. A nickname, used alike by her employers and their children, makes it constantly clear that she is neither of these things. Because she is not sufficiently ruthless, wary and cunning, she loses the first man whom she loves. Because she is too honourable, she loses the second. Her only children are the children of her employers and, later, an orphaned Italian boy whom she adopts. Yet, like the nanny "Simpson" in Edward Sackville-West's unjustly half-forgotten novel of that name, she finds in her surrogate children a satisfaction denied to many real mothers. She even comes to accept with calm resignation that the gratitude and affection with which "Old Fenny" is at first remembered will eventually become little more than a sense of obligation. "One has to have somebody to worry about," she tells herself at one moment, patiently and even gratefully shouldering the worry that her former charges cause her. She no longer dares to tell herself "One has to have somebody to love."

*Fenny* is in no way an autobiographical novel. Its protagonist, working as a school-teacher, a governess and a clerk in a travel agency, has none of her creator's intellectual distinction. Had Fenny returned from Italy at the outbreak of the war, instead of staying on there and suffering internment, she might indeed have been recruited into the Ministry of Food, like Lettice Cooper. But it is doubtful if she would have become a public relations officer. It is even more doubtful if, like Lettice Cooper, she would ever have become a weekly reviewer of fiction for the *Yorkshire Post*. Certainly she would never have become President of the English Centre of PEN, chairing its meetings with a robust mixture of tolerance, common sense and firmness. (After Lettice Cooper and the historian Jasper Ridley had attended a PEN Congress in Stockholm, a Swedish writer remarked to me "They are exactly what we think the English *ought* to be like—and so seldom are.")

But, although Fenny is not a self-portrait, there are nonetheless certain basic similarities between the fictional woman and the real one. Fenny and her creator share a moral sturdiness; a refusal to be shocked by any oddities or even aberrations of human behaviour; a relaxed and quiet courage; an ability to find consolatory pleasures in life even at times of grievous disappointment or sorrow. For a long period in the years between the wars, Lettice Cooper underwent psychoanalysis. Yet no one whom I know has a personality more firmly and surely integrated. Either she had a remarkable analyst or she is a woman of remarkable character. I opt for the second of these alternatives. When her beloved sister Barbara, with whom she had lived in Hampstead for more than forty years, died in 1981, many of her friends, myself among them, feared a crack-up. But just as Fenny has the inner strength to survive her losses, so Lettice Cooper had the inner strength to survive hers. "It was her nature to shove off quickly when she had run aground on unhappiness." The statement is as true of Fenny's creator as of Fenny. Neither would give way for long to the desperate pessimism of the young painter Daniel, who unburdens himself to Fenny, already in love with him, about "the terrible isolation of being alive, and the pointlessness of it, and the certainty of death being the only certainty".

Fenny and Lettice Cooper also resemble each other in the vividness and immediacy of their sympathy for the young. Soon after I read *Desirable Residence*, written by Lettice Cooper in her mid-eighties, I read the latest work of a famous novelist in his mid-sixties. It was the novelist in his mid-sixties who seemed to me to have been marooned by time on a bleak island of his own, from which he could only peer through binoculars, with fastidious and uncomprehending distaste, at the antics of a younger generation on the mainland. Lettice Cooper has always been there on the mainland with that younger generation, sharing in all its excitements, apprehensions and joys. Into her ninth decade she has preserved intact a sense of adventure and enterprise.

It was that sense of adventure and enterprise that led to one of the more amusing incidents of her early literary career. Reading that her then publishers, Hodder & Stoughton, were offering a prize of one thousand pounds for a novel on a religious theme, she sat down and wrote *The Ship of Truth* and then submitted it under a pseudonym. She was the victor. Hodder were less than pleased to discover that, instead of acquiring a new author, they had to pay out far more money than usual to an author already on their list. Decades later it was that same sense of adventure and enterprise that led her to respond so readily to Maureen Duffy's and Brigid Brophy's appeal to join their Writers' Action Group, of which I also was a founder member, and to exert herself so vigorously and effectively in our campaign for Public Lending Right. In arguing a case that, surprisingly, had opponents even among librarians and among writers now only too happy to receive their annual cheques, she was always trenchant but never ill-tempered or aggressive.

There is a candour and directness in *Fenny*, as in all Lettice Cooper's novels. There is also the ability to make a point unshowily but with telling impact in a single sentence or even phrase. "The kind of face that suggests a daughter taking after her father ..." "She was like someone hit by a wave and unable to see clearly until the water ran out of her eyes ..." "Unhappiness and perplexity came from him like a smell ..." Here is not merely a highly professional writer but a born one.

This novel is published to celebrate Lettice Cooper's ninetieth birthday. One can only wish her many happy returns of her novels in further editions, to delight generation after generation of readers.

*Francis King, London, 1986*

# PART I

1933

# CHAPTER I

Ellen Fenwick first came to the Villa Meridiana in April. Long before the train ran into the station at Florence she had been sitting on the edge of the seat, a starter poised for a race, handbag, overcoat and umbrella disposed on one arm, so as to leave the other free for her luggage. She recognized that she had not the same grip on the *wagon-lit* attendant as the companion who had shared her sleeper as far as Pisa. This woman, the wife of an hotel-keeper in Lucca, with a daughter married in England, had chattered to her in bad English ever since they found themselves in the same compartment at Calais, but she was a hardened traveller, who with one wave of her hand in its tight black glove subdued the unknown terrors of the journey and left Ellen free for enjoyment. Replying "Yes!" "Really?" "Do you?", "That must be nice for your daughter!", she sucked into her eyes the mountains of Northern Italy, the pink farms, and the interrupted glimpses of the sea, appearing between the rattling tunnels.

Now it was dark, and she was alone. To watch the Signora, who had been her family in space for twenty-four hours, stump away under the platform lights of Pisa between her husband and son who had come to meet her, was for Ellen the final parting from home.

As soon as the train left Pisa she opened the door of the *cabinet de toilette* and looked at herself in the mirror, partly to make sure that she was tidy, partly to reaffirm her identity. The mirror showed her an image which to eyes whose horizon was already widening appeared slightly comic. She had not cut her hair short, in the fashion, but wore it in two thick plaits, coiled over her ears. The new felt hat, which in the shop had seemed to settle harmoniously on the coils, now proved only to be comfortable if she allowed it to slip forward over her nose. She pushed it back, relentlessly driving the hairpins into her ears. The lifted brim exposed a candid forehead, delicate eyebrows and grey eyes, smudged beneath with fatigue and strain. The cheeks were too thin for the bone-structure of nose and chin. It was the kind of face that suggests a daughter taking after her father. Ellen, when

11

she looked at it again, always hoped that it would have improved since her last inspection, but did not often think that it had.

She put a finger under one hairpin and tried to relieve the pressure, but as soon as she removed the finger the hat drove the hairpin back. Well, she must suffer so as to arrive looking like a suitable governess, and perhaps at the villa she need not wear a hat. Mrs. Rivers had written that they were five miles out of Florence. She hoped that Miss Fenwick liked a country life.

Ellen had made an imaginary picture of Mrs. Rivers, seeing her, the mother with the little girl, an authoritative figure, much older and wiser than herself, invulnerable, the mother seen by the little girl. Ever since Lady Gressingham had told her that Madeleine Rivers was Rose Danby's daughter, the image had crystallized into something like Rose Danby's stage presence. This had been for Ellen the thing that clinched her decision to take the job for the summer. She had looked blank with astonishment when Lady Gressingham, telling her about Madeleine Rivers, had added, "Poor girl! It's not so easy, you know," the old woman remarked, "to be a famous person's child." But, Ellen thought, so interesting! She had always been stage-struck. The treats that she had enjoyed most from her first pantomime had been visits to the theatre. Rose Danby, whom she had seen whenever she had an opportunity, had stimulated her sense of life as it really was but was so seldom allowed to be. This made the prospect of six months in a villa in Italy as governess to Rose Danby's granddaughter so dazzling and so unlike anything that had ever happened to her as to outweigh the inevitable terrors of one desperately home-bound for seven years.

Besides, if she did not make a break now, when would she? "Are you wise," her mother's friends said, "to throw up a permanent position for a temporary one? Is it a good thing to let your place at the High School be filled, even for a term? Suppose they decide to keep on your substitute?" To her mother's friends, Ellen was always a girl doing her best, but not to be expected to do it well. To her headmistress Ellen's sudden desire to go abroad for a summer after her mother's death appeared a mild form of illness, the result of shock, which she treated with the sane and liberal understanding that Ellen had always admired and suddenly found intolerable. Only Alice, who would miss her most, said "Go!"—but Alice was fond of her.

Well, Ellen thought, suppose they don't want me back? Do I really want to stay here until the Board present me with a cheque and a set of coffee-cups? Until I am the only one on the staff who remembers the old girls when they come to their daughters' prize-giving? Is Ainley the world? Here, in this swaying train between two unknown foreign stations, at least it was not. The excitement that had been working in her all through the journey made her courage rise. Even if, by some mischance, nobody met her at the station—a possibility that had haunted her for several days—she had money, she had an Italian phrase-book; she was not a child! With resolution she shut the door of the cabinet on the face in the mirror that still betrayed some qualms, and collected her things.

She thought at first that there *was* no one to meet her. She stood on the platform by her suit-cases, and the mob of chattering, gesticulating Italians swept round and past her as if she were a stone dividing a stream. As the platform began to clear she saw a man unmistakably English hurrying towards her. In that second of impact before the whole stranger is refracted through speech, her impression of Charles Rivers, beyond the obvious facts that he was of medium height and broadly built, sunburnt and dressed in casual clothes, was that he was exasperated. At once she felt in some way at fault; perhaps, after all, her train was late, or she should have gone down to the barrier. As soon as he smiled and spoke to her cordially, the impression receded.

"Miss Fenwick? I thought you must be. I'm Charles Rivers. My wife was so very sorry she couldn't come down to meet you. Some people turned up unexpectedly for a drink and stayed late. I do hope you've had a good journey? Are these all your things?"

A porter appeared and swept her suit-cases on to a barrow. Mr. Rivers took her coat over his arm and said, "Got your ticket?" With relief she felt herself out of her own charge and in capable hands.

It was so much more of a relief than she would have been willing to admit that she felt dazed, and, as if half under an anæsthetic, heard her own voice replying that she had slept pretty

13

well in the *wagon-lit*, that her companion had been an Italian woman who got out at Pisa, that she had never been to Italy before, only once some years ago for a holiday to Belgium, and once to Paris for a week.

"I think you'll like it here," Mr. Rivers said as he shut her into the car and got in beside her.

The strange city through which they drove was the scenery of a dream. She saw tall, flat-fronted houses with shuttered windows, stone façades lit by street lamps. Mr. Rivers said, "The *Duomo*—the Cathedral," and she peered at a mass of building, improbably striped black and white—not her idea of cathedrals. It was only when she caught a glimpse of the arches of a bridge, of lights reflected in flowing water, and her companion said, "The Arno," that expectation burst in her like a bubble; what had been names and distance on the map suddenly assumed substance. She thought, This is Florence. I'm here! and longed for Alice rather than for a stranger with whom she was not yet ready to share her excitement.

As they emerged from the main streets and drove along the Lung'arno between the river and the houses, he began to talk to her about Juliet.

"I think you'll find her nice to teach. She's very bright—at least, we think so. I suppose she may be just like any other kid of eight, really."

At once Mr. Rivers slipped into focus. He was no longer a stranger, but a parent. Strangers might be formidable; but parents, with their assumed deprecation, their barely concealed conviction that their children were never ordinary, were not strangers: they were an annexe to what had been her life for seven years.

"I'm very much looking forward to seeing Juliet. Will she be up?"

"No, we thought you'd like to have your first evening in peace. Besides, it's rather late for her. She's been ill, you know. I expect Madeleine told you. She had a very bad go of measles and middle-ear trouble in February, and she's still a bit thin and tearful, not quite like herself. So we thought she should have a summer out of London, somewhere where we could be sure of the sun. Madeleine needed a holiday, too, after nursing her. And then

Helena Gressingham offered to lend us this villa; much too good an offer to refuse, as you'll see tomorrow."

"I've seen pictures of it."

She could see them now hanging on the faded green distemper of the schoolroom at Hawton Towers. To remember them brought back the smells of blackboard chalk and toast made by the fire. Those pictures had seemed to her so beautiful, the sky so blue, the big white house with its square, red-roofed tower a house in a fairy-tale, unlike any house she knew in the Northern county of grey stone. They had certainly played their part with Rose Danby in deciding her to come to the villa.

"Oh, those dreadful water-colours of Violet's!"

"Are they dreadful?"

He laughed.

"Well, didn't you think so?"

She could not explain that she had never seen them out of her own imagined context. She only said lamely:

"They were in the schoolroom at Hawton Towers."

"Yes, I'm sure they were!" He added, with a faint inflexion of surprise, "You know the Gressinghams quite well, don't you?"

"My father was the doctor for a big, scattered practice that included Hawton. I did lessons at the Towers with Angela Gressingham for two years before she went away to school. Since my father died and we moved into Ainley and Angela got married, I haven't been there so often, but I go over whenever Angela comes up to stay. Lady Gressingham has always been very kind to me." With an effort she added formally, "I was most grateful to her for recommending me for this post."

"She told us that we were very lucky to get you, and I'm sure we are."

They had crossed the river by a bridge, and seemed to be climbing steadily, a narrow road between the high walls of gardens and houses. Once they were crowded—Ellen thought that they would be crushed—into the wall by a car tearing down towards them at breakneck speed. She sagged now with fatigue, her head felt too heavy for her neck and her eyelids dropped. The journey had become a journey outside place and time. She could

15

not remember the beginning nor imagine the end. It merged with a journey out of childhood; she was back again in the big car that was bringing her home from the Towers after Angela's Christmas Party. Nearly lost in her mother's old fur coat that came down to her ankles, she hugged on her knee beneath it her present from the Christmas tree. They drove over a patch of moorland, and a blizzard swept across, plastering the window of the car with half-frozen snow. She saw the windscreen wiper climbing heavily under a wedge of snow, and heard old Carter grumbling to himself behind the wheel. Her feet in their bronze sandals were numb with cold, her nose and ears felt icy. She began to be frightened and to feel that she would never get home: the car would be stuck in the snow up here on the moors, and only after the thaw would her dead body and Carter's be found. Then, almost before she realized it, they were off the moor. The wheels were crackling on the ice in the village street; she saw the shape of the church thickened by snow; the Vicarage buried in snow-bushes; their own house with the curtains drawn back to show the lights, and as the car drew up, the door opened and her mother stood in the lighted doorway. Now, as she half woke, half dozed again, the two journeys were still confused, and she did not know if she were going towards an old or a new homecoming.

Mr. Rivers' voice saying, "Well, here we are," jerked her into the present. She stumbled out of the car, and stood on a sweep of gravel, feeling the air cool against her cheeks. In the pale façade that rose above them an archway sprang into light. Looking through, Ellen saw what seemed to her like the quadrangle of a college with round pillars, a vaulted cloister and pale walls. Servants—a man in a white coat, a girl with swinging print skirts —came to take the luggage.

Mr. Rivers said something to them in Italian of which she understood only, "The Signorina Fenwick from England." To her, "This is Ofelia. This is Gastone." Their welcoming smiles made her feel as if they were really glad to see her. "They'll bring all your things."

She walked beside him across the courtyard, roofless except for the cloister running down one side. Before they reached the door in the opposite wall it opened. A young woman, pretty as a

16

flowering tree, stood in the doorway, holding out both hands in a graceful gesture of welcome.

"Here you are, my dear! I'm so glad to see you. Welcome to your new home."

## CHAPTER II

"THAT'S ALL for this morning," Ellen said.

Juliet pushed her exercise book away and slid off her chair.

"Shall we go out now?"

"We'll just put the books away first."

"Then will you tell me some more about the girls at the High School?"

"If you like."

"Oh, I *do* like!"

Juliet skipped up and down. Her short plaits, with their scarlet bows, danced on her shoulders. Ellen had expected Madeleine Rivers' daughter to be fair, but the little girl whose head came round the door when her breakfast tray appeared on her first morning was dark, just beginning to grow leggy, with childish features still undefined. Ellen's first impression of her face had been of the very clear blue whites round her bright, well-opened brown eyes.

"Tell me some more about the play in the garden when the donkey's head got stuck!"

Ellen was kneeling on the floor before one of the low cupboards under the bookshelves. The library, being both scholastic and likely to be cool in hot weather, had been allotted to them for a schoolroom. They worked at the table where old Sir Robert Gressingham had gone through the farm accounts with his bailiff and sat late into the night reading the books on astronomy and astrology which filled half one side of the room. It was he, Mr. Rivers said, who had cut the narrow door in the outer wall so that he could step straight out on to the English lawn that he had made and look at the stars.

Juliet, with a pile of books in her arms, stood just behind her governess's neat back, looking down at the white shirt firmly and evenly tucked into the belt of the grey tweed skirt. A hair-pin fell out of one of Miss Fenwick's coils of hair and tinkled on the polished floor. She picked it up and put it back in the same place.

"Mummie would like to cut all your hair off! She says it's dowdy! But *I* think it's beautiful! Your plaits must be much longer than mine. Can I see them down your back some time? Grannie Rose has long hair. I don't like prominent waves."

"The word is permanent. It means that they last."

Ellen knelt for an instant without moving, feeling the first faint breath of chill on her glowing happiness. But not to take too much notice of things that children repeated was a piece of wisdom bought by her years of experience.

"Just a minute, Juliet. I want to make some more room in here for our books. Your mother said we could have the whole of this cupboard, but there's something stuck in this corner. Ah!"

She dragged out a ball of dust fixed in a hoop of metal to a dusty stand with a coiled flex clotted with dust and cobwebs.

"It's only a dirty old lamp!"

"Yes, but look!"

With the duster they had been using for the books, Ellen wiped off the thick coating. The lamp was a globe of the hemisphere made of dark blue glass, with clear glass for the stars.

"It's a map, do you see? A map of the sky with all the stars. We can plug it in somewhere, and they'll light up, and then we shall be able to find them in the sky."

"Is that a map? It's got no countries."

"There may be countries on all those stars. They may each be a world."

"Who lives there?"

"We don't know. We don't know much about them yet."

"But you know a lot of things," Juliet said kindly. "I like doing lessons with you better than school."

"I'm glad you do. I like teaching you very much."

The door in the wall opened and Charles Rivers put his head in.

"Have you done with her, Miss Fenwick? Juliet, there's a new calf in the Mandini shed, born this morning. Would you like to come and see him?"

18

Juliet skipped towards him, catching hold of his hand. To go anywhere with her father was always a treat, but she hung back in the doorway.

"Can Miss Fenwick come, too?"

"Of course, if she wants to."

"You show it to me another time, Juliet."

"She's glad to be rid of you for a bit," Charles said without conviction, and Juliet laughed at a good joke.

But it was true that Ellen was glad to be alone. This was only her third morning at the villa, and she needed frequent intervals of solitude, for she could hardly contain all the enchantment of her new life. It had begun on the first morning when she woke at dawn and saw the light coming between the curtains. She had jumped out of bed, sodden with sleep, and stumbled across to the window to see this unknown country which at bedtime the night before had only been darkness pricked by sparse lights. Now she saw that the villa stood on the crest of a hill with a valley below and the land rising beyond it. The serene lines of the Tuscan hills folded in like a stage set to enclose the formal garden, that sloped from beneath her window to a low wall. There were a few farms in the valley, and pale villas in clumps of trees spaced here and there on the hillsides, but no walls or hedges divided the fields, neatly patterned with the young veridian of corn or vine, broken by rows of silvery olives, or by the sharp, dark exclamation mark of a cypress. As yet untouched by sunlight, the scene lay in suspension, strange but familiar, so that Ellen, while transported with delight, felt at the same time that there was, after all, really no such thing as going abroad. She huddled back into bed again, and was asleep almost as soon as the bedclothes touched her chin, with that first half-waking vision of Tuscany printed for ever on her mind.

She stood now by the mahogany table holding the cold glass globe between her hands, fascinated by this solid piece of the magic. She stared into it as if it were a crystal and she might see in it what was going to happen to her in this new life. She could not believe that nothing would happen, that she would just teach Juliet for six months and go back to the Ainley High School in September. Already she felt different—in the clear light and the warm sun some heaviness had dropped from her body and spirit.

She felt like a balloon filling with air, ready to take off. In need of anchorage, for she had been brought up to suspect pleasure, she looked down at the exercise book on the table whose first pages were covered with Juliet's round hand. She picked up a pen and corrected a spelling mistake, then put the book away with the others, lifted the globe on to the window-ledge and went out to stroll in the sun on the English lawn.

From the lawn steps led down to the vegetable garden, a patch stolen from the farm where, between the olives year after year old Giovanni, who was both caretaker and gardener, planted tomatoes and artichokes for the family, although since Sir Robert's death they had never come to eat them. He came up now with a basket of salad for the kitchen. His face, which, like his clothes, was the colour of the Tuscan soil, crinkled into a smile of greeting. He answered Ellen's *"Buon giorno"* with a long sentence in Italian, which seemed to be about the weather. *"Non capisco,"* she said— it was one of the first things she had learned—*"Non capisco"*; but he only smiled and nodded, as though a necessary courtesy had been exchanged; what she had understood was his good will and the rest did not matter. After he had gone round the corner of the house to the kitchen, his wife, Angelina, a little old woman who seemed to live always in the same dark blue dress faded by the sun nearly to lavender, came out of the door of their house in the north wall of the villa. She carried a bowl full of scraps for her one hen, a precious fowl which roosted in the wood beyond the garden gate. On her way back with the empty bowl she, too, greeted Ellen, and told her something, waving her hand from the bowl to the hen, now picking pompously among the scraps. Ellen nodded and smiled and this time did not trouble to say, *"Non capisco"*, which in a way was not true, for she understood that Angelina, like Giovanni, was pleased to see so much company again after the years when they had lived like two mice in the corner of the empty house.

She saw a fair head and a pale blue sweater underneath the olive-trees. Madeleine Rivers came up the steps to the lawn, and Ellen went to meet her. It was perhaps the greatest part of her happiness that not only was Juliet such a dear little girl, but her mother was so kind, and so utterly charming—the most charming person Ellen had ever known. She had never expected Mrs.

Rivers to seem younger than herself, although actually a year or two older, to be so gay, so considerate, to treat her with such simple friendliness. She liked Mr. Rivers, and was beginning to be at home with him; he was kind to her and devoted to Juliet, and his dry humour often made her laugh, but for her he was not an illuminated figure. He was simply a necessary part of the happy family, which was something she had always been wanting, and had at last found.

Madeleine came towards her, smiling.

"Lessons over? Good! Where's Juliet?"

"Her father took her to see a new calf at the Mandini farm."

"Oh! He didn't ask me to go, too!"

"They've only just started. I expect you could catch them up in a few minutes."

"No. They didn't ask me to come, so I shan't bother. Let's go round to the *piazzale* and have our drinks in peace."

She slipped her hand through Ellen's arm. They walked along the flagged path under the villa's creamy wall.

"I do hope you don't find it dull teaching a baby like Juliet, after much older girls?"

"No, indeed; I shall enjoy teaching her. She's very intelligent, and I'm glad to have a change."

"Have you always taught at the same school?"

"Yes. Seven years. When I came down from Oxford I was going to America for a year. I got a scholarship to do some post-graduate work there, but my mother had her first heart attack just then, and I couldn't leave her. I had to get a post near her, and luckily there was one at the High School, which was my own old school."

"That was very bad luck, not being able to go to America!"

"It couldn't be helped."

"I suppose not. Didn't you get away from home at all in the holidays?"

"Sometimes for a few days when I could persuade a cousin to come and take my place, but it was too much responsibility for her in this last year or two. My mother was always upset when I went away, and it generally made her ill. It was very difficult."

"My dear, it must have been impossible! I don't know how you stood it."

21

"It wasn't as bad as that." But now, hearing it said by someone else, there rose up in Ellen a full realization of how very bad it had been. "I really like teaching. And there were other things that I enjoyed."

"What things?"

But Ellen felt that it was too difficult to explain to Mrs. Rivers a life so remote from her experience. Most of her pleasures had been unpremeditated: a walk to school on a blowing spring morning, with the cloud-shadows sweeping over the hills and the mill chimneys in the valley flying flags of smoke; a fireside tea or Saturday afternoon walk with Alice; a new perception stirred in her mind by some book that she was reading. Even the extra half-hour in bed on a holiday or the cup of hot coffee in the staff-room at break on a winter morning came back into her mind. They belonged to life in the Northern industrial town where beauty was incidental and happiness a by-product. Here, where everything was beautiful, where life was arranged as a series of pleasures, Ellen felt that they would mean nothing. She chose by instinct that part of her old life which seemed to connect with Madeleine's world.

"I had a lot to do with the Little Theatre. I used to help to produce plays, and produced one or two on my own, and I organized play-readings and so on. I used always to go there two evenings a week. There was a place where you could have coffee and talk. I enjoyed all that very much."

"I should think you would have died without it!"

Ellen, who thought that you did not die so easily, replied soberly:

"It made a lot of difference."

They crossed the courtyard and came through the archway on to the *piazzale*, meeting a wave of scent from the rose-garden, strong as the scent from a greenhouse, but fresher and sweeter.

"All these roses in April!" Ellen murmured, with a sigh of content.

Gastone brought the shaker and glasses. Ellen, accustomed at home to the occasional mild dissipation of a glass of sherry, had refused a drink on her first day, and asked anxiously for half one on the second. Now, with a feeling of abandoning herself recklessly to the stream, she allowed Madeleine to fill up her glass,

22

and drank it quickly. This at once put a slight haze between her and the edges of the world, and emboldened her to say something she had been wanting to say for three days.

"I've seen your mother act several times—twice in Leeds and once when we took the Sixth Form to Stratford. I do so much admire her! I don't think anyone is better in Shakespeare! So often people act well but don't give the lines their full value as poetry, but she does both."

It appeared to Ellen that Mrs. Rivers' face, now slightly swimming before her, looked pinched, almost haggard. She took a drink without answering. Ellen was conscious of some check.

"I expect you're tired of hearing people say these things."

"Oh, no, indeed I'm not! I'm always delighted and proud, especially when it's people who know something about acting and understand what they are talking about."

Ellen was inordinately pleased.

"I don't know much about it, really."

"Did you know that I was on the stage, too?"

"No."

The blunt negative dropped like a stone between them. Hazily aware of its fall, Ellen added:

"I was hardly ever able to go to London. I only saw the shows that came round to us. I missed so many plays and people I should like to have seen."

"Oh, I was never famous. I was only on for three years before I got married. I wasn't a success. In some ways I suppose I had a very easy start. I got parts, of course, without any difficulty because every management knew my mother. But in other ways it was much more difficult for me than for any other young actress starting. People expected too much of me. They compared me to my mother all the time, and watched to see if I was like her and if I was going to be as good. I always felt them doing that; I couldn't forget it. You can't imagine what it was like."

"I think I can, a little."

"Once, after I'd been playing Celia in *As You Like It*—the best part I ever had—and I thought I was doing it well, I heard two people talking. They said, ' Pretty little thing; but she'll never be another Rose Danby.' After that I just didn't know how to go on to the stage! It was torture! I couldn't sleep for dreading the next performance. Luckily I got tonsillitis the week after and fell out of the cast."

"But you were so young," Ellen said. "How could they possibly tell what you could develop into! Of course it would have taken a few years for you to establish your own stage personality apart from your mother's! But it would have come, and they would all have recognized it if you'd wanted to go on with a stage career."

"Well, I didn't. I married Charles. I never acted again after I was married. I know my mother and all her friends really think of me as a failure."

Ellen said diffidently:

"I should have thought that most people would envy your life."

Although still seeing the world through a slight haze, she was aware that some tension had relaxed. The charming face opposite to her was once again clear and smiling.

"I'm so very glad," Mrs. Rivers said, "that Helena Gressingham sent you to us. Juliet likes you so much, and I'm so looking forward to having your company this summer. Charles goes back next week, you know, when the Law Courts open. He can't come out again till the end of July. I was rather nervous before you came because Helena Gressingham said you were so clever, and I thought you might be too strict with Juliet and despise me for having no brains. But you're so sympathetic and understanding, I feel as if we'd known each other for a long time, and I'm sure we shall be real friends and have a lot of fun together this summer; don't you think so?"

It had never been Ellen's habit to make friends quickly. The people among whom she had grown up were chary of praise and reticent of enthusiasm, but such open-heartedness broke down her barriers, and she answered with sincere warmth:

"Oh, I do! I can't tell you how glad I am that I came. I think every moment of the day how lucky I am to be here."

"I'm so glad. I do want you to do one little thing for me. Will you?"

"If I can."

"Let me do your hair differently, or cut it off. Your head is such a good shape, and nobody can see it with those catherine wheels."

24

"Oh!" Ellen exclaimed, "I'm so glad you said that *to* me." She added non-committally, "I'll think about my hair."

"Yes, do. Let me give you another drink."

"No, no." Ellen shielded the glass with her hand. "I'm quite drunk already."

"You can't be! Anyhow, what does it matter? I'll give you half, if you like." She filled her own glass to the brim. "We'll leave the ice for Charles."

## CHAPTER III

THE CAR swung out of the back gates and into the main road that wound above the further valley. Here the hillsides sloped more steeply than those in front of the villa. The tiered vines ràn down between the corn like stripes on a print, to a little stream half buried in grass. The sun was hot, the sky made of dazzling blue light. They met a creaking cart drawn by two white oxen, and were only able to pass it by driving half-way up the bank.

"I don't know why we had to go to the Warners' again so soon," Charles grumbled.

"Well, darling, they're our nearest neighbours. This is country life."

"As a matter of fact, they are not our nearest neighbours. The Villa Caligari is a good mile nearer."

"It's a much worse road to Caligari, and the old Contessa gives me the creeps."

"So do the Warners give me! She's a bitch, and he's like some awful automaton. He's been dead for years, really. Why does he go on buying all that furniture and those pictures? The house is stuffed full already, and he doesn't care about any of them."

"He wants to have taste."

"Well, he never had, never can have and never will!"

"Lucrezia has."

"She has too much of it! She's been brought up to know the right things to like."

"Don't you see, Charles, Grant is trying to live up to her. He said something about it to me. He feels that she belongs to the old civilized Europe, that Rome is her proper setting, and that he has to make it up to her for taking her out of it. That's why they came back from America. He said that she just couldn't stand it; she couldn't live in that raw new world."

"Well, damn it, it wasn't the rape of the Sabines; she knew what she was doing when she married him. Boldoni probably left her very poor. I knew the parents when I was in Rome. They were living with one servant in the corner of a crumbling old *palazzo*. Lucrezia's got everything she wants from Grant, and manages to make him feel apologetic for giving it to her."

In the back seat Juliet asked:

"Fenny, who are the Sabines?"

"They were some people a very long time ago who plundered Rome and carried off all the women to be slaves."

"Did they get back again?"

"They didn't want to," Charles said over his shoulder. "They liked taking it out of the Sabines."

Madeleine turned round.

"Daddy's teasing! You'll both enjoy going to Bronciliano. I want Fenny to see the villa and the garden, and Juliet likes Shand, don't you?"

"Yes. But he doesn't like me much. And I don't like Donata and Bianca. Silly little dressed-up babies, always crying!"

"Shand, poor chap, doesn't like anybody much. He was certainly the eggs in that omelette."

"Lucrezia says he likes the new tutor. He's the third they've had since they've been here. The others couldn't do anything with him."

"I expect they've always got mugs. Shand's all right, really. They should send him to school."

"I can't think why Grant doesn't send him back to his own people in New England. I know he wants to go."

"I should think Lucrezia likes keeping the prisoner of the conquered country in her train."

"And, of course, Grant gives in to her about that, as he does about everything else. He's afraid of her."

Charles said with sudden vicious intensity:

"He ought to beat her. It would be very much better for them all."

26

"Mummy, do you like the Warners?"

They all laughed. Charles said:

"Mummy adores them. She isn't happy unless she can go over there two or three times a week. Lucrezia Warner is her greatest friend."

"No, Charles, don't tell her that nonsense. It's like this, Juliet. When you live in a town you choose the people you go to see, but when you live in the country you go to see the people who happen to be there because you must see some people, and there are always things you like about them as well as things you don't."

"When I'm grown up I'll live in a town. Will you live with me, Fenny?"

"We'll see when the time comes."

Madeleine turned to Ellen.

"The Warner family is a mix-up. Grant is American, Lucrezia's Italian. They've both been married before. Shand is—what is he, Charles? Twelve? He is the first wife's son. She was American, and after she died he lived with Grant's sisters in New England until the second marriage. Donata is a year younger than Juliet."

"A year and a half," Juliet interrupted fiercely.

"Well, a year and a half, then. She's Lucrezia's child by Boldoni, her first husband, who died. Bianca is the child of this marriage, born in America. Her name is really Blanche, and Grant always wants to call her that, but——"

"But," Charles said, "what Grant wants is of no consequence."

"I dare say," Madeleine replied sharply, "that Lucrezia puts up with a good deal we don't know about."

"I should think that's most improbable."

Ellen felt a momentary discomfort, without knowing why, as the car turned a corner and the Villa Bronciliano came in sight. She was looking forward to seeing this exotic family. The week that had turned her from Miss Fenwick to Fenny had made her very much at home with her employers, but had not dimmed her enchanted delight in everything around her. She did not say very much about it, for she saw that they enjoyed the villa and the countryside in a different way. To them this was one of many beautiful places that they had seen; they appreciated the loveliness, but took it as a natural part of their lives. Ellen, much as she liked them all, looked forward to those hours in the day when she could stroll out alone and draw into herself the shapes of the hills and the rounded tiles of a roof, the sun-faded apricot of a farm-house wall. Even in the villa she liked to wander through the rooms sometimes when they were out or resting, or to sit in the courtyard gazing at the contrast between the bright light and the violet-tinted shadow on the pale stone. She knew that she was gaping, and knew, too, that the Rivers did not gape, probably never had. Even in Juliet there was already a kind of experience that precluded more than a measure of astonishment. Juliet liked the animals and the farms and the wild flowers, but was indifferent to house or scenery. She enjoyed acting plays and stories with her dolls, hearing about the Ainley High School, or reading. Ellen thought she was too much with grown-up people, and was glad that they were going to a house where there were some children. In her opinion even babyish little girls and a difficult boy would be better than no young company at all for her child.

The Warners were in the loggia in front of their villa. Lucrezia Warner came running to meet them with cries of pleasure—excessive pleasure, Ellen thought—embraced Madeleine with fervour, and gave her hand graciously to Charles. Except for her corn-coloured hair and arched eyebrows, she was not beautiful, but she had an elegance that made Madeleine look suddenly young and unformed. An assured feminine confidence hung about her like her scent. She said, "How glad I am to see you, darling!" to Juliet, who submitted passively to be kissed. She shook hands with Ellen without looking at her, and Ellen disliked her at sight. Grant Warner, who came up very slowly behind his wife, was tall and grey, with a square, pale face and melancholy eyes. He seized at once upon Charles, and began to talk to him about a sale he had been to near Bologna. He had bought two *sopra porte* and had had them made into bed-heads, and he carried Charles off to see them. Lucrezia and Madeleine sat down in basket chairs under a tasselled wisteria.

Lucrezia looked at Ellen and Juliet.

"Juliet, my pet, wouldn't you and your governess like to go and find the children? I think they are in the lower garden."

"Would you take her, Fenny?" Madeleine's smile apologized for Lucrezia's abrupt dismissal. "You ought to see the garden; the view's so lovely."

But Ellen knew that Madeleine, too, wanted to get rid of them so that she could gossip with Lucrezia. She felt a small stab of jealousy as she turned away with the child.

On the other side of the villa, on a lawn bordered by a cypress hedge, two little girls, one dark and one fair, were playing with an elaborate dolls' dinner-service. The dishes were heaped with rose-petals and fading blooms of wisteria. The elder child, very like Lucrezia except for her dark hair, jumped up and came to meet Juliet with a good imitation of her mother's manner. The little one went on stolidly filling soup plates from a tureen of water in which floated daisy-heads and blades of short grass. The children were both dressed in white embroidered muslin frocks, much frilled and tied with coloured ribbons. Beside them Juliet in her grey flannel skirt and red shirt looked boyish and leggy, a school-girl with two nursery children, but Donata's gestures and movements were those of a little grown-up woman as she waved her hand towards the dinner-table inviting Juliet to join in the game. Juliet, who would have loved to have the dinner-service for her dolls at home, here gave it a disdainful glance, but could not refrain from saying, "You've got no vegetables. Why didn't you make a salad with green leaves?"

"But that would be charming," Donata said. "Let us get some."

They moved off together. The little one went on unconcernedly ladling the water into the soup plates with a fat but steady hand.

Ellen thought that the children would get on with each other better if she left them alone. She strolled down the steps into the garden. An avenue of green turf ran between the hedges of clipped cypress to a grove of lemon-trees in terra-cotta stone jars. In the middle was a fountain—a stone boy with his head thrown back playing on a reed from which a jet of water sprang into the air and curved down to the pool. At first Ellen thought that she was alone, but as she walked round the pool she saw a living boy sitting on the rim with a book on his knee. Hearing her footsteps he looked up and scowled. He was at that age, just beginning to shoot out of childhood into adolescence, when the growth seems to be mostly in the wrists and ankles. He was gangling, dusty-headed, with his father's square face, but with a wide mouth not in the least like his father's, and with very deep-set blue eyes. His scowl relaxed a little as he saw Ellen, but he looked wary, and did not close the book on his knee.

"I'm sorry I disturbed you. You must be Shand?"

"Yes. How did you come here?"

"I came with Mrs. Rivers. I'm Ellen Fenwick, Juliet's new governess."

"Oh, I see. I thought you didn't look like one of Lucrezia's friends."

Not sure whether this was to be taken as a compliment or not, but quite sure that he wanted her to go, Ellen said, "Oh, no. I haven't seen her before. I only came out from England a week ago," and was turning away, when he shut his book and put a hand on the rim of the pool.

"You can sit down here if you like."

"Thank you."

The stone was warm as new bread.

"What are you reading?"

"*Huckleberry Finn.* Do you like Italy?"

"So far as I've seen I love it."

"I hate it."

"It's the most beautiful country I've ever seen!"

"Perhaps you haven't seen many."

"No, I haven't; but I've seen enough to know how beautiful this is. Why, look there in front of us."

Before them, at the end of the garden, a gap in the cypress hedge opened to a view of the towers and roofs of Florence and the lovely valley of the Arno stretching away between sunny hills.

"I suppose that's O.K. But I don't like the Italians."

"I hardly know any yet, except the servants, who all seem very nice."

"Yes, servants are nice. But the rich ones are mean and greedy and treacherous and conceited and cruel." He seemed to have relieved his mind by this diatribe, for his frown relaxed. "Has Juliet come, too?"

"Yes; she's up there with your step-sisters. They're having a doll's dinner-party."

"Donata isn't even my step-sister. Her father was Italian, too. Blanche was born in America, and as soon as I can, I shall take her back there."

He said this with renewed defiance, but Ellen only replied, "Yes, I expect everybody wants to go back to their own country," and then wondered whether for herself in six months' time that would be true. "Oh, there's a fish in the pool."

"It's full of gold-fish."

She leaned over the water, watching the gleam of coral and silver under the surface.

From the terrace above them a man's voice called:

"Shand!"

"Hya!" As the echo died among the cypresses, Shand added, "That's Daniel, my tutor." The sullenness had altogether cleared from his face. "He's new, too. He's only been here a month. He's different from all the others. He's an artist, and he paints beautifully. Come and find him."

But Ellen hung for a moment longer over the pool, feeling the warmth of the sun on her bent head, catching the gleam of a bright fin. She put out her hand and caught in the palm the jet of water from the boy's pipe. The cold drop trickled from her fingers to her wrist and splashed on the stone beneath. Some instinct made her unwilling to mar that tranquil moment and go on to the next.

Then she looked up and saw a young man standing on the turf between the cypresses.

## CHAPTER IV

THE YOUNG man, walking warily, as if ready to fight or run, came towards the fountain. No taller than Ellen, he had a sharp face, very sunburnt and topped by an untidy shock of brown hair.

Shand made the introduction with affectionate pride, "This is Daniel Blackett."

"And you're Miss Fenwick? My opposite number at the Villa Meridiana? I was sent to find you."

"Oh, I'm so sorry! Are we late?"

"Late? What for?"

"For lunch?"

"Oh, Lord, no! I hope you're not hungry. We shall be lucky

if we get lunch before two. Some more people have just arrived, and they're all having drinks on the loggia. People don't come to lunch here until an hour after they're asked, and they don't go away until the end of the afternoon."

"Good gracious! They must waste an awful lot of time!"

"They've got it to waste. None of them has anything else to do."

There was a slight North of England inflection in his voice which Ellen recognized.

"I didn't know. I've only been here a week, and we haven't had a lunch-party yet."

"I should imagine that yours is a comparatively sane household."

A child's shrill scream came from the terrace above them.

"Donata," Shand remarked wearily.

"Of course," the tutor agreed, but Ellen ran up the steps ahead of them.

Juliet and Donata were standing up, confronting one another across the dolls' dinner-table. Bianca, sitting cross-legged on the ground, was trying to fit together two halves of a broken plate.

"No, I didn't. It's not true!" Juliet cried furiously.

Donata, seeing grown-up people approaching, wailed:

"She's broken one of my plates."

"No, I didn't, Fenny. I was holding it for Bianca to put some rose-leaf pudding on, and Donata suddenly snatched it away, and it fell on the ground."

"She ought to say she's sorry!" Donata shrieked. "Make her say she's sorry!"

"I shan't ask Juliet to say she's sorry if she didn't break it, Donata. But I'm sorry it's broken. I think it could be riveted at a shop in Florence."

"I don't want a mended plate!" Donata snatched the two halves that Bianca had laboriously fitted together, and hurled them against the balustrade, where they smashed to bits. She ran off round the corner of the house, sobbing hysterically, "Mamma, mamma, mamma!"

Daniel said to Ellen:

"I'm glad to see that you support your own side!"

"Juliet is a very truthful child."

32

"Well, nobody could say that about Donata."

Juliet and Shand, who had been exchanging friendly grins, moved towards each other, but Bianca, staring at the fragments of china, slowly realized that the plate was broken beyond repair, opened her mouth wide and howled. At once Shand turned to pick her up in his arms and comfort her, rubbing his cheek against hers.

"Never mind, Blanchie! It doesn't matter. Don't take any notice of Donata! We can buy another one." Over his shoulder he said, "I'll take her in to Maria."

He carried her off, and Ellen saw Juliet's disappointed face as she looked after him.

"Bianca's not a bad little kid," Daniel observed, "If she doesn't get spoilt, too. She's her father's pet, so I dare say that spoiling won't be so pernicious. Donata's Mummy's little darling, a bitch in the making."

Shocked at the freedom with which he spoke of his employers, but interested against her conscience, Ellen asked:

"And Shand?"

"Oh, nobody spoils Shand. That's why I like him. He's odd man out, the same as I was at home. Have you brothers and sisters?"

"One brother, an engineer in Liverpool. He's married and has two children."

"There are five of us, all boys, and I'm the youngest. The other four are all miners, like my father. We live in Durham. Have you seen a mining village?"

"Of course I have. I've lived in South Yorkshire. And I've been teaching at the Ainley High School for seven years. A lot of my pupils are the daughters of miners."

"Then you have an idea of the sort of life I wanted to get away from."

They had strolled to the end of the terrace, Juliet running ahead of them. From here they could not see Florence—a shoulder of land hid the Arno valley. The land below the garden shelved steeply down to the village; they could almost have dropped a stone on to the tiled roofs and the bell-tower of the church. On their left the cypresses of the avenue marched two abreast up the slope, breaking the repeating pattern of vine, olive and corn. Ellen put her hand over her eyes to shade them from the dazzle of light in the midday sky.

"Well, you have got away!"

"Not really. I never shall. I still dream of having to go down the mine, and wake up sweating. I was afraid of it before I could walk! I worked and worked at my lessons from the day I went to school because I knew even then that it was the only way out. I can remember quite clearly when I was about six, and got a prize for reading, thinking that I was moving a bit farther away from the mine. I knew other boys who got scholarships, you see, and went to other schools and to training colleges and universities and didn't come back. I had it all worked out then."

"I've known children like that. It was always a pleasure to teach them; when they knew what they wanted so early they generally got it, as I'm sure you did."

"Oh, yes, it wasn't difficult. I was a clever child."

They were leaning on the parapet, looking down over the valley. He ran one hand through his already untidy hair, and turned to Ellen a face which even without the ruffled crest would have looked distracted.

"At the same time I always feel less of a man than my father and brothers because I did get away from the mine. You won't understand that. You've seen houses like ours, but you've never lived in one. You don't know how all the life in them is directed towards the mine. Whatever you do above ground is only an interlude. It's like a religion. You eat to be strong for the mine, and sleep to be fresh for the mine, and beget sons to work with you in the mine. You get drunk on a Saturday night to forget the mine, and then you fight, and it's probably the mine you're fighting. When you're damaged and can't go down the mine any longer, you live remembering it and hearing the others, your sons especially, talk about it. You know, when a miner's children are young, he often likes the little girls best, and pets them, and is sharp with the boys. But as soon as the boys go down the mine with him they're buddies as well as sons, and it's a stronger bond between them than any other tie I've seen in family life."

"I can see it must take a lot of courage to go against all that!"

"There are things to make you. My father was badly injured

when I was eight. I was there when they carried him in on a stretcher. I hated him. I'd always hated him since I can remember, but I felt nearly mad then with terror and rage. I hated the mine for doing it to him. It clinched it for me. I wanted to blow the whole thing up, so that nobody could dig coal there any more."

His voice had roughened, the North-country inflection grew stronger as he talked of his home.

"Was your father killed?"

"No. He was crippled for life. After that he lived all day in a wheeled chair in the kitchen. My brothers carried him downstairs in the early morning and upstairs at night. It was the usual kind of terrace house, one room downstairs and two above. When I was working for my scholarship I had to do my work in a corner of the kitchen in the winter, when I couldn't bear the cold upstairs, and my father grumbled and cursed at me all the time for wanting to be different from the rest of them. I think in a way he was jealous because I was going to avoid the mine that had done for him. He used to call me a weakling, which, compared to him, I was. Then my two eldest brothers used to come in from the mine and kick my books across the floor and jeer at me. They and my father would talk to each other as if they were members of an exclusive club. Heaven knows I didn't want to belong to it. I wanted nothing less, but all the same I hated being left out—I felt blistered by their contempt. And I feel it still, all the time, everywhere. Even in this world here, where nobody knows or cares anything about that life, I feel as though I'd failed in the test that really mattered."

"It's difficult to shake off these things. But I don't think you should feel like that, because what you've done probably needed more courage than taking the line of least resistance and going down the mine."

"My father wouldn't have agreed with you."

"No, but it's your life, isn't it, not his? You would only have been a failure if you had let him and your brothers drive you off what you really wanted."

He looked pleased, but as if wishing to deny it said abruptly:

"You've probably heard too many prize-giving speeches, ending up with some nice quotation like 'To thine own self be true.'

35

That settles everybody's problems. Was that what you were going to say next?"

"No, I don't make the prize-giving speeches. I only see that my form get into the right seats and don't whisper or giggle while they're being made."

"Oh, you're a school-marm, are you, in real life?"

Juliet ran back to them and caught hold of Ellen's arm.

"Fenny! Aren't you coming? Are we *never* going to have lunch?"

With a guilty start, Ellen realized that for the first time since she took up her post she had forgotten all about her pupil.

"My hands are all dusty." Juliet held out her grubby palms. "Where do we wash?"

"I'll take you in," Daniel volunteered, "and get one of the maids to show you."

As they turned the corner of the house, he asked Ellen:

"Have you explored Florence yet?"

"No, not at all, really. We've been shopping several times, and once we had lunch in a restaurant. I've not seen any of the things I want to see yet, except that I just looked inside the Cathedral."

"I'll take you sight-seeing, if you like. When do you next have an afternoon off?"

"I haven't thought about one yet."

So far daily life at the villa had been so easily the best holiday she had ever had that beyond a vague wish to go and look at Florence with a guide-book some day, she had not thought of any free time for herself.

"But you must ask for an afternoon off soon. Don't be done out of your rights. You owe it to our profession to preserve solidarity. Try if you can get Saturday week, and meet me in the café in the Piazza Vittore Emanuele at three-thirty."

Surprised and pleased at the invitation from so scornful a young man on such short acquaintance, she accepted eagerly. She saw him smile, more kindly than before, and presumed that she had amused him, but did not know or care why.

"I shall die of starving in a minute," Juliet complained. She looked round the hall. "It's a very grand house, isn't it, Fenny? But not as nice as ours."

It was the most elaborately furnished house that Ellen had ever seen. There were more pictures than wall-space between them, statues and vases and porcelain figures filled every alcove and stood on brackets against the walls, with flowering plants in stone vases between them.

"He's got some very nice things," Daniel remarked. "But there's an awful lot of junk, too."

I shall never know which is which, Ellen thought sadly. She looked at Daniel standing in the middle of the tiled hall with his untidy head cocked, putting the Warners' possessions in their place by his assurance, and wished that she had the key to that world in which he was so much at home.

Juliet admired the green bath and the quantities of green-fringed towels, mirrors and stools in the bathroom to which they were shown, but she said as she splashed vigorously in the wash-basin:

"I wish we were going home to lunch. I don't like it much here. Shand has gone away, and Donata is an awful little cry-baby."

"Yes, she seems a bit spoilt. But Shand will be coming back: he only went to take Bianca to the nursery. I think he looks cross sometimes because he gets into trouble so much more than the little girls. But I'm sure he wants to see you, Juliet. He asked me at once whether you had come, too."

On a rare impulse, for she hardly ever caressed children, she touched Juliet's round, dark head as the child knelt on one knee to tighten the strap of her sandal. Juliet looked up and gave her a brilliant smile.

"Shall we go home in time for tea?"

"I should think so."

"And you and me have our walk together afterwards? Promise?"

"I expect we shall. I hope so."

The face that Ellen saw in the mirror as she firmly tucked a stray bit of hair into one of her cart-wheels was flushed and happy. There seemed to be several people who very much wanted her company in this enchanting new world.

Since it was Charles' last evening before going back to England, they made dinner an occasion. Wreaths of roses circled the candle-sticks, there was chicken and an iced cake from Florence to eat with the fruit. Juliet was allowed to dine with them on condition that she went up to bed when the coffee came. In her white frock, her eyes and cheeks brilliant, she contributed to the party an element of pure rapture that was like another burning candle. When she was told to go, she said good-night to her parents and demanded:

"Fenny, come up and put me to bed!"

"Not yet," Madeleine said. "You run up and get undressed. Fenny isn't coming until she's had her coffee."

Balanced on the fine edge of excitement that tips with a feather into tears, Juliet complained:

"I can't unfasten this frock."

Her father cut in sharply:

"Yes, you can, if you try. Run along at once!"

He seldom spoke to her in that tone, and she looked startled, recovered herself, said, "Anyhow, I wouldn't drink that nasty black coffee!" and whisked her muslin skirts out of the room.

"Poor Juliet!" Madeleine exclaimed. "We might have let her have another quarter of an hour. It wouldn't really have made much difference."

"Haven't you seen enough of spoilt children today?"

"But Juliet's not the least bit like Donata, is she, Fenny? And she never whines."

"Never. I haven't seen her cry at all since I came."

"That's because you're so good with her." Charles gave his coffee-cup an impatient push:

"All the same, I don't want her to grow up into the kind of woman who thinks she can have the moon whenever she asks for it."

"She's not likely to think that long. She'll soon learn that only men are entitled to moons. Unless she grows up like my mother, and manages to get her own way all the time, while she makes other people believe they're having theirs."

"I think that's unjust. Rose has always seemed to me remarkably unselfish."

"I should be the last person to deny that she's a good actress."

"If you . . ." Charles stopped, his face red and constricted. "All this isn't very interesting for Miss Fenwick."

"If I may, I'll go up to Juliet and see her into bed."

"Come out on to the terrace, Fenny, when you come down. I'm going to fetch a coat and try if it's warm enough to sit out there."

"I think I must write some letters to catch the post tomorrow, if you don't mind."

They were very kind. Madeleine especially was always asking her to join them, but she felt sure that on his last evening Charles must want his wife to himself. It was probably because he was leaving her that he was irritable. She was used to sparring between her own parents; she knew that it was part of family life; but it was easier for a third person not to be there. She went up to Juliet, and then to her own room. She was sorry for Charles because he was leaving this Paradise, but not really sorry that he was going. She looked forward very much to being alone with Madeleine and Juliet. They would, she thought, be very cosy together. They had already made plans. She and Madeleine were going to learn Italian together in the evenings. Reading and talking with Madeleine would be like enjoying continuously the pleasure that she had always enjoyed in snatches with Alice, only with the surprise and untouched bloom of a new friendship. She thought remorsefully that she had not yet written to Alice, and sat down to do so. She wanted to describe the Rivers, the villa, her life; but already the gap was widening; she would have to explain so many things that in a week she had learnt to take for granted. She persevered, but when she had finished she was tired, and decided not to write any more letters. She went to her window to look out at the night.

Her curtains were not drawn, and the window threw a fan of light over the gardens. Madeleine and Charles Rivers stood by the pool like figures illuminated on the stage. Madeleine was wearing a light coat, which seemed all of one colour with her blonde hair. Her back was towards Ellen, but Charles stood sideways; he appeared to be arguing or persuading. Ellen saw

Madeleine make a movement towards him; he put an arm round her shoulders, and they walked out of the fan of light into the darkness at the end of the garden.

She went back to her dressing-table feeling sad and lonely, reminded that however much they treated her as a friend, they were a family, and she was outside it. Now that her mother was dead, she was not part of any family. She took her hairpins out of her ear-phones, let the plaits fall, and began to brush out her kinked hair. The release and the rhythmical movements of the brush soothed her, and her depression began to lift. It was her nature to shove off quickly when she had run aground on unhappiness. She looked in the mirror at the face between the curtains of hair, and thought that it had changed already since her arrival. It was now lightly browned by the sun, the cheeks were rounder, the shadows were disappearing from under the eyes. It crossed her mind that she would like to look nice when she explored Florence with Daniel Blackett on Saturday week. She lifted her hair behind her ears, and held it in a bunch at the back of her neck, realizing with pleasure that what Madeleine had said about the shape of her head was true. She let the hair fall, plaited it again, tied the plaits neatly with blue ribbons, and got into bed.

## CHAPTER VI

"It's too bad to be going back on a day like this!"

Ellen and Juliet were standing by the entrance to the court-yard watching Gastone pack Charles' suit-case into the boot of the car. There had been a shower of rain in the early morning, which had freshened the air, but now the sky was again perfectly blue; everything glittered with light, light quivered from the pale façade of the villa and ran off the beams of the big bay tree, so that it was a relief to turn the eye to the black shadows of the cypresses.

"Oh, I don't know," Charles said; "I get tired of doing nothing. I like work."

Wearing a suit for the journey, instead of holiday clothes, he already stood apart from their life at the villa. Ellen had for the first time a conception of him as a personality distinct from the family pattern, a man in the working world, with his own achievements and disappointments. How little she had heard about that life of his in the past week! Perhaps he did not want to talk about his work on a holiday, but she felt sorry that she had not got to know him better, as she might have felt if she had been in a train and awakened to find that she had passed through an unknown town without seeing it.

"Juliet, run and tell Mummy that if she isn't here in ten minutes I shall have to start without her."

"You won't start without me? If I come back as fast as I can run?"

"No, but make her come, too." As she raced across the court-yard, he said abruptly to Ellen, "Teach Juliet to be punctual and to have some consideration for other people."

Confused by the implication, Ellen said hastily:

"I don't think I shall need to teach her. If we're going any-where, Juliet likes to be ready to the last hair at least half an hour before we start."

Her father smiled.

"Yes, she's generally ready for anything." Walking back-wards and forwards with short, quick steps, he jerked his wrist up and looked at his watch. He paused in front of Ellen. "You've quite settled down here, haven't you? You like it?"

"I love it."

"Well, look after them, and look after yourself, too."

Madeleine appeared with Juliet.

"Don't be fussy, Charles; there's heaps of time."

"Not if we meet anything on that narrow road."

"Oh yes, even then."

Marcella the cook, and Ofelia came running across the court-yard to join Gastone and wave good-bye.

"How nice they are!" Madeleine said as the car started. "They might have been with us for years. They seem so really sorry that you have to go back. They'll miss you now that they'll be reduced to my scraps of Italian. Fenny knows much more than I do already."

"Well, between you, keep an eye on the accounts when Gastone goes to market."

"You don't trust anybody very much, do you, Charles?"

He answered woodenly:

"I lived here for a year. I know the Italians."

"I didn't only mean the Italians."

Ellen waited in the car outside the station while Madeleine and Juliet went with Charles to the train. When they came back, Juliet was crying.

"Never mind, my pet!" Madeleine consoled her. "It won't really be very long before he comes back. We're going to have lots of fun together, you and I and Fanny. You'll see what a lovely time we shall have! There's an English company coming to do *Twelfth Night* in the Boboli Gardens, and I'm going now to get tickets for us. You'll like that, won't you? You've never been to a theatre out of doors at night, and after I've got the tickets we'll go and get an ice at Doney's."

Juliet accepted the ice, but ate it slowly, with a mournful expression.

"We shall be able to do much more sight-seeing now," Madeleine remarked to Ellen. "Charles doesn't like it. He was here for a year when he came down from the University, so he saw everything then, and he doesn't like being a tourist. But I do, don't you?"

"Yes, indeed I do; it's all so new to me."

"How lucky it is that we like the same things! I've got to leave you now for a bit, I'm afraid. Some friends of Charles' mother are staying at the Excelsior for a night on their way to Rome, and I promised to take Juliet to see them  Perhaps you'll like to look about. Shall we meet at the car at six?"

This was the first time that Ellen had been alone in Florence. She had not brought her guide-book, and without it did not know how to find the things that she wanted to see. She sauntered along the Via Tornobuoni looking in the shop windows. It was one of the fashionable hours. Elegant women—Italian, English, American—strolled on the pavement, shining cars nosed their way along the street. Elderly ladies in pairs, with elaborately veiled hats and antique summer dresses, tottered towards Doney's for their five o'clock cup of tea. It amused Ellen to watch this decorative world, but when she came opposite to a mirror in a shop window she was struck by the incongruity of her own sober figure, in the grey tweed coat and skirt, with her grey hat tipping forward as usual on her coils of hair. A few doors farther on she came to a hairdresser's, where there was a notice in the window that they spoke French and English. She went in and asked them to cut off her hair.

The first snips of the scissors seemed to denude her of a good deal of what had so far been her life. As the valences of hair slipped down over the cotton robe to the tiled floor and the scissors skilfully shaped the short locks, the head of a new Ellen, younger, prettier, more pleased with herself, emerged. She thought while she was drowsing under the drier of Madeleine's pleasure and surprise. She had done it to please Madeleine—she would have done almost anything to please her; but she also thought that she would like to buy a new dress: a light-coloured, less sensible dress, that she could wear when she was out alone, when, for instance, she came into Florence to meet Daniel Blackett. She did not know which shop to go to and how much it would cost, and decided to wait until Madeleine could advise her; but she bought in one of the shops a striped silk scarf of different colours, and knotted it loosely round her neck over the sober jacket. Carrying her hat, proud but self-conscious, she waited for the others by the car. Madeleine's, "There, I told you it would make all the difference!" Juliet's, "Oh, Fenny, you are beautiful!", confirmed her delighted sense of being somebody at whom people might, after all, look with pleasure.

That night the moon was full over the hills. They agreed that it was far too lovely to stay indoors, fetched coats and went to stroll in the garden.

"Poor Charles!" Madeleine said. "What he's missing! He'll be through Turin now, and having the second dinner on the train: he always has the second dinner—it's a fixed rule. He's going to stay with his mother in Kensington. It's convenient, and she likes it, and so does he; but I'm rather sorry, because she doesn't like me. She has always thought I was actressy and shallow and empty-headed, not the right wife for him. She would never say such a thing, of course—she couldn't approve of herself if she did—but she conveys it to him. Everything in the house conveys it. He's always different when he's been there. I really wish he was staying in our flat, but we've let it for the summer, so there Charles will be, soaking in silent disapproval of me."

"I think mothers of sons are always like that. My mother used to have a lot of little grumbles about her daughter-in-law, but she was really very fond of her, and knew that she was a good wife to Hugh; it didn't mean anything."

"Were your mother and father happy together, Fenny?"

"On the whole, I think they were. They were very different. He was much more light-hearted and casual than she was; he was impulsive and very bad at managing money. He trusted people more than she did, and was often let down. She was the prudent one who saved and strained to get us educated. He had a great capacity for enjoyment; I think he often felt that she restricted him; and she was sometimes impatient with him because he was too easy-going with people about paying their bills and didn't share her anxiety enough. He liked all kinds of people, and made friends with them, and she was reserved and didn't make friends easily. But there was a very strong tie between them, even when they clashed on the surface. They were knit together under their differences. I felt that as far back as I can remember."

Ellen sighed.

"I suppose there aren't any perfect marriages. Although my mother had one, apparently, just as she's had everything else. But, then, it didn't have to last a lifetime. My father was a soldier; he was killed in 1914, in the first week of the war. They had only been married ten years. I've often thought that if he had lived longer the glamour might have worn off; he might have got tired of being Prince Consort to Rose Danby."

"Perhaps not, if they'd been happy together for ten years."

"Fenny, do you really think that it's natural to go on living with the same person all your life?"

Ellen realized that she had always thought so. Of course, there were children at school whose parents were divorced and separated. They were marked in her mind as children with an unusual background who might need special care.

"I always have thought so," she said doubtfully.

"So has Charles. But in my mother's world—the stage world—it wasn't nearly so much taken for granted. They knew far more about feelings. They didn't expect them always to conform to

44

some impossible pattern. They were alive, and I often feel that Charles' family are all just stuffed dummies. I can't breathe in their world!"

"I expect Mr. Rivers' mother is glad really that he's so happy with you!"

"Oh!"

It was a cry of hysterical exasperation. Madeleine withdrew her arm from Ellen's and ran a few steps to the edge of the lawn, where the steps led down to the kitchen garden. The moonlight silvered her light coat and pale hair; she looked as if she were just going to throw herself over the edge, down among the tomatoes and lettuces. In a moment she turned back.

"It's getting chilly, I think, don't you? Let's go in. I'm rather tired; I think I'll go up to bed."

Ellen felt as if a door half opened had been shut in her face, and followed her silently into the house.

She was brushing her hair in her bedroom when she heard Juliet crying in the room that opened off hers. She went in and switched on the light. Half the bedclothes were on the floor, the rest in an uncomfortable tangle, above which rose Juliet's tear-smudged face. One of the plaits had come undone, and the curtain of dark hair falling over her cheek made her look forlorn and babyish.

"Fenny!" she wailed. "I woke up and thought there was no one here."

"I'm here, love; I've come up to bed. I'll leave the door open, if you like."

Ellen began to pull the bedclothes straight.

"My hair's all undone, and it's tickling my neck."

"Well, never mind; we can soon plait it up again."

Ellen fetched a comb and combed out the tangled hair. Juliet, still crying, wriggled against her shoulder.

"Were you too hot? Or did you have a bad dream?"

"No. I woke up, and the bed was all horrid, and I couldn't find my hair-ribbon."

"It's here underneath you."

Ellen tied the plait.

"I wish Daddy hadn't gone!"

"He's only gone for a short time, you know. He'll be back at the end of July."

"Where's Mummy? Has Mummy gone, too?"

"No, of course she hasn't. She's in her room going to bed."

The body in Ellen's arms was hot and trembling.

"Are you quite sure she hasn't gone away, too?"

"Quite sure. We've been walking about in the garden after dinner, and she came upstairs when I did. She's going to be here with you all the summer."

"And you will, too?"

"Yes, I shall, too. Now let me turn your pillow over, and you'll be comfortable."

Juliet turned over and buried her face in the pillow. She said something that Ellen did not catch.

"Where's Oliver?"

"I don't know. Who is Oliver?"

There was a fresh burst of sobs.

"I want Mummy! I want Mummy."

"I'll go and ask her to come and say good-night to you."

Madeleine had heard the sounds, and was coming along the corridor, tying the string of her dressing-gown.

"I think she's been dreaming," Ellen explained. "She woke up crying because her father had gone, and thinking that you had gone, too. Now she's asking about somebody called Oliver."

"Oh! I'll settle her down, Fenny. You go to bed."

Ellen went into her own room. The communicating door into Juliet's room was ajar, and the murmur of voices came through. As Ellen picked up her hair-brush she heard Madeleine, raising her voice, say with passion:

"No, my darling, no! Of course I'm not going away. I'd never, never leave you for anything, my precious one, my own little girl."

As Ellen heard this, a constriction gave way in her own heart. Her mother's death was something that she had not yet fully experienced. The experience had been insulated by shock. After the years of anxious care and foreboding, it had happened casually. Her mother had been reading a letter from Hugh and telling Ellen news of the grandchildren. Ellen had gone down to

46

fetch her some hot milk. As she took the empty glass, her mother had fallen back against the pillow. Ellen, as she put the glass down on the bedside table, saw the life drain out of her. There was left a doll with an unexpectedly small face, to be a subject for irrelevant discussion with undertakers.

Ellen had done all that was necessary in a suspension of feeling. Her mother in life had aroused so much emotion. There had been so much compassion for her feebleness, so much respect for her frosty integrity, so much resentment of her dutiful exactions and remorse for the resentment, at bottom so much yearning for her love. But up till now Ellen had been able to feel less about her death than she had felt during an argument with her as to whether she should or shouldn't go out with Alice on Saturday afternoons. The feelings that she had not been aware of having were a hard ball somewhere inside her; she felt their painful pressure without experiencing them. Now the ball suddenly dissolved; desolation, the sense of a deep root torn out of her life, was released. Long after Juliet's room was dark and quiet, Ellen lay face downwards, tears soaking into her pillow, until at last, worn out, she fell asleep.

## CHAPTER VII

WHEN THEY came out of the Spanish cloister at five into the hot, sleepy square, Daniel said:

"Now we'll go and get some tea. It's a mistake to try to see more than one thing thoroughly in an afternoon. We'll go to the café in the Piazza."

He did not ask Ellen if she agreed, and by this time she did not expect him to. She was delighted to fall in with his suggestion. She had listened with interest to his dogmatic comments on the Giotto frescoes, feeling that she was seeing more than she had ever seen in any painting before, but what she most wanted now was to sit down.

"After that we'll stroll across the Ponte Vecchio and have a look at the other side, and then we'll come back and have dinner. I know a good cheap place."

Ellen was delighted that their afternoon together was extending into an evening.

"That would be lovely! I needn't go home at any particular time."

"I should hope not! It's the first time they've let you out, isn't it?"

"It isn't like that at all. If I'd wanted to come out before by myself, I'm sure it would have been all right. I just didn't think of it. Mrs. Rivers is very kind. I feel more like a visitor staying with them than a governess."

"Yes, she's got better manners than her friend, Lucrezia. Your chains are gilded. On the whole, I think I prefer mine. It's a business arrangement. I do pretty much what I like because I'm the only person who can prevent Shand from being a nuisance to them."

"They must have been very stupid with him! I like Shand."

"Yes, he's worth the lot of them. When I leave at Christmas I shall try to make them let him go back to his aunts in New England."

"Are you only here till Christmas?"

"I came for a year. I teach in an art school in Newcastle, but I was ill last winter. I was told to get into the sun, so I took this job. It was a chance as well to see a lot of things I've always wanted to see. This was the only way I could afford it."

"Do you get any time to paint?"

"I make time, but I can't paint here! At least, I haven't done any good since I came. It's too overwhelming. There's too much to take in. It ought to be the perfect place, but for me it isn't. It makes me feel restless. I want to see everything, and I want to go away and digest everything I have seen, and between the two I can't settle down."

"But you will when you go home. I expect you're storing up inspiration now to use it later."

"Oh, don't talk that amateur's rubbish about inspiration!"

She felt crushed, and did not answer. A moment later he surprised her by adding:

"I dare say you may be right."

Ellen was encouraged to say:

"I should so much like to see some of your work."

48

"I don't suppose you would. You'd probably hate it."

Her spirits sank again. Evidently her ignorant comments before the Giottos had made him decide that she was hopeless about art. She was surprised and pleased when he added casually:

"I'll show you one or two things when you come over some time."

They sat down at a table behind the hedge of potted box. Daniel ordered tea with lemon for both without consulting her. She preferred milk, but it did not matter. After the years of being a stand-by at home and an authority at school there was a pleasure in being dominated. Daniel was the first person with whom she had felt able to share this holiday on equal terms. To him, as to her, such things were not a matter of course. His life had been very much harder than hers; his struggle must have been heroic. She looked at him, and saw how white and delicate his skin was wherever it was not burnt by the sun, how the bones stood out in his thin wrists, how jerky his movements were, as though all the nerves of his body were tightly stretched. She felt very sorry for him, and eager to give him whatever comfort and reassurance he needed.

"Go on," he said; "you're dreaming! Put some lemon in your tea and drink it up."

She obeyed. His casual, half-bullying manner made her feel alive and on the edge of laughter. She looked round at the tables filled with Italian and English, Swiss, American, German tourists. She cried out:

"What fun this is! Did you ever expect to find yourself in a place like this?"

"Certainly. I always meant to come. The Warners are just a means to my end."

"I came by the most extraordinary chance! The Rivers were lent their villa by someone I happened to know, and they told her that they wanted a governess for Juliet for the summer, and she recommended me. I still don't quite believe it."

"No, that's obvious. You look so idiotically pleased with everything."

"Why should it be idiotic?" Ellen replied with spirit. "People like Shelley and Byron and Landor found Italy wonderful. I should be much more idiotic if I didn't!"

"What I mean is that you shouldn't be so surprised at anything pleasant happening to you. You should make claims on the world, and expect them to be met. Women like Lucrezia and Madeleine Rivers are making claims the whole time. They think that other people are only there to give them what they want. Oh, don't look indignant! I know you've got a schoolgirl passion for Mrs. Rivers, and she asks nicely and Lucrezia doesn't. But you mark my words, they're the same sort of people underneath; you've only got to see them with their heads together, as thick as thieves. As for you, Ellen, you've been well brought up to share and take your turn, you go about enjoying everything and trusting everybody, pleased because the sun shines on you, and if you aren't careful, the pirates will plunder you all the time. You shouldn't laugh. I'm warning you."

"What about you? Do you make claims?"

"Of course. If I hadn't I should be down the mine. I'm a pirate, too, but I don't pretend to be anything else. That's why in a sort of way Lucrezia and I understand one another, and have come to terms without saying anything. 'The Empress Catherine and I are bandits!' I'd sooner be employed by the Warners, really, than by your nice Rivers. The Warners make no appeal to my better nature—not that I'm hampered with as much of that as you are. I'll pay for this tea, and we'll have dinner Dutch; is that all right?"

"Of course, but let's have everything Dutch. It's far better."

"No, I'll do this."

Daniel fished out a handful of small coins and beckoned to the waiter.

They had driven several times across the Ponte Vecchio, and Ellen had often wished to get out and look in the tempting little shops, full of jewellery, cameos, tooled leather and exquisitely embroidered underclothes.

"Tourist bait!" Daniel said scornfully.

"Well, I am a tourist! And I want to buy a birthday present to send to Alice, my great friend; we've been teaching at the same school for six years."

"And I suppose you go to one another's houses in the evening and make huge pots of tea and tell one another what the head mistress said and what you think about life. I suppose you were in love with each other. . . ."

50

"Certainly not!" Ellen cried, scandalized.

"And now Mrs. Rivers has cut her out."

"You do talk nonsense!"

But she resolved, with a tinge of remorse, to buy a specially nice present for Alice.

She expected him to be impatient with shopping or at best humorously patient, as her own brother would have been; but he came in with her, examined the trays of brooches and pins, sternly rejected several that caught her fancy, and finally directed her choice on to what he said was the only possible one. She was quite ready to believe that he knew more about these things than she did, and she listened, amused, as he bargained for her in what even she recognized as execrable Italian. She said as they came out:

"You seem very good at shopping!"

"Of course I'm good at shopping. I lived in Paris for a year on nothing. You soon learn that way what is worth buying and what isn't. I could housekeep for a week for the price of one of the Warners' meals."

"It would be fun to housekeep here! I know I shan't want to go back in September."

"Well, why do you? Get a room in Florence, get a bit of work teaching English, and you can live on nothing here, and it's a much pleasanter life. You're free, aren't you?"

"Yes, I'm quite free since my mother died."

"Then I can't see any earthly reason why you shouldn't live where you like."

The idea of pulling up her roots permanently was new and startling to Ellen, who was also inexplicably depressed by his readiness to consign her to a solitary life in Florence, while he, she supposed, would go back to Newcastle.

"Only," he said, "I don't know how long it's going to be possible to live here under Mussolini, for anybody who isn't Fascist. What are your politics, if you have any?"

"Of course I have. I'm a Liberal." Ellen's grandfather had been a supporter of Mr. Gladstone, her father had believed in Free Trade—had in fact been willing to believe in any kind of freedom, although between his wife and the urgent demands of a poor and struggling practice he had not enjoyed much. Ellen

51

had read the papers and talked to her Form about current affairs. "I've been secretary to the school Group of the League of Nations."

"Well, that's a dead hat, anyway. It was only a question of which nation would knock it on the head first, and now Japan has, with this business in Manchuria."

She detected a certain malicious satisfaction in his voice, an obscure desire to punish the world, and answered sturdily:

"A good thing, like the League—the only possible thing for the future, really—isn't finished by one reverse!"

"I'm not so sure. I think some good things never recover from the first blow."

"Anyhow, I don't suppose Mussolini will worry me much."

"You don't know what you're talking about, Ellen. You're still living in a Victorian walled garden; you haven't seen one brick after another crumbling from the walls."

What struck her most was that he had called her Ellen. She laughed, and he laughed, too; but he said:

"I'm not joking. I'm warning you. You can't go about the world like a lamb in a field of daisies. I don't believe you're stupid, really."

"I'm not stupid. I'm happy." The first time I've ever been completely happy, she realized, with surprise.

"Perhaps," he said gloomily, "it's the same thing."

"Oh, no, it isn't."

Of that she was sure, had always been irrationally sure. Happiness meant to her the normal, anything else was an accidental departure from it. She divined that it was not so for him, perhaps because of his difficult childhood, the struggle that had lined his forehead and stretched the skin tight over his bones.

They dined in a small restaurant on the Lung'arno, sitting at a table near the door which was open to the cool spring evening. Daniel chose the dinner with careful consideration. Ellen was content to leave the choice to him.

"Don't tell me you're one of those boring people who don't mind what they eat!"

"Oh, no, indeed I'm not; but anything to eat is so good out here, and I don't know all the dishes yet. I should like you to choose for me."

While he discussed the dinner with the waiter very seriously in his bad Italian, she watched him, amused, realizing that he was showing off a bit for her benefit, but was hungry and eager for a good dinner, as he must have been when he was a little boy and his mother stooped with the cloth in her hand to open the oven door.

Putting down the menu, he looked at her and smiled.

"You've had your hair cut off; it suits you. Only the way you had it before was like my mother when I first remember her. She hasn't got enough to do it that way now. I wish I could get her out here for a month, just to sit in the sun. She's always cold."

"Tell me about her."

She wanted to fill in all the blank spaces in her picture of his life.

"There isn't much to tell. She must have been very pretty when she was young. She still is when she smiles. She was a dressmaker's assistant in Darlington before she married. She liked dancing, and looking at the shops, and going to a theatre. She's had a very hard life bringing us all up, especially after my father was injured, and before my brothers were old enough to earn full wage. You know what a miner's pension is! And she hates the village being so ugly and grim; she's got a feeling for the look of things. She'll still wear a bit of bright colour if she can, and she always likes to have something pretty—flowers, or berries, or coloured leaves—in a jar on the window-sill. I used to go up the Fell and bring back harebells and heather for her, and anything else I could find."

"How pleased and proud she must be about your painting!"

"She's mostly pleased and proud that one of us hasn't gone down the mine. She feels that's her achievement, and so it is. It was the only thing she ever opposed my father about. She saved to help me with books without telling him. Lord knows how she managed it on what we had, but she did, and once or twice she got money from her own family for books for me. They kept a small draper's shop, and were very genteel and respectable, and sorry about the marriage. They thought my mother was fit for something better than scrubbing a miner's back. They didn't have much to do with us, and my father loathed them; but they did let me board there in the term after I got my scholarship—

my mother went on at them until they did, and kept them at it, although they didn't like me much, nor I them. I understood how my father felt about them. They were hardly alive. My mother was worth the lot of them!"

"Couldn't she possibly get out here to see you? I'm sure there must be a lot of spare rooms in the Warners' villa. It looks big enough for a school."

"Oh, I could plant her on the Warners all right. They wouldn't care. But even if she could afford the fare, or I could scrape it up for her, she wouldn't think it right to spend so much money on her own holiday. She's like you." He looked at Ellen with kindness. "She doesn't know how to make claims for herself."

Singing internally with happiness because she felt that he was approving her, Ellen said:

"Perhaps I shall learn to out here."

The sweetness vanished from his face as if a shutter had been pulled down. He replied curtly:

"You'd better be quick about it. It's perfectly true that the devil takes the hindmost."

He picked up the evening paper that the waiter had put down on the corner of the table and began to read it. Really, she thought, to be in his company was like being on a switch-back. You swung from feeling that he liked you to feeling that he loathed you in the space of a minute. There he was lighting a cigarette behind the evening paper and blowing smoke across the table into her face as though she wasn't there at all. She pushed her own chair back a little, scraping it on the floor in the hope of reminding him that she was; but he read on, inhaling and expelling clouds of strong Italian tobacco, his eyes straying across the page, his shock of hair falling forward to his eyebrows. Ellen wished that she had never come. It was clear that he was hopelessly bored with her. He was already repenting his suggestion that they should have dinner together. She felt desolate and then annoyed. For it had been his suggestion, and he should at least have made a pretence of being willing to go through with it. Ellen, who had never before smoked at the beginning of a meal, took a cigarette out of her bag, and leaned forward.

"Will you give me a light?"

"Eh, what?" He crumpled the sheets of the paper impatiently

54

together. "I thought you'd got a box of matches; you had some before." He felt in his pocket, jerked out a box and struck a match. "I suppose you thought I was rude?"

"Oh, no, I . . ."

"Oh, for Christ's sake! Why can't you be truthful and say 'yes'?"

By puffing furiously at the cigarette she managed to keep her lips from quivering and the tears out of her eyes.

"I haven't any manners," he said, with what sounded to her a curious satisfaction.

Several answers occurred to her, but not fast enough. Before she could make use of any of them, the elderly waiter brought their bottle of wine, smiling at them as he put it down, as if he was glad to give them an opportunity of enjoying themselves. It was white wine just off the ice, and the first drink was delicious to Ellen, who felt as if the cool, golden evening was running down her throat.

Daniel raised his glass to her.

"We must do this again!"

Unexplored visions of pleasure opened before her, like the corridors of a dream. Too much dazed by sudden variations of feeling, she smiled widely at him, and finished her glass. He grinned, as if he knew about the switch-back and rather liked it. He refilled both their glasses. The waiter put two plates of food down in front of them, and they began to eat and talk. By the time Ellen had finished her second glass of wine she felt as though she were beginning to float above the tables and the diners and would soon float out of the door and up above the Arno, the tiled roofs and the bell-towers.

. . . . .

She took the tram back to the village, and then walked the half-mile to the villa. There was a light behind the curtains, and Ellen ran up, eager to tell Madeleine about her afternoon and evening. She found her sitting on the floor, surrounded by paper patterns and pieces of silk. They had bought some stuff to make a frock for Juliet, and Ellen had promised to cut it out next day. Madeleine looked up from the litter of pieces.

"Oh, Fenny, there you are at last! I've been having such a time. The directions are all wrong on this pattern or something,

55

and I've cut two sleeves for one side. I thought you'd be back before I finished. Now I shall have to get some more stuff—if we can—but it was nearly the end of the roll. I don't know what to do," she wailed.

Her face had its pinched and peevish look. She thrust out her underlip like a sulky child.

Perhaps it was because of what Daniel had said, perhaps it was because she felt deflated, happiness going down inside her like milk in a pan taken off the fire, that Ellen saw Madeleine for a minute as she had never seen her before. She felt a touch of anger.

It was the first time she had been off duty, and she had promised to cut out the dress in the morning. Her mother had been like that: when Ellen came in glowing and rosy from a walk with Alice, how often she was met by complaints that the fire had got too low, that Ida had cut the bread-and-butter too thick for tea, that she could not write a letter because only Ellen had the address. Did one never get away from that sort of thing? Ellen stood checked, awkward, half apologetic, half annoyed in the doorway.

Then Madeleine pushed silks and papers to one side, and jumped up, laughing and shaking the bits from her skirt.

"Never mind! It's my fault. It was silly of me to start without you. We'll leave it till tomorrow, then I expect you can get it right. Come and sit down and tell me everything you've done. You look as if you'd had a lovely evening."

## CHAPTER VIII

In the growing heat of May the courtyard of the villa became more and more the scene of their life. Ellen and Juliet breakfasted there at a table in the corner, while Madeleine drank her coffee upstairs. Often Ellen came down early and found Angelina, always in the same faded blue dress, industriously sweeping the paving-stones with a broom of twigs. She had done this every day while the house was empty, and she was not going to relinquish this particular duty now that she was relieved of the others. Perhaps it was the only one she had ever cared to do. Ellen could imagine her wandering vaguely through the shuttered rooms, leaving her footprints like a bird's on the dusty tiled floors, occasionally opening a shutter and seeing in one of the Venetian mirrors the reflection of her own ageless face and neatly parted hair. Angelina always smiled and spoke to her. By degrees Ellen began to understand and to stumble out an answer, but whatever the answer was, Angelina only nodded and said " *Si, si, si,*" as though, like an animal, she listened to the voice rather than to the words. She never left the villa, she could not read or write, and Ellen never knew whether she had one dress which she washed by night, or whether she had a set of faded blue dresses, all exactly alike. Because, unlike other human beings, she never presented any difference to the eye, she had the absolute quality of a work of art.

Now that it was so warm they lunched in the courtyard, and began to dine there. The basket chairs by the archway that led to the *piazzale* were their meeting-place and point of departure. Books, hats, cameras, newspapers, handbags were thrown down there. As the midday sun grew too hot, they sat before lunch and after in the shade of the cloister, looking at the deep blue of the sky above the red-tiled roof, or watching the swifts fly in and out of the tower and swoop across the courtyard, their shadows falling like stones down the pale wall.

Outside the villa the hay stood knee high. Juliet came in with armfuls of yellow daisies and of the long-stemmed crimson clover. At night the fire-flies danced their unearthly ballet, and Ellen found glow-worms in the crannies of the wall. Juliet made friends with the Mandini children, Francesca and Marco, whose company she very much preferred to Donata's. She talked to them in some kind of English-Italian that they seemed to understand. Walking along the low parapet of the wall at the end of the garden was one of their favourite games. The two barelegged little girls and the half-naked boy could often be seen like figures on a frieze cut out against the hills and the sky. Every evening the sun set in splendour over the town of Florence, and as the red faded to rose and the last stain of rose died from a sky the colour of old turquoise, the sombre green cypresses became hard black shapes against the deepening blue and the appearing stars.

Ellen thought that Juliet should read *Twelfth Night* before she went to see it in the Boboli Gardens. She found that Juliet had already seen the play once and remembered it clearly.

"Grannie Rose was Olivia in a black dress and a black veil over her face. At the end she had a beautiful white dress. Gwenda Lucy, who is a friend of ours, was Viola. She has red hair really, but she had a brown wig to make her the same as Sebastian. I shall play Viola when I'm grown up."

Juliet meant to be an actress. She had a toy theatre at home which had been too big to bring to Italy, but of which she often talked, and she loved to hear about the plays that Ellen had produced at Ainley.

Madeleine did not encourage the idea of Juliet on the stage.

"There've been quite enough actresses in the family! I want her to be something else. I don't want her to act out all her emotions in public until there's nothing left for her real life."

Ellen thought that Madeleine was accusing her mother. Madeleine had built up for her a picture of herself as a sensitive little girl whose childhood was spent dragging along behind Rose Danby, constantly shaken by the excitements and disturbances of her career, like a small ship getting the wash of a big one. Ellen felt a good deal of sympathy for Madeleine, who aroused in her something of the same protective instinct that had been aroused by her mother's feebleness and fretfulness. She felt in herself far greater powers of endurance, and also accepted that it was part of her duty, as Juliet's governess, to stand between her employer and the vicissitudes of life. But she would not damp Juliet's childish ambition. If she wanted to be an actress, she must be an actress. It was what she would have liked best herself. She said so once to Madeleine.

"You?" Madeleine exclaimed, then hastily, "my dear Fenny, you're much too real a person, too worth while."

Again Ellen read an oblique criticism of Rose Danby, but she was not entirely convinced, for the impression of Rose that had come to her across the footlights was of a powerful sincerity, a poetry that made her a living channel for noble words, and she thought that she saw the beginnings of the same quality in Juliet.

When they opened their copies of *Twelfth Night* and she

explained, "You remember it begins with the Duke, Orsino," Juliet said, "Oh, don't let's read about him! Oliver was Orsino. I don't like him."

"Who is Oliver? Why don't you like him?"

"I did like him first, when he was my friend. He used to take me to sail boats on the Round Pond. Afterwards I hated him."

"What made you change your mind?"

Juliet would not say, and Ellen did not press her. She thought that Oliver was probably some young actor who had made a fuss of the child for a time and then forgotten her, leaving her with a sense of rejection. She tried instead to separate Orsino from Oliver in Juliet's mind by telling her about a performance at Ainley in which her brother had played Orsino and they had made him a cloak at home out of an old curtain. Juliet was always entranced by any story of back-stage contrivance, and seemed to have forgotten about Oliver when Ellen took up the play again.

Madeleine went that evening to dinner with the Warners. She dined there every week, and often went with Lucrezia to some opera or concert in Florence. Ellen did not mind being alone, but she always felt a resentment of which she was ashamed when Madeleine left her for Lucrezia. It was a different Madeleine who came back from Lucrezia, less natural and friendly. Lucrezia, when she came to the Villa Meridiana, made a great fuss of both Madeleine and Juliet, but her eye slipped over Ellen as over part of the wall. When Madeleine spoke to Ellen, Lucrezia was like someone waiting politely for an interruption to finish. Ellen could not understand how anyone so considerate and kind as Madeleine could stand her, and Madeleine criticized her a good deal, but unmistakably sought her company. Once or twice she had come home so distant and, Ellen could almost have said, artificial, that she would gladly have gone to bed before Madeleine came back if it were not that she always hoped to hear something about Daniel.

It was more than a fortnight since they had spent the Saturday afternoon together, and she had not seen him. She did not know what she had expected, but certainly not that he should just go out of her life again. She listened eagerly for any news of him.

Once Madeleine mentioned that he had taken Shand to hear Tosca. Once she came back from a concert and said casually, "It was quite a big party—the Roziani were there and Claud Flocton and the tutor and a girl I didn't know." Dismay ran up in Ellen like a sheet of flame. On that Saturday she and Daniel seemed to exist alone in a vacuum. But of course he would know girls, would meet at the Warners' villa young, beautiful, intelligent creatures who could both delight his eye and understand his pictures. In their company he had probably forgotten all about her.

This evening Madeleine was dining at the villa to meet some American friends of the Warners who had come from Paris.

"I wish you were coming too, Fenny. I'm tired of going out alone!"

Ellen also wished it. For the first time a conscious resentment at the difference between the lives of employers and employees disturbed her. She, too, needed friends. Gastone was out, but Ofelia brought her dinner into the courtyard, waiting on her with especial kindness.

"The Signorina will not be lonely?" she said.

She carried the lamp out on to the *piazzale* for Ellen, who took her Italian grammar and phrase-book and tried to work, but so many moths fluttered into the lamp that she switched it out, and sat listening to the cicadas and the more distant croak of frogs from the stream at the bottom of the hill. Close to the house a nightingale was singing in a plane tree; fire-flies wove their pattern of sparks above the flower-beds. A few weeks ago simply to be here on such a night would have been enough for Ellen, but the first rapture of astonishment was over. Now she wanted more: she wanted to share the pleasure, as she had shared it that Saturday. If she could not have Daniel's company, she would have liked to go to a theatre or concert among lights and people. The night, with its scents and nightingale and fire-flies, stirred too much longing. Ellen was lonely, and envied Madeleine her fun.

She heard the wheels of the car earlier than she expected. The light in the courtyard was switched on, and she went in through the arch. Her eyes were so dazzled after the dark garden that at first she only saw Madeleine, who was wearing a red cloak over an apricot dress, as a blur of light colour.

"Have you had a good evening?"

"Not very. Lucrezia really has some awful friends! These were the worst kind of globe-trotting Americans. And it was so hot, and dinner seemed to go on forever. I kept on thinking how much nicer it would be on the *piazzale* here with you." She slipped her hand through Ellen's arm. "Let's go and sit there for a few minutes. I've asked Ofelia to bring some iced lemonade."

"Were there any more people, then?" Ellen asked.

"Some man from Rome, a cousin of Lucrezia's. I've promised to go to Rome with her for three or four days soon. I haven't seen it since we were there on our honeymoon. You and Juliet will be all right here?"

"Yes, of course."

"Oh, I nearly forgot! I've got a message for you from Shand's tutor. He wants you and Juliet to go for a picnic with them at that ruined villa you can see from the back of the house. I think Donata is going, too, so Juliet won't be pleased, but you'll be able to keep the peace. I said Friday; they'll fetch you in the car at eleven. Will that be all right?"

"I'm sure it will. We shall enjoy it very much."

The world, which in the last few days had seemed to be closing in round Ellen more graciously but as inexorably as at home, suddenly expanded.

"Did Juliet seem all right at bed-time?" Madeleine asked.

"I thought she was rather tired, but this was the warmest day we've had; and we went for a long walk."

"She came into my room while I was dressing and begged me not to go. She said she didn't feel ill and there was no special reason, but she wanted me to stay. She got into quite a state about it. She never used to be silly about my leaving her, but she's had rather a thing about it since she was ill this spring. I suppose she got a bit spoilt. I thought it was best not to take too much notice. I knew she'd be all right with you, once I'd gone. She's been so much happier and more like herself since you came."

"We had a curious little upset over *Twelfth Night* this morning."

Ellen told her of Juliet's prejudice against Orsino. As she spoke she felt uneasily that something was wrong. In the dark she could

61

only just see the shape of Madeleine's head and cloaked shoulders, but she had an impression that they had stiffened.

"She means Oliver Farren."

"Oh!"

For Ellen, of course, knew Oliver Farren by name and fame, although she had never seen him act, and had not somehow connected him with the picture of a young man who took Juliet to the Round Pond.

"What did she say about Oliver?"

"Just that he played Orsino and she didn't like him, so she didn't want to read that part of the play."

"She's about far too much with grown-up people; she picks up all sorts of rubbish when she goes to my mother! When we get home I think I shall send her to play healthy games at a good no-nonsense boarding-school. I don't want any more lemonade, Fenny; help yourself if you do, but I'm going up to bed now. Good-night."

## CHAPTER IX

THEY LEFT the car half-way up the hill by the farm gate, and climbed the rough grass path between the olive trees. Daniel and Shand carried the picnic-basket between them. Juliet scrambled easily up the slope, but Donata hung back and complained that her sandal hurt her. Ellen made her sit down on a tuft of grass and examined it, but she found no trace of a blister, nor of anything to rub in the soft leather.

"I knew it was a mistake to bring you!" Shand said, glowering.

"Don't waste time on her, Ellen!" Daniel also scowled at Donata. "She's only doing it to attract attention."

"It's a steep climb if you're not used to scrambling. You go on, and Donata and I will come slowly."

Looking surprised, they picked up the basket again and followed Juliet along the path.

Juliet had reached a place where the olives gave way to brambles and sparse pines. They saw her pink skirt between the tree-trunks, then she turned back and came into full view. She stood,

62

a sculptured figure in the windless air, stretching out one brown arm to point ahead. She called Shand, but he trudged sulkily up the hill, gripping his handle of the basket and taking no notice of her.

"They're always horrid to me!" Donata whined.

Ellen thought that they were, and that Donata, although an unprepossessing child, had a good deal to bear for seven years old.

"We haven't very far to go now. Look, you can see the garden wall through the trees. You tell me the names of all your dolls and what colour their dresses are, and by the time you've finished we shall be there."

Daniel came back to help them over the crumbling wall. In the hayfield that had been a lawn in front of the villa Juliet and Shand were already unpacking the picnic lunch. Ellen turned to look back at the tower and roofs of their own villa across the valley. Daniel swung Donata over the wall and put her down in the grass.

"Run and help the others to unpack lunch." To Ellen, as he gave her a negligent hand, he said, "Don't let your maternal instinct spill over Donata. She's a thoroughly disagreeable child, as tough and greedy as her mother. All her whims are calculated."

"I know she's spoilt, but I don't think it does her any good to be bullied. Besides, it's bad for Shand."

"You haven't stopped being a school-mistress, have you?"

Without answering him, Ellen walked away from him towards the roofless villa. Tears that took her by surprise prevented her from seeing where she was going. She knocked her ankle against a broken stone pillar in the grass, and the sharp pain added to her desolation. From the beginning something had gone wrong with this meeting. The Daniel of that perfect Saturday afternoon and evening in Florence had been transformed during the fortnight's interval into a partly mythical figure, so that it was a shock to find him only a thin young man with untidy hair and an arrogant manner who seemed this afternoon to wish to shut himself into an alliance with Shand against the rest of the world. Her disappointment, like a cloud, took colour from the whole landscape. Standing among the broken stones, tracing with her eyes a jagged

63

crack that ran from window to floor in the weathered wall, she was angry. She said to herself that his manners were intolerable. She would tell Madeleine that she did not want any more joint picnics because Shand's tutor was rude to her, and Madeleine would perhaps repeat this to Lucrezia, and Daniel would be sacked. A little shocked at discovering such malice in herself, Ellen altered this to "reprimanded". He needed to be made to realize . . .

"Smell!"

A spray of rhynchospermum was thrust under her nose. Distractedly she sniffed up the sweetness of the Italian summer. She noticed the dark hairs on the lean wrist holding out the spray, and the bracelet of white on the sunburnt skin left by the strap of a watch. She said stupidly:

"Have you lost your watch?"

"Broken the strap. It's in my pocket. Aren't you coming to have lunch, Ellen? The children have got it all unpacked?"

She realized that the climb and the resinous air of the hill-crest had made her very hungry. Either from the scramble or from feeling, her knees were trembling. As she walked by his side, Daniel said:

"I had a colossal row with Lucrezia this morning."

She understood that she was receiving an indirect apology and, eager to sympathize, asked:

"What about?"

"Oh, I don't know. Nothing. She likes them. In a way I do, too."

She was silent, nonplussed, and obscurely envious. He held out the spray of rhynchospermum.

"Here! For you! Put it in your dress!"

She fastened it to the front of her cotton dress with the brooch she was wearing. As its sweet scent reached her nostrils again, she brimmed with happiness. A dislocation slipped into place, and the real young man at her side expelled the mythical Daniel who had grown in a vacuum.

The children had spread out ham, cheese, bread and fruit in the shade of a tall cypress, half throttled by the wisteria that had wreathed its trunk and was pushing up tendrils to the top of the tree. The flask of wine stood in the shade, its fat wicker belly

64

half hidden by grass and daisies. Juliet was making a daisy-chain, while Shand, sprawling in the long grass, picked handfuls of daisies and threw them into her lap.

"I want one! I want a daisy necklace, too," Donata cried.

"You can have this one. They're no use to wear; they only break. I just like making them."

"You should make one for yourself, you silly thing." Shand frowned at Donata. "You always expect everybody to give you everything and do everything for you."

But Daniel, uncorking the wine, said:

"Oh, shut up, Shand, don't be a bore! Let her alone!" He smiled across at Ellen and she smiled at him. "Hold out your glass." He lifted his. "To our next meeting, Ellen!"

They both drank. The three children were silent for a moment, looking curiously at their elders, struck out of their own pre-occupations by the visible exchange of feeling in the world lived over their heads.


## CHAPTER X

ELLEN'S ONLY evening dress, a plain black one, had appeared at every school dance and prize-giving for two years, but she had an old soft Paisley shawl of her grandmother's, a small diamond brooch that had been her mother's, and a string of good artificial pearls, her own twenty-first birthday present. As she brushed up her short, curling hair and pinned on the carnations that Juliet had picked for her, she was pleased with her reflection and felt light-hearted—a young woman going out for the evening.

"You look beautiful, Fenny!" Juliet said earnestly.

"Sit still a minute while I brush your hair. I want to make you look beautiful."

And you are, you will be, she thought, looking over Juliet's parting at the face in the mirror.

"Mummy is wearing her silver dress that Grannie Rose gave her for Christmas."

They were going with the Warners, who had guests staying,

and came to fetch them in two cars, so that Ellen and Juliet were put into the smaller car with Daniel and Shand. Ellen thought this arrangement perfect, and Shand, also now in high spirits, agreed with her.

"It's much more fun in here than with all those chattering parrots."

"Oh, yes." Daniel slumped down in the seat. "Always travel third for company."

He spoke with a bitterness which penetrated Ellen's state of bliss. She was sometimes annoyed when Lucrezia looked through her, but she also felt contempt, having long ago decided that Lucrezia was not only undemocratic, but also vulgar. She did not in the least mind being the governess in the nursery party, but she became aware of an angry tumult of feeling in Daniel. It had not occurred to her before that anyone so interesting and enlightened as she thought him could mind having been humbly born and kept in what his employers considered his place. She felt sorry for his vulnerable spirit and said:

"I agree with Shand! I think it's very nice having a car to ourselves! I hope we all sit together."

Her tone pleaded with Daniel to enjoy the evening, to do what her mother would have called "get rid of the little black dog on his back", and when he responded, sat up and began to tell her what to think about Shakespeare's Fools, she felt in herself an astonished sense of power at being able to recall him from one of his dark moods.

She was so happy that evening that she was almost unconscious. She seemed to be living on a level of her being below the surface of her mind. The coloured figures on the stage, the magic words were an emanation from Daniel's nearness, his shoulder a few inches from her own, his knees touching hers as he fidgeted in his seat. During the interval, as they were strolling in the gardens, they lost sight for the moment of Juliet and Shand.

Daniel said casually:

"What's happened to our children?"

The words gave form to a longing of which Ellen had been only half aware. She began to know what she wanted. She had hardly yet begun to consider whether it would ever be possible that she might get it.

66

As the applause died down at the end of the play, Madeleine came down the row to Ellen.

"I'm going back to supper with the company in Florence, Fenny. I should get Juliet straight to bed. Gastone was going to leave us some sandwiches; you'll find them in the *salone*. Don't wait up for me. Somebody will drive me home."

On the way back to the villa Juliet fell asleep in the car with her head against Ellen's arm, and Daniel had to lift her out. He said, "Good-night, Ellen, dear. I'll be seeing you soon. Next week sometime," and leaned out to wave as the car drove away.

Juliet murmured with drowsy pride:

"I must be up very late. It must be as late as midnight."

"It's after midnight."

"Ooh. The latest I've been!"

She hardly awoke fully as Ellen slipped off her clothes, sponged her face and plaited her hair, and her eyes closed again as soon as she was tucked into bed.

Ellen went downstairs to the *salone*, ate a sandwich and drank a glass of wine. She went up to her room, and looked in at Juliet, who was fast asleep. She did not feel sleepy. She put on her dressing-gown, brushed her hair, and sat by the window, in a trance of contentment, looking out at the still night. She could not have said what she was thinking about, nor how long she had been sitting there before she heard a car drive up to the front of the villa. She switched on the light and looked at her clock. It was half-past two. She was just going to get into bed when there was a cautious tap on her door. She went to open it. Madeleine stood in the passage, her cloak huddled anyhow over her shimmering dress.

"Fenny! I saw your light under your door. I didn't want to wake Juliet. Come to my room; please come! I want you!"

Thinking that she must be feeling ill, Ellen followed her quickly. The lights sprang up in the pretty bedroom, twinkling in the glass and silver on the dressing-table, where two large photographs stood: Rose Danby smiling in a low-necked velvet dress; Charles rather formal and severe, confronted them—a silent audience who had been waiting for the curtain to go up. Madeleine flung herself on the bed and broke into hysterical sobbing.

Utterly astonished, Ellen stood by her for a minute not knowing

67

what to do. Madeleine's sobs grew more violent; she clutched the pillow to her face, half stifling them. She writhed on the bed as if she were trying to burrow her way through it, and her feet drummed on the coverlet. Ellen put a hand on her hot shoulder.

"What is it, Madeleine, dear? What's the matter?"

A fresh storm of sobs was the only answer.

"I'll get you some water."

Ellen went into the bathroom and filled a glass. When she brought it back, Madeleine was still sobbing hysterically and clutching at the bedclothes as if to let go would be to slide over a precipice.

"Hush!" Ellen said sternly. "Stop it! You'll make yourself sick! Sit up and drink some water!"

The sharpness of her tone seemed to do some good. Madeleine's movements became less convulsive. She turned on her side, and let Ellen see her ravaged face. Ellen put an arm under her shoulders, raised her head and held the glass to her mouth. Madeleine's teeth chattered against the glass, but she gulped down some of the water, gasped and made a fumbling attempt to wipe her face with the sheet.

"Oh, Fenny, I'm so miserable! My life is such a mess! I don't know what to do! I wish I was dead!"

Ellen pulled up the pillows behind her.

"Sit quiet for a minute. I'll get a sponge and sponge your face, then you can tell me about it."

She bathed Madeleine's eyes and gently pushed back her ruffled hair. Madeleine was growing quieter. She reached out her hand for the glass and drank the rest of the water. Ellen gave her a handkerchief. She blew her nose, sat up against the pillows. She looked so forlorn and young, with her blotched cheeks and scarlet nose, that Ellen felt almost as if it was Juliet in trouble. She was divided between curiosity, pity and a faint enjoyment of which she was hardly aware.

"Won't you let me take your dress off? You'll spoil it; and you'll be much more comfortable in your dressing-gown."

Ellen shook out the dress, and spread it carefully over a chair, noticing with regret a long tear where Madeleine's drumming heel had caught the tinsel lace. As she turned back towards the bed, her eyes met the eyes of the photographs. Charles Rivers

68

looked disapproving, but the face of Rose Danby was the face of one who had seen a good many young women in a tantrum, and for a second an older, not yet associated Ellen wondered whether Madeleine's tragedy was really beyond repair. Then, seeing her huddled forlornly against the pillows, she forgot everything except her wish to comfort her. She sat down on the chair by the bed.

"Won't you tell me what's the matter?"

"It's Oliver."

"Oliver?"

"Yes, yes. Oliver Farren!" Madeleine's eyes filled again. "I can't live without him! I can't! I've tried so hard, but it's no good!"

"But—was he there tonight?"

"No, no, of course he wasn't. But it brought it all back again. Holbrook, who played Sir Toby, is a friend of his. They all knew him, and talked about him. They knew about us, of course. They said Oliver was looking very strained and thin. They meant I'd been cruel to him. I wish I'd never gone to the damned play! I wish I'd never gone!"

"But—is Oliver over here?"

"Oh, Fenny, you don't understand! We were lovers. We asked Charles to let me divorce him. But he wouldn't. He said he would divorce me and keep Juliet. Then she was ill, and I felt it was all my fault. When she had a high temperature she cried for me all the time, and wouldn't let me go out of her sight for a minute, and I felt I couldn't leave her. But I felt I couldn't let Oliver go, and I couldn't make up my mind. He was so impatient! If he could have waited a few weeks until Juliet was quite well again and I wasn't so tired, perhaps it would have worked out, but he got angry, and we had a furious quarrel, and parted. Then Charles was very kind. He said it would be a good thing for me to get right away from it all and have this holiday abroad, and he would be here as much as he could, and we would try to make a go of it again for Juliet's sake. And I have tried! It's been so happy and peaceful here, with you and Juliet! I thought my life could go on without Oliver, I thought I was getting over it! But tonight, with people who knew him and had seen him lately, it all came back. I knew I couldn't live without him! I wanted to throw everything up and go straight back to him."

69

She writhed against the pillows, and began to cry again.

"I'm young, Fenny! I can't let my life finish now! I can't go on being miserable! I can't go on with this! I'm not Charles' kind of person. I can't make myself into it! I've tried, but it's no use! Oh, God, what shall I do!"

"I'm sorry! I'm so very sorry!" was all that Ellen could say.

Her own feelings were in confusion. What had seemed to be a piece of firm ground, as solid as that in which her childhood was rooted, had suddenly proved to be rubble. Hazily she understood things that she had not connected before. Charles half concealed irritation. Juliet's underlying insecurity, the relief and rest which Madeleine had appeared to find in their peaceful life. She felt as though she had suddenly stepped out of her depth. There did not seem to be anything that she could say. She patted Madeleine's shoulder as she sometimes patted Juliet's when she could not go to sleep and, feeling that it might be a relief to her to talk, asked:

"Have you known him long?"

"I've only really known him for about a year. I met him before, of course, at parties. I used to dislike him on the stage. I didn't get to know him until he was in a play with my mother. She brought him to lunch one Sunday, and he took a fancy to Juliet, and used to call for her and take her in the Park in the afternoon; then, when he brought her back, he used to stay and have tea with me, and we began to see more and more of each other, and so it all happened. And then we told Charles."

She slid down again, and crushed her face into the pillow.

"Oh, Fenny!" she wailed. "What shall I do? I can't go on like this! I don't love Charles, and he doesn't love me."

Feeling unable to discuss Madeleine's relationship with her husband, Ellen said diffidently:

"There's Juliet."

"I do love her!" Madeleine sounded as if she were repelling an accusation. "I've ruined my life for her! But it might be better for her. It's not good for children to live with parents who hate each other. And we shall if we have to go on with it. I should often see her, and she'll soon accept it. She's devoted to her father."

"And to you. Juliet is a very loving little girl."

There was a long silence. Madeleine moved restlessly against the pillow.

"Christ, how my head aches!"

"Wouldn't you like to undress and get into bed? I'll go down into the kitchen and make some tea."

"Oh, no, don't do that! Marcella would hear you and be very shocked and get up and insist on making the tea. Probably toast, too. No, Fenny, dear, don't bother. I've got plenty of aspirin. I'll take some and try to go to sleep. You go to bed, too. You must be tired out! I'm sorry I've kept you up! I think I had too much champagne. It often makes me stupid. Don't think any more about this. We shall have forgotten all about it in the morning."

## CHAPTER XI

"WHY COULDN'T I go in to Mummy this morning? I always go in and have the coffee-sugar dipped in coffee. Why couldn't I?"

"I told you. Because she was very late back last night and the party gave her a headache and she asked Ofelia to tell us she didn't want to be disturbed."

Juliet looked dissatisfied.

"Who was she having a party *with*?"

"With some of the people who were acting in the play."

"Why didn't she come home with us? Who were the other people at the party?"

"I don't know. It doesn't matter to you, anyhow. Get on with your sums."

"I was only asking you about my own mother," Juliet replied with dignity. "You're very cross this morning."

Ellen for a moment felt like giving her a slap, but she looked at the indignant face confronting her boldly, laughed and said:

"I dare say I am. I was very late going to sleep, and I had a headache, too, when I woke up. I'm sorry, Juliet. But don't worry any more about your mother. She's very tired. She'll be coming down soon. I want you to get that sum right, but when you have, we'll have a run out to the *orto* and each pick six strawberries to eat before we start the next lesson."

Juliet nodded vigorously, licked her pencil and drove the point through the paper to show her willingness to fulfil her part of the contract.

Madeleine put her head in just before they finished lessons to say that she was going over to the Warners for lunch to arrange with Lucrezia about the visit to Rome. She was very carefully made up, and looked pretty, but subdued. She said that her head still ached, and would until she had had another night's rest. At dinner that evening she chattered about her plans for Rome, and went straight up to bed afterwards. For the next two days, before she went away, she was friendly but distant. Except when Juliet or the servants were there, Ellen hardly saw her. She helped her by keeping out of her way, sure that Madeleine must regret that unguarded hour in the night. She was sorry for the check in the relationship, but would have been more sorry if her own head had not been full of Daniel. She was on the alert for the sound of the telephone, or of a car on the gravel sweep, and her strongest feeling about Madeleine's visit to Rome was that she could not be sure whether she would be more or less likely to see him when Lucrezia was away.

The scene in the night had disturbed her, shifting her angle of vision. She felt less serene, realizing more sharply than ever before how much lies below the surface. She had been shaken, but also stimulated, and in spite of her compassion for Madeleine, she felt a kind of pleasure in a realization which, if it threatened, also seemed to extend her world. The impression faded as she saw Madeleine playing with Juliet, picking flowers and putting them in the rooms, making arrangements for the household in her absence. Ellen had a strong belief in the compelling power of what she thought of as ordinary life. It had been the recognized cure for her own occasional tantrums or bursts of inexplicable adolescent misery. "Why don't you help me to cover the jam!" her mother would say, "or finish your homework? Or go and play with Hugh?" It had been implicit in her upbringing that action was safe, but feeling was dangerous, and she looked on Madeleine as someone who in the night had nearly fallen off a tight-rope, but had managed to scramble back. Ellen was glad

72

that she was going to Rome, for this would make a break, and when she came home again the constraint between them would probably have vanished, and they would all be happy together as before.

In the full heat of June that was now upon them Juliet slept all the afternoon, and as she was often not hungry at lunch-time, Ellen allowed her to stay up and have dinner with her in the courtyard. Madeleine had spoken of staying three days in Rome, and of sending a telegram to say what time she would be back, but on the fourth morning after she left there were only picture postcards for Ellen and Juliet saying nothing about her return. Ellen hoped every day for some word from Daniel. Gastone could drive the car, and one afternoon she asked him to drive them into Florence and took Juliet to see the Palazzo Vecchio and to have tea at Doney's, but although they strolled afterwards in the Via Tornobuoni, they did not, as she had hoped, see any sign of Daniel or the Warner children. The Villa Bronciliano, only four miles away, seemed once again to have vanished into the blue air. Ellen lay half awake and half dreaming through the siesta, reliving her meetings with Daniel, or imagining new ones. At night, when Juliet had gone to bed, she wandered in the garden, where only an occasional fire-fly still flickered above the wilting roses. She found it difficult to concentrate on her Italian grammar—her mind slipped away from any book that she was reading. She sewed in fits and starts, looking up whenever she heard a footstep in the courtyard. Only when she was with Juliet, her attention was fully occupied. Juliet was happy.

As she lay down in bed on the fourth night after Madeleine's departure, she locked her hands behind Ellen's neck, pulled her face down for a good-night kiss, and said:

"You and I live nicely together in this big house."

She slept the next afternoon from lunch-time until five, and Ellen allowed her to stay up for an hour after dinner to find the stars on Sir Robert's globe. As she came down from tucking her up in bed, she heard a quick footstep in the courtyard, which was still partly lit by the lamp on the dinner-table. Her heart jumped; she knew who it was before Daniel came into the radius of the lamp. He smiled, seeing her, and the shaded light softened the contours of his bony face, making him look younger.

73

"I came over on my bicycle because we haven't heard a word from Lucrezia, and Warner wanted to know if you'd heard anything about when they were coming back?"

Almost too happy to remember what she had heard from Madeleine, Ellen took him out on to the *piazzale*, where Gastone brought fresh coffee, putting the tray down between them with a benevolent smile. They had forgotten to switch off the light in the globe, and Daniel knelt down by it and began with much more certainty than Ellen and Juliet to identify the stars. She hardly listened to what he was saying. She was absorbing again his physical presence. The world narrowed down to his face and the outline of his shock of hair in the ghostly illumination of blue light from the globe.

"There's the Great Bear," he said. Then, as she only smiled vaguely at the sky, "Look, you stupid, there!" He took her by the shoulders, and his arm shot up, directing her eyes. The excitement that drummed in all her pulses made the stars only a dazzle in the sky. She said, "Oh yes, I see!" and had no idea whether she was looking at the right one. He gave her shoulders a shake and let her go. She picked up the coffee-pot and began to pour out. He sat down on the step, nursing the little cup in his long hands. He said, "What a night!" She felt that he meant more than the warm, flower-scented air and the brilliant sky. She felt excitement running between them. Shyness pushing her into speech, she asked:

"Have you done any painting lately?"

"No, hardly any, except a few sketches when I'm out with Shand. I sometimes think I shall never paint again. It was fatal to come here. One feels one's own piddling efforts are simply an impertinence."

"I don't see why you should. If I could write a play or a poem, I should feel it was worth doing, even though I should know it could never be like Shakespeare."

"You're always so bloody reasonable!" Less deflated than she would have been six weeks ago, she was also less surprised when he added, "I suppose you're right. But it isn't only the skill. It's their damned conviction. You can see it in every line. Are you religious, Ellen?"

"No, not exactly. I was brought up to be. I was very religious

74

when I was confirmed, when I was about fourteen. Then at Oxford I rather grandly grew out of it. I made what I thought was a great stand, and wouldn't go to church when I was at home in the vac. My mother and I had fights about it. My father believed in letting people alone, and was too busy and too tired, and anyhow very shy of talking seriously. Now I just don't know, except that I feel there is something—a plan, a kind of pattern, something too big for us to grasp in this dimension. I don't think about it as much as I ought."

"My trouble is that I don't believe in what you call 'something', but I don't see how life's bearable without it."

"What is it that makes your life so unbearable?"

"It's not my life. I suppose I'm quite lucky. I've got some talent. I'm fairly healthy. That breakdown last winter was the first real illness I've ever had. I don't like teaching art to a lot of boneheads, but I like it much better than I should have liked cutting coal. I enjoy the use of my eyes in a way that you wouldn't understand—nobody does who doesn't paint. But the conditions of human life altogether seem to me intolerable, the terrible isolation of being alive, and the pointlessness of it, and the certainty of death being the only certainty, and human beings, whatever they were meant to be, are so degraded and spoilt! Look how nasty people are!"

"No, they aren't. They're mixed."

"By this time it's a poor mixture. That's why all personal relationships are unbearable."

"I think they're what makes everything worth while."

"Because you're romantic and inexperienced, because you don't know what people are really like. You haven't any idea what I'm like, for instance."

"Yes, I have. You want to be horrid, but you can't."

He laughed, and said in a lighter, teasing voice:

"I knew quite a lot about you, Ellen, the first time I saw you. I knew that your home was full of solid, Victorian furniture, very well polished, and old clean linen sheets, beautifully darned. I knew that all the bills were paid every month, and that you never read other people's letters, nor used scent, and would plunge into a burning house to save a child."

"Well, you were probably quite wrong about that. I'm

frightened of fire. It was always one of my nightmares that the house was burning."

"Mine was a black creature coming up from some dark place underground. The mine, I suppose. But I always expected it to come through the bedroom floor. I can remember now, when I was sent up to bed before my brothers, lying with every muscle pulled so tight that I felt as if they would crack. It was the only way not to go to sleep, and if I went to sleep, I thought my bogey would be up through the floor and on to me. Oh, well, adult life has its advantages! You said there were some glow-worms in the side garden. Take me to see them."

When they were walking back between rose-beds where only the white roses were triumphantly visible, Daniel said:

"It's rather peaceful at Bronciliano now Lucrezia's away. Grant and I sit and smoke together on the terrace in the evenings. I think he's quite glad to have company. He's not a bad old stick when you get him alone. I've been working on him to let Shand go back to the aunts in America when I leave. It's no use the boy eating his heart out here. Apparently the aunts had had Shand from a baby, and when Grant married Lucrezia they were discouraging because she is a Catholic, and they didn't want to give up the child. There was a meeting, and it went badly. I should think they and Lucrezia hated each other at sight. Anyhow, she carried Shand off, and won't hear of him going back to them. Grant thinks it's so noble of her to be determined to be a mother to the difficult step-son."

"Perhaps she does feel it's her duty."

"Perhaps, my aunt! Lucrezia's duties are what she wants to do. But Grant is interesting when he talks about his early life, before he made so much money. I'm sorry for him now. This isn't his *milieu* at all; he's quite disorientated. He did go so far as to say to me that he wished Lucrezia could have settled in the States. But it seems that Madame nearly died when Bianca was born, and after that her nerves wouldn't stand exile, and in about a year she wore Grant down. She's still on at him to go and live in Rome."

"I suppose they will in the end."

"It's the one thing, apparently, that Grant stands out against. I gather that all Lucrezia's family despised him as a vulgar

76

American and all tried to borrow money off him. He's not mean, but he takes money very seriously."

"I know a lot of people like that at home. My father had no respect for money at all. He used to laugh at them."

He answered sharply:

"My people never had any, so of course they took it seriously. You respect money all right if you can't afford a bit of meat in the middle of the week. That's another thing you don't know anything about."

"You tell me so many things I don't know anything about, I keep on hoping that one day you'll come across something I do."

"I might. I might tell you something you're really very good at."

She looked at him hopefully, but he only said:

"If my tyre's gone down, shall I be able to borrow a pump?"

They walked across the shadowy courtyard to his bicycle propped against the wall. He halted with one foot on the pedal.

"Can't you just see those two harpies in Rome? Trailing round the expensive shops, trailing from one restaurant to another with an escort of Italian cavaliers and people from the Embassy supplying their wants."

"Don't call Madeleine a harpy! She isn't!"

Ellen, who had been envying her St. Peter's, the Colosseum and the Sistine Chapel, paused to envisage a different picture.

"Why do you hate them so much? I don't like Lucrezia, but I don't think she treats you badly. You seem to do pretty well what you like. And you don't know Madeleine at all. You haven't really got a thing against her!"

"Haven't I? I have against all parasite women when I think of the life my mother led."

"Perhaps she has been happier." I could be so happy, Ellen thought, in a mining village with you.

"When she was forty she was old." He swung his leg over the saddle. "When am I going to see you again?"

Ellen's heart beat fast with pleasure.

"Whenever you like."

"What about Saturday afternoon and evening in Florence?"

"If they've come back. Otherwise I don't like to leave Juliet for so long."

"Oh, what nonsense! As if a houseful of idle servants couldn't look after one brat."

"I'm responsible for her."

"You're a prig, Ellen."

"Well, anyhow, I'm not a parasite; I'm trying to earn my salary."

"They ought to have to look after their own bloody kids."

"Then we should never have come to Italy."

"Perhaps," he said gloomily, "it would have been better if we hadn't."

"Oh, no, it wouldn't."

At the absolute conviction in her voice he laughed self-consciously.

"Well, Saturday, if they're back. If not, early next week. If they don't appear by then, I'll send a telegram to say that Donata's dying. I'll tell you one thing you are good at, Ellen dear. I always feel better for seeing you. Good-night."

## CHAPTER XII

IN THE long field that tilted down from the garden wall to the stream at the bottom of the valley, Ellen and Daniel watched the Mandini family cutting their first corn between the olives. Shand had established himself in the shade, and was sketching, his back propped against the big jar of aquarella to which the thirsty harvesters came at intervals. Juliet squatted by his side, sometimes scribbling imitatively on her own block, sometimes watching him as he drew the brush between his lips and narrowed his eyes at the brilliant light that seemed to burn into the air from the waist-high corn.

The heat, in which Madeleine had been languid and fretful ever since her return from Rome, made Ellen feel like a ripening fruit. As they moved into a patch of shade, she took off her big straw hat and with her fingers lifted the flattened hair from her damp head. She watched the curved blade, wielded by old grandmother Mandini with a man's skill and energy, slashing the tall stalks close to the earth, while ten-year-old Marco

Mandini, the muscles of his strong back rippling under the bare skin, worked in time with her rhythm between the next pair of olives.

"I wish I could do it, or do anything as perfectly as that!" Ellen sighed. "I should like to have been born a *contadina* on one of these farms. I should like to cut corn all day and go in at night to a huge plate of *pasta* with some wine, and then fall into bed."

"And fall out of it at four o'clock tomorrow morning to cut more corn?"

"I don't think I should mind much, in this weather. It's lovely in the early morning. I've been for a walk then several times."

"That's about my time for going to sleep."

"It wouldn't be if you didn't worry about so many things that don't matter."

"As if anybody's problems mattered to anybody else!"

"You know yours do to me!"

It was the kind of remark that generally provoked a snub from Daniel, but Ellen knew now that the snub was often automatic. Daniel said, "More fool you to add my troubles to your own," but he said it lightly, and smiled at her. When she answered, "Oh, just at the moment I haven't any troubles of my own," he said as if he meant it, "Long may the moment last! It suits you," he added, "being so happy," at which she became happier, and felt as if she was putting out flowers.

They had strolled into the shadow of the garden wall, and were startled when a voice overhead called to them. Lucrezia and Madeleine had come out of the house, and were leaning on the wall looking down at them. Madeleine's pink sunshade gave back to her face the colour that had been drained from it by the heat. She had pushed her hair behind her ears, and the austere line emphasized the beautiful curve of her cheek and jaw. Her bare arms and throat were honey-brown. She swung herself sideways on to the wall, and her bright cotton skirt spread like a fan over the stones. Lucrezia was bare-headed, the sun polishing her brassy hair. Her glance ran over Ellen and Daniel standing on the stubble below the wall. She said something to Madeleine and smiled and looked again, her sharp black eyes like nails driving her meaning home. Madeleine stared down at them with surprise. She lowered her sunshade so that the light fell on her face, which looked pale and pinched. Ellen was startled by that drawn look and thought, Madeleine really shouldn't come out till it's cooler, and then thought, But it's not the heat; she's unhappy. She's still fretting for Oliver. She had a feeling that she had been wanting in sympathy to Madeleine because of her own happy preoccupation.

Madeleine waved to the children and called, "Come along! Tea's ready on the terrace."

That evening, as they were strolling after dinner on the English lawn, Madeleine asked casually, "Daniel Blackett is nice, isn't he? And interesting? Lucrezia thinks he paints quite well and knows a good deal about painting. Really I hardly know him. When we go there Lucrezia chatters all the time, so that you can't attend to anyone else; and she always sends him off with the children. Juliet said the other day that Mrs. Warner always says, 'I am so glad to see you, darling; do run away and find the others.' But you've seen much more of Daniel, haven't you? Tell me about him."

Ellen was only too delighted to talk about Daniel. She began to tell Madeleine the story of his early life, his struggles and achievements, some of his difficulties. She realized suddenly that she had been talking for some time, and broke off, abashed.

"I'm glad you've made friends with him, Fenny. It sounds as though he'd always been rather lonely, and I'm sure the Warners and their friends can't be congenial to him. I often think I don't really like them myself. I don't know why I keep on going there. It's always a relief to get back to you and Juliet. I know perfectly well that Lucrezia is hard and egotistical and wouldn't move a hand for me if I was in trouble. So I can understand what it must be for Daniel to get right away from them and talk to anyone as sane and sympathetic as you are. It's nice for you, too, to have a change from our quiet life. You like him very much, don't you?"

Native caution and reserve kept Ellen from replying, "I love him," but her voice as she replied, "Yes, I do, very much!" said it for her. She added, "I do think if you talked to him without a crowd you would see how interesting he is, and what a lot there is to him. Every time I talk to him he makes me see things I never saw before. As if all my thoughts were like pieces of a jig-saw puzzle and he shook them together in a box and threw them out to make new patterns. It's exciting! I should so much like you to know him better."

"Why don't you ask him to come over by himself some evening and just have dinner quietly with us?"

"I should love to." To Ellen it seemed that it would be almost like bringing her young man home. She added, "I can ask him on Saturday—that is, if you don't mind my staying down in Florence to have dinner with him after the flower show."

"Why, of course! You don't get out nearly enough. When Charles comes back I think I shall send you to have a few days' holiday in Venice. You ought to see some more of Italy while you are here."

"I don't need a holiday. I couldn't be happier than I am here."

Not even Venice was going to tempt Ellen a week out of Daniel's reach.

Some friends of Madeleine's—a young actor and his wife from England on their way to Rome—came for the week-end of the flower show. Lucrezia and Donata were to join their party, but Shand had begged to go for a lunch and sketching picnic with Daniel, and Ellen was to meet Daniel in the square at six. She had bought a new dress: corn-coloured linen with squares of drawn thread-work. The colour suited her. She tied a new brown velvet ribbon round her wide straw hat, looked at herself in the mirror, and felt pretty. Not only Juliet, who was always firmly convinced that she was beautiful, admired her. Madeleine and the Sewells told her how much they liked her new dress. She started off in high spirits for the afternoon.

At the end of the flower show, Lucrezia, as she often did, began to complicate everybody's arrangements. She wanted to send the little girls home with Ellen and take Madeleine and the Sewells to have a drink with some friends of hers in one of the hotels, after which they would all have dinner together in Florence. Madeleine objected that Ellen had an engagement at six and wanted to do some shopping first. Juliet and Donata could be sent back to their house in the car. Jim Sewell, who had fallen in love with the villa, but obviously not with Lucrezia, offered to go home with Juliet. Lucrezia was not going to allow the only available man to abandon her party. Madeleine took Ellen aside, "Go along, Fenny, and get your shopping done and enjoy your evening! All this will settle itself. It's just a fuss about nothing." Ellen thankfully accepted, and went off across the Ponte Vecchio. Madeleine had seen and fancied a small china box in one of the antique shops, and if she could afford it, she wanted to buy it for her birthday next week. The box was quite as much as she could possibly afford—more, perhaps, than she could sensibly have afforded, but she was rather glad: Madeleine had shown her so much kindness. She bought it, and walked back towards the square.

She was a little before her time at the café. The waiter, who knew her by now, came and asked her if she wanted anything, but she said she would wait. She bought an evening paper for the sake of practising her Italian, but she kept on looking up at the colonnade where Daniel would probably appear. Once she unwrapped her present and admired the little box with its design of strawberry leaves. She planned to ask Ofelia to send it up on Madeleine's breakfast tray on her birthday morning. She had found out that Daniel's birthday was in September, and she began to wonder what she should give him—something he needed for his painting, some very special brush or canvas; she could perhaps find out in one of the art shops what he could want.

She looked at her watch, and saw that it was a quarter past six. It was not like Daniel to be late, and she did wonder for a minute if he had been knocked off his bicycle by one of the furiously driven Italian cars, but she thought it more likely that either he or Shand had stayed on to finish a sketch. It was too soon to be really anxious, but she no longer read the paper. She fished with her eyes in the chattering group that crowded the colonnade, hoping at any second to draw from among them the thin, casually dressed, quick-moving figure that for her carried magic. When the clock chimed the half-hour she grew really uneasy. Then a voice behind her said, "Fenny!" She turned and saw Madeleine and Daniel together coming towards her.

"Fenny, darling," Madeleine said, "I just came to tell you not to blame Mr. Blackett for being late, because it's all my fault! It was so hot in the hotel, and I didn't want to go on drinking. I slipped out and left them for a bit. I thought I'd go and buy one or two odds and ends in the straw market. Then I met Mr. Blackett, and you know how bad I am at bargaining in Italian. I asked him to come and help me to buy a table-cloth, and somehow it went on and on and took ages. We had to walk away twice and pretend we didn't want it, and I forgot the time. Please forgive me!"

"Of course; it doesn't matter a bit." Ellen was delighted that Daniel was here, after all, and pleased that these two, whom she loved, should have made a personal contact at last. She pulled back a chair. "Do sit down, Madeleine, and have a drink with us."

"No, my dear. Thank you. I couldn't possibly. I must go back and look after the poor Sewells before Lucrezia drives them mad." She turned to Daniel, "Thank you so much, Mr. Blackett. I'm awfully grateful! I do hate being done by these people. You are a wonderful shopper! I shall ask you to help me again. Good-bye, Fenny; don't hurry back. I'll tell Gastone to leave the door open. See you in the morning."

She moved quickly away, and her light dress and broad hat with its wreath of cornflowers were soon swallowed up in the crowd.

Daniel dropped into a chair and wiped his forehead.

"Florence is like an oven tonight. I feel absolutely done in!"

"I expect you rode too fast coming down."

"No, I didn't; but I've been standing about for half an hour in that blasted straw market, where they all shriek and pester you to buy things."

"I think it's rather fun; but not if you're tired, of course." Ellen seldom was, but had learnt not to be surprised at Daniel's habit of suddenly flopping into exhaustion. "I'm so glad you could help Madeleine."

"It's always the people like that, with lashings of money, who want to bargain down to the last lira."

Disappointed, yet obscurely relieved, Ellen explained.

"The Rivers aren't very rich, like the Warners. They can only have their holiday because the villa is lent to them; Madeleine told me so."

"I know, I know! They're terribly hard up, but they do get villas lent them, and they don't have to think twice about getting

83

there. What do they ever go short of? That woman who was selling the table-cloth that I had to beat down to the last lira could have told Mrs. Rivers something about being hard up!"

"But you told me it was right to bargain! You said the Italians expected it and put their first prices high on purpose, and despised foreigners who swallowed them."

"Yes; well, that's true. But somehow when I knew Madeleine Rivers was going off to eat a dinner that would cost what the market woman would spend on a fortnight's food, I felt revolted."

"She just didn't think of it that way, I suppose."

"I've no use for people who don't think."

"I hoped perhaps you were getting to know Madeleine a bit and like her better."

Jumping as if she had stung him, he replied:

"No, I don't like her. I shall never like her." He added unwillingly, "Except to look at."

He jerked his chair back.

"Ellen, let's get out of here; let's get out of Florence—it's too hot. Let's get on the *filo* bus and go and have dinner at Fiesole. I can pick up my bicycle on Monday; it's in the garage; and when it's cooler we can walk to Bronciliano, and I'll get a car and drive you home."

## CHAPTER XIII

THE TWO families had planned an expedition to the sea at Viareggio, but on the morning of the day Juliet was sick, complained of a headache and registered a small temperature. Ellen said that of course she would stay with her. Madeleine decided at first that none of them would go, but after a long telephone conversation with the Villa Bronciliano she agreed to let the Warners pick her up. She telephoned at lunch-time from a hotel in Viareggio to ask if Juliet was all right. Daniel put the call through for her. Hearing his voice for a minute before Madeleine spoke gave Ellen a pang. She turned away from the telephone with a sense of loss greater than the occasion seemed to bear, and with a faint resentment against Madeleine, which she told herself sternly was quite unreasonable.

Juliet slept all afternoon, and woke recovered and hungry. Thinking that she would sleep better at night if she got up, Ellen let her have her boiled egg and glass of milk on the *piazzale*, and was reading *Treasure Island* to her when Madeleine came home. She said that they had not missed much, Viareggio was twice as crowded as Brighton and not half so pretty; but she looked enlivened, as if the day had amused her. She had bought presents from the sea-side shops for both Ellen and Juliet.

"Did you bathe in the sea?" Juliet asked enviously.

"No, Daniel and Shand did, and the little girls splashed about on the edge with their nurse, but I thought it looked too crowded. I walked along beyond the bathing-huts with Daniel, Fenny, just before we started for home, and we talked about you. I hope your ears burned!"

"Her face is burning now," Juliet said seriously. "Perhaps Daniel is still talking about her. Would my ears burn if you and Fenny talked about me?"

"If we said something nice. Not if we said you were a little nuisance to have a headache and prevent poor Fenny going to the sea."

"*Fenny* wouldn't say things like that about me," Juliet replied with utter confidence. "It wasn't my fault that I was ill; I wanted to go to the sea, too, and bathe with Shand. Can we go tomorrow?"

"Well, not tomorrow, I think. Perhaps next week."

"This week, next week, sometime, never! I'm hungry now. Can I have some more toast?"

"If you like to go and ask Ofelia to bring it."

"I'll go." Ellen got up. "I want to put my present safely upstairs."

She really wanted to be alone for a minute or two. The uncomfortable flush which Juliet's quick eyes had noticed had not been entirely due to gratification, but to a feeling that Daniel's affection for her was something personal and private between the two of them, not to be handed to her on a plate by Madeleine.

When Juliet was in bed again, Ellen strolled out alone over the shoulder of hill behind the villa and down into the valley, where the *contadini* were cutting some of the last corn and stacking it in the middle of the field as if they were building a giant sand-castle. This was the road to Bronciliano. There was a field-path shorter than the road, and once or twice lately, when Ellen had walked this way in the evening, Daniel had walked down the opposite hillside to meet her, and they had talked by the stream until it was time for Ellen to go home to dinner. They had never made any arrangement to meet, but the back of the villa was visible from the Bronciliano windows, and once Daniel had said, "I saw somebody coming down the hill in a blue dress. I thought it must be you." Ellen slipped on her blue dress, before going out this evening, and hoped that Daniel might see her again and come loping down the steep path, but there was no sign of him. She climbed wearily back up the hill, which as a rule she hardly noticed. At dinner Madeleine was very affectionate to her and talked to her again about taking a week's holiday soon, to go and see Venice or Rome. Ellen, depressed, began to fancy that Madeleine was bored with her company and wanted to get rid of her, then rebuked herself for ingratitude. She felt as she went to bed that somehow it had been a very unsatisfactory day.

## CHAPTER XIV

FOR A few days Juliet, who seemed for the first time to be feeling the heat, was limp and fretful. They kept her quiet, so that she should be well for Madeleine's birthday celebration, and although Madeleine went over once to tea at Bronciliano, Ellen and Juliet did not go. Daniel telephoned to Ellen that evening, and hearing that she was not coming over, flew into a temper and raged against Madeleine's selfishness. Ashamed of being pleased, Ellen told him not to be silly. He calmed down—she could feel him over the wires subsiding from an abnormal mood into what she considered a normal one. They arranged to meet in Florence on Saturday evening.

Juliet was up early on the birthday morning. She could hardly stand still to let Ellen brush her hair. When they heard Ofelia going along the passage with Madeleine's coffee-tray, on which

Juliet had arranged both their parcels, scattered with lavender heads and rose-leaves, she flew to her mother's room. Ellen was tidying her own dressing-table before going down when Madeleine came in, radiant and lovely in a new pale pink dressing-gown from Florence, carrying the little box in her hand.

"Oh, Fenny! How naughty of you to spend your money like this; but how very, very sweet of you! I wanted it so much! I've been preventing myself from going back to the shop ever since I saw it. You shouldn't have done it, but you are an angel!"

She threw her arms round Ellen and kissed her cheek.

All the Bronciliano party were coming over to a birthday lunch. Juliet had a holiday, and spent the first part of the morning dressing her dolls in their best and crowning them with wreaths of flowers, which immediately wilted and had to be replaced. She and Ellen decorated the big table in the courtyard with an elaborate design of roses and vine-leaves. Juliet was eagerly watching for the post, which always came in the middle of the morning.

"Daddy's present isn't coming," she explained. "It's too precious to go in the post, and he's going to bring it with him, but I know about it; he told me in a letter. It's a pair of sapphire earrings! Mummy doesn't know yet; it's a secret, but she's going to get a letter today telling her. She'll be very pleased, I think, don't you?"

"I'm sure she will."

"I wish it was my birthday; but that comes in October, and I always have a party. If I had a party here I could have Shand and you and Mummy and Francesca and Marco and Daniel— and I might have Bianca, only she's rather too young, but I wouldn't have Donata."

"Poor Donata!"

"No. She tells tales about Shand. Oh, here's the post." Juliet ran to take the letters from Ofelia. "One for you, Fenny, and one for me, and a lot for mummy. That's Daddy's. I'll put it on top. I'll make her a birthday table." She placed the letters on a stool and laid two roses near them. "Now I'll tell her they've come."

She rushed off, and came back with Madeleine, who had been arranging flowers in the *salone*.

"Open your post," Juliet shouted; "open your birthday post. Then you'll know Daddy's secret. I haven't told you, have I?"

"No, you've only just hinted."

"All I said was it *might* be two of something that dangles. But you don't really know, do you?"

"No, I haven't an idea."

"Open and find out quickly."

"All right." Madeleine picked up the top letter from the pile. "Fenny, I was thinking it would be rather nice this evening if you and I and Juliet . . ."

She broke off with a quick breath and stood for a minute with her husband's letter in her hand, looking down at the others. Moving like someone walking in her sleep, she laid the first letter unopened on the table, and picked up the second. Looking at Ellen as if she did not know who she was and speaking as from a distance, she said:

"I've got something to do. I'll come back."

Carrying the letter she walked off into the house.

"Why has she gone?" Juliet exclaimed. "She hasn't opened Daddy's letter, and there's one from Granny. I know hers by her blue envelopes." She picked up the discarded letters. "I'll take them to her."

"I should wait. I think she'll be coming back in a minute. I expect she remembered something she wanted to do."

"But doesn't she *want* to open her birthday letters?" Juliet's lips trembled.

"Yes, of course she does. But you know she's busy getting the party ready. Look, Juliet. Viola's wreath has quite faded. Don't you thing you'd better throw it away and get some fresh flowers for her hair? She looks rather messy."

Juliet glanced doubtfully from the doll to the letter.

"I want to see Mummy open Daddy's letter about the surprise. But poor Viola must have a wreath. I'll tell you what, Fenny. I'll just get one red pomegranate flower for her, and you call me if Mummy comes back while I'm getting it. Promise!"

"Yes, I promise."

Left alone she thought, "Oh, dear! Was it a letter from Oliver? It must have been! Oh, what a pity! Just when Madeleine seemed to be getting happier again! Why can't he leave her alone?"

She felt angry with this unknown man who threatened the stability of her family, and especially of her child.

Madeleine came back while Juliet was arranging the pomegranate flower in Viola's matted hair. She opened Charles' letter, and was astonished and pleased about the earrings to Juliet's satisfaction. She gave Juliet messages from her grandmother and read them amusing extracts from the other letters. Ellen wished that she did not feel as though in all this Madeleine was acting a part, while she was alight with some inner excitement. A few minutes later they heard the car, and all went across the courtyard to meet the guests from Bronciliano.

"How your birthday suits you, *carissima*!" Lucrezia exclaimed, and Ellen saw that it was true.

She had never seen Madeleine's beauty more glowing. She herself was happy because Daniel had come, although she saw that he was in one of his nervous, jerky moods. At their first greeting he almost shied away from her, but he seemed to settle back into himself as he walked by her side across the courtyard towards the chairs in the shade, while Gastone, smiling with pleasure in the occasion, was putting down the cocktail tray.

Juliet leaned entranced against the arm of Madeleine's chair to watch her unwrap the luxuriously fitted vanity bag from Lucrezia and Grant. She smiled with unusual amiability on Donata as she presented a box of chocolates from herself and Bianca with a graceful little speech.

Lucrezia cried out:

"But Daniel has a present, too! Where is it, Daniel?"

Without speaking, almost rudely, he thrust a flat parcel against Madeleine's hand.

When she unwrapped it, she exclaimed:

"Oh, Daniel! Oh, no! You shouldn't give this to me."

Ellen, too, was surprised. It was one of his own paintings, and one which she herself liked almost best, because it was one of the very few that he had done in Italy. It was a small, charming sketch of a woman filling a jug of water from a well outside one of the houses. It was full of the peculiar quality of the Tuscan evening light, and of a serenity that seemed unattainable in his own life.

89

"You must keep that for your first exhibition," Madeleine said; "it's far too good to give away."

"How can he think anything too good for you, darling!"

This was one of the flattering remarks that were ordinary conversational counters with Lucrezia, but she said it with emphasis, her shrewd black eyes travelling from Daniel to Madeleine and back again to Daniel, her thin, painted lips parted in a smile of too much meaning. From them her eyes moved to Ellen, who met them squarely, hoping to disconcert her. Lucrezia only shifted her gaze back to Daniel and still smiled. Hatred of Lucrezia—it must be of Lucrezia!—rose like nausea in Ellen's throat.

"I've given it to you, Madeleine," Daniel said, the words jerked out of him as if under some compulsion.

He got up and moved away, taking a packet of cigarettes out of his pocket. Ellen saw his hands shaking as he lit one.

"Have you brought a picture for Mummy, too, Shand!"

Juliet's clear young voice released the grown-up people from the unexplained tension; they moved, smiled, picked up glasses.

"No, it's for you." Shand held out the oblong parcel.

"It's not my birthday!"

"It doesn't matter. You can have a present, too. This is my best one so far. I did it on Wednesday afternoon."

"Oh, thank you, Shand! Oh, I've got a picture of my own now! I'll hang it up in my bedroom. Look, Mummy."

"How lovely, darling! Aren't you lucky! It's the one you were doing last time I came to tea, isn't it, Shand? It's very nice! You *are* getting on!"

"Look, Fenny! My own picture!"

Ellen saw a steep path, a box hedge, a cypress, a blue sky interrupted by a pudgy white cloud, and two sketchy figures seen from behind, the upper half of the woman conveniently hidden under a pink sunshade, which had probably been easy to draw, the man a blob of brown head above a blue shirt.

"The cloud was difficult," Shand said with modest pride.

"Who are those people, Shand?"

"Your mother and Daniel. I did it when they didn't know. They were so busy talking to each other on the terrace after tea. I thought you'd like this one because she was in it."

Juliet said reverently;

"I'll buy a frame for it in Florence."

Ellen moved away from the group, out of the archway into the glaring sunlight of the garden. She was like someone hit by a wave and unable to see clearly until the water ran out of her eyes. She did not yet think what she felt, her mind, beginning to clear and steady, told her unconvinced heart that it could not be true.

"Ellen!" Daniel was standing just behind her. "Here's your drink."

"Thank you."

The ice-chilled glass against her fingers brought her another step back to full consciousness.

"Ellen, don't forget about Saturday! I want to see you again! I want to have one of our evenings together, just the two of us! I want some peace!"

## CHAPTER XV

DANIEL RANG up and told Ellen that he had got seats for *Madame Butterfly* on Saturday evening. She was pleased that he had thought of a treat for her, but half sorry that they would spend most of the evening in the theatre, and have so little time to talk. They had not had a good talk for some time, and she believed that if they did, everything—she did not define clearly what she meant by everything—would come right again.

She had all the North-country love of dramatic music, had heard *Madame Butterfly* several times when Carl Rosa came to towns within her reach, and enjoyed the performance far more than Daniel, who, although he talked grandly in the interval of opera heard in Paris, had no ear, and was displeased to find himself less knowledgeable than Ellen. In her state of unexplored tension and quivering feeling, she was moved by the opera as never before, and cried a few concealed tears during the last act. Daniel was fidgeting in his seat, and once or twice murmured that it was too hot. He jumped up with alacrity at the end and hurried out of the theatre without troubling much about Ellen, who was separated from him by a family party, and found him waiting impatiently for her in the street.

"Oof!" He was wiping his forehead. "I was glad to get out of that! Really in this weather these places are impossible. Let's go and get a cool drink in the square."

As soon as they were sitting down he began to rail against Elena Farona, who had been singing Butterfly:

"An old sow like that waddling about the stage! Really, it's ridiculous!"

"But such a lovely voice! And such a good singer, too!"

"As a matter of fact she wasn't. She was flat all through that last act."

By now aware that he hardly knew flat from sharp, Ellen replied shortly:

"I don't think she was."

"You should get your ear trained, my dear."

For the first time in their acquaintance she was irritated by his masculine assumption of superiority. She opened her mouth to tell him that she had sung in a choral society for several years and had had some training, but he closed it by saying with finality:

"Puccini's nothing but a musical-comedy writer, really! Mozart's the only opera worth hearing."

She knew that he was only parroting some dogmatic friend; he would not be able to distinguish an air from either composer. With more self-assertion than she had ever shown in any discussion with him, she said:

"I like Puccini. I enjoyed it enormously." She added, "Thank you so very much indeed for taking me. It was a great pleasure."

"Oh, that's all right."

He did not sound as though it had been any pleasure to him. He ordered two iced lemonades, and until they were brought, swung half round in his seat, with an arm over the back and his face turned away from her. She could examine, if she wished, his sharp profile cut out against the lights and movements of the square. For a second, before she got a grip of herself, she saw it blur and tremble.

He turned round when the lemonade came.

"You see," he said, "I can't really enjoy anything on the stage, however it sounds, if it doesn't *look* right. That fat old *hausfrau* padding about was a blot; you can't get away from it! Butterfly ought to be a lovely, fair, slender, graceful creature with great blue eyes."

"Oh, no!" Ellen cried. "That would be all wrong! She was a Jap. Japanese women are small and dark."

"I suppose they are, if you want to be literal."

He made it sound what Ellen at once felt it was: a dull thing to be. Daniel sucked up the last of his lemonade. With despair she saw the evening slipping away from them, leaving them in this unsatisfactory state, out of touch, with some unexplained hostility between them. Trying to bridge the gap she said:

"Of course, you're right, really, that Farona didn't look the part; and for you, being an artist, I expect that does ruin it. But I did think I'd never heard the last part, when she's waiting for Pinkerton's return, more beautifully sung. It was most moving."

"I wasn't moved. My sympathies were with the American. There's nothing more exasperating for a man than to be expected to re-live an episode that's over."

Thinking forlornly that this evening they could not agree about anything, Ellen picked up her shawl and bag.

"I mustn't miss the last tram. I think I'd better go now. I expect you want to catch yours?"

"I've got my bicycle down here. I'll walk to your tram stop with you."

This seemed like a reprieve, and her spirits rose. She knew by now that he often enjoyed her company more than he was able or willing to show. That he wanted to be with her to the last minute was perhaps a sign that below the surface he liked to be with her as much as ever. Encouraged, determined somehow to break down his unsociable silence, she began to tell him about an adventure that she and Madeleine had had the day before. They had received from the Contessa Caligari a card, yellow with age, saying "At Home", and out of curiosity had gone to the Villa Caligari, to find no other guests, the servants, if any, all out, and the Contessa, with her ancient silk skirts tucked up to her waist, feeding the hens in the courtyard with grain from a tarnished silver soup tureen. This she had thrust into Madeleine's arms, muttering something about a dog getting into the garden, and had vanished.

They had fed the hens, and then, after exploring dusty, shuttered rooms for another entrance, had discovered the old Contessa fast asleep in a dilapidated garden chair with a volume of Racine's plays, its leaves crumpled and dog-eared, lying beside her on the grass. Ellen was pleased to find that Daniel had come out of his black mood.

"This is a fascinating story," he said. "Go on. What next?"

"Madeleine said we couldn't go home without saying good-bye, but we didn't like to wake the old lady, and we sat down one on each side of her chair. After a bit she opened her eyes and looked at Madeleine and said in French, 'My dear, where is your husband?' Madeleine was rather surprised, because Charles had never been there, but she said, 'In England.' The old lady said vaguely, 'The Marquis in England! How strange! But why did he not take you with him? It was a mistake to leave you alone here,' and she said, '*Tu es si belle!*' She had got all mixed up, you see, and thought Madeleine was somebody in her own family long ago, perhaps."

"She wasn't so far out, though"—and he repeated half under his breath, "'*Tu es si belle!*' I suppose the other one was beautiful and not to be trusted a yard."

Ellen was silent, disconcerted.

"Well," he said, with a return to his impatient manner, "is that the end of the story?"

"We weren't sure that she ever realized who we were or how we got there, but we said good-bye and came home."

"I suppose a lot of the villas round here are full of old ladies like that." He added, "Here's your tram, and it looks as though it's going to start in a minute. You'd better hop on, quick."

Now that the evening was coming to an end, she had an unhappy sense of it having failed to bring them nearer together again, and of this having been her fault, as though she ought to have been able to grasp the intangible barrier between them and pull it down. She thanked him again, climbed on to the tram and turned to wave to him.

Under the light of the street lamp she saw his face strained and unhappy. He smiled at her—the first affectionate smile he had given her that evening. The smile broke up in a contortion of anguish. He took a step towards her, making a gesture as if he would pull her off the tram. She had what seemed to her an insane wish to jump, to be with him again and talk to him, find out what was wrong, comfort him, even if it meant sleeping on a bench in Florence or walking five miles home. A lifetime of not doing anything extravagant kept the wish insulated. She smiled and waved. The tram started. He turned abruptly away, and she pushed through the crowd standing near the door to try to find a seat.

## CHAPTER XVI

MADELEINE WENT out a good deal in the next day or two, and did not take Juliet with her, so that Ellen was seldom alone. When she was, she went unhappily in her mind over the last evening with Daniel, sometimes feeling that it had been disastrous, sometimes thinking that she had exaggerated a passing mood, and that next time they met everything would be as before. Madeleine went out to dinner at Bronciliano, but came back very late, and said nothing about her evening. She seemed restless, and spent more time than usual in Florence, returning to complain of the heat there. Once she brought Ellen a present: a yellow straw handbag to match her new linen dress. Ellen was pleased, but Madeleine turned abruptly away from her thanks.

"I don't think it's very nice, really. Those things look so pretty when they're all hanging up together, but when you get them home . . . I wish I'd brought you a white one, to go with everything."

Ellen, working her way as a daily exercise through the Italian newspaper, saw that Oliver Farren was making a film in Rome. She did not know whether Madeleine had seen it. She had picked up much less Italian than Ellen and Juliet. She was content prettily to call herself stupid and to let them find the words. Her reading of any newspaper was spasmodic, but the stage and film news was the part she was least likely to miss. Charles was due to arrive in ten days. A month ago Ellen would have been sorry that she would no longer be Madeleine's chief companion in the evenings. Now she was glad. Charles' presence would dispel an uneasiness that Ellen had felt since the night of Madeleine's revelation, and a sharper, more personal uneasiness that she was determined not to feel. She was sure that it would be a good thing when Madeleine had a husband again.

When she was at home Madeleine always kept Juliet with her for the hour before her bed-time, and Ellen was free. This did not happen until the Thursday after the visit to the Opera. She felt certain that Daniel would come down to the stream to meet her that evening. She went early to her room and washed her hair, pleased because it went well under her fingers and shaped itself prettily around her face. She put on her blue dress and ran up to the tower. From here she could always see if Daniel was coming. It was easy to distinguish against the hillside the shirt of bright blue—the colour which he nearly always wore. The path from Bronciliano zigzagged backwards and forwards between the cornfields, the path from the Meridiana was straight, so that it took longer for Daniel to reach the stream. There was time for Ellen, after she first saw him, to wait a minute, enjoying anticipation, before she went down through the fields to meet him.

The corn was all cut now. The threshing-machine had been thrumming since four o'clock that morning, and the air still vibrated with the sound. In the upper storey of the tower, with its glassless windows open to the sky, Ellen leaned on the hard sill and looked down into the valley, while the swifts that nested in the roof of the tower flew in and out, almost touching her hair.

She saw what she hoped to see: the spot of bright blue appear on the opposite hill. She saw it disappear in a clump of olives and emerge, now distinguishable as the figure of a man, small as a toy in the Perugino landscape. Her beating heart echoed the drumming beat of the threshing-machine, her body felt alive and light with joy. She waited a minute longer, watching Daniel's progress along the winding path between the fields of close-cut stubble. He would get to the stream first, and then he would watch as she was watching now, and see her blue dress coming towards him down the hillside. She turned to run down the tower staircase, and then stopped. There was another figure in the landscape. A rose-coloured parasol above a white skirt was moving down the path from the Villa Meridiana towards the bridge over the stream.

Struck into stillness, Ellen leaned on the stone. The blue shirt moved aster; she knew so well the loping walk with which Daniel had often covered the last hundred yards of the path. The parasol was loitering. The two met at the rough wooden bridge that crossed the stream. Ellen knew the weathered wood of the hand-rail, the dry tufts of yellowish grass that fringed the stream, and the pattern of pebbles from which the water had receded with each successive week of summer. She saw the blue shirt and the rosy parasol together for a few moments by the bridge. Then, still together, they moved slowly along the path by the edge of the stream. The path wound down the valley to a place where it broadened out between two fields of trellised vines. There was a farm standing alone there on a slant of hill, and at this time its windows always caught the evening sunlight, so that Ellen had often walked with Daniel towards a house with windows of gold. Now he walked towards it with Madeleine. As Ellen watched, the slope of the ground hid their sauntering figures from her sight.

Anger swept her like an Italian thunderstorm, and the upper story of her gentle, reasonable life went down in wreckage on the flood. Her wish leaped out to kill them. It never occurred to her for an instant that the meeting by the stream might be casual and unimportant. It was something that she had always known; it had been waiting for her under the surface, and with it this naked feeling into which, as into an unbearable pain, her being dissolved. She did not know that she was walking backwards and forwards across the floor of the tower room, her hands gripping the front of her dress. When she re-entered her body she was leaning on the window-ledge, looking down the valley, while the cooling air of evening dried the sweat under her hair.

She watched the valley for the returning figures. She saw them reappearing round the shoulder of the hill. The stream was now in shadow, and Madeleine had furled her parasol. They paused by the bridge and leaned side by side on the rail, looking down at the stream. They were close together, the man's bare head and blue shirt, the woman's white dress and fair hair. Ellen saw Madeleine point with her parasol to something in the shingle, perhaps to one of the lizards that she and Daniel had sometimes watched streaking between the stones.

All her anger was focused on Madeleine. *You*, she thought, *you*, who pretended to be my friend! You've got Charles, you love

Oliver—or you think you do! You don't want Daniel; you can't love him! You never thought about him until you knew I was interested in him! You've been so kind and charming to me! I was so fond of you, and all the time you've been spoiling the best thing that ever happened to me, for vanity, or some queer kind of jealousy, because you can't bear to be left out of anything, or see other people happy when you aren't! You're cruel—to me and to Daniel! You must be tormenting him, and he is tormented enough already! He could have been happy with me if you'd let us alone. I love him. There's nothing I wouldn't do for him. I could make everything so different for him. I could make him believe in himself. I could make a home for him; we'd have children. All you'll ever give him will be a humiliating experience!

The instinct that told her that this might be an experience for which Daniel was willing to throw away everything else was for Ellen the sharpest point of anguish, so sharp that as she leaned over the window-ledge the idea crossed her mind of throwing herself down on to the stones of the courtyard.

But that was outside her nature, a thought blown in from the knowledge that other people had ended their troubles in such a way. There was something else that she could do. She could still stop Madeleine. In the last ten minutes a good deal of latent knowledge of Madeleine and of herself had become clear. She knew that she was in many ways the stronger. She knew that Madeleine was a coward who wouldn't face a direct attack. I'll go down now and meet her! I'll tell her what she's doing and what I think of her! I'll tell her to leave Daniel alone! I can make her do it if I frighten her. I know I can! It did not enter her mind for one moment that Madeleine was her employer and could send her back to England tomorrow. She was below the level of feeling where such things mattered.

She saw the two of them by the bridge separate, saw Madeleine begin to climb the path up the hill and turn to wave her hand to Daniel, who stood looking after her. Ellen ran down the staircase of the tower.

In the passage from the kitchen she met Ofelia, carrying a tray of silver to the dining-room. Ofelia spoke to her, but she did not hear, nor see the girl's look of surprise as she brushed past her. She went out of the library door. Juliet was on the lawn, playing with a scrawny kitten, that she had borrowed from Francesca Mandini. She had a cotton-reel on a string, which she pulled in jerks over the parched grass. At every jerk the kitten pounced forward with splaying white paws. Juliet ran towards Ellen, bobbin and kitten bouncing after her.

"Look, Fenny! Look how Tomasino likes the cotton!" She stopped, staring up at Ellen's face, indifferent for the moment to the kitten making an assault on her ankles. She exclaimed in a frightened, inquiring voice: "Fenny?"

The scared tone of appeal from the child penetrated. With a great effort Ellen answered:

"It's all right, Juliet. I'm just going for a little walk. You go on playing with Pussy."

She walked on. As she passed through the gate on to the path she saw without comprehension that Juliet was staring after her. She had picked up the kitten and was clutching its wriggling body to her chest.

But that brief contact with Juliet, the moment of re-entry into her everyday life, had brought Ellen back nearer to the surface, and on the surface she was somebody trained to control herself, trained to distrust violent feelings. She stood still at the corner of the path, her conviction dissolving into doubt. Was she crazy? Was there really only casual friendliness between Madeleine and Daniel. Had Madeleine known nothing at all about their meetings by the stream? Had she just strolled down the hillside by chance? Ellen herself had no right to assert any claim on Daniel. She began to have a horror of making a scene and exposing her own reticent feelings. Suppose she attacked Madeleine and the whole thing turned out to be a fantasy of her own imagination. What was really happening?

Madeleine, swinging her parasol and smiling, came round the corner, and Ellen had her answer. Madeleine stopped dead, her cheeks blanched, her expression of guilt and fear was unmistakable. She said:

"Oh, Fenny!" murmured something about "out for a walk," looked away from her eyes and moved uncertainly forward.

Ellen, her voice dead, her body weighted down as in a nightmare, let her pass.

Madeleine murmured, "It's late, I think I—I must go and

change," and scurried round the corner. A minute later Ellen heard her voice high with relief speaking to Juliet. Anger merging into the pain of loss, Ellen stumbled weeping down the path between the olive trees and into the shade.


## CHAPTER XVII

IN A world irrevocably changed, Ellen forced herself the next morning to give Juliet her lessons as usual. Every time she heard a step in the courtyard she hoped ardently that it might be some-one coming with a telephone message from Daniel, even with an invitation to all of them to go over to Broncliano, where at least she could see him. Nobody came. The interminable morning dragged on to lunch-time. Ellen was glad that Madeleine was out to lunch. She found it difficult to attend to Juliet, but Juliet luckily had her own preoccupation. Francesca Mandini had given her the kitten. While they lunched in the courtyard, it slept, curled in a ball in one of the basket-chairs, and Juliet could hardly take her eyes off it. She was satisfied with Ellen's mechanical assents to her raptures, and went up to rest happy in the prospect of playing with Tomasino again at tea-time.

Through the hot afternoon Ellen lay wakeful, trying to subdue her raging tumult of feeling to something that she could deal with. She wanted to think that if Madeleine had been playing with Daniel's feelings, it was a passing thing that would be over when Charles Rivers had arrived, and Daniel would be his old self and turn back to her. She did not really believe this. She had a sicken-ing fear that Madeleine and Daniel were together now somewhere. When at tea-time Madeleine came back, bringing some English friends with whom she had spent the day in Florence to see the villa, Ellen felt such relief that her spirits began to rise. She had been making a complete fantasy about that day; could she be making one altogether? At dinner, while she talked to Madeleine of Juliet and the kitten, and listened to her repeating her friends' gossip from England, she observed her with a painful curiosity, almost as if she was noting her beauty for the first time and getting, as Daniel must have got, the fresh impact of her charm. After dinner Madeleine went to write letters, and Ellen, tired out, to bed.

She did not see Daniel or hear from him that week-end. She had never telephoned to him at Bronciliano, and was trying to make up her mind to do so when a message came from Lucrezia asking her to take Juliet to tea with Donata that afternoon. Madeleine was out, and Ellen over-ruled Juliet's objections.

"You'll see Shand, too, you know, and Bianca as well as Donata. You don't mind Bianca."

"I shouldn't mind her if she wasn't so young! Can I take Tomasino?"

"Oh, no, their dogs might be rough with him and he might run away and get lost in the garden."

"Well, I'd rather stay with him. He misses me when I'm out. Please, Fenny, ring up to say we can't go."

"No. It's good for you to see other children."

Juliet sighed, and then startled Ellen by saying:

"I expect you want to see Daniel. I'll ask Ofelia to give Tomasino some milk at tea-time, but it won't be the same to him as having it with me."

Lucrezia was on the terrace when they arrived. To Ellen's surprise, she did not dismiss them both to the nursery party. She said, "Juliet, my darling, you will find the children by the fountain; they have a picnic tea there." To Ellen she said, "Soon they will bring our tea. Let us walk a little in the shade." She put her arm through Ellen's. Ellen disliked her touch and disliked the wave of scent that came from her. She made her elbow as stiff as possible, but Lucrezia held on.

"Signorina Fenny, I want to ask your advice because you are a very sensible woman and a friend of Daniel Blackett, and I am sure that you are as worried as I am. What is to be done about this madness?"

Ellen's heart leapt into her chest so that she could hardly breathe.

"What do you mean?"

"Why, the poor young man—you must have seen? He is quite crazy with love for Madeleine. He does not eat, he does not sleep. He does not look after Shand. I have not spoken to him about that because I know how these feelings are. I am sorry for him, but perhaps—what do you think?—I should send him back to England."

Moving her dry tongue with difficulty, Ellen answered:

"I don't know."

"You see, I know that I can speak to you freely, because you are the friend of us all and you are so kind, so calm, so wise. But I do not know what to do. Every day he goes to meet her somewhere. I expect that they are together in Florence now. She has not spoken of it to you?"

"No. But she doesn't . . . she can't . . .!"

"Oh, of course she does not love him; it is this Oliver that she loves, as you must know."

"Her husband is coming back next week."

"Poor Madeleine! Yes. Well, that is something that they must arrange between themselves."

"But, there isn't anything to arrange. I mean . . ."

Lucrezia shrugged.

"I don't know. But I want you to advise me about Daniel. You see, he is altogether *boulversé*! He is highly strung, he has been very ill last winter and I do not think he has been much in love before. I am afraid that he might have a breakdown, or perhaps try to kill himself."

"Oh, no!"

"You think not? But I think that he is the type. I am not sure. Such things happen. What should I do?"

"Have you talked about it to Madeleine?"

"Of course, and she says that it is not her fault. She was not thinking of him at all. He is a young man, her countryman, your friend, and she wished only to be friendly to him. Now she is afraid to refuse to see him because she sees that he is possessed. She does not know what he will do."

"What a lie!"

The words leaped out before Ellen could stop them. She jerked her arm away from Lucrezia's hand and turned to face her. She became aware of a gleam of enjoyment in the small black eyes.

"You think that she cares for him? But I am sure that she does not. You think that perhaps she has amused herself a little with him?"

"I can't talk about it. I think you had better send him back to England."

"I do not want to do that because Shand is very fond of him. He has not been difficult at all while Daniel is here, and also it is important for Daniel to have this year in a warm country."

Ellen, in a turmoil of feeling, detected something sinister in this benevolence, but was too shaken to know what Lucrezia really wanted.

"It is so strange," Lucrezia said, "that Madeleine had not spoken to you of it when you are alone in that house together except for the child, and when she has made such a companion of you!"

Ellen's heart cried, Stop tormenting me. But she had a feeling that Lucrezia, for some reason of her own, was an ally, and she was ready to clutch at any help.

"Why don't you talk to him, Mrs. Warner?"

"No, because he hates me! It is of no importance; I have ignored it for the sake of Shand, but now I can do nothing. No, Signorina Fenwick, I think that you should talk to him; you are his countrywoman and his friend."

"I have no right to interfere."

"Oh! Right! You would not say that if you saw him walking in his sleep and about to fall from a window? Well, that is what you do see. You are too English. You think too much of your own good behaviour! You should think of your friend!"

There was a silence. Then Lucrezia said:

"Let us go and have some tea."

"Will you excuse me? I don't think I want any. I'll just see if the children are all right."

"They will be all right, but as you please."

Unable to bear her company another minute, Ellen escaped round the corner of the house. She glanced at the picnic party by the fountain, and then turned down one of the walks between cyprus hedges that led to the end of the garden. She was shocked to her heart by this confirmation of her fears. There was a gate at the end of the path, opening into a narrow lane that ran down to Florence. She leaned on the low stone wall by the gate. She believed everything that Lucrezia had told her, except that Madeleine could not help it. She remembered the afternoon when she and Daniel had been happy in the cornfield, and Lucrezia had called Madeleine's attention to them, the pinched and whitened look on her face that she now realized she had seen before, when people praised Rose Danby, when Juliet had a letter from her father. Madeleine had broken up the growing relationship between Ellen and Daniel because she could not bear to be left out of anything. Probably now she was half afraid because she had raised a stronger feeling than she could deal with, but that she had not tried to raise it in the beginning Ellen did not for a minute believe. And she was still playing with the feeling, probably seeing him somewhere every day, coming back to Ellen, who had been her friend. Oh, if I had only stopped her the other night! Ellen thought—I could have: she was afraid of me. Lucrezia is right: I ought to have done something to save Daniel. Hearing footsteps, she looked up, and saw him wheeling his bicycle round the bend of the lane.

When he saw her, he frowned. She was horrified to see how dreadfully ill he looked. His eyes had sunk into his face, and his skin was grey. He wheeled his bicycle slowly forward. Ellen opened the gate and went a step or two to meet him. All her anger against him melted away, and she felt only a longing to comfort him. She did not think at all about what she could say to him; she moved towards him, and a cry of appeal, of sympathy, of love, sprang from her heart:

"Daniel!"

His face quivered, seemed to break up, and for one minute she saw in his eyes an agonized entreaty. Then his features hardened again into their mould. He was close to her now. She put a hand on his arm, but he shook it off.

"Let me alone!"

He wheeled his bicycle through the gate and slammed it after him, leaving Ellen standing in the lane.

# CHAPTER XVIII

THAT EVENING Ellen went to Madeleine in the *salone* and told her that she wanted to go home.

"I know that I ought to give a month's notice, but I don't want the month's salary. I should like to go at once."

Madeleine, who was sitting on the sofa with an unopened novel, looked up, looked quickly down again, fiddled with the clasp of her handbag, and said nervously:

"Oh, dear! I hope there's nothing wrong! You haven't had bad news from home? Your brother's family?"

Ellen had decided not to give any explanation, but she was not going to encourage such insincerity. Madeleine knew perfectly well why she was going.

"No, I've had no bad news from home."

"Then, are you sure? It's so nice here . . . there's such a lot you haven't seen . . . I wanted you to go to Rome . . . Venice . . ."

Her voice trailed away.

"I should like to go the day after tomorrow, please."

"You couldn't go as soon as that! You wouldn't get a *wagon-lit.*"

"That doesn't matter. I can go without a *wagon-lit.*"

Madeleine pulled her cigarette-case out of her bag with a jerk, so that it fell on the floor. She picked it up, and lit a cigarette. The flame of the lighter shook so that it nearly caught her hair. Seeing her so disconcerted, Ellen felt some triumph even in her desolation.

"Fenny! Do sit down! I can't talk to you when you're standing up there!"

"There isn't anything to talk about. I've only come to tell you that I'm going home!"

"Fenny, please. You don't know how bad I feel."

Ellen stiffened all over.

"I don't want to discuss anything. I'm going up to bed now."

"Yes, yes, of course. I understand."

Madeleine twisted in her seat and then looked up for the first time at Ellen's face. Her eyes were full of tears.

"Fenny, I wish you would let me tell you! I've been so wretched, I've hardly known what I was doing. But never mind that now. I haven't any right to, but I want to ask you a favour. It isn't for my sake; it's for Juliet's."

She wiped her eyes and made an effort for control.

"Listen, Fenny. I do pray and beg you to stay with Juliet just until her father comes. It's only five more days; I had a letter this morning. I won't bother you, I promise. I shall be out a lot. I've got things to do in Florence. On Sunday I promised to take Juliet to the sea for a day. You could have the whole day in peace to do your packing. Fenny, please! This isn't something that doesn't matter! It isn't for my convenience! Juliet's very happy now with the kitten and looking forward to her father coming. I want him to see her like that. She's very fond of you. If you go, so suddenly, it will be an awful shock and spoil all her pleasure!"

Ellen knew that that was true. Both she and Juliet would feel the wrench of parting. She hesitated.

"Please, please, Fenny! I wouldn't ask you for myself. Please do stay until Charles is here, and please don't tell Juliet you are going until after he has arrived. I have a special reason for asking. I can't explain."

"There's no need to explain anything. Mr. Rivers comes on Tuesday, doesn't he? I will arrange to go on Thursday."

"And you won't tell Juliet until he is here?"

"Not if you think it's better for her," Ellen replied doubtfully.

"I know it is. I'm absolutely certain."

"Very well, then. Good-night."

Ellen turned towards the door, but Madeleine, now really crying, put out her hand in a blind gesture to stop her.

"Fenny! We've been very happy together! I'm very fond of you! Don't be more angry with me about anything than you can help! You don't understand! You don't know how miserable I am!"

"Good-night."

"Fenny!" Madeleine's voice rose to a wail. "I can't bear you feeling like this about me! I must tell you . . ."

Seeing her trembling and weeping, Ellen had a sense of power, of satisfaction in her own hardness. She repeated, "I don't want to hear anything at all. I will stay until next Thursday. I shall go and book a place tomorrow, but I won't say anything to Juliet before her father comes. I'm going up now. Good-night."

## CHAPTER XIX

Wʜᴇɴ Mᴀᴅᴇʟᴇɪɴᴇ and Juliet came back from Viareggio on Sunday evening, Juliet ran to find Ellen, who was sitting on the window of the tower, looking across the valley. Juliet hugged her, gave her three shells she had picked up on the shore and a small china jug that she had bought with her own money at one of the sea-side stalls.

"This has been one of my best days that I ever had!"

Ellen thought that it had been one of her worst. Perhaps Juliet felt this, for she added sweetly:

"Only I did wish you had come, too. There was a boy there who had a live monkey doing tricks, and I wanted you to see it. Will you come with us another day?"

"We'll see. I'm very glad it was so nice, and I'm delighted with the shells and the jug."

"I chose it myself because you like yellow. Where's Tomasino?"

"I saw him out on the lawn climbing up an apple-tree."

"I've bought him a saucer for his milk. I must go and give it to him."

She scampered down the tower stairs, and Ellen was left alone.

Packing all the afternoon in the heat, she had felt desperate. On Thursday she would go, and that would be the end. She did not know whether Madeleine would have told Lucrezia or Daniel that she was leaving. She did not know if he would care. Perhaps he now only thought of her as an embarrassment out of his past, and would be thankful when she was out of his sight. Perhaps in his preoccupation with Madeleine he did not think of her at all. That possibility made her angry, and it was so painful to find herself angry with him that she turned away from the thought to intensify her anger with Madeleine. Her hands trembled as she folded the respectable garments she had brought with her, and the few prettier and livelier clothes she had bought in Florence. Sweat dripped from her eyebrows on to the tissue paper which she had first spread in her suit-cases only a few months ago with such hopeful anticipation. When she had finished she went up to the tower, saying to herself that she must have a breath of air. She sat for a long time looking out at the stream in the valley and the opposite hill. She had a wild hope that she might see Daniel coming down the hill, that she might run to meet him, and that the nightmare in which she was living might evaporate. He did not appear, and she was nearly sick with the long tension by the time Juliet arrived home.

But the child's affectionate greeting after the day of lonely brooding revived Ellen's spirit, and made her unwilling to give up hope. Why should she let Daniel go out of her life without a struggle? She would write to him this evening and tell him that she was going on Thursday. If the letter was posted tomorrow, he would get it on Tuesday. There would be time for him to come over or to write; he might even come and see her off at the station. She would give him her address in England. With recovering spirits, she remembered that he would be going back to Newcastle at the end of the year. Newcastle was not far from her own part of the world; they might meet again, when the Rivers were safely back in London and their Italian summer had become a fantastic memory to the school-mistress and the art teacher back in their everyday lives.

She wrote the letter after dinner that evening. She wrote affectionately, telling Daniel that she was leaving, thanking him for all his kindness to her, and saying how much she would have liked to see him before she went. She realized that she had no address in England to give him. The house in which she and her mother had lived was let to new tenants, her furniture was in store. She had meant to go into rooms in Ainley for the autumn term, look for a small flat and move in at Christmas. She gave him Alice's address. She could go there until she found somewhere to live. Madeleine's treachery increased the value of this true and sturdy friend, but although she would be glad to see Alice again, the thought of going back to the rest of her old life was infinitely dreary. She still had a feeling that something might prevent it. It was with a revival of hope, for which she could have given no reason, that she went to bed.

Her letter went on Monday, and she knew that it could not arrive at Bronciliano before midday on Tuesday. She had to fix her attentions on Juliet's lessons on Tuesday morning, although Juliet was too much excited by the prospect of her father's arrival to be able to learn anything. She was writing her dictation when

Madeleine came in, wearing one of her more formal dresses and a hat, as if she were going out to lunch.

"Fenny, I'm so sorry to interrupt, but I'm going to Florence. I shan't be back to lunch. Will you take Juliet down in the car to meet her father at the station? Gastone will bring it round at half-past three. I'm going to have my hair done, and I've got one or two other things to do. If I'm not at the station by the time the train comes in, you'll know I'm not coming. I'll be taking a taxi straight home, so don't let Charles wait for me."

"Very well."

Ellen thought that she might have got her hair done earlier and come to meet her husband, but she felt indifferent. In two days, except for Juliet, whom she very much hoped to see again, she would have done with the Rivers.

Juliet, who never liked dictation, welcomed the interruption.

"Oh, Mummy, what do you think Tomasino did just now? He jumped on the table and pushed my pen with his paw so my writing went squiggly! We had to put him out on the lawn!"

"Did he, darling?" Madeleine lingered in the doorway. She said, unnecessarily, Ellen thought, "Fenny, you'll look after her?"

"Yes, of course."

"I shall see you later on, Juliet." Madeleine ran back from the doorway and hugged her. "Good-bye, my little girl, bless you!"

Juliet casually turned up her faced to be kissed, remarking cheerfully:

"Now I've made another blot! Good-bye, Mummy! Oh, look, Fenny, this blot's like a spider! My dictation's spoilt today, isn't it? First Tomasino and then Mummy!"

"It is, rather. I think you'll have to turn over and begin a new page."

They went down to meet Charles, and kept a look-out for Madeleine as they walked up and down the platform, but she did not appear.

"It's a good thing we're here," Juliet said importantly; "or there wouldn't be anybody to meet poor Daddy. Who met you when you came, Fenny?"

"Your father."

"How funny! You didn't know me then, did you?"

There were a good many other things, Ellen thought, that I

didn't know. Was it really less than three months since she had stepped out on to this platform so full of vague anticipation?

The train came in, and Juliet, darting into the crowd, found her father.

"Where's Mother?" he asked when he had shaken hands with Ellen.

"She's getting her hair done."

"She had some business in Florence," Ellen added; "she said if she was not here by the time the train came in, would you not wait for her, as she would go straight home in a taxi, and meet you there?"

"Business in Florence? She never does business anywhere. Dressmakers, I suppose. Well, come along. Let's go home to tea. How brown you are, Juliet; and you've grown about a foot since I saw you."

"Yes, my frocks had to be let down."

Ellen was glad that Juliet chattered all the way from the station, and although Charles spoke to her once or twice, saying that he had been glad to hear that she liked Italy so much, and asking if she minded the heat, he was occupied with the child, and she was left in peace. When the car drew up before the villa, Ofelia, all smiles, came to help with the luggage and Charles asked if the Signora had come home. Ofelia said no, but she had left a note for him in his room. Tea was ready on the *piazzale*.

"Will you and Juliet go and begin, Miss Fenwick? I'll be down in a minute."

He did not appear, and Juliet was impatient.

"Isn't Daddy coming to tea? I want to show him Tomasino. Shall I go and fetch Daddy?"

"I should wait until he comes. I expect he felt very hot and tired and is having a bath after his journey."

But as half an hour began to slide into three-quarters, Ellen, too, was surprised. She wondered whether Madeleine had come back without them hearing her and was talking to her husband upstairs.

Gastone came to fetch the tea-things, and said to Ellen that the Signore had some urgent letters to answer and that he had taken him some tea upstairs. Would they go for their walk and he would see them later? He added with meaning in his quick brown eyes:

"The Signora has not returned."

Ellen pacified Juliet's demands for her father as best she could, and took her for a walk down the field path in front of the house.

She found it difficult to satisfy Juliet's impatience, because she herself was in the grip of panic. She felt sure that Madeleine was with Daniel. Probably she had gone to meet him in Florence for the last time, and they had not been able to part. Perhaps he was so desperate that Madeleine did not know how to leave him. Perhaps, after all, she had some feeling for him. To Lucrezia it had seemed out of the question that Madeleine could love a poor tutor, but Lucrezia was like that. It did not seem to Ellen impossible that anyone should love Daniel. Something was going on, Ellen was sure, and it must be something that involved Daniel, and could only end in his greater unhappiness.

"Are you listening, Fenny?" Juliet was grumbling. "Why couldn't I show Daddy Tomasino before we came out? Why hasn't Mummy come back?" Only child that she was, she was accustomed to plenty of grown-up attention, and she complained, "Everybody is *molto stupido* this evening!"

When they came back, Charles was walking up and down on the English lawn. He called Juliet, and Ellen went in, leaving them together. Her bedroom was still shuttered against the heat, but the sun was now off the front of the house. She unfastened the shutters and let in the evening light. The heat, which had made her body glow when she was happy, now oppressed her; she was tired of the unchanging blue skies and of the menacing sun, against which they had to protect themselves from breakfast to tea-time. She lay down on her bed and closed her eyes.

She began to imagine herself climbing one of the steep roads out of Ainley that led to the moors. She passed the last terrace of grey stone houses, clinging to the slope like outcrops of rocks. A wet wind blew in her face. The road came to an end. There was only a track across the moor; she walked, lifting her feet between the tough stems of heather that whipped her ankles. She turned to look down the valley, where smoke should be rising from the mill chimneys, but there was no smoke, and she thought, The mills have closed down; what has happened? She woke with a jump as Ofelia, carrying a freshly washed cotton dress, came into the room.

"Ah. *Scusi!* I thought that the Signorina was in the garden!"

Ofelia slid the crisp dress on to its hanger and closed the wardrobe door. Ellen, still only half awake, blinked at her.

"The Signora has not yet come home," Ofelia said. Like Gastone, she spoke with meaning.

Ellen sat up and pushed the strands of hair off her face. Did everybody know something she didn't know?

"I suppose she has been kept in Florence."

"*Sì, sì.*"

Ofelia politely accepted an explanation that was no explanation at all, and went out. Ellen heard her speaking to Gastone in the passage, and a moment later she knocked at the door.

"The Signore would be glad if the Signorina Fenwick would go to him in the *salottino*."

Charles was standing by the window when Ellen came in. He pulled a chair round for her and then again turned towards the window, speaking to her without looking at her.

"Madeleine has been unexpectedly called away to Rome, to an old friend there who has been taken seriously ill. I shall be going down there by the night train, and I have to leave in half an hour. I want you, if you will, to stay here with Juliet until you hear from me, or until I come back. You'll want some money. I'll leave you a cheque you can cash at the Bank. I'll write to you in a day or two. I don't quite know when I shall be back. I've explained to Juliet, and she will be quite happy here with you. I know you will look after her. Is that all right?"

"Well, I had made arrangements to go home to England on Thursday."

"You were going home! But I thought you were staying with us until the middle of September."

"I only arranged it with Mrs. Rivers two or three days ago."

"Oh, Christ!" He turned round and looked at her sharply. "Was it necessary for you to go for private reasons—something happening in England—or has there been anything to upset you here?"

Sure that the seriously ill old friend did not exist, not yet able to see what had happened, and how Daniel fitted into the picture, Ellen said slowly:

"I wanted to go for personal reasons; but there's no urgent need for me in England, and if you have to leave Juliet, of course I can put off going for a short time, and stay with her."

"Can you really? Without too much inconvenience? I can't take her with me, and I don't want to leave her with servants. I shall be most grateful if you could stay, even for a few days. Until I know where I am. I mean until I can get back here and make some arrangements."

"I will certainly stay with Juliet until you or her mother get back."

"Thank you. It's very good of you. I really shouldn't know what to do . . ."

He turned to pick up the cheque lying on his desk. Ellen saw him rub his hand across his face in a gesture of weariness.

"I'm so sorry you have to make another journey tonight!"

He did not seem to hear her. He gave her the cheque.

"I'll send you my address as soon as I know where I am staying. I shouldn't bother too much with lessons, in this heat. The great thing is if you can keep the child happy."

After putting Juliet to bed and eating her solitary dinner without noticing it, Ellen went out into the garden. She was obsessed by one idea that excluded everything else—the idea that Madeleine and Daniel had gone together to Rome. Both she and Lucrezia must have been wrong. Madeleine had fallen in love with Daniel, and had not been able to part from him. Perhaps when Charles was arriving she had meant to put an end to it and they had met in Florence for the last time to say good-bye, perhaps he could not bear it, and she had been overcome by his distress, and had let him persuade her into something that she might afterwards regret. But Ellen was sure that they were together. She saw them at the station, in the train, walking along the pavements of an unknown city, as clearly as she was accustomed to see her own face in the mirror. Charles, of course, was going after them. She did not know what would happen when he got there. The whole thing was too far outside the range of her experience. She thought, since she still believed in the over-riding power of marriage and family life, that he would probably bring Madeleine back. And Daniel? Daniel would be left alone in despair and humiliation.

Entirely possessed by these images, she walked up and down without noticing how long she had been out, until she suddenly became aware that her legs ached with fatigue. She looked at her watch, and saw it was after ten. She was crossing the courtyard to go in when Gastone came out and told her that she was wanted on the telephone by somebody at Bronciliano. She flew to the *salone* and picked up the receiver, all her convictions turned upside down. Daniel! It must be Daniel! After all, he had not gone; it could only be he who wanted to speak to her! But it was a younger voice that came over the wires, and at first, in the shock of disappointment, she could not grasp who it was or what he was saying.

"Fenny! Can't you hear me, Fenny? It's Shand."

"Oh, Shand!"

"Fenny, is Daniel with you?"

"No! No, I haven't seen him."

"I thought perhaps he might have come over to see you. We're worried because we don't know where he is."

This confirmation of her fears made her feel so sick that she could hardly hold the receiver.

"What do you mean?"

"Well, of course, it's because of what's happened. Lucrezia had a note from Mrs. Rivers. It was brought in when we were all on the terrace before lunch, and she opened it and told us."

"Told you what? What?"

"Well, you know she'd always tell anything! She just said, 'So Madeleine has gone to her lover: to this Oliver Farren in Rome!' Then Daniel looked as if he'd gone mad. He shouted 'It's a lie!' and snatched the letter and read it and crumpled it up and threw it on the floor. He rushed straight out of the house, and we haven't seen him since. My father's away in Milan. Lucrezia says she's sure Daniel went off to kill himself. She's quite hysterical. If he isn't back by tomorrow morning I think perhaps I ought to telephone to the police or go out with the servants to see if I can find him! Do tell me, Fenny? What do you think I ought to do?"

## CHAPTER XX

At LUNCH-TIME next day Shand telephoned to Ellen to say that Daniel had been found and was safe. Her relief was so great that nothing else seemed to matter.

"*I* found him!" Shand said importantly. "When he didn't come back at all last night, I got up at five and rang the police, and I got our own people, the servants and gardeners, out looking for him. I went round with Roberto in the car, and I suddenly thought of trying the ruined villa. You know we used to go there a lot to sketch. He always said it was a good place to go and get away from everybody. He often went up there alone. Well, we found him lying under the wall of the villa among those broken stones. I was frightened when I first saw him, Fenny! I saw a bit of his blue shirt as we got over the garden wall. But he was all right. He was in a sort of coma. He'd wandered about in the heat all yesterday afternoon and half the night, until he was completely exhausted. We gave him some brandy and got him into the car and took him home and fed him, and he's in bed now, asleep. Lucrezia's furious with him, but I shan't let her go near him. I'm managing this while my father's away."

Shand sounded pleased with himself, as indeed he had a right to be. Ellen could have hugged him, and congratulated him warmly. She felt giddy with relief. Not only was Daniel safe, but the whole fabric that she had built up in her imagination had proved to be a fantasy. Whatever might be the result of Madeleine's flight, it was all over between her and Daniel! It must have been a painful shock for him, and Ellen was sorry for him, but could not be sorry that it would make him angry with Madeleine! He would get over it—there would be nothing else to do—and she would still be here, ready to comfort him and give him real love. She felt almost grateful to Madeleine for making this decisive end. Then she remembered Juliet, playing happily with the kitten in the shade of the courtyard. For her, unless Charles brought Madeleine back with him, this was a disaster. How like Madeleine, Ellen thought, to beg her to stay on because she had to leave somebody to pick up the bits! But the bits were precious, and Ellen was only too glad to be still here. She went to tell Juliet that she might sit up to have dinner with her in the courtyard—one of the child's great treats.

There was no more news that day either from Rome or from Bronciliano. Ellen rang up the Warner villa next day at lunchtime and asked for Shand, but he was out. The butler told her that the Signore Blackett was better. Ellen was content to wait.

The next morning she gave Juliet a holiday and took her into Florence. Her father had given her some money to spend, and she wanted to buy a basket for Tomasino. She could not persuade him to sit in it, and spent most of the day lifting him back into it after he had escaped to his chosen perch in one of the garden chairs.

In the evening, when Juliet was playing with the kitten on the lawn and Ellen was picking flowers for the house, they heard a car coming up the drive.

"Mummy's coming back!" Juliet shouted joyfully, and ran to meet it, followed almost as quickly by Ellen, who hoped it might be Daniel, but it was Lucrezia who got out with Donata.

"Juliet, my darling, I have brought Donata to see you!" Juliet's expression was unenthusiastic, but Lucrezia waved them both away. "Run and play on the lawn."

Lucrezia took Ellen's arm.

"Signorina Fenny, let us go and look at the roses in the front garden."

"They're mostly dead with the heat."

"Well, we shall sit in the chairs on the *piazzale* and look at the view."

Ellen unwillingly offered to have cocktails brought.

"No, no, thank you. We must only stay a few minutes; we have friends who arrive. But I must ask you whether you have any news of Madeleine?"

"No, I haven't heard anything."

"Poor Madeleine! It was a good thing that she made up her mind at the last. Tell me about Charles. He was very angry, very distressed?"

"He naturally didn't talk to me about it."

Lucrezia shrugged her shoulders, as if she did not think it at all natural.

"Anyhow, it is better if the marriage is to end."

"I don't think so."

"Oh, you are thinking of the child. But children that age soon forget, and adapt themselves. I know, because she often spoke of it to me, that Madeleine suffered very much about Juliet. But what could she do? She no longer loved Charles nor he her. A woman like Madeleine cannot live without love; that, too, I understand."

Why should it be assumed, Ellen thought with fury, that women like Madeleine and Lucrezia are different from the rest of us? She would have liked to get up and walk away and leave Lucrezia, except that there was one question she wanted to ask.

"You do not know whether Charles is still in Rome? I suppose that they are arranging the divorce?"

"I don't know anything; and I am sorry, but I'm afraid I can't discuss their affairs."

Lucrezia made a graceful gesture of acceptance.

"You are always so honourable! I have a great respect for you, Signorina Fenny! I wish that I could find someone like you to teach Donata and Bianca. The nurses spoil them, and so far they have learned nothing. It is time that they should have a governess." She gave Ellen a sharp glance. "And now we have to find another tutor for Shand."

"What!"

"Oh, yes. Did you not know? Daniel Blackett went back to England this morning."

In her reeling world, Ellen was upheld by one strong spring of determination to show nothing to Lucrezia. Her own voice sounded cool and distant as she heard it inquire, "Was he fit to go so soon?"

"He was not at all in a good state, but we could not stop him. You see, he felt that he had made a fool of himself, and everyone knew it. He was very inexperienced, poor young man! He believed that Madeleine loved him. Perhaps he believed that they would soon be lovers, even that she would divorce for him. You see, he is quite romantic! He does not know anything about these things! And then that he should rush off like that, and we should all be searching the countryside for his dead body—that, you must admit, was ridiculous! No, I think that for him it is better that he should go. And because he is so upset, and, after all, he is always a very discourteous young man, he goes like that, without saying good-bye to his friends! And Grant is away! Shand, of course, is in a fit of sulks because when anything goes wrong he thinks that it is always my fault! So now we must call the children and I must go home."

Only Donata came running when Lucrezia called. She said:
"Juliet will not come to say good-bye."

"Well, be quick and get in. I am late now!"

As they drove off, Ellen went slowly round the corner of the house towards the lawn. She did not know where she was going. She was half stunned. There was a rush of footsteps, and Juliet, sobbing in gasps, threw herself into her arms.

"Oh, Fenny! Oh, Fenny!" she writhed, choking, like a child who has had a bad fall and cannot get breath to cry.

"What is it, darling? Have you hurt yourself?"

"Oh, Fenny! It isn't true, is it? It isn't true?"

"What?"

"Donata says . . . Donata says . . . that Mummy has gone away to Oliver Farren and she'll never come back to me again!"

When the storm of sobbing was subsiding and Ellen had done the best she could, explaining that of course whatever happened Juliet would see her mother, and see her often, that her father would be back soon and Juliet would be with him, the child lying against her shoulder, exhausted and sodden with crying, said urgently:

"But you won't go and leave me, Fenny! You'll stay with me!"

Ellen held her close.

"I shan't leave you now. I think your father will want me to stay with you till he takes you back to England. I shall ask him to let me."

"But after we go back to England! Oh, Fenny, don't go away, too; don't leave me! I must have somebody! Please, please! Don't go away."

Torn between the wish to relax the taut string of the child's anguish and a conviction that it was wrong to lie to her, Ellen said slowly:

"I don't know what your father will arrange, but I'm not going away now. And even if I don't live with you afterwards, I shall never forget you. I shall always love you and think about you and write to you wherever we are, and if you want me, I shall be there."

"Promise!" Juliet's hands clutched her with desperation. "Promise faithfully?"

"I promise faithfully," Ellen replied.

# PART II

1937

# CHAPTER I

Leaning on the wall at the end of the Bronciliano garden, Ellen watched the sun set behind the towers of Florence. In the field below her the *contadini* were carrying the last load of hay. She heard the creak of the ox-cart as it moved off, rocking beneath the green swags that dripped on either side feathery grass and crimson headed clover. This was her favourite hour of the day. While Maria was putting Bianca to bed, while Donata chattered to her mother and helped to amuse the guests who so often came for a drink, no one made any demands on Ellen, unless it was Shand, and his were always welcome.

She turned round and saw him now coming towards her along the grass path between the clipped cypresses. At sixteen he had grown as tall as a young tree, but had not yet filled out with muscle and flesh to match his bones. Tramping across the turf, he looked like a man; she saw him for an instant as his future, but when he came near her, into the light of the flushed sky, he was the scrawny, overgrown boy who sometimes surprised her by an unexpected maturity, at other times by lapses into childhood.

"I guessed I should find you here, Fenny!"—he was the only person who still called her Fenny.—"I've brought your mail."

She glanced at the two envelopes, one of which was addressed in a child's hand.

"From Juliet!"

She was going to open it, for Shand always liked to hear Juliet's unrevealing news, and the letters often ended "P.S. Love to Shand." But she saw that he was preoccupied.

"Look, Fenny! There he goes, damn him!"

The shining bonnet of a Bugatti nosed out of the front gate. The car gathered speed and shot down the avenue. They could just see the uniformed figure in the driver's seat, and another figure in the back of the car.

"When did he come?"

"After lunch. I heard the car when I was taking the girls upstairs for the siesta."

"Fenny, don't you think that when my father comes back I ought to tell him?"

I don't suppose, she thought, that you could tell him anything he doesn't know.

"I don't think I should interfere. She isn't your own mother. Besides, you don't know . . ."

"Oh yes, I do. Everyone knows, even Donata."

Ellen sighed. There were many obstacles in the way of educating Donata like a good English girl.

"It's the way she flaunts him here, it's the insult to my father that I feel bad about."

He had never been very close to his father. Lucrezia had seen to that. Ellen thought that Count Paolo Vascani had roused in him a personal passion, perhaps because he was on Ciano's staff and stood for the regime that Shand hated.

"I'm afraid there's nothing you can do, my dear."

"Anyway, Fenny, I've made up my mind when my father comes back tomorrow I'm going to speak to him again about letting me go home."

Ellen did not feel hopeful. The argument about Shand's return to America blew up every six months, swept the household like an equinoctial gale and subsided, leaving everything as it was, except for a deeper silt of resentment in Shand. Lucrezia was determined that he should not go until he was eighteen, and Ellen knew that Grant would not stand against her.

"You see, Fenny, if I went back now I'd have time for a year or two of schooling there before I went to college. It would be better than going right there from Europe. And, then, my aunts will be glad to have me around the place. They're both older than my father, you know—there's ten years between him and Aunt Gertrude. And Aunt Emily was pretty sick last winter. It's a big old house, and a big garden, and there's the farm; it would be better for them to have a man about the place. There's a lot of things I could look after for them."

Ellen had heard it all before, but did not mind hearing it again. At least while she was there the boy could talk.

"It's not as though anybody wanted me here."

She could have answered, I want you; you are the one thing that makes my life here worth living—but she did not say it. She had all the time been very clear about the essence of their relationship. Shand was not there for her, but she was there for Shand.

"I think your father wants you here, more than you realize. He's very reserved, but you're his only son. It probably means a lot to him to have you growing up in the house with him."

"He's not interested in anything but making money."

"No, I don't think that's true. He has great ability, and likes to use it. After all, he's not an old man; you wouldn't expect him to sit about all day doing nothing, would you?"

She understood why Grant had given up buying pictures and furniture, and turned to making a place for himself in the Italian industrial world. Lucrezia's husband had suffered a good many humiliations. He needed to return to a field where his judgment carried weight and could command success. He needed the conferences in Milan and Rome, the office in his house, his secretary, the telephone calls and cables. These things made a protecting wall round his self-esteem. He should be able to understand Shand's need to establish a separate life, but Lucrezia told him that Shand was a tiresome, moody boy, ungrateful for her motherly care, and he believed her. Yet both he and Shand went short of affection. If only the gulf between a father driven back into himself and a son tossed in the rough seas of adolescence were not so difficult to cross!

"My aunts wrote me that they're keeping my old room always ready for me. It's the big room over the porch. You can look way down the avenue between the trees to the paddock. I used to look out first thing every morning when I woke when my pony was there. But he's dead now, of course."

It was no use saying that the magic of those mornings might be dead too. That home of his childhood was Shand's romance. Sometimes Ellen wondered if his faithful memory had transfigured the aunts who had mothered him as a baby, if he would find strangers in the two women ageing together in the big, shabby house. From their letters, which he often showed her, they were upright, narrow and kind. Certainly they had given to their boy, even from a distance, the warmth of being loved.

"Try to discuss it calmly and sensibly with your father, Shand, without losing your temper. Talk to him as you talk to me."

"I can't. I feel all gummed up with him. I can't talk to anyone

123

here except you, Fenny! If you hadn't come here, I should have died."

A thrill of pleasure warmed her, but she answered:

"Oh, no, you wouldn't! Healthy young people don't die so easily! But when you get into rages it helps to make your father think that you aren't old enough to go away alone."

"Maybe, but it isn't only my father."

No, it wasn't, and Ellen did not believe that the most reasonable manner, even if Shand could sustain it with her, would move Lucrezia.

"Only I thought that perhaps while she's so taken up with Vascani she won't care whether I go or not."

Ellen was unwilling to dash a hope that she did not share.

"I suppose we'd better go in now."

"If I go, Fenny, what would you do? You wouldn't want to stay here without me, would you?"

She smiled at his young egotism, but what he said was true. It was mostly for him that she had stayed over three years at Bronciliano. Perhaps, too, she had stayed partly from inertia.

"I don't know what I should do. We'll get you off first if we can."

"You'd stay in Italy?"

She looked back at the grape-coloured shadow of the valley, the serene line of the hills against the fading sky.

"Yes, I think I should stay in Italy."

"It's the only thing we don't agree about! I hate the goddamned country! I want to be somewhere where people can say what they think without finding themselves in prison or beaten up next morning. I can't bear to think we're living here and paying taxes to Mussolini so he can send a few more planes to drop bombs on decent folk in Spain! Europe's rotten, and I want to get out of it! I just can't wait to be a hundred per cent American!"

She thought, You never will be. You can't wipe out these ten years. You'll take some of it with you.

"I don't think you'll always hate it. I think some day you'll want to come back again."

"I'll come back and see you, Fenny!"

He was looking at her now with the face that should have been his so much oftener, all his natural sweetness in his smile and in his deep blue eyes. She saw him now as some girl would see him in a few years' time, and there stirred in her envy of all that grown-up life to which he must go without her.

"Oh, of course you must come back and see me. Come along, we're going to be late for dinner."

They walked across the garden and went into the house, which, with its elaborate furniture, its scent of freezia, and floor-polish, always seemed to Ellen to close round her, giving her a slight feeling of imprisonment.

## CHAPTER II

IN HER own room upstairs Ellen read her letters. She wrote to Juliet every month, and at some time in the month Juliet faithfully answered her. In four years her handwriting had lost size and roundness. She now covered two sheets instead of one, but the letters still told nothing except facts:

"I got a prize for history and dancing. Granny Rose gave me a camera. I went to three parties and a circus. I've got a grey kitten called Smoke. We went to stay at the sea in Wales."

Ellen could not tell if behind this laborious recital of events there was a happy or unhappy child.

The photograph that had arrived at Christmas showed Juliet smiling in a bridesmaid's frock, her head beautifully erect under the cap of leaves and berries. She lived with her father and his mother at the house in Cranleigh Gardens, and was going next September to St. Paul's School.

She went at intervals to stay with her mother, and news of her came obliquely in Madeleine's occasional letters to Lucrezia. Madeleine had married Oliver Farren as soon as the divorce was through, and they had a son, now two years old. Juliet was shooting up, and very sweet. She adored her baby brother.

Madeleine was longing to go on the stage again, but Oliver

wanted her to wait until Stephen was a year or two older, or until he could find a suitable play in which they could appear together. The letters hinted dissatisfaction. Ellen was glad—she could not endure the thought of Madeleine triumphantly happy. Sometimes it surprised her to realize that her hatred of Madeleine was still so much alive when her love for Daniel had faded. She had, she supposed, done what people called getting over it, but there was a dreadful death in the end of feeling.

After he left she had written to him twice, addressing him care of the Newcastle School of Art, but she had had no answer. Later she had asked Alice to find out from a friend in Newcastle if his name was still on the staff list. It was not, and she knew no other address. She always looked in the English papers for the names of artists exhibiting, but the name of Daniel Blackett never appeared. For a long time after he went home she had watched for the post each day with a suffocating anxiety, followed, when no letter came, by a drop of the heart that left her each day a little farther below the level at which life is worth living.

It had been very bad that winter in Florence after Charles Rivers had taken Juliet home. So long as the child was there, and she was absorbed in trying to give what security and philosophy she could to someone of eight years old abandoned by her mother, she had kept herself from being submerged by her own trouble. When the train curved away along the platform, carrying the last glimpse of Juliet's face and waving hand, she walked out of the station to confront her own life. There was a little money to come from her mother, but the lawyers had not yet cleared up the estate. She kept herself by teaching English in two schools, and lived in a cheap *pension*, where the clientele were mostly students, with one or two elderly English spinsters living in Italy on tiny incomes. She shrank from these as from ghosts of her future, and the very young gravitated naturally together, and perhaps sheered off from her unhappiness. She was very lonely.

Still she did not think of going back to the Ainley High School. That for her meant going back defeated, and the instinct of her bruised being was to hide. Also she felt in some way tied to the place where things had happened to her. She told herself that she would be very foolish to go without learning Italian thoroughly. Another language was always an asset. One thing that remained

126

to her was her growing love of the country and the people. It seemed easier to be unhappy here than in England. Even in the biting cold of January and February, there were days of sunshine and soft colour that revived in her a belief that life might one day again be bearable. In the last fortnight of February she had a sharp attack of 'flu and reached her lowest ebb of wretchedness.

Soon after she had struggled back to work again she was walking along the Via Tornobuoni on a March afternoon of warm sunshine and blue skies, when she turned a corner and came upon Lucrezia Warner. She was surprised to find herself glad to see her. She was also surprised by Lucrezia's friendly greeting. "Miss Fenwick! But this is charming! I did not know that you were still here! I am delighted! But how thin you have become! You have been ill, perhaps? Let us have a cup of tea together!"

She found herself with Lucrezia's hand through her elbow, Lucrezia's familiar scent in her nostrils, being steered into Doney's. By the time they came out she had accepted the post of governess to Donata and Bianca, which she had now occupied for over three years.

She never quite knew why she had accepted Lucrezia's offer. It was partly that she had grown heartily sick of the *Pension*, and was ready for any change. But it was much deeper than that. It was a feeling of picking up again one of the strands of her life. She hoped that through the Warners she might get in touch with Daniel. She found that they knew nothing of him. Shand, too, had written letters, but had had no answer.

"It is not to be wondered at," Lucrezia commented. "He was a conceited young man and he made himself very foolish here. He would wish to forget."

Ellen was afraid that Lucrezia must be right.

She stayed on. Donata and Bianca were not Juliet, but Donata had a precocious intelligence, Bianca was a nice little girl with a good deal of character. Lucrezia, except in an occasional fit of petulance, treated Ellen with respect, and it was a much older, less defenceless Ellen who came to her after that winter than the girl who had been governess in the Villa Meridiana. Then, too, Lucrezia valued Ellen as she had once valued Daniel, as someone who kept Shand from being too much of a nuisance. He was only her pupil for English, but the schoolroom, whether the little girls were there or not, soon became his refuge. To Ellen he was at first a legacy from Daniel, soon dear in his own right. All the warmth that had been driven back into her heart by the shocks of her first Italian summer seeped out again for Shand.

She put away Juliet's letter in the writing-case of Florentine leather that had been her last Christmas present from Lucrezia. Shand had given her the tooled leather frame for Juliet's photograph. She had filled her bookcase with her own books that she had had sent out to her, with new Italian books and English books, presents from Alice and other old friends. This bedroom had become a home. Even the creak of the wardrobe door as she opened it to take out her evening dress was a familiar part of the day's routine.

She slipped the plain black dress that she wore every night over her head, shook herself into it, and automatically fastened the string of pearls behind her neck. She was putting on her governess's uniform for the long, formal dinner which she often found wearisome. She went to the dressing-table to smooth again the hair that had been ruffed by the dress, and looked at herself as indifferently as she did every evening at that time to see that all was in order. Tonight something made her prolong the look. The bloom and roundness that the unfolding of her spirit had brought to her face in that summer at Meridiana had faded with its end. The face that confronted her, except that it looked older, was the face that she had often seen in the mirror of her room at Ainley.

Dismay stabbed her. I thought I was making such a complete break with my own life when I came out to Italy, but did I really? Am I living in just the same way as I was at home, earning my living, but half dependent, protected by the Warners, instead of by my parents, a child's life? She knew that after that first dreary winter on her own she had been glad to come even to Lucrezia. She had said to herself that she would try it for a few months until she felt better and could decide what to do next. And here she was after three years, still in the house of Lucrezia, whom she neither respected nor liked. She had been half paralysed, she began to realize, after that disastrous summer. She had retreated so far into herself that even the growing menace in the outside world, the Abyssinian war, the fighting in Spain, the monstrous growth of Nazi Germany had been to her like history read from a distance.

Now she was beginning to wake out of her apathy. It is not too late, she told herself, to do something different with my life! When Shand goes, I will take a small flat in Florence, and work up a teaching connection. It will be much easier now. I only had a beginner's Italian last time. Now I could teach English in Italian schools and give Italian lessons to English and American visitors. I've got a bit of money to start with. If I had a place of my own I could have people from England out for holidays: Alice, Hugh's children, Juliet, perhaps. And I should make friends! She had no friends. People came all the time to Bronciliano, but they did not show more than civility or indifference to the governess in the background. She would have been very lonely if it were not for Shand. At the thought of Shand a conviction of point and purpose in her life came back to her. I can't go until he does, and he won't go for another two years. I shall have saved enough by then to furnish a place of my own.

Her room had two windows. A big one opened on to the garden with a distant view of Florence. This view was one of her untiring pleasures. She could see it when she sat up in bed in the morning drinking her coffee, and she knew it in every changing light. The other, smaller window looked over the valley to the Villa Meridiana. Ellen did not often look out of this window, but now, as she passed it to hang up the dress she had been wearing, she stopped and looked across the darkening valley to where the square white tower rose above the trees. All that the Villa Meridiana had meant in her life was over. Her heart rebelled. Why should it be, when such things were not over for Lucrezia? But it is not the same thing, she told herself. Lucrezia does not really love Paolo Vascani, or anybody but herself. She never has. Not the same thing, but disturbing! Lucrezia's new lover was a stone thrown into the pool of their life at Bronciliano whose ripples did not only reach Shand.

At dinner Lucrezia was unusually silent. She lit a cigarette as soon as she had finished her soup. The light from the candles glittered on the improbable but effective gold of her hair. Her sharp black eyes under the fine brows were almost dreamy. She is as ugly as a weasel really, thought Ellen, but so sure of herself, so little vulnerable. Lucrezia turned to her and spoke kindly: "Miss Fenwick, you are looking tired. You have been too long with these tiresome children without a break. Tomorrow I go to Rome but when I come back I think I shall send you then to my brother-in-law's house for a few days to have a holiday. They will be so glad that you should make them a little visit."

The kindness seemed genuine, and it was not in Ellen not to respond to it. Perhaps it would be rather nice to have a few days' change. She began to thank Lucrezia warmly, but Shand interrupted.

"Fenny wouldn't want to stay in that house with a lot of god-damned Fascists!"

Oh dear, thought Ellen, now we're off. She hated the shouting matches between Lucrezia and Shand that were so often an accompaniment to their meals. But this time Lucrezia did not bother to answer. She only lifted her eyebrows, shrugged her shoulders under the transparent black lace, and blew a smoke-ring, watching it go up into the air above the roses and candles with a secretive smile, as if her content made her impervious to a school-boy's rudeness.

## CHAPTER III

LUCREZIA LEFT the next morning for her visit to Rome. Donata and Bianca were allowed to break their lessons to go and see her off from the front door.

"She isn't really going to the station," Donata told Ellen as they settled down again at the schoolroom table. "Roberto is going to take her to Doney's and Count Paolo is going to meet her there and move her luggage into his car and then he's going to drive her to Rome. Roberto told Maria."

"Donata, you shouldn't listen to servants' gossip about your mother."

"Roberto and Maria had another terrible quarrel, and they did not speak to each other for two days, but when he told her about this, naturally she was interested and they became friends again."

Bianca, who was devoted to Maria, inquired with concern:
"Will they quarrel every day after they are married?"

"No, of course not, *stupida*, because they will not then be so much in love."

"Donata!" Ellen rapped on the table. "Go on with your translation."

Donata never disobeyed Ellen openly. Only the hint of a sigh, a barely sketched gesture of resignation, showed with how much reluctance she abandoned an interesting subject for the labour of putting a page of Italian history into good English.

Grant came home that evening, but if he was disappointed to find Lucrezia away, he did not show it. He was no more silent than usual at dinner, but Shand, who was always liberated by Lucrezia's absence, talked a good deal with an undertone of suppressed excitement. When Ellen went upstairs afterwards, he ran after her up the first flight.

"Fenny! I'm going to speak to my father now! Wish me luck!"

"Of course I do!"

But she did not expect him to get it. She went on to the schoolroom, and sat down at the table to write a letter.

She had finished and was reading, when she heard a slow step in the passage and a ceremonious knock at the door. Grant did not often visit the schoolroom, and now looked around the dim walls outside the circle of light from Ellen's lamp as if he did not remember what shape they were and was surprised to find himself there. He looked too large for the schoolroom chair into which he lowered himself. He had grown heavy; the fleshy padding of his face masked the bone structure and decreased his likeness to Shand. There were dark pouches under his eyes, and the thin strands of hair, usually arranged with care over his scalp, were ruffled as if he had been holding his head in his hands. Unhappiness and perplexity came from him like a smell, and Ellen wondered if he was really as entirely absorbed in business and as remote from what went on in the house as he always seemed.

"I hope I'm not interrupting you, Miss Fenwick? If you're not too busy, I'd like to have a little talk with you about Shand. You've always been very, very good to the boy. His mother and I appreciate what you've done for him, as well as for the girls."

"I'm very fond of Shand. I think there's a lot in him."

"I'm glad to know you think so. He's a difficult boy, but maybe things haven't been all that easy for him." Grant hurried on as though the admission had slipped out of him against his will, "I expect you know that he's been talking to me this evening about going back to his aunts in New England. You know, of course, that his mother died when he was born and my sisters took charge of him until my second marriage, when he was six years old. Now, I don't need to tell you that Lucrezia has always been a mother to him. I'm very, very grateful for the way she made that boy her responsibility and treated him as one of her own. But I suppose it was a big break for a child of that age, and I don't reckon he's ever been quite at home with us here. A growing boy in his teens isn't at all that easy for a woman to control." He paused and looked uncomfortable, face to face with some thought that he did not want to admit. "Well, that's how it is. He's been talking to me tonight. He put it to me that his aunts were very good to him when he was a baby, and that it's hard he's never seen them since, and they keep writing and hoping he's coming over, and I'm thinking of letting him go back for a few weeks this fall to pay them a visit, only I don't know whether he'll come back more unsettled than before. I'd like to have your opinion."

Ellen's heart leaped for Shand.

"I'm sure it would be a good thing, Mr. Warner! I think it would make all the difference in the world for him. He's very fond of his aunts; he's never forgotten them. He's an American; it's natural that he should want to go back sometimes to his own country. He'll learn to love Italy some day, but just at present I think he feels trapped here. He's old enough now to enjoy the idea of going off somewhere by himself, it will be good for him to be more independent. Do, do let him go!"

"Only for a visit," Grant said hastily. "His mother feels he ought not to leave us till he's eighteen at least, and I agree with her. But I might let him go in July and August, when we go to the sea, and then he could come back and start his classes again in September. That way he won't miss much of his schooling."

He won't, Ellen thought, once over there he won't come back. But the visit was an excellent idea; it would save everybody's face, and there was a possibility that Lucrezia might agree to it. As for missing classes, Ellen did not think that Shand was learning much except for the English he read with her. He went three times a week to a tutor in Florence, a retired English clergyman, who bored him, and was, Ellen suspected, rather frightened of him, since he never seemed to venture more than a mild remonstrance about homework scamped or undone. Shand had a good brain, but a life spent permanently in opposition was blocking half his mental energy.

"I am quite sure you are right to let him go."

Grant seemed relieved by her certainty.

"Well, I told him I would consider it. Of course, only if his mother agrees."

Moved by Shand's interests to what she considered outside her province, Ellen pleaded:

"Of course he feels that he is *your* son and that he belongs to your country. I expect he wants to abide by your decision. A boy can't feel quite the same about a step-mother's authority, however good she has been to him."

Grant flinched from the implication.

"She's been a mother to him, and he owes her a son's duty."

Ellen thought that she had only done harm and was silent. Suddenly, as if the words were pushed out by uncontrollable feelings, Grant muttered:

"Maybe now she won't care."

Ellen saw sweat start on his forehead, unhappiness and impotent fury in his eyes. Then he wiped his forehead and straightened his heavy shoulders.

"I mean, she may feel he's old enough now to have some say in his own affairs. There wasn't much friendship between her and my sisters when they met. They're good women, but they haven't travelled, and some of their ideas are narrow. But I'm sure Lucrezia will see that the boy owes them something, and a couple of months' holiday over there would please him, and please his aunts, and do no harm." He got up to go, looked around the room again as though recalling its purpose, and asked, "Does Blanche make progress with her lessons?"

It was a long time since he had called Bianca Blanche, and Ellen recognized another sign of revolt.

"Yes, she works very steadily, and doesn't forget what she

133

learns. She's particularly good at arithmetic. She's nearly up to Donata in that, although she's so much younger."

"Ah, Donata! But she's clever in her own way, as clever as a cartload of monkeys!" He added with sudden vehemence, "If I thought Blanche was getting too much like Donata, I'd pack her off too to her aunts in New England."

"I don't think Blanche is very much influenced by Donata, and she goes her own way. They have very different temperaments. But Donata is an intelligent girl."

He seemed to suppress something he was about to say. He moved towards the door.

"I'm glad to hear that they're both getting on well." His tone was formal, the employer concluding the interview. "I'd like you to know, Miss Fenwick, that we're very grateful for all you do for them. We're very fortunate to have you with them, and it's been a fine thing for Shand. I'm afraid I've kept you up late. Goodnight."

She waited up in the schoolroom, knowing that Shand would come. A minute after she heard his step in the passage he burst in, wild with excitement.

"Fenny, did he come and talk to you?"

"Yes."

"He said he would. I knew you'd say the right things! What did he say?"

"He said he thinks he will let you go over to America on a few weeks' visit to your aunts, if your step-mother agrees."

"She must, she will, if it's only supposed to be a visit! And once I'm there they won't get me back!"

"That's something you'd better not say!"

"Of course not, only to you."

Restless with excitement, he walked to the window and back, flung his loose limbs into the chair that his father had just left. He swung himself sideways, his legs over the arm, kicked off his sandals, and stretched his big jointed toes to the floor. This was his favourite position for talking, and Ellen, who was sleepy, resigned herself to one of the sessions that she was never really too tired to enjoy. They were generally at the end of the evening. These were the times when he was able to forget his two obsessions, or the two ends of his one obsession, his step-mother and

134

going home. He talked about books, about politics, about his philosophical and religious gropings, and about his plans for his future. He should have been talking like this, Ellen often thought, to companions of his own age, but there were none about with whom he cared to make friends, and she alone enjoyed his confidences, the more keenly because she knew they could not last. Sooner or later he would be in America, spilling out his inexperienced enthusiasms to girls and other boys, which was as it should be. Ellen never allowed herself to forget that she was only a station waiting-room for Shand.

Tonight he did not start one of their discussions. He was silent for a minute and then broke out:

"It would make so much difference! I'd be glad to quit acting the way I do here all the time, I don't like it! I even get sick of myself always feeling mean about Lucrezia! I'd be glad not to have any feelings about her at all! But so long as I'm here, I just don't seem able to stop! Only sometimes when I'm up here with you, when it's peaceful after the kids have gone to bed, I can let go for a bit and think about other things. When I try to do it other times, I can't. Wherever I go I almost seem to smell her! It's like it was when I had whooping cough, when I was bored with the thing and yet I had to go on doing it, till I felt I could scream! So now if I could get out of it! Even if it was only for a visit! But once I'm there, I don't see how they'd get me back again. By the time we'd all done arguing about it, I should be eighteen."

By no means sure that Lucrezia would be unsuspicious enough to agree to the visit, Ellen could not bring herself to discourage him. He did not seem to want to talk any more, but lay back in the chair, swinging his legs and whistling gently. Ellen began to put her things together.

"I've been writing to Juliet."

"She was a nice kid, Juliet. That was the best summer we had here when you were all at Meridiana, and Daniel Blackett was here, and we all used to do things together. Do you remember, Fenny?"

"Yes, I do."

"I often wonder what's become of him. I wish I could have heard from him again."

"It's getting late, my dear; I think we'd better go to bed."

"Fenny, why do you think *she* likes him?"

Ellen, who had been very far away in her own thoughts, dragged herself back.

"Who?"

"Vascani."

"Well, he's handsome in his way, you must admit. And very dashing and slick." She was going to say "And Lucrezia's getting older and she hasn't had a new admirer for some time," but substituted, "And sometimes he's amusing."

"He never amuses me! I think he's a conceited fool! I hate his guts!"

"Well, you won't be seeing him for a bit now; anyhow until after Lucrezia comes back."

"And then I'll be off myself, as soon as I can get a passage. And good riddance to the lot of them! Except you, Fenny. I shall be very sorry to leave you. But I'm going to fix it with my aunts that you come over and stay with us for a spell in America. I know they'd love to have you. You'd come, wouldn't you?"

"We'll see. You'd better get there yourself, first."

"Oh, I shall. I've got a hunch they really are going to let me go this time!"

## CHAPTER IV

WHEN LUCREZIA arrived back from Rome she came into the schoolroom wing with presents for the little girls and for Ellen, but they saw at once that she was in a bad temper. She said sharply that Donata must not stoop over her work and get round-shouldered. She rated Maria in the passage because Bianca's hair looked as if it wanted washing. She said that the journey had given her a headache and that she was going to lie down till dinner-time. She gave the impression that she could not bear the sight of anyone at home. Ellen hoped that Shand would have the sense to put off pleading his cause until the next day.

But he had not yet come to this kind of sense. After dinner he followed his father and his step-mother into the *salone*, with an air of desperate resolve that made Ellen smile, even while she sympathized. She went up to the schoolroom and sat down to her accounts. To record her modest spending was a habit that she had been taught early and had never since broken. It was the only way, her mother had told her, to keep out of debt. The very sight of the figures brought back the dining-room table in their old house before they moved into Ainley, her mother's greying head bent over the book, herself a school-girl standing near, waiting to see if she would be able to have the new winter coat or the new dress for the end-of-term party. Her mother would draw her lips into a thin line as she remarked bitterly that the Browns' account had been outstanding for more than a year. "I can't get your father to do anything about it. He ought to send them a solicitor's letter." And that night there would be an argument, with her father pleading that the Browns had had so much trouble, and her mother maintaining, "Your own children ought to come first." Ellen had sided with her father for she loved him better, and felt that there would be something dreadful about having her new winter coat at the cost of more trouble for the Browns. Now she understood better how her mother had felt, and how much of her father's generosity, real as it was, was also that unwillingness to make trouble that she knew in herself, that had lost her, she sometimes thought, Daniel.

There were times when she wished that Shand would not stir up the old argument; but how right the boy was really, to fight for his own life! Had she been too much inclined to soothe him and counsel patience? Ought she to have given him stronger support? But if she did, she might have to go, and that would leave him stranded, without a friend. She suspected, all the same, some reluctance of her own to face a crisis and make a break with a life in which she had every comfort and only a subordinate's responsibility She turned to the end of her account book and considered her savings She should have enough by the end of the year to furnish a flat simply, she had her small regular income from England, she was guaranteed now against starvation. She resolved that no want of enterprise of her own should prevent her from doing whatever seemed best for Shand.

She had put away her accounts and was darning a stocking

137

when there were hasty footsteps in the passage, and the door flew
open. One glance at Shand's face told her what had happened.
He lurched into the room, picked up an empty chair by the table
and banged it down on the floor.

"The bitch!"

He shook the chair till Ellen thought it would come to pieces.

"She won't let you go?"

"No. Goddamn her, she's talked my father round!"

"Not even a visit?"

"Not even a visit. She said I was too young for my age, not to
be trusted to go to America by myself. The aunts would turn me
against her and my father. I was their responsibility until I was
grown up. I was too unbalanced for my parents to inflict me
on any other household. I'm not to go for another two years.
She's angry with you. She thinks you're in it, too! I told her this
was my affair and no one else's." He gripped the chair again, the
muscles of his lean hand straining through the flesh. "I could
have strangled her! I looked at her and thought just where I
would put my hands on her stringy neck!"

"No, my dear, don't talk that nonsense! But I'm so sorry,
Shand! So very sorry!"

"And my father! Just sitting there, saying 'It's for your mother
to decide!' Mother! Letting her ride over him, when all the time
she's making a fool of him with her lover, when she only sticks to
him for his money! And he expects me to obey HER. . . ."

His face, screwed up like an angry child's, suddenly quivered.
Ellen saw that he was on the point of tears, but he managed to
check them.

"It's very hard. I'm very, very sorry. But it will only be two
years to wait. It isn't so long, really."

He said less violently, but with a conviction that made itself
felt:

"I can't stand another two years."

"Perhaps even before that . . ."

He kicked the chair back into its place. With an effort of
control that made him suddenly look older, he said:

"Well, it's no use talking about it any more now. I'd book a
passage on a ship to New York and go without telling them if I
had the money, but I haven't. I suppose there's just a chance she

138

might change her mind. I'll see if I can do anything with her tomorrow. I'm going to bed now. Good-night!"

She heard his step going heavily away along the passage. She was very sorry for him; she knew that at his age two years is a tunnel almost without end. She began to wonder if any third way was possible, if the Warners would agree to let him board with a tutor, or to go to school in Italy, or even in England, for two years. She did not believe that they would. Lucrezia, for some reason of her own, was determined to keep him. Ellen was thinking mostly of him, but she was conscious on her own account both of disappointment and relief, since her plunge into the outside world was postponed. For the next two years she was pledged to stay with Shand.

If she was allowed to. She heard the brisk click of heels in the passage. Lucrezia swept in. She was wearing over her black dress a bright magenta shawl which did not suit her skin and made her dyed hair look garish.

"Miss Fenwick, I must ask you not to encourage Shand in this foolish plan of going back to America! I know that he talks a great deal to you, and that you have great influence over him; I am sure that you are very kind to him, but I think you have not been very wise."

"I am obliged to say, Mrs. Warner, that I do think it would be good for Shand to go away from here."

"That is not something for you to decide!"

"I know it's not. But Shand is one of my pupils, and if you come to talk to me about him, I must say what I really think, even if it is something you do not wish to hear."

"And what is this that you really think?"

"I think that his present life isn't doing Shand any good. He isn't developing in the right way, he isn't learning anything, he doesn't make friends of his own age, because all the time he is fretting to get away from the place. He doesn't like this country."

"To a child one country is the same as another."

"But Shand is hardly a child."

"Do you think of him, then, as a man?"

Lucrezia pointed the question with a sharp glance of her black eyes.

"I think of him as a boy at a difficult age going through a

difficult phase, in a kind of life that doesn't suit him and in which he is not happy. I think he would do better in his own country, or anyhow at school with other boys."

"Shand will not go away until he is eighteen, of that you may be sure! You can see for yourself that while he is so hysterical we could not send him back to his aunts in America. Two old spinsters!" Lucrezia said viciously. "They would not find again at all the little child of whom they think so sentimentally. He would give them terrible shocks! No, of this you can be sure. Shand will stay here, and I must ask you not to encourage him in his stupidity. He is discontented, and of course he wishes someone to sympathize, and you, I know, have a sympathetic nature; but that you should sympathize with him against his father and me, that is not good."

"If you are not satisfied with my handling of the children, Mrs. Warner! . . .?"

"No, no, no!" Lucrezia sounded less belligerent and more fretful. "I am very satisfied. For Donata and Bianca I could not find anybody better. They learn, they are obedient and content, there are none of those screams and scenes that were always with Donata and the nurses. All I ask is that you should use your good influence with Shand to try to prevent these arguments which only make bad feeling. It is because he will take notice of what you say that I ask you to help him to accept what he cannot prevent. When he is eighteen his father has promised him that he shall go to Harvard University. Until then he stays with us, and it is better for everyone if he makes up his mind to it. Thank you for your good care of the children while I was away, Miss Fenwick. I must arrange that you have a little holiday soon before you take the children to the sea. Good-night."

## CHAPTER V

The next day was Thursday—the day that Ellen took the little girls to their music lesson in Florence. She felt, as often nowadays, glad to be out of the house for a time. It was partly to prolong her own relief, as well as for their pleasure, that she took them afterwards to have an ice in Doney's. When they returned to the villa and came in to the hall, they at once heard angry voices behind the half-open door of the *salone*. Lucrezia's shrill torrent, interrupted by Shand's voice, which had lately broken and in moments of agitation still ranged from a growl to a squeak.

Bianca remarked placidly, "Mamma and Shand quarrelling again. They're always quarrelling."

"Like Maria and Roberto." Donata observed with a side glance at Ellen.

Ellen lost her temper.

"Run upstairs at once, both of you! You try to meddle far too much with things in this house that aren't your business!"

She very seldom spoke to them with anger. They were startled, and scampered upstairs to get away from her.

It was so hot in Florence, Ellen thought, but I shouldn't have let myself speak irritably to the child. The quarrelling voices pursued her as she climbed the stairs, and rasped her nerves. Really, it's getting too much for all of us; this house is intolerable! For a moment she was annoyed not only with Lucrezia, but also with Shand.

He must have flung out of the house after the argument, for he did not appear at dinner. After she was in bed she heard his footsteps going along the passage of the schoolroom wing to his room.

In the next week she saw very little of him. He stayed down in Florence after his classes. On the days when he did not go, he went walking over the hills alone. He had friends on the farms around; he sometimes went off for a whole day to lend a hand with the hay-making, or with anything that was going on. Ellen hoped that he was working off his feelings in some such way. She thought, too, that he might be avoiding her for fear of getting her into trouble. He sent a message by Bianca to excuse himself from his next English lesson, and she did not press it, nor attempt to break his reserve. At meals he looked strained and silent. It was clear that he was going through some kind of crisis, and though she ached to help him, she thought it was better to wait until he was ready to come to her. She missed his companionship terribly. His withdrawal showed her how much she had come to depend on it for any real life in that household.

Towards the end of the week he came for his second English lesson, which he always had at six, when the little girls had finished, and were out in the garden. At first Ellen felt as though he were not there. She talked to an older, graver mask of Shand, who made automatic answers. Stimulated by her pleasure in having him back, she used all her powers to interest him, and gradually he relaxed, the spirit filled the shell, and the boy, the Shand whom she loved and knew, was with her again. When the lesson was over he flung himself back in the chair and slewed his legs over the side, ready to talk.

"Fenny, I haven't given up. I've thought of another possible way, but I haven't quite made up my mind. I shan't tell you anything about it, because if I decide to do what I think I shall, I don't want you to be involved in it."

"You needn't worry about that! But don't do anything foolish, my dear!"

"Can you think of anything more foolish than going on with another two years of this?"

She was not sure that she could, but she felt uneasy. Below his forced calm, she detected a rash wildness.

"I won't ask you what you are planning, but will you promise me that before you do anything drastic you will tell me what you're going to do?"

"No, because whatever I do, I want you to be able to say afterwards that you didn't know anything about it. Then they can't take it out of you."

"They can't anyhow, because I don't really care; they don't matter to me. But you do. Promise me, Shand, whatever you are thinking of doing, you will tell me about it before you do it?"

"No, I shan't promise. Maybe I shan't do anything at all, maybe I shall just stay rotting here."

"Well, don't expect me to put wreaths on your tomb!"

He looked affronted for a second, then his face broke into a grin.

"I suppose," he conceded, "I *might* survive two years, even. But I'm pretty sure I'm not going to try!"

They heard a car coming up the drive. Shand strolled to the window, and looked out.

"Vascani! I thought we'd got rid of him!"

"So soon?"

"I thought even a fool like that would finish with Lucrezia when he got to know her!"

"Shand, my dear, it doesn't really matter to you. In a year or two you'll go away and begin a new life in America. Then you'll be surprised how unimportant all this will seem. Can't you make up your mind to concentrate on getting ready for that and looking forward to it? Lucrezia is only your step-mother. Her private life isn't really anything to do with you."

"My father is her husband."

"Yes, but you're not!"

"If I was I would kill myself . . . or her."

"I don't think you're a suicidal type, nor a murderer either. Anyhow, your wife is probably now about as old as Donata, and going to high school, in America, in bobbysocks. Try to put Lucrezia and her affairs out of your mind and make the best life you can here for another two years. We shall be going to the sea next month, and she isn't coming with us for the first week or two, I know."

"Where is she going? Off with Vascani somewhere?"

"I don't know. I think she said she was going to Switzerland. But we shall have a happy time at Portofino, and you always enjoy the fishing and bathing."

"Yes, I do; only this year I can't imagine myself enjoying anything. But anyhow it doesn't matter, because I shan't be there."

"Well, promise to let me know of any plan you make."

"I won't promise to tell you what I'm planning. But I promise I'll never leave here without letting you know where I'm going."

"Leave here?"

"No, don't ask me any more. I dare say there's nothing I can do; but if there is, I'll let you know before I do it."

And with that concession she had to be content.

## CHAPTER VI

A few days later Ellen had to take Donata to the dentist in Florence. The car was to pick them up at Doney's after Donata had been consoled with tea and ices. Shand, who was going to his tutor, arranged to meet them there.

Ellen had not realized that it was a Fascist Party Festival, but the streets were full of uniforms, black shirts, banners and Party badges, and they had difficulty in making their way along the crowded pavements. Donata, in high spirits because the dentist had relieved her toothache without hurting her much, was excited by the stir, and when she heard the distant music of a band, wanted to stay and see if a procession was coming.

"No, we can't wait, you won't have time for tea, and Roberto won't be able to keep the car standing when the streets are so full. They're all very silly, anyhow; we don't want to watch them."

Thinking them silly had for some time been a defence that Ellen had built up against thinking them sinister.

When they came out of the café, the police had cleared the street of cars, and the procession was passing, cheered by spectators packed on the pavements and in the shop doorways and the windows above. A group of young Fascists went by, military and smart in their uniform jackets and top boots. They were boys of Shand's age or less. Some of them looked very hot, the sweat rolled down their solemn young faces under the peaked caps, but they carried themselves proudly, their limbs swinging in perfect time, their heads erect under the swaying banners with their portraits of the Duce, the Roman wolf, the fasces and the ever-repeated inscription, "*Credere, obedire, combattere.*"

"How well they march!" Donata said with exaggerated fervour and a mischievous upward glance at her governess's unsmiling face.

Ellen saw Shand on the opposite pavement. In his flannel trousers, sandals and open-necked shirt—clothes which he always wore untidily—he could not have looked a more complete contrast to his marching contemporaries. He was frowning at them with open hostility. Behind the marching boys there was a brief gap in the procession between their rear rank and the leaders and foremost banners of the *squadristi*, who followed them. Through this gap, as the movement of the procession brought it opposite to him, Shand slouched coolly across the road.

Luckily there were at the moment no policemen nor Blackshirts just outside the door of Doney's. A young man wearing a Party badge shook his fist at Shand, and began to pour out a torrent of abuse. He evidently thought him English, for the word "sanctions" kept on recurring. Two or three of the bystanders joined in, and there was a movement towards them from the back of the crowd. Ellen pushed Donata inside Doney's and pulled Shand after her.

"We'll wait inside until the procession has passed."

At that moment Roberto appeared, wriggling his way out of a gap in the crowd, his face hot and anxious. He followed them into the shop and said that he had left the car behind the building; they could go through and out by the back door.

"*Scusi*, Signorina, but we should make haste; it is not a good day to leave the car unattended."

"How stupid you were, Shand!" Donata scolded. "We might all have been arrested! You quite spoilt the look of the procession!"

"I hope so. I'm glad."

Roberto shut Ellen and Donata into the back of the car and got into the driving-seat beside Shand. He seemed on wires. He said that the Blackshirts had been making arrests in the outskirts of the city. He drove by a devious route through the quiet streets, swinging the car sharply round the corners, and braking noisily as the bonnet nearly touched an old woman who bolted out of a doorway and scuttled like a hen across the road.

"Roberto is driving badly," Donata remarked, "But he is *nervoso* because this morning he had news from his family in Perugia that his brother has been thrown into prison."

"What for?"

"They do not know. So far there is no charge against him."

"How infamous!"

"Oh, well, I suppose that he has been a Socialist, or has perhaps spoken against the Duce."

"He ought at least to be told what he is accused of!"

"In England," Donata offered in a bored voice, "I suppose that he would be."

"Of course!"

"Ah, well, here it is all so different!"

With a feeling that Donata had left her nothing to say, Ellen looked out at the glaring dusty streets, and was seized by nostalgia for her own country. She also felt distressed for Roberto, and

145

vaguely guilty. Life went on in Bronciliano and in the English and American society round Florence as if Mussolini hardly existed. This was the first time that the finger of the Fascist State had touched the life of anyone whom Ellen knew personally.

They were driving along a shabby street of tall houses, evidently let off as flats or apartments, when a door flew open, and a party of Blackshirts erupted, hustling between them a man who stumbled over the doorstep and slipped down to his knees on the pavement. One of his captors, with a hand in his collar, hauled him to his feet. He wore a black striped suit, and looked like a clerk. He was elderly, paunchy, round-shouldered, with tufts of grey hair sprouting from a bald head. His face was distorted by panic, a stream of prayers and excuses poured from his open mouth, in which a gold-stopped front tooth glinted back the sunlight. One of the Blackshirts struck him hard on the mouth. He covered his face with his hand, and blood trickled between his spread fingers. He stopped with a groan, but a kick in the small of the back from heavily booted feet sent him staggering forward. Again he stumbled and fell, and was jerked, sagging and bleeding to his feet.

"Stop, Roberto!" Shand cried. "Let me out!"

Roberto, muttering, shook his head and trod harder on the accelerator.

"Stop!"

Shand grabbed the brake. The car slewed into the gutter and slowed down.

Ellen leaned over and gripped Shand by the shoulders.

"No, Shand! You can't do anything! Go on, Roberto!"

Roberto had already released the brake and swung the car back into the road.

"*Niente a fare!*" he said. "*Niente a fare!*"

"It's no use, Shand." Ellen kept hold of him. "There are six of them, grown men, and there will be more within call. They'll only take it out of him."

The Blackshirts and their victim had disappeared round the corner. Roberto, driving at a reckless speed, left the street behind. Shand shook off Ellen's grip.

"*Niente a fare! Niente a fare!* That's all anyone says, and so it

146

goes on! You don't care as long as we're all safe! Nobody cares! Jesus Christ! I wish I was in Spain!"

Ellen leaned back in her seat, trembling, aware at first only of thankfulness that the moment of so much danger for her charges had passed.

With an imitation of her mother's voice, and manner Donata complained:

"Shand is always so hysterical."

But Ellen felt with shame that what he had said was true, and that she had been blind or asleep for the last three years.

As they turned into the avenue of Bronciliano and saw the honey-coloured walls above them among the trees, Shand said bitterly:

"Those are HER friends!"

## CHAPTER VII

VASCANI'S CAR was standing outside the front door. Ellen went into the house and up to her room. She took off her hat, sponged the dust of Florence off her hot face and neck and arms, and combed back her hair. The shutters were still closed, and in her familiar, dim room the scenes of the afternoon began to fade. One part of her—the part that had been content to live at Bronciliano for three years—wanted to forget them, but something else in her, returning to life, urged her to remember.

Shand, she thought, is always treated as a naughty child in this house. Even to me he has been often a child in trouble, though not trouble of his own making. Yet in some ways he is the only grown-up person here. He makes me feel ashamed that I have been drifting on with my eyes shut. But he must go! How can I make them see it? He can't contain himself much longer, and one day soon he will get into serious trouble, he will see something like what we saw today, and get involved with the Blackshirts, get hurt, killed before anyone realizes that he is an American. Why won't Lucrezia understand!

She went downstairs to look for the children. In the hall she met Lucrezia, carrying a letter.

"Miss Fenwick, I was looking or you; I have some news here that will interest you. Charles Rivers is to be married again."

"Oh!"

"You are not pleased?"

"I was thinking about Juliet."

"You do not think it is good that Juliet should have a step-mother? Perhaps, like Shand, you do not think very much of stepmothers? But you could not expect Charles to remain for ever with his mother, unmarried. It is much better for Juliet when she will be a girl growing up that there should be a home for her and a woman who will be able to advise her, and entertain her friends, and perhaps find her a husband."

"Does Mrs. Farren tell you anything about the new wife?"

"Yes, she has met her. You are very welcome to read the letter. Perhaps you will take it out to the loggia. The *avvocato* has called to see me, and I have left Count Paolo there with the children. I see that Shand has come back from Florence in a bad mood. I do not want him to give Paolo any impertinence."

Ellen was not at the moment aware of either Vascani or Shand. Whatever this new stepmother was like, this must be a great upheaval in Juliet's life! She had come first with her father for four years. Standing in the hall, Ellen anxiously read the letter, which was full of exaggerated terms of affection, with the usual undercurrent of complaint.

"Charles is engaged to a woman called Lorna Marshall. Quite clever, I believe: she has a job in the Civil Service or something. He met her on some legal commission. We all had lunch together, only Oliver was kept late at rehearsal, of course, just when I wanted him, and I had to meet them alone. Juliet was at home with chicken-pox, poor pet! Lorna is about thirty-five, nice-looking but not pretty, clothes good but dull. I should think she is the sort of person Charles really likes and he has found it out at last. I can just see her in the house at Cranleigh Gardens, getting on so well with his mother! Well, I suppose this is good news really. Of course I don't grudge Charles his happiness, and this Lorna seems to be the kind of woman who will feel obliged to do her duty by Juliet, which is all that matters."

148

But it wasn't: it was only the beginning of what mattered! Juliet, so warm-hearted and loving, needed much more than someone doing her duty by her. But, then, this was Madeleine's story, and Madeleine always felt other people's happiness an assault on her own, and would naturally dislike her successor. Ellen could well imagine that this might be a woman with a longing for children who would open her heart to a ready-made daughter.

The light slap of a child's sandalled feet on the tiled floor of the hall roused Ellen from this distant world. Across the big bowl of full-blown roses on the table, Donata was looking at her with eyes narrowed in mischief.

"Count Paolo and Shand are having a terrible quarrel!"

"Where are they?"

"On the loggia."

Ellen went quickly out, Donata with an air of pleasureable anticipation skipping by her side.

At first Ellen only saw Vascani. He was standing at the front of the loggia, one hand resting on the wooden pillar, wreathed with wisteria, that supported the roof, the other on the leather belt of his elegant, waisted uniform. He looked very angry, but was covering his anger with an assumed nonchalance. Then she saw Shand, behind the table where Giorgio had put the tray with bottles and glasses. Shand was leaning forward with the fanatical look on his face that he often wore when he quarrelled with Lucrezia.

". . . glorious Empire!" he was shouting. "Built on mustard gas, used on a lot of poor blacks that hadn't any chance of fighting back!"

"Since I am a guest in this house, and you are a child, I do not choose to answer."

"Because you can't! I've been growing up here for ten years, and I've seen what your Fascist State has been doing to this country! Making slaves! Slaves and bullies! Your prisons are crammed with people who've never had a trial and never will have! They'll just rot to death! This afternoon I saw your god-dammed Blackshirts, half a dozen of them to one poor little devil of a clerk that they were knocking about! You've got spies in every factory and in every village!"

149

"Shand!"

Ellen pulled his arm. He jerked it away from her.

"Count Vascani, please go in."

Vascani's temper was getting out of control. Beneath the sunburn the red went up his handsome face to the roots of his hair.

"You should remember that this country has given you hospitality!"

"Hospitality! Only because I can't get away from it!"

"Shand! Stop it, Shand!"

"Hospitality! I'll say we pay for everything we get twice over! What with everybody lying and cheating, and with the taxes we pay to your god-damned Duce . . ."

"Be silent, or I will whip you! What do you understand, you who come from a vulgar civilization that is decadent before it is mature!"

The table went down with a crash of glass. Donata shrieked. The two struggling bodies were on the edge of the tiled floor. Ellen, taken by surprise and startled by their violence, could not see how to interfere. Panting, clutching at one another, uttering half-finished ejaculations, ridiculously like a dog-fight, they went over the edge of the loggia floor, and crashed into a bed of zinnias four feet below them. As Ellen ran down the steps she heard Donata's scampering feet and her voice shouting, "Mamma! Mamma!"

The fall had for the moment knocked the breath out of them. Ellen caught Shand by the arm and pulled him off Vascani. She spoke to him as she might have spoken to one of the little girls.

"Shand, go upstairs at once!"

He scrambled up, looking dazed and a good deal astonished at his own behaviour. He glanced doubtfully at Vascani, now getting on to his knees among the crushed zinnias.

"Go into the house, Shand!"

To her immense relief, he turned and walked slowly in, absently rubbing one elbow. Vascani, scarlet and furious, stood up, turned his back to her and began to brush soil and petals off his uniform.

"I hope you are not hurt, Count Vascani?"

Ellen could not make her voice express much real concern.

"Of course not!"

He walked away from her on to the terrace.

Lucrezia, with Donata, came out of the door of the *salone* on to the loggia. She looked at the overturned table. The tiled floor was strewn with broken glass, and a stream of vermouth from a bottle lying on its side, dripped over the edge of the floor on to the bed of zinnias.

To Ellen's surprise, Lucrezia looked more amused than angry. "They had a fight?"

"Well, a scuffle. It was my fault, really; I was reading your letter indoors. I should have come out sooner to see what was happening. They fought about politics."

"Oh! You think so? Perhaps if you are going in, you will take Donata, and ask Giorgio to come and clear up this mess and bring fresh drinks."

She walked across the terrace towards the angry back of Vascani. Her voice, saying his name softly in a tone between reproof and entreaty, reached Ellen as she went indoors.

## CHAPTER VIII

ELLEN HEARD Vascani's car going away before dinner, at which Shand did not appear. Donata, who had pleaded that it was too hot to go to bed, dined with them, and kept up a stream of chatter to which Lucrezia listened more indifferently than usual. Ellen wondered what was in store for Shand. It was difficult to see what punishment Lucrezia could devise for a boy too big to beat or to shut up in a room on bread and water.

Ellen went up to the schoolroom afterwards to write to Juliet. She would not mention her father's marriage until she had heard of it from the child. She wrote to tell her that she was sorry to hear she had chicken-pox because she wanted, in a changing world, to give her an assurance of love. Ellen had never had a real holiday since she came to the Warners; she always went to the sea with the children in July and August, but now she thought that she would ask for a week or two in the autumn, and go over to England, to see her family and Juliet. She felt that she needed an interval of peace away from this house, away even from Shand. She longed to know what Juliet was really feeling. Her father's remarriage might be a very good thing for her in the long run; it almost certainly could not seem so now. Juliet, shut up in quarantine, scratching or trying not to scratch her spots, must be feeling dispossessed.

Shand came in as she finished. He grinned at her in a shame-faced way, but looked on the whole relieved, as though he felt better for having released pent-up feeling.

"Haven't you had anything to eat, my dear?"

"I didn't want anything. Later on, when I'm hungry, I'll get Giorgio to let me have some bread and cheese."

He flung himself into the chair.

"I suppose I shouldn't have done it!"

"Well, he is a guest. How did it begin?"

"Oh, I don't know. He had been swaggering to Lucrezia about some big review of the Fascist militia he'd been to with Ciano, and then she was called away, and he went on telling me about it. I suppose he's just too stupid to know that I hate the lot of them, or else he doesn't care. He went on and on, and I guess I lost my temper. I just can't stomach his insolence, coming here when my father's away and behaving as if he has a right here."

"I know how you feel, but I think you'll have to try to keep out of his way."

"Not for long, I hope. At least I hope I'll be really out of his way soon. Fenny, I've made a plan. I'm going over to Livorno next week to have a look round and see what the chances are of getting on to an American cargo-boat and working a passage home."

Ellen smiled. It sounded a little too much like a story in a boy's magazine. But he was entirely serious.

"I can pass for an Italian, you know."

"You can speak like one, but you don't look like one."

"I could, I think. I'd wear my oldest clothes and hang about the dock, and bribe some agent to slip me in when they're taking on extra hands."

"But you'd have to have papers."

"Well, I've had a passport since I went to Switzerland in January."

"Yes, an American passport. You can't show that if you're

trying to go as an Italian seaman. And there are other things. You'd probably have to belong to a seaman's union."

"Well, anyhow I'm going over to Livorno next week to spy out possibilities and have a look around."

She said no more, for she suddenly perceived that he did not believe in the plan himself. It was a fantasy that he had made to comfort himself, as a man in prison might look at the window and think that some day he would saw through the bars. Boys had run away to sea, but Shand, in many ways the spoilt son of a rich man, had not even had to book his own railway ticket when he went to Rome. He had never been away to school, he was far less used to taking himself about than an English boy of the same age would have been. Let him go to Livorno and find out the difficulties for himself. Perhaps they could be surmounted, but she did not think that he would know how to surmount them, or that he more than half believed in his own scheme. When he found it impracticable, he would perhaps come back more prepared to settle down, and in a month at the sea, with the schoolroom party before Lucrezia joined them, he would be happier, and she might be able to persuade him to accept the next two years with some sort of philosophy. They had no chance to discuss his plan any further, for Giorgio came and asked them both to go and speak to the Signora in the *salone*.

"I suppose," Shand said, "You're going to catch it, too, because you didn't stop me. I shall tell her you weren't there until the end and had nothing to do with it."

With an air of one conducting his troops into battle he led the way downstairs. Ellen followed him, feeling as if they were both in disgrace and going before the headmistress. She could almost fancy that she, too, had tumbled Vascani into the zinnias.

It was an anticlimax to find Lucrezia sitting on the curved Empire sofa in the lamplight with coffee-cups and brandy-glasses on a little table before her. She welcomed them graciously.

"Ah, that is right; now let us all have a cup of coffee together."

She beckoned Ellen to the sofa beside her and pointed to a chair that had been pulled up opposite for Shand. He slumped into it, looking disconcerted and wary. Lucrezia gave them coffee. Ellen refused brandy, but Shand took the big glass and nursed it in his big, bony hands with so childish an air of being grown up that Ellen's heart was touched, and she thought that Lucrezia's might be. Lucrezia began to tell them a leisurely account of an encounter with some friends in Florence that morning. Ellen saw the tension increasing in Shand, and did not herself pay much attention to what Lucrezia was saying. The story came to an end. Lucrezia sipped her brandy and lit a cigarette.

"Well, I have asked you to come here, and I have asked Miss Fenwick to come, too, because she is such a good friend to you and I know wishes what is best for you. I am sure that she will always give you good advice. So now I must ask you why did you throw poor Paolo into a flower-bed? His feelings were much offended, and tomorrow it will be necessary for the gardeners to dig up all those zinnias and buy more in the market."

"I lost my temper."

"But, and I think that Miss Fenwick will agree with me, it is not good that you should lose your temper with my guests."

"I can't help it if you will have that kind of guest."

"It is not for you to decide who I shall ask to the house."

"When my father is away I have a right to represent him."

Shand gave Lucrezia a glance of meaning that ran off her like a rain-drop.

"I do not think you have ever seen your father throw people into flower-beds?"

Shand swallowed the rest of his brandy at a gulp and muttered, "More's the pity!"

Lucrezia did not choose to hear.

"No, your father is always most kind, most courteous, an excellent host. Now listen to me, Shand. I wish to say to you that a thing like this must not happen again. You are allowed very much freedom. You go to Florence, you come back from Florence as you like. I do not ask you what you do. I do not inquire of your tutor whether you go to him or not."

"Of course I go to the old fool!"

"Yes, well, when you wish to, you go off for the day to walk or to work on the farms with your *contadini* friends. It is not what I should choose, that you make friends only amongst the *ignoranti*, but again I do not interfere. I am only telling you that you think you are very unhappy in this house, very badly treated, but you are really very fortunate. A boy of your age at school in England or America would not have nearly so much freedom. Your aunts, whom you cannot really remember, would be much more strict with your behaviour than I have ever been. But"—her voice hardened—"I will not tolerate that you insult my friends. So I have been thinking that unless you can control yourself, we must make another arrangement. We must get a tutor for you who will live here, and will be a companion for you. And we shall make a separate schoolroom for you. It is not right that Miss Fenwick and your sisters should be disturbed by your tempers. Do you understand me?"

Shand leaned forward and spoke earnestly.

"Listen, Lucrezia! I know I've said it all before, but I guess I'll say it once more and try to make you understand. Maybe I shouldn't have started anything with Vascani, but I don't like him, and I don't like his politics, and he got me riled. If I have to stay on here I can't promise that something like that won't happen again. I don't like living here. I like the folk on the farms around, but I don't like this Government and the fancy-dress parades and the spying and the cruelty. I can't learn or grow right here. I almost feel I can't breathe. I'm an American. I want to go back to my own country. I hate being in a house where I'm not wanted. I don't blame you for not wanting me. I feel so driven and boxed in that I know I act like a clod, but I don't want to. I'm sick of it all. Let me go, Lucrezia! It's the last time I'm going to ask it."

"I am glad," Lucrezia said coldly, "that it is the last time you will ask it. I, too, am very tired of all this, although I have been very patient, as Miss Fenwick well knows."

Shand got out of his chair and moved impatiently to the long windows as though he needed to breathe. Ellen saw that he was making a great effort to control himself.

"For God's sake, Lucrezia! I don't want to be here! You don't want me! I'm sorry I started on Vascani, but if I stay on I might do worse than that. You'll all be much happier without me. Let me go!"

Lucrezia got up and with a light rustle of silk moved to join him at the window. She put out a hand towards him. To Ellen the hand looked like a claw.

"What makes you think that I do not want you here?"

Shand turned on her.

"I was wrong. You do want me, God knows why! You want to torment me! You don't want me to grow up in my own way! It pleases you to have me in your power, so that I can't get you out of my mind for a minute!" His voice was now running up and down the compass. "You keep me here because you hate me! And I hate you! I hate you!"

Laying her hand on his arm, Lucrezia said softly:

"No, you do not altogether hate me, Shand."

Ellen saw him stare at her as if he saw something that horrified him. He made the beginning of a movement towards her, then he brushed her hand off his arm as he might have brushed off a mosquito, put his hand over his eyes and stumbled out into the dark garden.

Lucrezia came back to the sofa. Ellen felt an anger that she could hardly control.

"These adolescent moods!" Lucrezia sighed.

"It is because the life that he is leading is not right for him."

The air between them was charged with hostility.

"That is for me to judge. You teach the little girls very well, Miss Fenwick; but if you continue to encourage Shand to rebel against me, I shall have to make some other arrangement."

Ellen longed to say, I should like to make it now, but in the last five minutes she had seen clearly something she must do before she went. She replied:

"That must be as you wish, Mrs. Warner!"

"Well, I do not wish it at all. But we cannot go on like this. You had better think over what I have said. Now I am very tired and I am going up to bed. Good-night!"

Ellen waited in the schoolroom for Shand, determined that he should hear what she had to say to him before he went to bed. She picked up a book, but was unable to keep her attention on it. The night was very hot. Mosquitoes and other insects, attracted by her light, buzzed continually against the netting of fine wire that protected her window, and irritated her taut nerves, so that she turned out the light and sat in the warm darkness, feeling the sweat springing in her armpits and under the roots of her hair. It was nearly one o'clock before she heard Shand go quietly along the passage to his room. She followed him and knocked. He did not answer at once, and she knocked again. His voice sounded half-extinguished with weariness as he called, "Come in."

She opened the door and saw him leaning against the end of the bed, his hair dark with sweat, his face showing nothing but exhaustion. His room was unlike any other room in the house. In his general rebellion against the world in which he was obliged to live, he had done all that he could to make it not look Italian. He had turned out half the painted Venetian furniture, and had discovered somewhere a big, plain, English cupboard that looked as though it might once have stood in a harness-room. He had pinned a large map of the United States above his bed. On the chest stood a photograph of his dead mother, photographs of his aunts in old-fashioned silver frames, and a snapshot of Ellen herself with Bianca, taken in the garden. A home-made shelf held battered boy's books, mostly English and American. Golf-clubs which had been bought to occupy him but which he never touched, a portable easel that he had used when sketching with Daniel occupied one corner of the room.

"Fenny," he said with apathy rather than surprise. He yawned and slumped against the bedpost. "I've been walking . . . somewhere. . . . It's pretty late, I suppose. I'm all in."

"You must get into bed. But I just wanted to tell you, before you go to sleep, that I am going to buy you a passage to America. I should have thought of it before. We'll go to Florence tomorrow and find out about boats, and you must just go without telling anybody and leave a letter for them. "

He looked too sleepy to absorb the suggestion. He said vaguely:

"But I couldn't take your money. And you'd get into fearful trouble."

"I want to leave, anyhow. And I have plenty of money to buy you a ticket."

"I don't know . . ."

"Yes, it's settled."

She had known that he might hesitate; she understood better since this evening the double pull of attraction and repulsion that held him. With all her will now she was going to make him go. He was too tired to decide anything this evening, but she would leave the idea with him.

"We'll settle all the details in the morning. But I wanted you

157

to know before you sleep that in a week or two you will be free. Good-night, my dear!"

She longed suddenly to take him in her arms and comfort him. She turned towards the door.

"Yes," he said, "we can talk about it tomorrow." Then, making an effort to rouse himself, "Thank you Fenny. Good-night!"


# CHAPTER IX

"There's the bell, Fenny. You'd better go ashore!"

"It's only the first bell."

"Well, you don't want to stay down here. Let's go up on deck."

Shand, Ellen thought, looked too long for the bunk. There seemed to be no room for his one small suit-case in a cabin strewn with the more plentiful belongings of his travelling companion. Generous but not reckless, Ellen had booked him a second-class passage, not realizing that it would be a new experience for Grant Warner's son. His hastily concealed surprise had disconcerted her, and although common sense told her that his quarters were perfectly all right for a healthy sixteen-year-old boy, she had a foolish wish that she had lavished the best on him. He stood there trying to look manly and adventurous. She knew that at this moment he felt forlorn and that the prospect of travelling with a stranger was making him feel more so. Yet this was one of the things that she had done it for: that he should be less sheltered, should have a chance to grow up and stand on his own in the outside world. She said again with the weak repetition of parting moments:

"I hope he'll be nice."

"It doesn't matter. Let's go up."

As they climbed the stairs he said:

"I've posted the letter to my father in the station. They won't get it till tomorrow morning, so you'll be back. I said I'd borrowed the money from a friend in Florence. I asked him to say good-bye to you for me. I don't see why they should guess."

Ellen could think of several reasons, and in any case meant to tell them, but she did not want him to know, and was glad that he was satisfied.

"I said 'a visit'. Then, if they did happen to fix it on you, there'd be less fuss. And maybe they'll leave me there for a bit and then settle down to the idea of it. And I'll send the money as soon as I arrived. My aunts will give it to me."

"There's no hurry about that, my dear. You must send it when it's convenient."

"You'll come over, Fenny? Next year, perhaps? My aunts will write to you. Maybe you could come next summer? If not, I'll come and see you when I'm through college. If there isn't a war in Europe by then. And if there is I might be coming anyhow. We'll be in it sooner or later, if there is one."

"I don't want you to have to come back that way!"

"I wouldn't mind cleaning up Italy. You'll write me about Roberto's brother, if he gets out of prison or if there's any news of him?"

"Yes, I will."

"And tell Blanche I'll fetch her over some day."

After three years together, Ellen thought, we have only three minutes. She would have liked in those minutes to say something that would express all her grief at parting, all the affection and kindness of the three years. She said:

"There's hardly any wind. You're going to have a calm start, anyhow."

"Oh, I shan't be sick! I never was when I was a kid."

"No, I'm sure you won't be!"

She wanted to tell him how eagerly she would always watch for his letters, how much it would mean to her to know that he was active and happy in the new world. If she could not, as somehow she could not, say any of these things, she wanted to leave him. The precious moments should be used to the full or cut short, but they trickled away at their own halting pace.

"It will be cooler when you get out to sea."

"Yes."

"I wish you'd been able to bring more of your things."

"It doesn't matter. I've got enough for the journey. There's the second bell!"

"Yes, I must go, or I shall be sailing with you!"

159

"I wish you were!"

"Good-bye, my dear! The best of luck!"

He threw his arms round her and kissed her.

"Good-bye, Fenny! Thank you for everything, more than I know how to thank you. We'll meet again soon!"

She stood on the quay while the gangway was raised and the churning water widened between the ship's side and the stone. Leaning on the rail, looking unnaturally tidy and grown up in his grey flannel suit, Shand waved to her, and she waved back until his face was only a knob on the rail in a line with other knobs. Still she stood waving as long as there was any chance that he could see her yellow scarf floating out on the breeze. Then she burst into tears.

She knew that in more ways than one she had said good-bye to him. They would write, they would probably meet again, but he was going to a life in which she would soon be "old Fenny", remembered with a gratitude and affection that would gradually become an obligation. This was how it should be, but for the last three years he had needed her every day. She could even feel jealous of the aunts whose place she had filled. But she was sure that what she had done was the best thing for him, and this sustained her as she made her way alone through the busy station and found a seat on the train.

She dozed in the train, relaxed by the sense of something accomplished, but never quite losing her consciousness of loss. She got back to Florence early in the evening. She had asked for the whole day off, and did not want to go back to Bronciliano in time to see Lucrezia that night. No one yet would be concerned about Shand; he had often spent a day working on one of the hill farms and slept there, but Ellen did not want to make her confession until the morning, and did not feel able to behave as though nothing had happened.

With a sudden irrational lift of her spirits, she decided to stand herself a good dinner. She had some money left after buying the dollars with which she had supplied Shand. This was not the moment to save it; tomorrow she would be sacked—she had no doubt about that—and would have to throw herself upon the world with her depleted savings. Perhaps it was the stimulus of approaching change that made her feel that this was not the moment to save; it was the moment for extravagance. Moderate extravagance. She did not intend to go to one of the expensive restaurants where the Warners had sometimes taken her. She thought that she would go to the little restaurant on the Lung'arno where she had always dined with Daniel but had never been since. First she would sit down in one of the cafés in the Piazza della Repubblica and have a long, cool drink.

The café was very full and very noisy, but this suited Ellen's mood. She had a feeling that after being submerged in Bronciliano for three years she was coming up to breathe. Her interest, which had been canalized by Shand's crisis, was free to extend to the rest of the world. She noticed at once a couple who sat at a table close to her own. The girl was very young and very beautiful, with the face of a Botticelli Madonna, set on a long, slender neck. Her fair hair was brushed back from her face and clustered in curls behind her neck. She looked as though she had come fresh from school—a convent school, Ellen thought—but there was nothing schoolgirlish in the finished grace of her movements, or in the way that she wore her expensively simple linen dress. The man with her, who had a thin, dark, clever face, might have been fifteen years older than she was. They were so unmistakably in love and so happy that Ellen watched them with amused sympathy.

They were arguing about whether they should or should not go to a film. The girl was making a parade of wanting her own way, which she was obviously ready to abandon.

The man protested, "No, no, Graziella; we shall die of heat in there!" but was clearly glad to do whatever she wanted.

Still playing at wilfulness she said:

"Well, at least I shall look to see what time it starts."

She got up quickly; her skirt caught Ellen's glass, which the waiter had just put down, and sent it into her lap.

At once all her light and laughter were extinguished, and she looked disproportionately upset, like a child about to cry. She flushed all over her neck and face, made desperate apologies and tried to wipe Ellen's dress with a small handkerchief. Ellen assured her that it did not matter in the least; the dress would wash, was dirty anyhow, for she had just come from a journey. The husband brought his larger handkerchief to help. He was divided between apologizing to Ellen and reassuring his wife.

"It was entirely my fault, Signorina: I pushed my chair back at the wrong moment. It was very stupid of me. Look, Graziella, it will not leave a mark."

Suddenly he said to Ellen in her own tongue:

"You are English, Signorina?"

"Yes."

"I know England well. I was at the University of Oxford for two years after I had finished my course here. My wife is very much distressed at the accident, but I do not think your dress is spoilt, really. I hope at least you will let me order you another drink. Let me turn your chair to our table." To Graziella, now beginning to recover her spirits and smiling timidly at Ellen, he said with enormous indulgence, "This comes of your mad passion to go to the cinema at all hours."

What Graziella saw in Ellen's face seemed to reassure her. She passed in a minute from apologies and shyness to happy confidence. Before their fresh drinks arrived, she told Ellen that they had been married three months, that her home was at Padua, that she had one sister and two younger brothers; that Arturo was a very learned professor at the University, and was it not surprising that he should have married anyone like herself, who could not even remember what was in a book after she had finished reading it?

"No, I don't think so," Ellen said sincerely.

Graziella's fluctuating colour ran up her long neck again, and Arturo gave Ellen a warm smile of gratification. She felt for a minute that she and he, two older people, were close together in their admiration for the charming child.

Perhaps Arturo thought that Graziella had chattered enough about their affairs, for when the drinks came he said to Ellen:

"You are here on holiday, Signorina? You speak Italian so well that you must have been here often before?"

"I live here. I have a post as a governess. At least"—she was swept into a rare communicativeness—"I have had up till now, but tomorrow I shall be sacked."

"Why, what have you done?" he asked, laughing.

When he laughed, his thin face crinkled up, his eyes, which

162

were grey, almost disappeared between his high cheek-bones and his thin, straight brows. Graziella looked at her with friendly concern.

She told them what she had done. It was a comfort to her to tell it, for while in her heart she felt that she had been right, her professional governess's conscience accused her of doing wrong. She was soothed by Graziella's uncritical sympathy.

"But, of course. The poor boy! What else could you do? How glad I am that he has escaped! How grateful he must be to you!"

Arturo said more thoughtfully:

"It must have been very difficult for you to decide, Signorina Fenwick. It is always difficult when there is a clash of two loyalties. But it seems to me that people more often go wrong by not having the courage to keep to the deeper loyalty and following the surface one instead. That you have not done. But of course," he added briskly, "that does not help you with your employers. Naturally they will send you away. Since you only stayed for the boy's sake, I suppose that you will be ready to go? But, excuse me, what are you going to do?"

She told him that she planned to work up a teaching connection, and as soon as she could afford it to get a flat.

"It is difficult now for an Englishwoman to get teaching in Italy. You would not be employed in the schools at all, the Government would not allow it. But you might get some private pupils. I shall be glad if I can be of any help! Let me give you my card."

She looked at it and read, "Professore Arturo Marelli" and an address in the Costa San Giorgio.

"And of course," Graziella said, "if they turn you out and you have nowhere to go, you must come and stay with us! Our flat is very pretty; it is at the top, and there is a garden on the roof with lemon trees. It is just outside the window of the guest's room where you would sleep. It is pleasant to look out on something green."

Ellen thanked them warmly for their kindness. It was a passing encounter, she would never dream of accepting the hospitality that Graziella offered so freely, but their sympathy and evident liking were an immense encouragement to her at this moment of new departure.

"And now"—Arturo stood up—"Since you are so determined, Graziella, we will go to the film."

They asked Ellen to come with them, but she wanted her dinner, and thought, too, that they did not really need any addition to their company. As they walked away across the square, Graziella turned back to wave to her. Then they both disappeared in the crowd milling on the pavement.

Ellen made her way to the restaurant. She expected to see the old waiter who always used to serve them, but it was a brisk young man, a stranger, who came forward to her. He was going to escort her to a table near the wall, but she said, "No, thank you, I prefer to be in the window," and went to the table where she and Daniel had always sat.

The legend of those evenings seemed to be written in the half-illegible, purple scrawls on the menu. For a minute the feeling was so intense that she half believed that she could look up and see the harsh outlines of Daniel's face, softening into a smile for her. There was only the waiter, helpfully trying to recommend dishes to ears that for a minute had not heard him. Ellen chose her dinner and ordered a bottle of Orvieto.

What a long time it seemed since the morning! Did it seem as long to Shand, now probably sitting next to some stranger in one of the ship's dining-rooms? Was he daunted, perhaps a little homesick for her, even, perhaps, for the disliked but familiar home? Or was he feeling, as she did, a certain exhilaration. The chance encounter with the Marelli had been an omen, reminding her that there was a whole world outside Bronciliano in which she might find friends. There was even a slight relief in being free of her concentration on Shand. She was thirty-one, and probably had more than half her life before her. She could not spend the whole of it on younger lives. Perhaps it was because she wanted to pick up again the current in which things had happened to her that she had drifted back to this table where she had sat with Daniel, for she knew that Daniel was the only thing that ever had happened to her at a certain level of her being. She longed for him to be here at the table with her, yet knew that one does not go back. Her sorrow for his loss was mellowed by time, by fatigue and soon by Orvieto. Her second glass comfortably dulling her anxieties gave her the courage to think of facing Lucrezia without a qualm.

I've beaten her, she thought, I've beaten her! It was a victory that seemed in some way to be long overdue. It added to her unexpected exhilaration as she sat on in the window drinking her coffee, and looking from the bright lights of the restaurant at the figures passing outside the glass in the darkening street.

## CHAPTER X

She woke next morning to the full realization that Shand had gone. She felt hollow, tired and rather sick—far less ready for a scene with Lucrezia than yesterday evening she had supposed herself to be. It was better to get it over. She sent a message to ask if she might see her as soon as it was convenient. Her heart jumped as she put out the books for the day's lessons and settled Donata and Bianca at the schoolroom table. Donata gave her a sharp glance.

"Do you know where Shand is, Miss Fenwick? Last night he did not come home."

"Never mind that now. Let me hear you say what I gave you to learn yesterday."

Donata liked reciting poetry. She stood up, smoothed her frock over her flat stomach, and began:

"The quality of mercy is not strained."

The door flew open. Lucrezia in her dressing-gown, her hair in a net, her face, not yet made up, yellow in the morning light, stood in the doorway with a letter in her hand.

"Children, go out into the garden!"

They looked at her, Bianca like one not believing her luck, Donata with lively interest.

"Quickly! Go!"

At her tone they scampered to get out of the door, jostling one another. Through the slap of their sandalled feet Ellen heard a man's footsteps in the passage, and saw Grant in the doorway.

"This is *your* doing!"

Lucrezia leaned across the table and struck Ellen with the letter in her face.

"Don't!"

Trembling with fear and anger, Ellen stood up, and with an instinctive movement put the chair between them. Grant came up behind Lucrezia and caught hold of her arm.

"Sit down, Lucrezia." He pushed her into a chair, where she sat panting, her hand on the thin breasts rising and falling under the lace of her nightgown. Grant said to Ellen half apologetically:

"Mrs. Warner has been very, very upset by this letter we have had from Shand."

"You need not tell Miss Fenwick. She knows. For what did she ask for a holiday yesterday . . . to see him off! Where did he get the money? He says from a friend in Florence. He has no friends in Florence who could lend him so much. His friends have always been the peasants, the *ignoranti*! Only they, and this woman who would do anything for him, who has most likely been more than a friend! How do we know what has been going on in this part of the house, where the children have been left to their so trusted governess?"

"How dare you suggest such a thing! I am twice as old as Shand. My relationship with him has always been entirely appropriate."

"Yes! It has indeed been appropriate. You have encouraged him, always, against his parents, who are your employers. You have taught him to deceive us; you have given him the money with which to disobey us. You . . ."

"Lucrezia!" Grant's hands pressed heavily on her shoulders, holding her down in the chair. "Please wait a minute. We don't know yet what has happened. Miss Fenwick, did you know that Shand had gotten this fixed?"

"Yes."

"Did you lend him the money for his passage?"

"Yes." She added, "I had no intention of deceiving you about it. I had already sent a message to Mrs. Warner asking if she would see me as soon as possible. I was going to tell you what I had done."

"No doubt! No doubt because, now that it is too late to prevent it, you wished to flaunt your triumph in my face! You

166

wished to tell me that you had got him away from me! Because you knew that I must find out anyhow, and so you would have the pleasure of telling me!"

"I did not expect it to be a pleasure."

"Now, to add to everything else, you are insolent!"

"Lucrezia!" Grant still kept his hands on her shoulders. "Miss Fenwick, you must see that Mrs. Warner has every right to be angry. What you have done is very serious. We have always treated you with great confidence. Mrs. Warner has often gone away and left the children entirely in your care. Many a time she has said to me what a great thing it was to be able to leave them with somebody we could trust. This has been a big shock for her."

"I know it has. I know quite well that what I have done in my position seems quite unjustified."

"Seems!" Lucrezia shrieked.

"Perhaps it is. I know that you have always trusted me with the children and that I have betrayed your trust. And of course I must leave. . . ."

"You will not 'leave'. You are dismissed! Without a reference! You will go today . . . this morning!"

"Certainly. But listen to me, please." For a moment Ellen dominated them, and they were silent. "I haven't ever been sure myself that what I did was justifiable, but I did it to save Shand, because I saw that the life here was destroying him; it was not the life any boy of his age should have, and I thought it might ruin him if he stayed here another two years. I knew that it was against my duty as your employee, but I thought I had another duty to Shand that ought to come first."

"As a lover, perhaps!"

"You know that's a lie! Don't say it again! No, it was the duty of one human being to another, particularly of a woman to a child."

"And so you, who have no children of your own . . ."

"Lucrezia," Grant interrupted, "there's no use in going on with this. We have to think what to do about Shand. We must write to my sisters, and maybe I'll have to go over in the fall and fetch him back. But we came here to find out whether Miss Fenwick knew about this and had helped him. She says she did. I guess we all feel that the sooner there's an end to this conversation the better. We must ask Miss Fenwick to leave us. I don't think she can have expected anything else."

"It is no matter what she expected. She goes this morning."

"Maybe this evening would be . . ."

"No, this morning. Without seeing the children. I will not allow that they speak to her again. I shall tell Maria to keep them in the garden until she has gone. Miss Fenwick, you will be out of the house by lunch-time."

"Certainly, Mrs. Warner. I shall be glad to leave as soon as possible."

"And I must tell you that you will not again be able to find pupils among my acquaintance. You had better go now to your room and pack your clothes. Anything else will be sent after you. I will not have you coming back to the house. I do not wish to see you again."

She got up to go, putting her hand to her head.

"I am become quite ill with all this!"

"Go right along to your room, Lucrezia, and lie down. I will come. I will just write a cheque for Miss Fenwick's salary to date."

"Which she has indeed richly earned."

Lucrezia rustled out of the room.

Sick with agitation, Ellen moved to the window and leaned against it, shutting her eyes for a minute against the bright blue of the sky. Behind her Grant took out his pen and cheque-book and sat down at the schoolroom table.

"Miss Fenwick."

"Yes?"

"How much is my son's debt to you?"

"No!"

"You must tell me, please, how much you paid for his passage, and for anything else you gave him."

"I would rather not."

"Then I shall make a rough estimate."

"If you do I shall tear up the cheque. I won't take money for working against you."

Grant made the resigned but impatient movement of a man beset by hysterical women.

"I hope you will not be so foolish!"

"I mean it."

He looked at her doubtfully, shrugged his heavy shoulders and wrote.

"Very well. Here is your salary. Please order the car to take you where you wish to go."

She took the cheque out of his hand.

"Yes," she said listlessly. "Thank you."

She waited for him to go, but he stood by the table. She felt irritated—she wanted to be alone. She glanced at him and saw without much interest that he had something else that he was trying to say to her.

"Mrs. Warner," he said, "is very, very nervous and highly strung. She has always made Shand a child of her own. Naturally this has been a great shock to her."

He seemed to be waiting for her to say something, so she said indifferently, "Yes," and looked at the door.

"Both she and I regret this. And we are very grateful for the progress the girls have made in these three years."

Ellen was silent. "Oh, do go *away*," a voice screamed within her.

Grant held out his hand.

"I'll say good-bye."

"Good-bye, Mr. Warner!"

He turned towards the door and then stopped. She saw him wipe his forehead. He said:

"I know the boy wasn't happy here."

The door closed behind him.

Ellen went to her bathroom and was sick. In her bedroom, shuttered against the day's heat, she switched on the lights, and slowly, with tired, dragging movements, packed her clothes and small belongings in her two suit-cases, which had appeared in her room, presumably by Lucrezia's orders. She scribbled a note to say that she would send for her books and left it on her desk. Maria, who had heard the news and was fond of her, came in crying.

Ellen gave her some money, kissed her and sent her out to the children in the garden, asking her as she went to order the car at twelve to take her to the *pension*.

# PART III

1938–1939

# CHAPTER I

A̲T̲ ̲H̲E̲R̲ desk in the offices of the Universal Travel Company in the Via Tornobuoni, Ellen picked up the telephone. The client in front of her, a middle-aged American woman, smartly armoured in expensive clothes and make-up, looked annoyed, obviously feeling that whoever was attending to her ought not also to have to answer the telephone. With an apologetic smile and gesture to her, Ellen spoke into the receiver. "Yes, Mrs. Crookshank? Yes, it will be all right about the sleeper for the 18th, but I'm afraid I cannot give you the ticket until they send it down from Rome. Oh, yes, it is certain to come in time. There are still ten days. I shall be going on holiday myself next week, but it should come before then, and if not, will you please ask for Mr. Muswell! I will leave all instructions. Yes, it starts at eleven-forty. Yes, certainly. Good-bye."

"Some folks," the American woman remarked acidly, "seem to think you've got nothing to do but run after them."

She proceeded to go through her folder of tickets with Ellen, asking every conceivable question, and interleaving her inquiries with explanations about her visit to England and with reminiscences of other journeys, blissfully indifferent to the fact that another client was shifting impatiently behind her.

Ellen looked past her to say, "I won't be long," looked again, and realized that she knew him. When, where had she seen before that thin, clever face with the high forehead and the high cheek-bones?

He smiled at her from behind the American woman's back with a slight shrug of amused resignation, and she remembered the meeting in the Square on the evening of Shand's departure a year ago, Professore . . . ? Yes, Professor Marelli, and his lovely young wife, who had been so kind to her.

". . . A disgrace, considering what we have to pay for a first-class ticket, that you can't get a cup of early morning tea on these trains!" The metallic voice clattered on.

"Perhaps you could take some tea in a thermos?"

"I can do that, of course, but it's the inefficiency . . ."

She went off at last with her folder of tickets. Marelli took her place.

"*Buono giorno*, Signorina Fenwick! Do you remember that we have met before?"

"Of course I do, Professore; I was just remembering."

"While the Signora Americana was complaining because the world was not arranged for her! You must require great patience! But I am so glad to see you again. I hope that all has gone well?"

"Yes, very well indeed, thank you. I have so often thought of that evening. I hope that the Signora Marelli is well?"

"I cannot give you good news of her. She is in a sanatorium in Switzerland. She developed tuberculosis after our baby was born dead in the spring."

"Oh, I am so sorry! Oh, how dreadful!"

"Yes, it is a tragedy!"

She noticed now why she had been slow in recognizing him. His face was thinner, older, and without the patina of gaiety that had been a reflection of Graziella's, had returned to an austerity that seemed more natural to its bones.

"I *am* sorry. Next time you write, do please remember me to her, and tell her I do hope she will soon be better."

"She so often spoke of you, and wondered what happened when you went back to the villa. She will be delighted to hear news of you. But I do not wish to imitate the lady who has just gone. . . . I came to ask for a ticket to Davos. At what hour do you lunch, Signorina?"

"Today at half-past one."

"Would you do me the pleasure of lunching with me? Then I can hear all your news, and I shall be able to send it to Graziella. I will wait for you at our old meeting-place in the Piazza della Repubblica."

She found him his train, and transferred her attention to two people who had come in after him. Over their shoulders she saw his thin figure disappearing briskly out of the doorway.

When Frank Muswell came back from his lunch to relieve her, she combed her hair and powdered her face in the slip of cloak-room at the back of the office.

She was filled with sympathy for the Marelli, for the tragic interruption to the happiness that had warmed her heart on that summer evening a year ago. She was also very glad that she was wearing her new dress—the only new dress that she had ventured

174

to buy this year. Liberated from the dependant's life, she had felt that she need not keep to her sober governess clothes, and the dress was of honey-coloured linen that threw up the lights in her brown hair. Carefully reddening her lips, she saw in the square of mirror a very different woman from the Signorina Fenwick of Bronciliano. She put on her broad-brimmed hat and went round to the Square.

. . . . .

"I can see," Marelli said, "that what you have to tell me is good. You have, if it is not impertinent to say so, a different face."

Ellen threw her hat on to a chair beside her, and pushed up the damp hair from her forehead. This year she had recovered her old pleasure in the hot weather. Her body, which had been languid and inert during the summer months at Bronciliano, glowed with energy in the stifling streets and squares of Florence.

"Yes, I have been very lucky; I got this job almost at once by sheer chance. There's a young man, Frank Muswell, who works at the Universal; he and his wife were staying at the *pension* I went to when I left Bronciliano, and they come from my own part of England. I made friends with them. He told me that there was a job going, and I went straight round and got it."

"You like it?"

"Very much indeed. It's such a complete change. It's amusing to see the variety of clients who come in, and I like the feeling of being a spider in a network of threads stretching out to places all over the world. I have nice people to work with, and I like being quite free after the office closes. I moved into a little flat of my own in the spring, on the Lung'arno, and I have one or two private pupils who learn English. They can come there in the evenings. I was very busy when I was moving in and working at the same time, but I've enjoyed it all! It's been a new life."

"That I can see, and I am very glad. We were afraid, Graziella and I, that just at first after you left your employer you might have a hard time. Was she very angry?"

"Furious! It seems funny now, but at the time it didn't."

"That I can understand."

"I did feel partly guilty. After all, it is impermissible for a governess to smuggle a pupil out of the country."

"That was what Graziella and I so much admired! That

evening after the film, when we went home to our supper, she was preparing food in the kitchen, and she began suddenly to laugh and said, 'I am thinking so much of what they will say when they find that the good English *signorina* has kidnapped the boy.' We wondered often if he got safely to America and was allowed to remain there?"

"Yes. He's there, and very happy! I believe they cabled and wrote angry letters and ordered him back, and threatened to go and fetch him, but they never went. He's doing well at school, and going to Harvard next year. From his letters, and from what his aunts write to me about him, he seems to be a different boy! He only needed to get away from his step-mother. There was something about her and about that house! I didn't fully realize it at the time, but it stultified you; it was like being shut up in a conservatory. I feel as if I'd escaped, too, into the fresh air!"

"That was the first thing I thought when I saw you again— that your life had expanded and become altogether different. I am very glad for you!"

"You and your wife were so kind to me that evening. I was feeling very lonely, having just said good-bye to Shand, and having no other friends here. I was very much touched by your wife's offer of hospitality to a stranger. Meeting you was like an omen. I wanted to break away from the Warner household, but I was cowardly about it, too. If it hadn't been that I had to get Shand out, I dare say I should be there now. Your kindness made me feel that I had been missing such a lot, shut up there, and that I should find friends in the outside world."

He said to her very kindly:

"But of course you will always find friends; you are sympathetic, talented, brave. Yes, Graziella has a gentle heart. She was sincere in her invitation. If you had come she would have been so glad to see you. She is one who makes up her mind about people at once, and she will do anything for her friends."

"I am so very sorry about her illness. Did it come on suddenly?"

"She was never well while the baby was coming, but we thought that after the birth she would be stronger. She longed so much for the child. It was a terrible blow to her to lose it. She did not gain strength, and always she was feverish at night, and she lost weight. They took an X-ray, and found that the consumption had developed very rapidly since the birth; both lungs were affected, one seriously. It was necessary to get her into a sanatorium as soon as possible. That was very hard, for she had never been away from me since we were married. She loved her home, and she was shy with strangers. I took her there, and she wept so bitterly at being left in that cold, impersonal place." Ellen saw tears in his own eyes. "I have been up there twice to see her, but I have my work; we are not rich—neither I nor her parents. She writes that she is becoming used to it, and they write me that she is cheerful and that she is less disturbed when I do not go; but I think that she counts the minutes till my next visit."

"I am sure she does. But they are hopeful about her?"

"They are professionally hopeful in these places. But they assure me that so far they have decided not to collapse the lung, and that there is every reason to believe that she will be cured in two years."

"It must make a great difference that she is so young and that she looks forward so much to coming back to you. She has everything to get better for. In the meantime it must be very lonely for you!"

"I have been living this term with friends, and going back to my own flat only to work, but it is too difficult, I do not like to be a guest always, and I am accustomed when I do not sleep to work in the night. I must have my books at hand. Next term I go back to my own home."

"And now that it is the end of term you will be able to go and be with Graziella?"

"I go next week to see her, but I cannot stay. I have other work here that goes on all the time. Let us go now and have lunch."

He took her to a small restaurant that she did not know. "It is not expensive here, but the cooking is good."

It seemed to be a meeting-place of his friends—scholars she thought, and probably, like himself, working at the University. Several of them spoke or waved to him as he led her across the room to a table.

When they had ordered their lunch she said:

"Next week I am going on my holiday to England."

"For how long do you stay?"

"Three weeks. I have a brother in Liverpool, I am going to him for a week, then to friends in Yorkshire, and I shall finish up with a few nights in London. I come back in the third week of August."

"If there is no war."

"You think that it might be as soon as that?"

"I personally think that Hitler will march against Czechoslovakia early this autumn; and that England, France and Russia cannot allow."

"I can't believe that he means to take them all on! I think he will go as far as he can without fighting. I have never believed that he wanted war against us—against the British Empire."

"No, I find that is a usual belief among your countrymen. I think that perhaps you have not seen so many exiles from Germany as I have."

"I've been so busy with my work and getting settled in my flat that although of course it's always been there in the background, I haven't perhaps kept my mind on it enough. I know we're living on the edge of it—war might break out at any time—but I feel that one can only go on with one's own life as though it wasn't going to happen."

"It is true now that we live on two levels. On the one we plan for life as we have known it; on the other we expect such a life as we have never known. Perhaps you are right that we must go on as though the worst would not happen. But you, who have made your life outside your own country, are in a peculiar position. You would not wish, if war broke out, to be cut off from your own people in a country friendly to their enemy, probably fighting with them as allies?"

"You think if there was a war Italy would come in?"

"I am afraid that Germany would drag us in with her. It is not for me to advise you. But if I were in your position I should, while in England next month, make arrangements to remain there, or to return before long, while it is still possible for you."

Ellen was silent, wanting to disbelieve him. She felt a furious resentment against the course of history for threatening to interfere with a private life which seemed to be expanding on all sides, and she was ashamed of the feeling.

He turned away from the subject and began to talk about some new books that had been sent to him from England.

"I like your English poets so much. I have always read them a great deal. I was even tempted sometimes to read them too much when I was at Oxford studying philosophy for two years."

They talked about their favourite books, and she thought how easy he was to talk to. His mind reached far beyond hers, but learning had not destroyed his simplicity. He had none of the arrogance of a fixed attitude, and seemed to listen to Ellen with as much pleasure as he talked himself. Their conversation was like a winding road through varied country, and as they sauntered along it kept on turning a corner and presenting a fresh view to their eyes. Ellen was glad when he ordered more coffee, sorry when at last he beckoned to the waiter for the bill. As he paid it, she asked him for Graziella's address.

"I expect any letter makes a break in the day, when she is in bed? I should like to write to her, and perhaps some English books or magazines would amuse her? She reads English?"

"Yes, she reads English. But, please, if you are going to be so kind, send her some fashion magazines! Those she would pore over by the hour. It was not just frivolity: it is her craft. She makes her own clothes. It is a most serious business! She would look at many pictures and look at them again before she made one dress. She is a beautiful needlewoman. She made all the clothes for the baby. Now I think she can sew only a little; she is in bed and will not want clothes for a while; but she will like to plan them for when she gets up again, and to have some different fashion papers from England would, I am sure, be a great pleasure."

"Of course. I'll send her the best I can find."

He wrote Graziella's address on the back of the menu, in a fine, scholar's hand.

"And I hope you will have a very good holiday! When you return—if you do return—I shall look forward to the pleasure of seeing you again."

On her way back to her flat she stopped to lean on the wall to look over at the thin stream of water in the shingly bed of the

Arno. The city behind her was drowsing in the siesta. Only a few indefatigable young tourists wandered the streets, dismayed to find the Galleries closed and the shops shuttered. Only a few urchins played languidly in the river-bed among the hot stones. Against the unbroken blue of the sky the houses on the opposite bank were cut out in irregular shapes of amber and tawny gold.

"I only half want to leave it," Ellen thought, "even for three weeks I only half want to go home."

## CHAPTER II

It was not until some time afterwards, when she looked back and saw the track her life had followed, that Ellen realized that she returned to Italy in that August of 1938 to see Arturo Marelli again. She seemed to herself to spend her holiday making up her mind whether to stay in England or not. Her brother in Liverpool, swallowing a hasty supper between his day's work and his A.R.P. Instructor's training, warned her emphatically of the danger of getting stranded in a foreign country at the outbreak of war.

"You've evidently no idea what it would be like getting back! You might never get a place on a train or a boat at the last moment! And the Channel would be full of submarines, and our ports and railways probably bombed. You might never be able to start at all; nobody knows what Italy will do. You might be interned, or stuck over there without any money, for years! You're mad to think of going back, with things looking as they do!"

He glanced at the clock, swallowed the rest of his beer, threw down his napkin and hastily brushed his wife's cheek with his moustache.

"Don't wait up for me, Mavis. I have to see Harding after the lecture about the supplies for the First Aid centres."

After the scramble to get his food quickly and the whirl of his departure, his wife and sister came up slowly, like trodden grass.

"Do have a little more custard, Ellen? Or a biscuit? I'm just

180

going to see if the children have started their home-work, and I'll make us a cup of coffee. Poor Hugh! He seems to have been out nearly every night about one thing and another now, with this Anti-gas and everything. It's a lot at the end of his day's work; but what can you do?"

Left alone, Ellen found herself thinking resentfully that Hugh enjoyed it. She took another biscuit, not because she wanted it, but in the futile hope that it might taste more interesting than the rest of the meal. She felt a petulant distaste for the stodgy house and the stodgy food, and for the complete lack of interest which her brother and his family had shown in everything that had happened to her in the last five years.

Mavis came back, carrying two cups of coffee.

"I'm sorry I've been so long. I've just been talking to Brenda; she says she wants to leave at the end of the month and go into munitions with her sister. You can't blame her; they get far more money. I expect it will be difficult to get another maid. Well, I can manage all right, with Hugh and the two children out all day. If it comes, we shall all have to put up with things." She added, "I'm sure Hugh's right, you know, Ellen. It isn't safe for you to go out of the country till we see what happens. I still hope there won't be a war, and if there isn't, you can go back later. You'd be sure to get a good job in Liverpool, and you could always live here for a time. One extra won't make any difference to the work, and you and I would be company for each other in the evenings, when Hugh has to go out. If war really comes, we shall just have to do the best we can, and we'd better all keep together. You want to be with your own people in war-time."

Her sturdy acceptance of possibilities and her kindness made Ellen ashamed.

"I expect it would be sensible to stay in England, and you're very kind, Mavis; if I do I should like to be in Liverpool and be near you all. It's difficult to decide. I've got my flat out there, you see, with all my things in it, and I've got my job. I don't want to lose that if Hitler's only trying how far he can go."

"All that wouldn't matter much compared to a war. But you must talk to Hugh about it at the week-end, when he's got more time. He's worried at the idea of you going out of the country again just now. I know that."

181

She was, or thought she was, still undecided when she left their house, without regret, for Hugh was too busy and pre-occupied to give her problems more than perfunctory attention. Mavis, though kind, had never looked outside her own world, and perhaps because she hardly saw them without their parents, she never succeeded in breaking down the barrier of shyness or indifference that divided Sheila and Roger from Aunt Ellen-from-Italy. She had felt in Liverpool that it might be her duty, as well as prudent, to come back. In Ainley she felt that she wanted to. Her own hills and valleys, the windy skies, the grey stone houses, the broad voices of her own people, tugged at her heart. She wanted to be here with old friends in a time of stress and danger. Alice, to whom she had written regularly during the last five years, and who had shared and sympathized with her joys and sorrows, was nearer to her than her family, and was able to visualize, at least to some extent, the world that Ellen might have to leave. She, too, both for Ellen's sake and for her own, very much wanted her to stay in England.

She said at once that she was not coming back with Ellen to Florence for the rest of the holidays, as they had planned.

"I couldn't think of it, Ellen! If there's any likelihood of war this autumn, I couldn't leave Father, and I've signed on as an ambulance driver. Besides, I don't want to go and stay in a Fascist country."

"In a way Fascism doesn't seem to interfere much with their daily life."

"Well, that must be because there's something wrong with their daily life! Besides, that's nonsense! It does interfere with some people's. I know what's going on; I've read about it. Anybody over there that's worth while is bound to come up against it. I'm sure I couldn't get on with the ones that don't, and that would make it awkward for you." She added sadly: "You've changed a lot, Ellen. You look very well and very nice in a sort of almost foreign way: I can see that you've branched out a lot and met different kinds of people. You seem more worldly, somehow. I expect you've found a kind of life that suits you. But you don't seem to have the same ideas any more. You don't seem quite to be part of anything here or there; you just seem to drift along having a private life."

"I think that's all I want to do."

"Yes, but you can't now. There aren't going to be any more only private lives."

Ellen looked at Alice, who from a rosy, healthy-looking woman in the twenties had become a rosy, healthy-looking youngish woman in the thirties, slightly thicker of body and skin, a little less flexible of thought and speech, still teaching at the Ainley High School, still coming home at night to her father, who from being elderly had become old. Ellen thought, perhaps you will be glad really if people can't any longer have only private lives. Like a good many of her recent thoughts, this made her ashamed. That evening when she and Alice walked over the moors and watched the sun go down behind the interlocking hills they broke through the crust of strangeness and renewed their old steady intimacy. In the ten days that followed, as Ellen read the English papers and went about the valley, seeing old friends and re-entering her early life, she thought that she was making up her mind not to go back to Florence, or only to go back to fetch her things and wind up her commitments. She more than half believed this as she leaned out of the window of her carriage in the London train and said good-bye to Alice.

"I expect I shall be back again in a few weeks."

"No, love," Alice said sadly; "you won't, unless you're driven to it. Take care of yourself!"

At that moment Ellen felt her friend much more mature and based on reality than she was herself, although there had been many times in the last ten days when Alice had seemed to her young for her age, inexperienced and sheltered. As she settled in her corner and watched the mixed West Riding landscape of town and country fly past, she perceived how tentative, fragmentary and diverse is that inch of the universe which each person warms for himself and calls experience.

In London for a day or two away from family and friends she felt both lonely and released. She enjoyed one or two theatres, visited some cousins, strolled in the parks and looked in the shops. She posted off a parcel of magazines and a pretty bed-jacket to Graziella Marelli, and found that she had every intention of going back to Italy. The news grew more threatening, and there were moments when she told herself that she was crazy, or when she felt that she ought not to be deserting her own country. In these moods she told herself that she was only going back to wind up her life there. As she trailed rather wearily about the London streets, oppressed by the sense of impending disaster, her anticipation became more and more concentrated on the afternoon that Juliet was to spend with her—her last afternoon in England.

She had saved money for this outing all through her holiday, and planned the day most carefully to be a series of treats for the child. They were to lunch at the gayest restaurant that Ellen knew, see *The Tempest* at the Open Air Theatre in Regent's Park, and come back to tea at Rumplemeyers. Everything was to be done to make it a memorable afternoon, to show that Ellen had not forgotten, and would never forget, the little girl who had clung to her when her mother abandoned her, and for whom Ellen still felt a protective compassion. Perhaps she had forgotten that the young have all the charms of a daily expanding universe to balance their tragedies. Perhaps she had indulged too much a fantasy of herself coming to the rescue of a forlorn child, but she experienced a sense of shock when she was shown into a pretty drawing-room, where a handsome woman of about her own age and a long-legged school-girl in a grey flannel suit and a black velvet beret rose to meet her from the sofa where they had been sitting side by side, looking through a book of patterns. One thing that had never really entered into Ellen's anticipations was that she might find Juliet and her step-mother on the best of terms.

She was so confused by the difference from an imaginary picture of which she had not been wholly conscious that she found nothing to say to Juliet, who smiled and shook hands like a polite stranger.

"It's so nice to see you!" Mrs. Rivers said. "Juliet has talked so much about you! She has been looking forward immensely to her afternoon with you. It's very good of you to ask her."

Ellen felt herself made into the stranger. She did not want to linger in this alien room, but she found herself accepting a glass of sherry and a cigarette, answering questions about her life in Italy and her journey. As from a distance she felt that she might have liked this new Mrs. Rivers if she had met her in other circumstances, but now she felt something almost like hatred of her because she was in possession of Ellen's child; it was she who was making a bridge for the shy Juliet to cross.

She showed Ellen the patterns.

"We've been choosing a new party frock for Juliet for the Christmas holidays: once the term starts there is so little time for trying on. We both like this buttercup-yellow taffeta, do you?" Ellen wished that she could say that she didn't, but the coloured pattern was charming, as Lorna Rivers held it up against Juliet's clear skin and dark eyes. "Juliet is doing very well at school especially in English and verse-speaking. She won a prize for it last term—a beautiful Shakespeare. Do fetch it, Juliet; I am sure Miss Fenwick would like to see it."

Juliet jumped up, as if it would be a relief to get away.

"I think we ought to be going. We haven't very much time before the theatre." Ellen heard her own voice sounding stiff and repressive.

Juliet sat down again on a stool, stretching out her long, silk-clad legs. They had cut off her plaits: her dark hair hung in a short, straight bob. On her knee she held a grown-up-looking handbag and a pair of grey gloves. Suddenly Ellen saw, half-hidden by the collar of her shirt, a little Italian necklace of silver beads—her own Christmas present four years ago. The sight encouraged her; it was like a message saying that there was something of the child she had known in this tall, strange girl, and she felt more able to attend to what Mrs. Rivers was saying to her.

"Charles had to go down to Bristol, and won't be back to-night. He asked me to give his kindest regards to you; he was so sorry to miss you. Perhaps next time you are in London you could spare us a night or two."

"Thank you; it would be very nice. Please remember me to Mr. Rivers."

Ellen heard herself sounding stiff and gauche. She swallowed the rest of her sherry, and repeated:

"I think perhaps we ought to be going."

"Do you think you had better take your mackintosh, Juliet? It looks rather like rain."

As Mrs. Rivers got up and moved to the window, Ellen saw that she was pregnant. She felt a flash of irrational anger because this woman was bringing an interloper into Juliet's house, as well as a stab of more personal jealousy. She fancied pity and patronage in the voice that spoke to her pleasantly, felt that Juliet's step-mother was conscientiously doing her best with the ex-governess who, in the manner of her kind, was still interested in the pupil who had grown beyond her and almost forgotten her. It was a relief to Ellen to say good-bye to her and to find herself alone with Juliet on the pavement outside the house. It was also alarming, for Ellen suddenly felt as shy as Juliet. The apparent difference between the imaginary situation and the real one had not somehow made a good beginning to the afternoon.

They did not establish any true contact over lunch. Juliet chose chicken, ginger-beer and strawberry ice, but she did not seem very hungry, and refused a second ice. She was exceedingly polite, but Ellen realized that lunch in a restaurant—a great treat in her own school days—had been a commonplace for years to the prosperous London child. Their conversation consisted mostly of questions by Ellen and answers by Juliet which did not lead to any further talk. When they were eating their ices, Ellen began to tell Juliet about her time at Bronciliano, about Donata's ways, and as much as she thought suitable of Shand's story. Juliet seemed to enjoy hearing about them, laughed and asked questions. Ellen began to tell her a little about her own life in Florence, but lost conviction from a feeling that Juliet could not be interested. After all, she was only thirteen—too young to think yet of her old governess's life, except in relation to her own.

When they came out of the restaurant it was raining heavily.

"Oh, well," Ellen said. "Perhaps it's only a shower. We must get a taxi."

Unfortunately everyone else had had the same idea. They stood on the edge of the pavement, both sheltering under Ellen's umbrella, which dripped on to their shoulders. Passing cars splashed the muddy water from the gutter over their ankles. Ellen made ineffectual signals to taxis which were already full or moving to take up a fare. She felt the day again slipping from her control.

"Do you think," Juliet suggested, "we should ask the man at the door to get us one?"

"Of course! How stupid of me!" Ellen felt flustered and

186

provincial. Juliet said with the gentleness of someone much older:

"Oh, no, I don't think he was there when we came out. I didn't see him."

Her words and the intention behind them relaxed a taut string in Ellen's disturbed heart.

She was a little disappointed to find that this was the third performance of *The Tempest* that Juliet had seen, and more disappointed that, as the rain was still pouring down, the play was in the marquee. They walked under the umbrella across the sodden park, and took their seats beneath the roof of wet canvas. She had planned for a sunny afternoon, the magic enhanced by the light splintered through the leaves, and by the casual flight of moth and bird. A conscientious but uninspired performance in a wet tent was a very different matter, and she was bitterly afraid that Juliet, who reminded her more and more with every look and movement of the little girl of the summer at Meridiana, was courteously enduring rather than enjoying her afternoon.

At first her anxiety made her unable to take pleasure in the play at all. The lovers looked too old, the clowns seemed awkward, Ariel a stage contrivance rather than a thing of air and fire. She felt as though she were hardly seeing it herself, but only through Juliet's probably disenchanted eyes. Gradually there stole into her from the words a beginning of serenity. She had allowed herself to be shuttered up all day with her trivial worries. It needed only a movement of her mind to push open a shutter and let in the air. She turned her head and looked at Juliet, at her clear young profile, at the two rows of dark lashes between which the rounded orb of the eye reflected light. She forgot to wonder whether Juliet was bored with the performance, or disappointed with her. Her heart went out in love, not only to the child of her memories, but to the young girl whom she was just beginning to know. Juliet turned and smiled at her, with affection and confidence.

The rain was stopping when they came out, though there was no break in the sky. They walked through the dripping, lush green of the park to the entrance, Juliet chattering now, about the play, about the play her grandmother was acting in, about performances at school.

"Do you remember, Fenny, how you used to tell about the Little Theatre Plays at Ainley when we went for walks in Italy? I did use to hate it if the Warners came over just when we were going for a walk, and I had to stay and play with Donata."

Juliet had become, Ellen thought, several years younger than she had seemed in the morning. At tea she was cheerfully greedy and took her plate back for more cakes. The afternoon had slipped somehow into focus and become like one of their old expeditions five years ago.

Still, Ellen thought as they left the teashop, I don't know anything about her life. Does she miss her own mother? Does she really like her step-mother? Is she happy? They were questions that Ellen, who respected privacy, even in a child, could not ask.

A watery evening light was breaking through the clouds that still threatened heavily.

"We'll get another taxi."

Ellen looked about this time with more confidence, but Juliet suggested:

"We could get a bus and then walk." She added, "It would take longer."

In the bus Juliet asked what Shand was doing now, and Ellen, who had lately had a letter from him and one from his aunt Gertrude, told her all that she knew about his American life.

They both became quiet as they walked from the bus towards the house. Suddenly Juliet said:

"Lorna, my step-mother, is going to have a baby."

"Yes. Do you want a little brother or a little sister?"

"Oh, a sister! I've got one brother. Mummy and Oliver have a boy. Stephen. He's three now."

"Is he nice?"

"Yes, he's quite sweet. I take him out sometimes in Kensington Gardens." She added, "Both Lorna and Daddy want a boy very, very much. They'll be awfully disappointed if they get a girl. They say they don't want to be beaten by Mummy and Oliver. Lorna says if they get a girl she'll drown it."

Suppressing a wish to comment that Lorna looked like the sort of woman who talked in clichés, Ellen suggested:

"I suppose they don't need another girl because they've got you."

"No, I suppose not . . ."

Ellen thought that she spoke without conviction.

"Juliet, I hope very much that, if things are all right, your stepmother and father will let you come out and stay with me in a year or two. It would be lovely if you could come and have holiday with me in Italy. Do you remember it?"

"Oh, yes, a lot! I remember the villa, and Florence and our walks, and that tumbled-down villa where we had picnics, and the Bronciliano garden with all the lemon-trees in pots. I still remember quite a lot of Italian. I talk it to myself in bed sometimes."

"I have a nice little flat with a spare bedroom. I should love to have you, as soon as ever they think you are old enough to come."

Juliet said soberly: "If there isn't a war. What will you do if there is?"

"I suppose I should come back here."

"Daddy thinks there won't be."

Again Juliet spoke without much conviction. Ellen was reminded that she already knew that the worst could happen.

They turned into the square, and approached the Rivers' front door. Juliet said to Ellen with a return of her grown-up politeness:

"Will you come in?"

"No, thank you, my dear. I have to go back to my hotel and pack."

Juliet rang the bell and turned round.

"Thank you so very much for taking me to the play, and everything. I did enjoy it all."

Ellen saw the door opening and held out her hand.

"I've loved having you. Good-bye."

Juliet, like the child she used to be, threw her arms round Ellen's neck and hugged her.

"Good-bye, Fenny! Good-bye! I wish you lived here! I do wish you weren't going!"

"I shall be coming back again, and you'll come out and see me in Florence whenever you want to. I shall be writing to you of course. Good-bye, Juliet, darling. Good-bye."

# CHAPTER III

CROSSING THE Channel on a day so clear that she seemed only to turn her head from the diminishing cliffs of Dover to the swelling line of France, Ellen felt homesick, and afraid of the plunge into an unpredictable Europe. She could not afford a *wagon-lit*, but the train was half empty. She had a whole side of the carriage to herself after Paris, and dozed uneasily through the night, disturbed by the chill of the mountains which crept through her tweed coat, and by haunting dreams of war. Italy, in the morning sunshine, was lovely and welcoming. An irrational relief stole over her as she drank her coffee in the restaurant car and looked out at the hill towns, the burnt-rose and apricot houses. It was only five years since she had first looked at this countryside with the astonished eyes of a stranger. Now she was coming home.

When the *portière* dumped her two suit-cases on the floor in her flat, and she was alone again in the sitting-room that she had painted herself, she felt an illusion of safety, and a great relief at getting back again into her own life. Her arm-chair, her books, the straw mat on the floor, the desk that she had bought at a sale with so much trepidation and triumph, seemed to promise continuity. She had found three letters in her letter-box. One, from Shand, broke into her flimsy illusion, for he wrote that everyone in the States thought that war was coming, and offered Ellen the hospitality of his aunts' house in New England for as long as she cared to make it her home. A formal note from Miss Gertrude endorsed the invitation. Ellen put these letters down half-read, gratitude tempered by her resistance to what they apparently saw with so much certainty. There was a note from Betty Muswell to say that Frank was giving up his job and they were going back to England in a fortnight. Would Ellen come to supper with them one evening before they went?

"It's been lovely having this year here, I shall always be glad we were in time to have this bit of Italian life, but Frank thinks we'd better not risk it any longer; he wants to be home if there's going to be trouble."

Here, too, was the note of finality and warning. The third letter was addressed in a handwriting which Ellen had only seen once, but instantly recognized. Arturo Marelli enclosed a graceful note of thanks from Graziella.

"She was so much pleased with your letters, and with the charming gifts you sent her from London. She does not know your address, and asks me to forward this to you. I am not sure of the date of your return, but I hope you will let me know. I trust we shall meet again soon."

Still holding this letter in her hand, Ellen went to the window. Shand's letter and Betty Muswell's had brought back with renewed sharpness her sense of a threatened world in which she was far from her own people. But happiness was in the air; it was reflected in the water of the Arno as it flowed under the ancient arches of the Ponte Vecchio, it hovered over the tiled roofs of the houses that sheered up from the opposite bank, it ran like music in the voices of the people passing below on the pavement. I'm glad I came back, Ellen thought, even if I've only got a few weeks, even if the worst happens and I have the most appalling difficulty in getting to England, I'd rather have a little more of this! She sat down to write a note to Arturo Marelli telling him of her return.

.　　　.　　　.　　　.

"So you have come back, Signorina," he said, "in spite of everything."

"I think I am probably foolish."

"I think, so, too. But it is a great pleasure to see you again, and to be able to thank you in person for your kindness to Graziella. I hope that you enjoyed your visit to England."

"No. Not much, really. I don't seem to belong there now. I feel that I belong here."

She looked happily across the crowded café tables to the life and movement of the Square, where everything that could reflect light sparkled in the brilliant sunshine.

"I hope that you will be able to remain here."

She realized that he did not sound hopeful, but this evening she was full of a gaiety that would not admit the worst possibilities.

" How did you find Graziella? "

"I did not think that she was any worse. They say that there are signs of improvement and that she has begun to accustom herself to the life, though she was very unhappy when I came away, *poverina*! Your letters from England gave her great pleasure. She has never been there, and it was something quite new to distract her mind. You describe so well places and people. . . . I hope that if you can spare the time you will continue to write to her."

"Of course I will! I am only too glad if I can do anything for her!"

"You are very kind." He broke off to order their drinks. "I myself was very happy in England, in spite of the damp in my bones. But Oxford is as beautiful as any city I have seen, and both my father and I received much kindness there."

"What made you decide to be a philosopher in the first place?"

"I suppose because to me the most interesting thing is to try to find out the meaning of life, and to study what wiser men than I have thought about it."

"Did you always know that that was what you wanted?"

"I think that I always had some idea since I was old enough to have ideas at all; but it was first given definite shape by a German friend of my father's, one of the many intelligent people who came to our house in Rome. He used to talk to me and lend me books. That was when I was about fourteen. He has since gone back to Germany, and I have been much afraid for him under the Nazis; he was not a man who could dissemble; but lately I have heard that he has gone to America."

"Was your father also a professor?"

"My father? Oh, no, he was a journalist—the editor of a Liberal paper. Politics were his great interest, and economics. But he was a man of many sides: he was also much interested in music and painting, and he had a gift for friendship. Our house was full of people of all occupations who came in and out; there was a lot of good talk; it was very interesting for my sister and me. But although my father was moderate in all his views and in his expression of them, he had great integrity and was not willing to compromise. He did not hesitate to criticize the Fascisti, and after the murder of Matteotti he was warned to leave the country

192

at once, before he could be arrested. I was then at Oxford, and he came to join me. Later he went to Paris. I returned to Italy to look after my mother and sister. My mother went afterwards to Paris to live with my father. He died there in 1935."

"It was hard to die in exile!"

"He felt very much the separation from my sister and me, and from so many friends. After he died my mother returned to Italy, and I found a flat for her in her home town Padua." He smiled. "That was how I first encountered Graziella! I went to stay with my mother for her first Christmas there, and we went to a party at a friend's house. Graziella had just come home from her convent where she had been at school. She had only arrived in the afternoon, and there had been no time to buy a grown-up dress for her—she was in her white school-girl's dress, and she told me afterwards that she cried in bed that night because she thought I should have considered her a child and should not have noticed her." His smile broadened until his eyes nearly disappeared between his eyebrows and cheek-bones. "But I had noticed her."

"It is a good thing," Ellen said thoughtfully, "that you were interested in philosophy. It would have been so dangerous if you had been interested in politics, too."

His smile vanished, and she noticed how the lines of his face made him look stern when he was not smiling.

"Of course I am interested in politics. Life, it seems to me, is not divisible. One cannot dissociate oneself, especially in these days, even if one does not take active part in them."

Ellen felt as if she had been rebuked.

"I know! I often feel ashamed of those years I spent in the Warners' house, never thinking about all these things that were going on around. We might have been in Italy as it was thirty years ago for all anyone cared. Except Shand."

"I should like some day to meet Shand. But I do not think you should blame yourself. You had not been so very long in this country; you were not among people who were aware of what was happening, and no doubt you had your own problems."

She had a strong wish to tell him the story of her first summer, about Daniel and Madeleine and the disaster that had sent her reeling, half stunned, into Lucrezia's house; but she was withheld

193

by the feeling that she did not know him well enough to talk about her most private affairs, and by an instinct which kept her from showing to him the picture of herself discarded and defeated. She only said sadly:

"I think I am one of the people who always see things too late."

"I think that perhaps you have an unsuspicious heart."

Her spirits rose, but, with the shyness that often made her withdraw from what seemed to be meant as praise, she asked him:

"Does your sister live in Padua too?"

"Lucia? No, she married a doctor, who now lives in Milan. She is very happy, I think, and they have a daughter. But to me her husband is not *simpatico*." He made a dismissing gesture. "I do not often see him."

She had begun to realize that something crisp and astringent about him would enable him always to extricate himself from people he did not care for. She was the more pleased when, as they both got up to go, he suggested a time and place for another meeting.

. . . . .

The mounting tension in Europe that September was a forcing-house in which her friendship with the Marelli shot up like a beanstalk. Graziella seemed to be as much a part of it as if she were there. Ellen wrote to her, sent her books and papers, showed her answering letters to Arturo. The letters were affectionate and graceful, sometimes lit by natural gaiety, sometimes very depressed. Graziella began to say to Ellen what she did not say to Arturo, that the sanatorium was "So cold, so cold, and like being at school after you were too old for it." She always added, "Don't tell Arturo that I feel sad. I shall feel better tomorrow." Ellen once or twice left a despairing letter behind when she met him, and filtered the news which she realized that Graziella always modified in her almost daily letters to him. She never succeeded in deceiving him; he seemed able to pick up out of Ellen's mind anything that she withheld from him about his wife. Once when Graziella wrote to her, "Don't tell Arturo, but I feel as if I should die just of being here before the end of two years," Arturo, whom Ellen had not told, postponed two of his lectures, packed a bag, and travelled up to Switzerland one night and down the next to spend the intervening day with Graziella.

194

He brought Ellen a handkerchief in one corner of which Graziella had embroidered the initials E. F. in a small circle of flowers.

"She enjoys your letters so much, Elena. All that you tell her about the amusing people who come into the Universal. She says that your letters more than any others make her feel still part of the outside world. . . . Not," he added with a shrug, "that it is altogether a privilege at the moment to be part of the outside world."

That was on the day of Chamberlain's first visit to Hitler. Ellen had been working until nine o'clock at night, for the Universal was crowded with English and American visitors and residents frantically booking any place on the trains to get home. I should be one of them, Ellen thought, and her two suit-cases were packed, but she did not take her ticket. The thing seemed too monstrous to happen. In this week Arturo withdrew from her. He was much with a family of Czech friends who had come down to Florence from a holiday in Switzerland, instead of returning to Prague. His withdrawal intensified Ellen's anguish as each day she tried to make up her mind whether or not to start for England, and each night found her still in her flat, where, after sleepless hours of panic and indecision, she would fall near morning into a short spell of half-waking sleep.

When the crisis was over at Munich, and the immediate tension had slackened into a dismayed unease, Arturo took Ellen out for a drink again, and they compared notes about their letters from Graziella. He said very little about Chamberlain's agreement with Hitler, and Ellen knew that he felt that she had suffered a national disgrace. She thought that herself; she felt that her country had betrayed Czechoslovakia, and sorrowful and angry letters from Alice and from her brother confirmed her sense of shame; but she was unable to help an immense personal relief, as she unpacked her suit-cases and hung her clothes again in the wardrobe. Even if, as Alice and Hugh wrote, and as she knew Arturo thought, the necessity was only postponed, her blood and nerves, defying conscience and judgment, rejoiced in the postponement.

.  .  .  .  .

She usually met Arturo, not by arrangement, but by a movement as automatic as a tide, for a drink in the Square in the evening. Often he had friends with him, most often his great friend, Carlo Pirovino, a lecturer in history, a gentle, shy young Jew, who in the hit-and-miss-way in which things still happened in Italy had not been dismissed from the Faculty when most of the Jewish staff were expelled in the spring of that year. Sometimes they were accompanied by Filippo Ceseri, a young journalist lately come to Florence, and recently married. In the week of Munich his wife, Benedetta, bore their first child. Ellen herself had made a friend, a Swiss woman, Sophie Brille, who worked in the offices of a shipping company. Occasionally the whole group would go round to Ellen's flat for supper, or would meet there later to drink coffee and talk. Much as Ellen enjoyed these gatherings, she was always glad when she and Arturo met alone. At such times he poured out to her his hopes and fears about Graziella, or talked to her about their brief married life. Ellen felt almost as though she had been part of that life or it had been part of her, so vivid was it to her imaginative sympathy. At other times she felt as though she and Arturo were parents, talking about a beloved and distant only child. She began to know Graziella so well that she thought of little things to please her that did not occur to Arturo. She sent her a length or two of bright-coloured ribbon to tie back her hair, a frilled shell-pink pillow-case, a picture of Padua, her home town, to hang by her bed. She spent many an odd half-hour looking at the clothes in the shop windows, and drew sketches of the fashions to amuse her. She wrote with all the warmth and tenderness with which she might have written to Juliet in distress to this girl who was only a few years older than Juliet. At this time in her life she was carried on a tide of unexamined feeling; she did not know how much she did these things for Arturo's pleasure as well as for Graziella's. They were hardly separate in her consciousness, and nothing was too much trouble for these exciting new friends.

· · · · ·

At the beginning of November she took Arturo out to see the Villa Meridiana, which she no longer wished to avoid. Since that summer five years ago no one except Angelina and Giovanni had lived there. Lady Gressingham was crippled with arthritis, her son in India with his regiment. Luigi, the bailiff, still looked after the farm, and occasionally hired a man to help Giovanni clear the garden of weeds. A bonfire was burning when they arrived—thin blue smoke went up behind the trees of the orchard where windfall fruit rotted in the long grass. Angelina's broom of twigs leaned against the wall in the courtyard, and she herself came out to meet them, wearing the same faded blue dress or a successor to it. She looked, if anything, smaller, Ellen thought, but otherwise no older; the hair that had always seemed to be painted on either side of the sunburnt parting still looked as if it had been polished with black lead. She brought them some wine, the *vino secondo* of which she and Giovanni were allowed to keep a cask. They drank it standing by the stone well in the courtyard. While Angelina went to fetch Giovanni, Ellen took Arturo out of the side archway into the garden, and showed him the folding back drop of the Tuscan hills. The creeper on the wall of the *contadino* house was scarlet. There were still late roses in the beds, and the diospero tree was like one of the golden trees in the Garden of the Hesperides. Above them the November sky still kept a depth of blue, and there was warmth in the sunshine.

"When I first arrived here," Ellen said, "I thought I'd got into a house in a fairy-tale."

"I am not surprised. I have not seen one more beautiful."

Giovanni came, more bent and aged than Angelina, still wearing his old brown gardening clothes. He welcomed them with a fine courtesy, and he and Arturo began to talk about the weather and the olive crop. Ellen looked on smiling, pleased because she saw that Angelina and Giovanni were charmed with Arturo, and that he liked them as he liked anyone unpretentious and friendly. After a minute or two Ellen slipped away and went into the house. She wanted to be alone to re-open that chapter of her old life.

She ran upstairs, went into the bedroom that had been hers, and unfastened the shutters. Old-fashioned, holland dust-sheets, bought in Sir Robert's time, covered her bed, dust lay on the dressing-table, and lightly clouded the mirror. Ellen wiped the glass with her scarf, and saw a woman who seemed to have only a distant connection with the Ellen who had lived in that room. She went out along the corridor. The door of Madeleine's bedroom at the end was open; light came through an unshuttered window. Probably here Angelina had stopped in her bird-like pattering, duster in hand, when the visitors came. Half unwilling to go into the room, and half drawn there, Ellen stood in the doorway. She could fancy that if she opened the wardrobe doors she would see hanging there the row of pretty dresses which she had often admired and sometimes envied. She imagined that Madeleine's scent still lingered in the air. She walked back along the corridor, and up the staircase to the tower.

Here no one had attempted to clean: feathers and bird-dung spattered the floor and cobwebs vaulted the corners of the wall. Ellen leaned out over the window-sill, looking over the Perugino landscape towards Bronciliano. She tried for a moment to re-enter her own past; for a moment it seemed possible that there was no barrier, and that Daniel was still coming down the hillside to meet her at the bridge over the stream. She saw him again walking away from her with Madeleine along the valley. The old happy expectation, the old pang of loss and pain of fury still lingered in the air, but they were outside her. She turned and went across the tower to look down from the other window into the courtyard. Arturo was sitting on the edge of the well, a glass of wine in his hand, the other, holding a cigarette, gesturing as he talked to Angelina and Giovanni. Ellen called down to them. The three faces went back on their necks; she saw Arturo's tilted against the pale stone like a face on a pillow. He shouted "Come down, Elena! We should be going!" She looked once more round the tower, shivering a little in the sharp chill of the shade, then turned and ran down the staircase to the courtyard.

. . . . .

She had never known anyone like him: anyone who touched life on so many sides and had such power to illuminate them for her; anyone who was so gay and so serious, so astringent and so gentle; so simple and so wise. By this time, like a good dancing partner, she was adapting the steps of her nature to his. Because he enjoyed roaming about the countryside and talking to anyone he met, she disinterred an old love of long walks, and discovered a new pleasure in casual encounters. Wordsworth was his favourite English poet, and that autumn she read Wordsworth as though she had never read him before. Colours that he liked began to appear in her wardrobe—wine red, peacock-blue, amber. When he noticed the new jersey, the scarf, the string of beads, as he

198

never failed to do, they acquired a special quality, different from her other clothes, as if they had been blessed. She had always been a good cook. Since Arturo and his friends sometimes came to supper at her flat, she became, where his favourite dishes were concerned, an inspired one. She went to look again with an enlivened eye at pictures and churches that he liked. The world was recreated for her by what she still thought of as this satisfying new friendship. The sun had never shone more richly on the tawny stone, the contrast between the clarity of the light and the darkness of the shade had never been as sharp. Books and poetry discovered a new meaning, food had more flavour, grapes had been pressed to enhance their meetings.

At all these meetings Graziella made a shadowy third, and it was often Ellen who invoked her. "Have you ever brought Graziella to see this?" "Wouldn't Graziella like this? What a pity she can't see it!" Sometimes when they were discussing ideas and books she would ask, "What does Graziella think?" and he would reply, smiling, "I don't know that Graziella thinks about such things." At these moments Ellen would feel the relief of one who moves from a cramped into an easier posture, and would think of Graziella as of a beloved child.

Sometimes when she left Arturo she was moved by a poignant sadness and sense of loss and disappointment; but there was always another meeting to look forward to; she woke first thing every morning with a joyful sense of happiness and expectation. Only, as news came of Hitler's increased pressure on his neighbours, as the Rome–Berlin axis visibly strengthened, and German uniforms became more numerous in the streets, as Mussolini stepped up his threats against France, and Italian students howled obediently for Tunis, Nice, Djibuti, Ellen was daily conscious of the cordon tightening round her private world.

## CHAPTER IV

IN FLORENCE the day before Christmas Eve saw the first onset of biting winter cold. Arturo was going up to Switzerland by the mid-day train. Ellen had arranged to see him off and to hand over to him at the station the parcel she had been preparing for Graziella. He had suggested that they should meet half an hour before the train was due to start and have a cup of coffee together in the station. Ellen had hardly seen him for the last few days. Since the end of term he had been exceptionally busy with his other work. He never talked to her about this other work, but she had gathered or had concluded that he did a good deal of private coaching, perhaps, she thought, to raise the extra money necessary to pay the sanatorium. She had seen so little of him in the last week that she felt faintly resentful of his neglect, and looked forward with heightened eagerness to meeting him before his departure.

Her stove had gone out during the night, and the kitchen felt like the inside of a refrigerator. She pushed wood into the stove, and heard a hopeful crackling, but it always took some time to warm the room. She stood about wearing a jersey under her dressing-gown and warming her hands on a cup of coffee. For her own Christmas she had asked Sophie Brille to come and eat a chicken with her—a prospect which was pleasant without being exciting. She had decorated a small Christmas tree with silver bells and red candles. As she moved about the room the flap of her dressing-gown shook out from the branches a thin carillon of sound, the candles glowed like pomegranate flowers in a patch of warm sunshine, but the tree was nothing until Arturo could see it; at the New Year she would buy more red candles and give a party for him and Carlo, and the Ceseri and Sophie. In the meantime the real excitement of her Christmas was the preparation of her parcel for Graziella. She had made her a nightgown—not as exquisite, she knew, as those made by the needlewomen round Florence, but it was very pretty. She had made and iced a small cake, and bought sweets in bright tinfoil. She packed all these things carefully in a box, wrapping them in fresh paper and tying them with red ribbon. She imagined Graziella opening the parcel with Arturo sitting beside her, smiling at her pleasure.

She put on her thick tweed coat, pleased that the crimson scarf and knitted cap that Alice had sent her had arrived early, so that she could wear them for the first time. They looked warm and gay, and suited her. Taking her parcel under her arm, she walked to the station. In the biting wind, everyone she passed appeared rather miserable: women huddled in furs, men with scarves up to their noses and hat-brims pulled down over their smarting eyes. But she felt invigorated, enough heat generating in her body by her own movement and by her eager expectation. She saw, when she arrived at the station, that she was five minutes before her appointed time. She took her stand by the bookstall and watched the entrance.

In the next half-hour she went through the progressive stages of slight impatience, disappointment, doubt about the meeting-place, and growing dismay experienced by anyone waiting in vain. She inquired if the time of the train was correct. She went to the restaurant to see if she had made a mistake and Arturo was waiting for her there. She hurried back to the bookstall, afraid that she might have missed him. As the time for the train drew nearer, and she began to realize that even if he arrived now they would not be able to have coffee together, she felt a shattering disappointment out of all proportion, for he was only going to Switzerland for four days. She began to feel angry with him, and then to think that something had happened to him—he was ill, or he had been run over in the narrow streets by some reckless driver. Distractedly she hurried to the station entrance, and back again to the platform where the express for Milan, in which he must start his journey, was now standing. Growing angry again, she thought of going away, but even if she could have borne to do this, she had Graziella's parcel. She returned to the bookstall and saw that there were only three minutes to go. Suddenly a hand gripped her elbow; she found him beside her. In overcoat and scarf, with his face whipped grey by the chilling wind, and his hair ruffled, he looked unlike his usual composed and attractive self. She saw him for a second not as her exciting friend, but as a thin, agitated foreigner in a hurry.

"Elena! I am so sorry. I could not help it! Will you come with me to the train? I must not lose it. I must tell you as we go. There is very bad news! Filippo has been arrested!"

"Filippo! What for?"

"We do not yet know. Probably for something he has written. They took him late last night. I have been with Benedetta this morning to the last minute. She is quite crazy with distress, it was difficult to get away," he added as they scurried down the long train between the waving groups and slamming doors. "And you have had no coffee! You have been waiting in the cold!"

"Oh, that doesn't matter!"

Nor did it, now that she knew that he was safe and had not willingly disappointed her.

He found a seat in the middle of a carriage, near the engine. Ellen gave him her parcel; he took it with hurried thanks. There was a general upheaval in the carriage as the people already in possession made a space for his bag and for the parcel on the rack. Treading carefully between their feet, he came to the window and stretched out an arm. His hand in a woollen glove caught Ellen's; she found herself holding it in both hers.

"Elena, will you go and see Benedetta, and try to soothe her? Persuade her that she must be brave for Filippo's sake and for the child."

She was glad that he asked it as if he had a right to demand her help.

"Yes, of course; I'll go straight round there now."

"Thank you! I hope that you will have a very happy Christmas."

"And you, too. Don't worry about this more than you can help!"

What was the use of saying that, for of course he must worry about Filippo. Such words were only clumsy vehicles for a desire to heal!

"Give my love and best Christmas wishes to Graziella!"

"Yes, I will be sure to do that. She will be so pleased with her parcel."

The train began to slide past the platform. Ellen ran a step or two beside it. Arturo, with a final wave, drew in his head and hand; the train gathered speed and bore him away. The last half-hour, with its varying agitations, had broken down the barrier which Ellen had managed to erect between her feelings and her mind. She knew, as she saw him go, that she helplessly loved him, that she would hardly be alive until he returned, that she wanted to spend Christmas with him, that it was intolerable that he should be bound to Graziella, and that there was nothing at all to be done. She turned away and walked out of the station.

# CHAPTER V

On a fine evening in March, Ellen left work late, but since she had not seen Benedetta for a week, conscience obliged her to go round by the Ceseri flat. She often reproached herself that she could not do more for Benedetta. She pitied her sincerely, but was not fond of her, and she was aware of a want of spontaneity in her attempts to help and console that often made them ineffectual. She could not find the right words that she so often found in her letters to Graziella. The acute, submerged tension in her own life broke out sometimes in an impatience that she had never shown before. She went to see Benedetta partly to relieve Arturo and Carlo. They were all a little weary of her exactions; she seemed to be so much more preoccupied with her own situation than with Filippo's. He was still in prison, but at least he had not been transferred to the Lipari Islands. Neither had he been definitely charged, and they had no idea if he was to be brought to trial. They could write, send him papers, food and cigarettes. Benedetta had been allowed to go and see him, once alone and once with Carlo. She said after the first time that it made her feel worse, and would have refused to go again, but they persuaded her that Filippo ought to have that comfort, and with difficulty suppressed their indignation because she was so reluctant to give it to him.

The Ceseri flat was on the ground floor of an old *palazzo*. Ellen rang the bell and waited for some time. Presently Benedetta herself came to the door, looking peevish, her head wound up in a towel.

"Ah, it is you, Elena! Since you have not been this week, I have given up expecting you! Lena is out. I sent her to buy food: we have nothing. The *bambina* has been so fretful all day that I could not go out. I think she has a little fever. I am washing my hair, as you see. Will you come up and sit with me while I dry it?"

The March day had been warm, but warmth had disappeared with the evening sun. The wood fire barely impinged on the big, shadowy room, with its stone walls and tiled floor. The baby's crib was on one side of the hearth. Ellen and Benedetta squatted down on the rug, and Benedetta unwound the towel, and let the soft chestnut mass flow over her shoulders.

"Your hair is lovely!"

Benedetta looked pleased for a minute, then her narrow, pale face, only pretty when she was cheerful, fell again into its fretful lines.

"It is coming out all the time since I have been so anxious about Filippo! I have never had to live alone like this before! And Lena is so stupid! Only this morning I have discovered that there is no more wood, only what will last till the end of the week. It was always Filippo who ordered that. I do not know where to buy such things, and perhaps it will cost too much! Yet in this great cold place we must have fires, until the end of April in the evenings, and I think that Nella has already a little chill, she is so flushed."

"Perhaps it is a tooth." Ellen looked at the sleeping face in the crib with a tenderness that she could not feel for the mother. "I expect that Arturo and Carlo will see about the wood for you."

"They have not been here for three days. I have been quite alone. I have spoken with no one but Lena."

"They are sure to be coming. They are so very busy."

"It would be better if they were not!"

Ellen resented the implied criticism of Arturo, and replied:

" The news of Graziella is not good. The sanatorium have written to say that she is making no progress. They think that they may have to collapse one lung."

"It is not surprising, since she must always be anxious. If Arturo and Filippo thought first of their wives . . ."

She seemed to Ellen to be talking wildly, obsessed with her grievance. She swept back her heavy, damp hair, and then, putting both hands in the mass, tugged at it as if she would pull it out by the roots.

"Oh, how my head aches! Tonight I could scream! But then Nella would wake, and I cannot any more stand her crying. Elena, how is it that you are always so calm, so composed? Do you not lie awake all night thinking of them working there?"

"I don't understand. Who? Working where?"

"You know very well what I mean! You need not be discreet with me!"

"I haven't any idea what you are talking about!"

"You do not know?" Benedetta swept the hair off her face, sat back on her heels and stared, incredulous. "I thought that you and Arturo . . ."

Ellen bent forward to throw another log of wood on the fire.

"I have told you that we have hardly any wood," Benedetta said crossly.

"I am so sorry! I wasn't thinking what I was doing. What is this you are talking about?"

"Arturo has not told you what they do by night, and sometimes by day?"

"I know about his work at the University, of course."

"No, no, no! You do not know what they are doing in the cellar in the Via Camina?"

"No, I don't know anything they do in the Via Camina," Ellen forced herself to add. "If it is something you have been told privately, Benedetta, you had better not repeat it to me."

"But, yes, I shall tell you!" Benedetta cried with rising hysteria. "Why should I alone bear this anxiety? And perhaps you can persuade them to stop. For they are *pazzi, pazzi* . . . all of them!" Her voice had risen to a scream, and the child whimpered and stirred. "I warned Filippo when he first told me! How is it possible to keep such a thing secret for long? Anyone may hear the noise of the press: anyone who happens to climb over the wall to make love in the garden or to take the fruit! And of what use can such things be against the Duce?"

"Benedetta! What *are* they doing?"

"They have a secret printing-press in the cellar of an empty villa, where they print all the time leaflets against the Fascisti, which are smuggled into the factories and the docks. They all worked there together—Arturo, Carlo and Filippo. It is not for that they have arrested Filippo, or he would now be on the Islands, but at any time they may find the press and take the others, and if they should discover Filippo's part in it while they have him in prison! *Now* do you see why I am out of my senses!"

The shrieking note on which she finished woke the child. Benedetta lifted her out of the cradle, and hushed her with more impatience than gentleness in her arms. This gave Ellen a few

205

minutes in which to absorb the shock of Arturo's danger. She was hurt that he should not have thought her fit to be trusted with a secret that had been entrusted to Benedetta, but that feeling was nothing beside her fear for him. Her mind raced to envisage terrible possibilities. She had almost forgotten Benedetta, until she saw that she was laying the child back in the cradle. Her outburst seemed to have calmed her. She began to plait and twist her hair.

"I am surprised that Arturo has not told you." She looked at Ellen as if readjusting a preconceived idea. She added uneasily, "I hope he will not be displeased with me. Perhaps you had better say nothing."

Ellen was not going to enter into a conspiracy with Benedetta against Arturo, but she felt remorsefully that she ought to have been less impatient with the poor girl, who really had even more reason to be wretched than she had known. She wanted to go home and be alone, but she made herself listen to a repeated round of complaints. Lena's stupidity, the coldness of the room, Nella's screaming fits, the shabbiness of all Benedetta's clothes and the unkindness of former friends, who would not speak to her since Filippo's arrest. Ellen felt as if she were half dazed and the stream were washing over her, but she must have given some comfort by listening, for when Benedetta, her hair now pinned up into a gleaming coronal, said good-bye to her, she thanked her with unusual warmth, and begged her to come again soon.

    .     .     .     .     .

Ellen walked slowly home, cooked her supper mechanically, and ate it without noticing what she was eating. Her chief feeling was an itch to see Arturo, if only to reassure herself that he was still safe and free. As if in answer to her longing, there was a ring at her door-bell about half-past nine, and she found him standing on the door-mat.

"I have been working all day," he explained. "And tomorrow I must go to Pisa. I have a letter from Graziella asking me to get some things for her, and I came to ask if you would be so kind as to do it for me."

"Of course! Do come in, Arturo, and have some coffee. Sit down by my fire while I bring it."

He hesitated, looked in through the door at the bright fire in the pretty room, and said, "Thank you, only for a few minutes. I have more work that I must do this evening."

Shivering as she thought of what the work might be, and imagined the *sbirri* shining their torches down the cellar steps in the Via Camina, Ellen brought coffee, and put it down on a small table between them. Arturo gave her Graziella's list and some money. Then, looking very tired, he leaned back and closed his eyes, relaxing like one at home and free to behave as he felt. For an instant Ellen was unwilling to disturb his peace, but she was driven on by anxiety and also by anger.

"I went to see Benedetta this evening."

"Ah, yes," he murmured. "Benedetta. I have not been this week. I must try to go. *Poverina*, she is very wearying with her endless complaints, even though she has good reason for them."

"Yes, she has! More even than I knew. She told me this evening about the printing-press in the Via Camina."

His eyes jerked open; he sat bolt upright.

"I might have known! I suppose it is only surprising that she has not told you before." He saw Ellen's face. "You must not begin to think, Elena, that I do not trust you. I have not told you all this time because it is always better, in my opinion, that as few people as possible should know about these things. No one at all should know but those working there. Graziella knows nothing. When Filippo joined us, he promised that he would tell no one, not even his wife; but he has proved, poor Filippo, less discreet than he seemed. Telling Benedetta about the press was his first mistake. The article for which it seems he must have been arrested was the second one. We must hope that he will not make a third," Arturo added drily.

"He was not arrested for anything to do with the press, you are sure?"

"No, no, they would have searched the villa and taken us—Carlo and myself, too. It is possible that they have suspicions."

"And he might let it out, by accident!"

"It is always possible. It would certainly be by accident. Filippo is brave and honourable. But it is better, when questioned about anything, not to know the answer. That was my other reason for not telling you—it is easier to be ignorant than to feign ignorance."

"Yes, I see that, but, Arturo, now that I do know, please tell me about it. I shall be less anxious."

"There is not much to tell. We print leaflets urging the people of this country not to let Mussolini drag them into war at Germany's heels, and explaining very simply the nature of Fascism."

"How do you get them into the factories?"

"That it is better for you not to know. Filippo did not know that, only Carlo and I."

"It must be very dangerous!"

"Others have encountered far greater dangers."

"Couldn't I help in any way? I should be so glad!"

"No. It is better that as few people as possible should be concerned in it. I regret very much that we ever included Filippo, but he understood the working of the press and was exceedingly useful. Since he left we have been much slower. But he had not the self-discipline necessary for such work. Our lives are far more unsafe since Benedetta knows. Tomorrow I shall speak to her about telling you, and make her swear secrecy again. But what is the use? She is not capable of it!"

The idea of him rebuking Benedetta for sharing his secret with her stung Ellen like boiling water.

"I hope you won't do that!"

"Certainly I shall speak to her! She has broken her promise to me!"

She was suddenly very angry with him, and in a curious way her acute fear for him intensified her anger; she had a despairing sense of being outside everything in his life that really mattered to him. He loved Graziella; the rest of his heart was in the dangerous work from which he was determined to exclude her. The tension of the last weeks surged up in her, and she exclaimed:

"If you tell Benedetta that you don't trust me, I'll never see you again!"

"Elena! . . . Have I not said that I trust you."

"Yes. But you don't, or you wouldn't be so much upset at my having found out!"

"How can you say such a thing! Do you not see that I must stop Benedetta's mouth if I can? I am glad, if she must speak of it to anyone, that she spoke of it to you; but tomorrow if she has a fit of nerves she may tell Lena—anyone!"

208

"I suppose you think I shall go round and give information to the police?"

"Elena!"

She felt nearly as much astonished at her own behaviour as he looked. She was glad that he was startled, glad that she had shaken him out of his fixed idea of her as always calm, kind, sympathetic, sensible. An uncontrollable impulse drove her on; she felt aghast, as if a carefully built up erection were tumbling in ruins. She also felt as if she were dancing on the ruins.

"Do you imagine that a few badly printed leaflets can overthrow a Government?"

"They are not badly printed!"

He was very exact in all small doings, he disliked careless movements and minor inefficiencies. He looked outraged at the suggestion.

"I expect they are, now you haven't got Filippo! But anyhow, the whole thing is ridiculous! What difference can leaflets make? Nobody will dare to act on them."

"What do you know about it? What do you know of Italy's Socialist movement, one of the strongest in Europe? How do you know what a word of encouragement and support may mean to a group in a factory, to someone feeling himself isolated from those who think as he does?"

"They will only get into trouble if they are found reading them!"

"Of course you think that we should all stand aside and do nothing! It is what your own country has done! You betrayed us in Spain, in Czechoslovakia! You yourself have been living happily for years in the household of a woman whose brother is a notorious Fascist!"

"There! I knew you didn't trust me! I wasn't happy there! You know I wasn't! I hated her! And don't you talk to me about *my* country, when yours started the whole thing in Abyssinia! *We* haven't used mustard gas! We haven't got a dictator!"

"No! You have an ignorant and foolish old commercial traveller!"

"You don't trust any of us! You do think I shall go round to the police!"

They were both on their feet now and facing one another. He

shouted. "Be quiet! Will you speak no more of going round to the police! It is nonsense. I . . ."

"No, I won't be quiet!"

He took her by the shoulders and shook her. The shaking, like the breakdown of her self-control, gave her an intense pleasure.

"You think I'll always be quiet, don't you, don't you, Arturo? You don't expect me to have any feelings! You think I'll just be there when you want me, and listen to you, and do things for Graziella!"

"It was your own wish to do things for Graziella! I shall ask you no more! Give me that list!"

"I won't."

"Give it back to me! Now! Immediately!"

"I shan't!"

She clenched it tightly in her hand. He snatched her hand, uncurling her fingers roughly from the palm, twitched the bit of paper out of it, and stuffed it in to his pocket. She slapped his face hard.

He stepped back from her, rubbing his cheek with the knuckles of one hand, looking startled and absurd. Then his face set into a hard shape of anger, and without speaking he walked past her towards the door. She heard his footsteps going down the first flight of stairs. Let him go! They were enemies! She hated him! She had hated him for weeks; hatred had lurked in the dark underneath their friendship! She stood panting, both hands clutching the base of her throat. She was glad that they had quarrelled, glad that he had walked out! She never wanted to see him again! She heard him on the landing at the bottom of the first flight, then on the lower staircase. She ran out of the room and tore after him at such reckless speed that she nearly fell headlong down the narrow stairs.

"Arturo! Arturo!"

He did not turn. His hand was on the latch of the door. She caught hold of his sleeve and pulled his hand away. Nothing mattered except that he should not leave her like this.

"Don't. . . . Come back. . . . Don't go!"

He pulled his arm away, and she clutched it again frantically. For an instant they struggled clumsily in the narrow, badly lit entrance, their grotesque shadows swooping on the wall. Then the anger between them dropped as a squall of wind drops, the two shadows ran into one another and became one large one on the pale surface.

## CHAPTER VI

ELLEN LAY in bed, staring at the oblong of light thrown by the street lamp on her ceiling. There was a bourdon of distant traffic in the city, but voices and footsteps had long ago faded from the Lung'arno. A little while ago she had heard the clocks strike two. A breeze, blowing in along the valley of the Arno, disturbed the curtains, the cool air of the April night made her draw the bedclothes up to her chin and lunge down with her feet until she found a water-bottle that kept a lingering warmth. She still shivered, all the heat of her body concentrated in the feverish indecision of her mind above her conflict of feeling.

"What harm should we be doing," Arturo had said, "to Graziella?"

Could she believe that true? She would not have felt it in Graziella's place. People were supposed, now, to feel like that, but she did not believe that they ever did. Even in this fortnight of indecision she had found it difficult to write to Graziella, and Graziella had felt the difference without knowing it. Something stilted and unspontaneous had crept into Ellen's letters since the evening of the quarrel had shifted her relationship with Arturo, so that instead of running steadily between banks, it tumbled over rapids, making her battered and breathless, tossed between new heights of joy and depths of pain. Yesterday Graziella had written, "Your letters are always such a pleasure, but you must not feel obliged to write to me when you are tired or busy." The words had sprung up in Ellen's face from the paper, an accusation. There had always been a sense of responsibility mixed with her affection for Graziella, as if the girl were Juliet, or Shand, or any other child in her charge.

But perhaps, she argued, that is only my feeling, only because I am partly afraid. We shouldn't do her any harm; she will never know. Even if Arturo wanted it—and he doesn't—I am not the kind of woman to break up a marriage. I am not Madeleine! The feeling broke through, how I wish I were! I wish I could just take what I want, without all these scruples and hesitations. Arturo was right last night when he was angry and called me a prig, and said that I didn't really love him. Oh, but that's not true!

Her head was hot, while the rest of her body shivered. She rolled over and pressed her face into the pillow. The movement released her inexperienced imagination. An invading drowsiness relaxed the grip of the censor, and in a half-dream she felt Arturo physically near her, her body and spirit merging with his; then separate but together they were walking along a valley towards a house whose windows seemed to be on fire; something— a sound outside, a movement of the curtain—jerked her back into wakefulness. She pulled herself up against the pillows, hugging the bedclothes round her. Like a clock that had stopped for a minute or two and then begun to go on again, the argument restarted its motion in her mind.

How can I refuse him? He is lonely, in danger all the time; he may be arrested, imprisoned, shot! Perhaps I am only hesitating because I am a coward, turning away from life. And all life is threatened now. In a few months there will be war. When the whole world is going down in ruins, how can it possibly matter what two people do?

No, I shall never really believe that! It will always matter, or there is no meaning in anything. I ought to go home! I am living here in a self-indulgent dream! I should go back to my own country and share whatever comes with my own people. But how can I go and leave him, and perhaps never know what has happened to him? Even if there is only a short time left, we could be so happy! I might have a child! If I did, Graziella should not know; I would take it away, look after it myself, make no claims on him. I would never be possessive; I would not let myself be— for she knew that an integral part of love is to want possession.

The pulse beating in her head seemed like the pendulum swinging of her mind. Exhausted, she longed for it to stop, longed to slide into the sleep which had evaded her for several nights, so that her eyelids felt hot and sore and her limbs ached with fatigue.

How stupid all this hesitation would seem to a lot of people—to

Madeleine, Lucrezia! They would despise me; and perhaps they would be right. I let my happiness slip last time for want of courage. I won't do it again; I can't. Arturo is right: we shan't hurt Graziella. I can't do without him; I have my own life, too. I must. . . . Her body knew before her mind that she had come to a decision; her tensed nerves relaxed, and in a few minutes she was asleep.

She was walking upstairs in the house at Ainley carrying something on a tray. She was going to her mother's room, but when she reached the top of the stairs there was a long white corridor with doors on either side; she knew that she was in a sanatorium. She had to go into a room, the door of which stood open. She saw through the doorway the outline of a woman lying on a bed with a handkerchief over her face. Someone said that it was Graziella, and that Graziella was dead. She knew that she must go up to the bed and lift the handkerchief, but she felt herself on the verge of a naked panic that she had been looking away from all her life. With the dragging reluctance of dreams, she went up to the bed, put out a hand to the handkerchief, and woke with a jerk, her heart beating wildly. Slowly the nightmare dissolved, and the solid shapes of the actual world re-formed around her. It was morning, she had slept late, and she felt as if she had been ill for a week. She stumbled out of bed.

She pulled the bedclothes together hurriedly without any of her usual neatness, and dragged on her clothes. As if she had been hypnotized, she went to her desk and pulled out a sheet of paper. Her usually, firm, clear writing sprawled on the page as she wrote to tell Arturo her decision. "I can't, because I feel that I should be treacherous to Graziella. I am going away into the country for a few days."

She gave the note and a few lire to the *portière* and asked him to take it round at once to Arturo's flat. Then, with a sense of going on mechanically with a life that would never again have any meaning, she telephoned to the Agency to say that she was ill, packed a small bag, and took a bus out of Florence.

.    .    .    .    .

For a day or two she felt like someone walking in her sleep, but as she roamed about the hills between Florence and San Gimignano in the exquisite spring weather, the numbness broke, and she

213

experienced an agony of desolation. It was like that first winter at the *pension* after Daniel, only then she had been younger, so that there was more round the corner. She had felt herself at that time the victim of circumstances. Now she felt that she had deliberately maimed her own life, and, what was worse, hurt Arturo. She did not know whether he would be angry or understand, whether he would forgive her, whether it would be possible to meet him again or how, what, if they never saw one another, she should write to Graziella. The time was too short for her to come to terms with her own feelings. It was her nature to scramble for some kind of hope, even if she did not know what she was hoping for. She was glad when the end of her week came, and as the bus tore down the steep hill and she saw the Arno Valley, and the glittering towers of Florence, she was impatient to be back in her flat, to be at work, to fill her emptiness with any kind of rubbish that might be better than the void.

She ran upstairs to her flat and scrabbled in her letter-box. She did not know how much she had hoped for a word from Arturo until she saw that among the half-dozen letters waiting for her there was nothing in his handwriting. She threw the letters on the table unopened and walked to the window. She stood there with her hands to her head, pushing back the hair from her hot temples. Outside in the brilliant sunshine voices and footsteps were lively, the tiled roofs on the opposite bank were warm with colour, the river, full fed with spring rains, ran smoothly by. Of course, she thought, he would not know how long I was going for, nor when I should be back! She was turning away from the window, when she caught sight of Benedetta hurrying along the pavement. She was stumbling; she cannoned off a woman, who passed her without appearing to notice; she had one hand on her chest, the other holding the ends of a scarf thrown over her brilliant hair. She saw Ellen at the window and made a wild gesture.

Ellen ran downstairs, knowing that she ran to meet disaster. In the daytime the doorway on to the street stood open. Benedetta, her face channelled with tears, reeled into Ellen's arms.

"What is it, Benedetta? What is the matter? What has happened?"

"They have arrested them! The police raided the cellar before it was light and found the press! They have arrested Arturo and Carlo this morning!"

## CHAPTER VII

At mid-day on Sunday, September 3rd, Ellen went to drink a vermouth with Sophie Brille in the Piazza della Repubblica. This had become a habit, and was almost her only diversion in the week. This morning she went earlier than usual in search of news; she had no radio, and had heard nothing since the evening before. The square was crowded; she heard the word "*Guerra*" repeated as she pushed her way through the gesticulating groups under the colonnade. She saw that although she was early, Sophie was waiting for her at one of the café tables.

"You have heard?" Sophie said. "England has declared war on Germany."

Ellen realized that however certainly you have expected something, there is still a great gap between the event and the expectation.

"What will you do, Ellen? You will have to go home? At once, while it may still be possible."

"I cannot leave Graziella."

"She has her parents."

"Her mother has had a stroke and is incapable. Her father is terrified of getting into trouble with the police. They cannot help her to try to make contact with Arturo. Here in Florence there are people who knew him, and through whom in time we may be able to get word to him. Graziella believes that there may be a chance of planning an escape for him."

"It is impossible!"

"People have escaped from the Islands."

"Not many. And now they will be even more closely guarded. It is certain that sooner or later Italy will come into the war. Arturo will not escape. It is a fantasy with which the poor girl consoles herself."

I do, too, Ellen thought, but she did not say it. Her friendship with Sophie Brille went up to a point, and no farther. There was a good deal in her own mind that she would not expose to so much practical common sense.

"I do not think that Graziella will recover. She should certainly go back to a sanatorium."

"She will not leave Florence."

Sophie sighed, but added energetically:

"You must think of yourself now, Ellen. You do not wish to be interned here as an enemy alien. You will cause great distress to your family in England if they are uncertain about your return."

But my family, Ellen thought, is here. Graziella has become my family, and to look after her is all that I can do for Arturo. Besides, we may be able to help him, find some way of communicating with him, send him money or food or papers. In Italy if you have some money there are usually ways to anything. But money was going to be a difficulty, for Graziella now had only what her parents could give her, which was not very much, and Ellen's work would come to an end.

Sophie Brille picked up her thought.

"And what will you live on? You will not get your money from England, perhaps, now that there is a war."

"No, that will be difficult; but I suppose that I can get work in one of the hotels."

"You are mad!"

"Perhaps."

"It is not 'perhaps' at all," Sophie said crossly. "It is certain. It is a great pity that you ever encountered these Marelli."

No, no, it isn't, Ellen's heart cried. One does not regret the times of deep feeling in one's life.

"I must go home now, Sophie, and get some lunch for Graziella."

She walked back to her flat through the hot sunshine, thinking of her own country, of Juliet, Alice, Hugh and his family, as she might have thought of people on a ship far out on a stormy sea. But she had chosen to make her life apart from them, and soon perhaps, as Sophie said, she would have no choice.

She had left Graziella in bed after a bad night, but found her dressed and sitting by the window. Her once bright hair had lost its colour and hung limply, her neck was so thin that Ellen could almost have encircled it with her hands. Only when she smiled was she recognizable as the shadow of the happy girl whom Ellen had first met two years ago in the Square.

"I have heard them saying in the street," she said, "that England has declared war." Then, as if she had gathered all her resolution to say it, "You must go home, Elena. Quickly! Arturo has always said that if there was a war Italy would be dragged in by Germany. It would not be good for you to be here!"

"I am going to stay here."

A relief which she struggled to hide spread over the girl's face.

"You must not stay here for me. Nor even," Graziella added gently, "for Arturo."

In the firm tone in which she always settled matters for the young, Ellen replied:

"We needn't talk about it any more, my dear. I'm not going home."

# INTERLUDE

1945

# INTERLUDE—1945

As Ellen climbed down from the high step of the tram at the end of the village, the blinding glare of the sun came back at her from the white road and hit her between the eyes. She loosened the handkerchief on her head, and pulled one flap forward to protect her face. The rocking of the tram had intensified the headache that in these last weeks had never left her. She knew that she would have been wiser to have waited until later in the day, but a febrile impatience, made unbearable by Dino's hungry clamour and by the wailing of the Lucchesi children, had driven her out of the stuffy, cluttered kitchen into the early afternoon. She grudged the tram fare when every lire was wanted for bread. Anna Lucchesi had given it as willingly as she gave everything, and Ellen was obliged to take it. She knew that she could not walk five miles. To reach the Villa Meridiana had become for her more than a visit to the Headquarters of the Allied Relief. It was a journey back to the familiar, a return home. She had no money for the tram-ride back into Florence, but it would be cooler then, and she might be able to walk it by slow stages. She hoped for a lift in one of the lorries and jeeps constantly passing on the road. The Americans, now bestriding the land like careless gods, were often kind.

On the right-hand side of the road, where the land shelved away to the valley, she saw men and women cutting the corn in the sloping fields. On the left the throb of the threshing-machine came from one of the farms hidden by a shoulder of hill. Everything was as it had been in that first summer, as no doubt it had been every summer while the Germans were there, driving their well-cleaned cars over these ruts between the indifferent fields, where the *contadini* would perhaps pause for a minute and glance warily under the sweat dripping from their eyebrows. At least that oppression was off the land, but for Ellen the glow of liberation had soon faded, extinguished by exhaustion and by the difficulty of keeping herself and, still more, Dino alive.

She had never seen him looking as a child should look. All the children in the Internment Camp were hungry towards the end of the war, but her first impression of Dino had been of a wolfish

221

hunger staring at her from his big dark eyes over the palliasse where his mother lay frowning in uneasy sleep in the earlier stages of typhoid. Later that night, when Ellen was giving her some soup, Margherita's eyes, open now and heavy with fever, had the same avid stare as she put two hot fingers on Ellen's wrist and asked:

"You come from London?"

"No, from the North. Yorkshire."

"Ah! I from London. Soho. My father is Italian, a *cameriere*, a waiter. But I have worked here in Italy for ten years." She let her head fall back and pushed the cup away. "After the child was born I was ashamed to go home. He has no father," she added in a drowsy, complaining voice. "I have had to support him always since he was born."

Ellen saw the boy's eyes, resentful and unsatisfied, still staring at her from the opposite side of the bed. She had sent him out to play with the other children, but he had stolen back to his mother, and squatted there with a concentrated stillness very unusual in one of his years.

"What is your name?"

"Dino."

"How old are you, Dino?"

"He does not understand much English," his mother murmured. "Since I am here I speak always Italian."

Ellen repeated the question in Italian.

"I am seven, Signorina."

"You are very tall for seven!"

He looked faintly gratified, but he did not smile. He said— it was a statement rather than a question:

"She is very ill."

"Yes, but she must sleep and get well. You should go now and have your supper with the other children; it is better not to disturb her."

"I shall not disturb her."

Through the days of his mother's increasing illness he was always there, a silent presence, watching her, watching Ellen. She often tried to send him away when Margherita was delirious. She asked one of the women who helped to look after the children to keep him with her, but he always came back to the kitchen of

222

the derelict farm that served as a makeshift sick bay. Yet he never showed any ordinary sign of affection to his mother, and she, as she emerged from a torpid sleep or in the lucid intervals of delirium, seemed hardly to be aware of him. She was entirely absorbed in her own predicament. Her imploring looks, her fretful cries were all directed to Ellen. She implored her to do something to allay the pain and thirst and fever.

There was very little that Ellen could do. There was no doctor in the camp, and at this stage they had no supplies, no medicine, that had not been used up long ago. The Italian guards were very sympathetic. They came and looked, and exclaimed, "Ah *poverina!*" They were always willing to help Ellen to lift Margherita or to move her palliasse. Once a day the commandant came. He was a middle-aged man, a store-keeper who had been thrust into uniform late in the war and whose strongest emotion was fear of his superiors. Ellen asked him to send for a doctor from outside, but he muttered that he had no instructions, and seemed to think it impossible. He looked daily more harassed, and Ellen hoped that he had bad news of the war. The internees knew that the Allies had occupied Rome, and expected every day to be released by their victorious army marching northward, but the Army never came, and they did not know what was delaying it. They felt that they had been forgotten by everyone, even by the Germans, for the commandant muttered something about having sent a letter asking them for medical supplies, but having had no reply. There was nothing to do for Margherita but to keep her clean, give her such of the poor food as she could take, soothe her and drive off the mosquitoes that were the plague of the camp from June to October. Seeing that she could not keep Dino out, Ellen made a fly-whisk for him from a branch of one of the neglected olives round the farm. He sat for hours moving it backwards and forwards above his mother's face.

One evening when Margherita had been delirious all day and had fallen into a sleep that was half stupor, Ellen went out of the farm to get her own supper. As she walked across the baked ground from which the internees had long ago trodden all the grass, she felt a hand touch her arm, and saw Dino's black head at her elbow. He did not look up at her, but said, again a statement rather than a question:

"She will die."

"I hope not, Dino. We will do all we can to get her well."

But Ellen thought that she would die. This was not the only case of typhoid that she had nursed. The first had been a little girl, whose mother, the English wife of a shopkeeper in Bologna, had proved to be hysterical and useless, so that Ellen had undertaken to nurse the child. Brought up in a doctor's house, she had some rudimentary ideas of what to do. The child recovered, and Ellen was called by the Italian guards to a woman they suspected of typhoid, but who proved only to have jaundice.

These two cures established Ellen's reputation as a nurse, and though she afterwards nursed several who did not recover, she was always called on for serious cases. This gave her prestige. She was listened to when she gave advice about keeping huts and cooking utensils clean. She was able to organize a makeshift school for the older children; there were no books, and several of the instructors knew very little more than the children, but they were all glad of the regular occupation. A habit of dependence on Ellen that grew up in the camp gave her a sense of value that made a kind of happiness.

On the day that Margherita died she seemed in the early morning to be a little better. She had some less restless sleep. Her temperature dropped a point. She drank half a cupful of tinned milk and water. Her heavy eyes, moving incuriously over Ellen, turned to the left side of the bed.

"Dino?"

"He is asleep. He was awake very late last night keeping the mosquitoes off you."

"*Poveretto.*" Her eyelids dropped, and then painfully lifted again. She said in a dry whisper:

"But for me he has no one."

"I was going to ask if you have any friends or relations, so that I could try to get a letter or a message to them telling them how you were going on?"

"No, there is no one, unless Anna Lucchesi . . . but I do not know. . . ."

"Who is Anna Lucchesi? Can you tell me her address?"

"Firenze."

Her eyelids dropped and she seemed to be dozing. Suddenly

224

her eyes opened wide and she clutched feebly at Ellen's hand. Her face, now a frame of bone for the stretched yellow skin, contracted with terror.

"I shall die!"

"Hush! You are better this morning. Your temperature is down."

The paroxysm of terror passed, but her fingers still held loosely to Ellen, her eyes, so large in her shrunken face, entreated:

"Dino?"

"He will come when he wakes."

"No, no."

The effort to explain was too much for her. Ellen answered what she believed to be the prayer in the eyes.

"I will look after Dino."

Margherita's hand dropped to her side. Soon she was delirious again. Ellen had often listened carefully to her rambling, and listened again, hoping to pick up something to link Dino with the world outside, but although here and there a name bubbled up to the surface of the hoarse, whispering speech, there was nothing to tell who these people were. Dino slipped back into his place on the other side of the bed a few minutes later, and as the morning grew hotter, he worked the branch untiringly above her twitching face.

At noon Margherita fell into a coma. Dino sat back on his haunches, and wiped his dripping forehead with the back of a grubby hand.

"She sleeps," he said, with a sigh of relief and exhaustion.

"I should go and get your lunch now, Dino."

"You will be here?"

"Yes, I shall be here; I'll have mine later."

She knew that it was not a healthy sleep.

Fanning with a slow, rhythmical movement, Ellen allowed her own eyes to close. It was a week since she had had more than an hour or two of sleep. Her wrist slackened, the branch, its leaves already withered and rattling, though Dino had picked it fresh that morning, slipped down on to the bed. Ellen woke with a jerk. There was no visible change in Margherita. Then her eyes opened wide, her jaw dropped. Ellen raised her head and wiped her face; she tried to give her water. She clutched the limp body closer to hers, as if to convey some living warmth to it, but she knew that there was no more to be done. She laid Margherita down, closed her eyes and crossed her hands on her breast. Every nerve in her own body, tensed for the last ten days' defeated struggle, relaxed, and she crouched, exhausted and faint, by the dead woman's side. She did not hear the child's bare feet until he was near. She saw him staring at the bed, his eyes dilated, shivers running all through his skinny frame. He stopped and picked up the branch, which lay where it had fallen across his mother's body.

"You slept!" he cried accusingly.

He struck at Ellen with the branch; she felt the twigs whipping her face and dry leaves in her mouth. She pushed it away and took him in her arms.

"Dino, *bambino*, there was no more that we could do for her. She feels no more pain."

Rigid in her arms he thrust away from her and threw himself down by the bed. He uttered a desolate cry.

"*Mammina!* What shall I do?"

"You will stay with me. I promised your mother that I would look after you, Dino. You will be my child."

.     .     .     .     .

As she turned in at the gateway of the avenue, a jeep driven at a reckless pace passed her, whirling up the dust that flew into her nose and hair, and settled on her parched lips and in her eyes. She sat down for a minute in the long black shade of a cypress and wiped her face. Dust would always be one of her memories of the war; dust blowing off the trodden floor of the camp, settling on the beds and the cooking-pots; dust always in her throat and under her finger-nails; dust on the high roads as she and Dino walked the long miles from the camp to Florence after the release; dust in Florence, where the Germans had blown up the buildings at either end of the Ponte Vecchio, and her flat, with a hole in the roof, was an uninhabitable mess of debris and broken glass at the top of a deserted, bomb-shaken house. There had been nothing else for it in this war-dented Florence, empty of everyone that Ellen knew, but to take Dino to Anna Lucchesi, of whom he remembered that she kept a greengrocer's shop by the market, that she used to give him oranges and was always kind.

The greengrocer's shop had vanished, but neighbours directed them to the room on the ground floor of the tall, narrow house whose windows were festooned with ragged washing. The girl who opened the door to them looked both frightened and stupid, and seemed as if she was going to close it again, but a deep voice in the room behind her called out, "Who is it?" As Ellen and Dino limped into the room, and saw Anna Lucchesi, with a child in her arms, heaving her big body up from a chair, and turning towards them a face of unmistakable dignity and benevolence, Ellen had for the first time for years the forgotten feeling of coming home.

. . . . .

She struggled to her feet again, pulling down the faded cotton dress that had shrunk with so much washing. They were always washing in the Lucchesi kitchen, old Anna and Ellen trying to make up by vigorous rinsing in cold water for the lack of soap. They had cut down the shirts of the dead Matteo to make garments for his two-year-old son, and for the baby daughter, born after he had been killed when the Partisans attacked a bridge above Trento. It would have been so much better, Ellen thought, if Dorotea had stayed with the children on her parents' farm, even if it was in the middle of the fighting, but Matteo had left her with orders, if he should be killed, to go to his mother in Florence. The cow-like girl had obeyed, and somehow, heavy with one child and dragging another, had managed to make the journey, to crawl into the Lucchesi *appartamento*, and a few weeks later to bear her daughter, Anna Maria, who was now six months old.

That effort of will and energy seemed to have exhausted Dorotea. She sat all day in the rocking-chair, taking very little part in what was going on. She suckled her baby mechanically, but only looked vaguely irritated when either of the two children cried. It was old Anna, then, who snatched them up in a passion of brooding love, the same love with which she gazed at the photograph of the dead Matteo and his living brother, Giuseppe, still fighting with the Partisans. Ellen had seen the look of tenderness on the old woman's face on the day of their own arrival as she lowered her dropsical bulk down on to the floor to bathe Dino's blistered feet, and from that moment had loved her. It was

227

some weeks before she learned what Dino's connection with the Lucchesi was. Margherita had been betrothed to Matteo before the crazy week with a passing commercial traveller who had fathered Dino, and vanished. Matteo had flung away from the girl, but old Anna had visited her in hospital, and shown a steady kindness to the unwanted child.

. . . . .

Ellen staggered with giddiness as she walked on up the avenue. I couldn't go on much longer, she thought; and then what would become of them? Old Anna could hardly drag her dropsical limbs to the end of the street. Dorotea was frightened of going out of the house alone and almost too stupid to buy a piece of bread. It was because she felt her own strength failing that Ellen had decided to go out to the villa where she had been told that the Allied Relief were setting up their headquarters. If she were out of action there would be no hope of their getting any share of the food-tickets distributed in the town. They needed regular help until Ellen could find a way of earning money again.

She put her hand into the pocket of her dress and fingered her talisman, her out-of-date British passport, and a pre-war cheque-book on her Italian bank. These had been in her handbag when she was swept off to the camp, and she had been allowed to keep them. She would show them to prove that she was not asking for charity. There must be money, her small income from her mother, in her bank in England untouched for four years. She needed tinned milk and beans and flour, but eventually she could pay for them. She rehearsed carefully what she was going to say, for her head felt so confused that she was afraid that she might not be able to present her case right, might forget even the number of the Lucchesi house and the name of the street. Lately, especially since she had heard that Arturo had been shot in 1941 while trying to escape from the Islands, she had been subject to fits of blankness, when the inside of her head seemed to be made of cotton wool, and she would stare about the kitchen wondering where she was, until a word from Anna or the sight of Dino's black head recalled her. Her fingers tightened on the passport. The five years in the camp had not obliterated her conviction that anybody English could not be entirely stranded in a foreign country. It had been a surprise to her, when she came out of the

228

Internment Camp like somebody coming round from an anæsthetic, to find Americans, even more than her own countrymen, dominating the scene.

.    .    .    .    .

Trailing up the avenue which had been churned into deep ruts by traffic too heavy for it, she came abreast of the Mandini house, and saw an old woman sitting in the doorway with a child on her knee. She recognized Grandmother, probably now great Grandmother Mandini, smaller, shrunken, almost bald, with a few white hairs strained back across her skull. Her face had contracted to half its size, much less than that of the plump child sleeping in her arms. How round and well fed the baby looked, compared to Dorotea's!

"*Buona sera*, Signora Mandini. You remember me? The Signorina Fenwick who was here with the Rivers one summer many years ago?"

The old woman stared, shook her head, and moved her lips over her toothless gums.

Ellen touched the baby's head.

"Whose child is this? Is it Marco's?"

The old woman nodded. A tear came out of one corner of her eye and trickled down her cheek.

"Marco is dead."

"Oh, I am so sorry! Was he killed in the war?"

The old woman muttered, "*Partigiano*." She looked at Ellen without curiosity or recognition. She was so old that probably nothing outside her own family was real to her. Ellen longed to ask her for a glass of water, or a piece of bread—anything to clear her head and give her strength to achieve her purpose. She longed to ask permission to sit down inside the house for a few minutes, but was withheld by a doubt as to whether, if she once stopped to rest, she would be able to go on again.

She asked slowly and carefully:

"The English and American soldiers are at the Villa?"

"*Tedeschi*," the old woman nodded. "*Tedeschi*."

"No, the Germans cannot be there now. . . ."

"*Si, si.*" The bald head went up and down. "*Tedeschi*."

"No, the Germans were there, I know, but they have gone away. Now surely the Americani have come?"

The old woman suddenly drew a wrinkled claw from the baby's back and pointed up the Avenue towards the villa.

"*E rotta*." Again a tear trickled out of the corner of her eye. "*E rotta*."

Ellen said good-bye to her and walked on again up the avenue. There seemed now to be a great distance between her head and her feet. She looked down at her lean, brown legs, and at her broken and dusty sandals. I am a scarecrow, she thought, and then, I can't do it, I can't go any farther. She stumbled, but by an effort that wrenched her body, saved herself from falling. She saw across the table in the Lucchesi kitchen Dino's eyes, avid and reproachful, as he swallowed the last mouthful of the slice of bread that was all she had to give him at mid-day. She saw the shoulder-blades sticking out from his body of skin and bone as if wings were sprouting. She drove herself on.

Everything seemed very quiet. A sudden fear that the report might have been untrue, that the English and Americans were not, after all, here shocked her heart. The iron gates at the head of the avenue stood open. Their posts were half covered by trailing briars from the unpruned roses, and a tangle of briars buried the oleanders that had so delighted Ellen that long-ago summer when they were the first that she had ever seen. In front of the villa a jeep was parked on the gravel sweep, now green with weeds. Ellen saw it with a relief that sent the blood to her head. Thank God the Americans were here!

Her eyes travelled over the façade of the villa, and what she saw stopped her heart. The side of the villa looking on to the garden was a shell, in which what had been windows were blackened holes. Madeleine's old bedroom had fallen in a heap of rubble across which she could see the magnolia trees in the garden.

She leaned against the gatepost, unconscious of the briars that scratched her cheek and plucked at her skirt. She shut her eyes. Of course she had seen plenty of houses damaged in the war, but this was personal damage, obscene and terrible, as if she had done it herself. In spite of the heat, she shivered; cold, starting from her skin, crept inwards towards her heart. She thought vaguely that she was fainting, but an inner voice said, "Dino!", the child's face hovered among the veils of blackness that were falling before her eyes. With an effort of will she drove back the faintness. Turning her head away from the damaged side of the house, she walked unsteadily across the gravel, past the jeep and through the archway, into the courtyard.

It was empty and still in the sunshine. As she held the waves of faintness and nausea at bay, she lost touch with the present; she expected to see Juliet come running out of the opposite door, or Angelina with her broom of twigs sweeping the yard. As always, swifts were flying in and out of the windows of the tower, and swooping across the open square; their shadows, as of old, dropped like stones down the sunny wall. She pressed her hands over her eyes, struggling to get back to some purpose that evaded her. It was terrible that the place was empty, but she did not know why, nor what the urgency was that held her shaking limbs together. Then she realized that the villa was not entirely empty. She saw a figure move across the unglassed window of the tower, and heard a distant voice somewhere behind the house call "Hya!" It was a man's voice, but it brought to her confused brain only an idea that Juliet and Shand were playing up and down the steps of the tower. A voice from the tower called "Harry! Come right up here!"

The voice was American and recalled her to her errand, or at least to a hazy knowledge that this was what she had come to find. That voice meant help for Dino and the babies. She moved uncertainly towards the door at the foot of the tower stairs. There was a heap of debris piled near it, as though someone had made a half-hearted attempt to clear the yard. The brightness of the sun on the pale wall hurt her eyes; she closed them, and stumbled against something hard on the edge of the heap. The pain of the knock aroused her. Looking down, she saw that the thing she had stumbled against was the globe of stars, lying on top of the debris with a great crack across the blue glass. A fresh wave of faintness swept over her; she tried to shout, but no sound came from her dry throat. The cold crept inwards again from her skin. She felt herself falling, but did not feel the stones bruise her flesh as she sagged on to the pile of rubble.

For an instant, as her body relaxed, the curtains of darkness lifted before her eyes. Voices were speaking above her, from a long way off through a roaring sea. A khaki trouser and the

231

blond drill of a sleeve moved across her sight. She tried to speak. A strong arm under her shoulders raised her head, far off, through the roaring sea, a voice cried, "My God! Fenny!" She saw blue eyes in a brown face above hers, murmured "Shand", and sank into the engulfing darkness.

# PART IV

1949

# CHAPTER I

"You see, Fenny," Juliet said, "I wanted to make a clean break."

She sat sideways on the window-seat of Ellen's sitting-room, hugging her knees. She wore her hair brushed back from her face and tied with a bit of black ribbon behind her neck. At first Ellen had thought this casual austerity a pity, but now she was coming to like it. She looked at the beautiful outline of head and profile, tilted against the luminous sky.

"Yes, my dear?"

Juliet had arrived three days ago, and this was the first time she had offered any real explanation of her sudden telegram. "Could you do with me next week for visit? Please be sure and say if inconvenient." The words had sprung out at Ellen from the slip of paper like something that she had been waiting for. When, at the station, there stepped from the train, hatless, smiling, in a long scarlet coat, a young woman who said, "It is good of you, Fenny, to let me take you at your word like this. I felt I couldn't wait any longer to see Italy again." Ellen knew that this was not all that Juliet had come for. But she only said that May was a perfect month and she hoped Juliet had come for a long visit. Then she waited. Three days had worn off the strangeness between them, had made her acquainted only on the surface with the grown-up Juliet who was both unexpected and familiar, but they had left her in no doubt that the girl was unhappy.

"I seemed to have come to the end of everything!"

Ellen was careful not to smile.

"Your grandmother's death must have been a very great loss. You had been living with her all the time you were at the Drama School, hadn't you?"

"Yes, since the end of the war. She was always my family, ever since I was old enough to know what I wanted. It was easy to arrange to live with her. Both the other families, Mother and Daddy, moved outside London during the war, and they haven't moved back. It was much easier for me to be in town. Anyhow, neither of them really wanted me. I don't mean they wouldn't have had me. They've always been kind. Remorsefully kind.

235

But Granny wanted me very much, and I was fonder of her than of anyone in the world. You never knew her, did you, Fenny?"

"No, I only saw her on the stage."

"She was the most fully alive person I've ever known. You know how often you have the feeling with most people that only part of them is functioning? They seem like cars with their jets partly choked. What comes out into living is so much less than it could be. But Granny's jets weren't choked. She was such fun! Just for her to be in the room made everything stir and open out. People were quite different when they came near her—more themselves."

"You could feel that from the audience. The whole stage lighted up when she came on."

"That was what made it so awful at the end. Not the dying, but the way that she diminished before she died. At the end she was under morphia most of the time, but when she was conscious she was absorbed in what she felt. People came to see her, but she wasn't interested in them at all. Everything that had always gone out from her to other people was over before she was. She liked to have me there, but she seemed right out of my reach."

"Yes, dying is a private business."

"It makes a nonsense of everything."

"I don't think it does if you can accept it."

"How can you tell whether you can accept it until you come to do it? And then you've got to."

"Yes, of course, nobody knows what it will be like for himself. But I think I mean if you can accept the fact that life has to be lived on those terms, a short journey with that certain end. If it is an end."

" 'Brief life is here our portion' was all right when people were religious and could count on eternity. Now we don't feel that we can count on three years."

"Nobody ever could, Juliet. The atom bomb hasn't really made any difference to that. Only to our consciousness of it."

"Well, perhaps the world can't stand being more than a certain amount conscious."

"Sometimes I think perhaps it has to be fully conscious of despair before it can go on to the next stage. What Keats called 'dying into life'."

236

"Do you think there is a next stage?"

"Yes, I feel sure there is."

Juliet clicked her lighter, and lit another cigarette. Ellen saw that her hands were trembling.

"Were you alone with your grandmother all the time that she was ill?"

"There were nurses, of course—two of them in the last months—and her maid, who'd been with her for twenty years."

"Wasn't your mother there?"

"Of course Mummy often came to see her. But . . . this was one of the things that was so awful, Fenny. Mother was very queer. She hated my going to live with Granny—not that she wanted me to live with her and Oliver; she was jealous the other way round. She couldn't bear my being a kind of daughter to her mother. She was never the same to Granny after I went there. She was always arranging to come and see her and putting it off. She used to grumble and make a great fuss if Granny had rehearsals or engagements at any time when she suggested coming. My being there made her angry with Granny all the time, before she was ill and even afterwards. She wasn't angry with me until just the end."

"What happened at the end?"

"I haven't told anybody until now. I couldn't. Mother wasn't there when Granny died. She'd been up to see her the day before, and she saw the doctor; he didn't expect it to happen so soon. Then, very early in the morning, the night nurse woke me and said I'd better come. I telephoned to Mummy—they live out near Farnham—and told her, and she said she'd come at once; but Granny died quite peacefully at the end—she was under morphia—half an hour before Mother got there. I went downstairs to meet her and tell her. She had a sort of hysterical fit, and shook me and raged at me. She said I had pushed her out of her place and taken her mother away from her. She said she was the one who ought to have been here all these last months, and not me, that I was so jealous and possessive, I hadn't wanted her and hadn't let her know in time on purpose, and that Granny was the only person she had ever loved in her life, and now she wouldn't ever be able to tell her so, and it was my fault. I can't tell you; it went on and on like a nightmare, and I couldn't stop

237

her. I felt quite numb. At last the nurse came in and got her some brandy and calmed her, but she wouldn't really speak to me again before she left."

"It was shock, Juliet. She didn't know what she was doing or saying."

"It was shock all right, but she was saying what she really felt. In a way, you see, it was true that I had taken her place with Granny, although I don't think at the end she really wanted to be there too, or of course she could have been. Granny worried about her a lot. She always felt it was her fault that Mother wasn't happy."

"Isn't she happy?"

"Mummy? Was she ever?"

"When I first knew her I thought she was the happiest and luckiest person I had ever met. But no, I realized afterwards that she wasn't really."

"She's one walking grievance. She went back on to the stage, you know, at the end of the war, in a play with Oliver. He didn't want to put on that play, but she was set on it. It only ran a few weeks. She had . . . quite kind notices. She looked lovely—she still does—but nobody said a great deal about her acting. When the play came off she got it into her head that Oliver hadn't tried on purpose because he wanted it to. I don't think he did act as well as usual, but I don't think he had a chance: she was in such a state of tension about the whole thing that he couldn't relax, and he always thought it was a bad play, which it was. Then Mummy had an affair with the playwright, an awfully silly young man, and Oliver went off in a pet and had an affair with Francia Fothergill, and they talked about a divorce and decided not to for the sake of Stephen. I always felt it must have been a great relief to Francia and the playwright; I'm certain they didn't want to get really involved, they must have been shaking in their shoes; and so it all blew over. But Mummy's line now is that she sacrificed a brilliant stage career to be a good wife and mother, and she doesn't let Oliver forget it, poor devil!"

Ellen said untruthfully:

"Juliet, I don't like to hear you talk about your mother like that."

"Oh, Fenny, you are restful!"

238

"Restful?"

"Yes. Nobody says that sort of thing nowadays."

Ellen was silent, feeling herself the old governess, stuffy, out of date. Perhaps, after all, she had nothing to give this girl except an Italian holiday.

She saw then that Juliet was crying. She was pulling fiercely at her cigarette while a tear trickled down her cheek. She put up an impatient hand to brush it away, but another followed. Ellen went to her and put an arm round her.

"Oh, Fenny, I didn't want it to be like that! She is my mother, after all! I wanted to be friends! After the funeral I asked if I could come and stay with her for a bit. I've got a job with the Liverpool Rep in the autumn, but nowhere particular to go till then, and after all we did both love Rose! I felt we couldn't go on being strangers and almost enemies! I wanted to be friends! But Mummy said she couldn't do with me because the spare rooms were going to be done up and after that they had people from America coming for most of the summer. And I felt . . . I know it sounds very silly, but I felt thrown overboard, as if there wasn't a place for me anywhere . . . and I came to you. . . ."

Ellen's arms were round her, the dark head relaxed against her shoulder.

"Of course you came to me. Don't cry, Juliet, darling." She could have said "I want you, I love you," but knowing that that would not touch the vital need, she said, "Your mother cares much more about you, I'm quite sure, than just now she is able to show. Loss affects people in different ways. She'll be longing to see you when you go back again. And meantime you're here with me, and I'm delighted to have you. You can stay just as long as ever you like. You must think of this as another home."

.     .     .     .     .

When Juliet came back from washing her face she found Ellen slicing tomatoes into a pan.

"Can I do anything to help you, Fenny?"

"No, thank you, my dear. I thought we'd go out to dinner, for a treat. I haven't taken you yet to my little restaurant. The food is very good there and quite cheap, and we can sit outside; it's warm enough this evening."

"That would be lovely!"

239

Juliet, Ellen thought, looked tired, but much less taut.

"What are you cooking for, if we are going out?"

"I want to leave something ready for Dino. I expect he's with the Lucchesi, and he won't get much there."

"He can cook perfectly well for himself!"

"Yes, but he won't bother if he comes in late and I'm not here. He's growing so fast he needs a good meal at the end of the day."

"You do spoil him, Fenny!"

"I want to make him happy. He had such a difficult start."

"I suppose it must have been hard for children in that camp!"

"I don't only mean the camp. His mother seems always partly to have resented him. His coming upset her life, it prevented her from marrying Matteo Lucchesi, who at that time, when they had the greengrocer's shop going well, could have given her a comfortable home. She had to work hard to keep Dino, and because of him she was ashamed to go back to her parents in England."

"Poor Dino! Wasn't she at all fond of him?"

"Oh, I'm sure she was. They were very fond of each other, but there was a lot of resentment mixed with it on both sides, and it's hard for a child to accept so much double feeling."

"I don't think it's easy for anyone. I wish Dino didn't mind my being here so much!"

"He'll get over that. He's an only child, and to him you're another child coming into the family. He was the same when my nephew came. But Roger doesn't speak a word of Italian, and is very insular and snobbish; he was only here for a fortnight, and they never got on terms. But your Italian's coming back, and that makes him feel more at home with you, even though he does speak English well. And you can understand his difficulties!"

"I shouldn't mind if he wasn't so often rude and sulky with you. Why do you let him be, Fenny?"

"I talked to him about it last night. He isn't generally as bad as this; it's a kind of protest because you're here. Be patient with him, Juliet; he hasn't many people to be kind to him. That's why I let him go so much to the Lucchesi, though I don't think Giuseppe is good for him. I expect he's there now, and going to stay all the evening, as a protest because I spoke to him last night. I don't take too much notice. He'll settle down."

"I hope he will, because I can see it worries you."

"One has to have somebody to worry about! Now come along, let's go out."

Inside the front door of Ellen's flat two letters lay face downwards on the floor. Juliet picked them up.

"Both for you, Fenny!"

At the sight of an American air-mail envelope Ellen exclaimed with pleasure:

"Shand! I was just thinking it was rather a long time since I heard from him. Will you excuse me a minute, my dear, while I see what he says?"

Taking out of her bag the spectacles which she had only just begun to wear, and which were still an irritation to her, she carried the letter to the window.

"Oh, how lovely! He's coming here!"

"Shand?"

"Yes, for a vacation. He's passed his final law exams, and he feels he must come over and see Erina. She's the widow of his great friend in the Army, Harry Jackson. It's a very sad story. Harry married this Italian girl.—Well, she was older than he was, about thirty—and he got a job in the American Embassy in Rome, and then, a year ago, he shot himself, no one knew why. Shand hasn't seen his widow since, of course. And he's coming to Florence to see me, too. I'm so glad he's coming while you are here! We used to talk about you in '45, when he was stationed in Florence, and he's often asked for news of you in his letters. You remember him, don't you?"

"Of course I do. I remember trying to sketch because he did. And all those picnics and games we had together. It will be very nice to see Shand again."

## CHAPTER II

"And you're really getting along O.K. now, Fenny?"

"Perfectly all right, thank you, my dear. I got back to my own profession soon after you left. I teach English two mornings and one afternoon a week at the Swiss school at Santa Barbara, and

241

there's a Madame Lamorne who takes about a dozen girls from sixteen upwards. I go there two mornings a week, and I have as many private pupils as I can take. I teach Italian, too, to some of the English and American people living round about. Some of them find it less daunting to learn from somebody who isn't Italian. I'm never short of work. I'm allowed to have my little income out again from England. I'm a resident, you know. It is less than it was before the war, but it's a help. There's quite enough to keep Dino and me in modest comfort. And all those parcels you and your aunts sent have made it luxury! You've been far too generous! And your letters have always been such a pleasure! And now you're here! Oh, Shand! It's lovely to see you again. It was so nice of you to come straight round here."

"Why, where else should I go in Florence? I just checked in at the hotel and threw my grips down. I didn't wait to unpack. This flat was always another home."

He looked round the cool, shuttered room.

"Do you remember what it was like when we first got you back in here? Do you remember the inches of dust on everything, and the great heap of rubble in that corner under the hole in the roof? Do you remember Harry collecting the broken crocks and glass out of the kitchen into your laundry basket, and going out right away and buying you a tea-pot?"

"Yes, indeed I do. I've still got it. I often think of that day when I use it. I am so very sorry about Harry, Shand."

"I still can't get around to it! It seems to me like the kind of thing that can't really have happened. Especially here, where it would seem natural for him to walk in at the door at any minute. When I think of all the times we reckoned we were going to be killed, and how we'd look at each other afterwards and think what luck we'd had! And then, with the war all over and Harry married to a grand girl like Erina, and with a good job in this country that he'd been crazy for from the first moment, then for him to walk out without a word to anyone and shoot himself . . . it just doesn't make sense."

"I suppose he must have had some sort of nerve-storm; a delayed after-effect of the war?"

"That's what Erina thinks. Maybe it's true. Harry always seemed kind of naked to the war. Some guys enjoyed it, and some

242

got along by growing a kind of protective skin, and doing what they had to do, and shutting out the rest. But I don't think Harry ever forgot for an hour that what it all worked out to was how many human beings you could kill. I remember him once in North Africa going through the pockets of a German prisoner who died as we were bringing him in, and turning out a lot of photographs of two kids playing in a garden, and crying. But then, when it was all over, to go and shoot himself like that, without leaving a word to Erina or me! It seems such a selfish end for Harry!"

"I think probably when people are desperate enough to kil themselves they are past thinking of anything but their own state of mind."

"Yes, I suppose that's true, but I can't help thinking we don't know all the story."

"Were he and his wife happy together?"

"I'm sure they were. He used to write me a lot about her. Erina's just knocked flat. She says there's nothing for her to go on living for. That's why I've come over, as well as to see you. It's the last thing I can do for Harry—to try if there's anything I can do for her."

"Where is she now?"

"I found a letter waiting for me. She's gone with some friends to Sicily, but she'll be coming up here in a week or two. I'll write this evening and let her know I've arrived."

"Do open the shutters, Shand. It will be cool enough now, and I want to see you better than I can in this dim light."

He unfastened the catch and leaned out to hook the shutter back against the wall. The late afternoon light came into the room, and with it the voices and footsteps of people passing on the Lung'arno below. Ellen's eyes explored affectionately the tall young man in the blond summer suit, the face that was like Grant's without the padding, a face browner than his dust-coloured hair, a little older this time than the young soldier's of four years ago, as though an invisible edge had been taken off it by the end of dedication and by the more confused issues of civilian life. Of the school-boy's brooding sullenness there was no trace. Shand was a fine young man, who looked honest, confident and kind. Ellen felt proud of him. He, too, was examining her.

"You look a lot better, Fenny, than when I saw you last. You look younger!"

She touched her hair, which had grown grey in the camp. "I was a scarecrow then!" Lately she had felt the flesh thickening round her bones.

He leant out of the window to fasten back the other shutter.

"Do you remember telling me, Fenny, when I thought I hated it all so much, that I should be glad to come back here some day? You were dead right! When I'm over there, I'm surprised how often I feel home sick for the smell and the look of it. I want to see a hill with a little town with a church tower on the top of it, or white oxen ploughing up a slope between the olives, or just any street here with the flat-fronted houses. There's a little water-colour in the spare room at my aunt's that my grandmother did over here on her honeymoon; it's only a girl's sketch of a corner of a road and two cypresses behind a garden wall, but every time I look at it I want to pack my grips and take the plane for Europe. It wasn't Italy I hated; it was the set-up at Bronciliano."

"Do you see much of your stepmother nowadays?"

"Only a duty visit now and then. I went to see her just before I sailed. She's got a house in Brooklyn always full of folk, but I should think she may be pretty lonely, really. Donata married, you know, just before my father died. And Blanche is at college, going to be a doctor. She goes her own way."

"Yes, she always did."

"Lucrezia was ready to go out to dinner when I called. She was got up with diamonds and orchids, but she looked rather yellow and stringy. She gave me a drink and hustled me out; she was afraid I should make her late. I was glad to get off with a call; I was all set to take her out to dinner if she wanted to go. Isn't it queer, Fenny? When I go to see her now, it's like going back to a place that you haven't seen since you were a kid—everything half the size you remembered. When we were at Bronciliano she just had me paralysed. I felt as if I was in a trap and shouldn't ever get away from her. Without you, maybe I never should have. And now I can't see why she made me feel like that. She's gone right out of my life; she's just someone I feel I have to be polite to sometimes. I feel rather sorry for her.

But what a dope I must have been to let her get a hold of me like that!"

"You were at a difficult age then, my dear. Things get out of proportion in your teens. Dino is just getting to that stage now. He's thirteen, you know. I want you to see him. He's growing a fine, tall boy."

"He was a skinny little dead-end kid when I last saw him. What are you going to do with him?"

"I don't know. In some ways he's precocious, in other ways very much a child. I want him to stay on at school for a bit. He goes to the monks at San Marco. I'd have liked him to stay right on and then try for a scholarship to the University here, or even in England, but he's not clever on paper or interested in learning. At present he's full of dreams about being a film star. I think perhaps soon I ought to have him taught some trade. I don't know what his bent is. I'm hoping you'll be able to help me to find out. He needs a man to take an interest in him."

"I'll certainly be glad to do anything I can. You've taken on something!"

"There was no one else to do it."

"My God, you're a good woman, Fenny!"

"No, it's not that at all. Dino is as necessary to me as I am to him!"

She went to the window and leaned out. She saw Juliet strolling along the Lung'arno, her full cotton skirt swinging out above her bare legs, her big straw hat dangling from her hand. She saw her freshly with pride, as if through the eyes of someone about to see her for the first time. Juliet looked, waved and smiled. Ellen beckoned to her to come up, and Juliet moved faster.

Ellen turned from the window.

"I've got a surprise for you." Shand was wandering round the room looking at the things he remembered. "Oh, what's that?"

"Somebody you don't expect to see here. Somebody you haven't seen for a long time."

"Dino?"

"No, not Dino."

They heard a light step in the hall. Juliet opened the door and stood in the doorway.

"Am I late, Fenny?"

"No, but look who's here."

"Shand?" Juliet exclaimed.

The young man towering behind Ellen looked puzzled.

"Don't you remember her? Don't you know who it is? It's Juliet, Shand."

## CHAPTER III

IN THE rough grass under the olives at the end of Giovanni's *orto* Ellen sat beside the picnic basket. The old couple had fled from the house when the district was being shelled, and wherever they had taken refuge—it was difficult to make out much now from Giovanni's mumbling speech—Angelina had died. He had crept back to the room in the wall of the empty villa, and somehow kept his thread of life going. He still pottered weakly in the vegetable garden and contrived to raise a few tomatoes and onions among the weeds. But he had evidently had a stroke which had partly disabled him and seemed to have scattered his wits; he did not recognize Ellen nor understand when she tried to remind him of that long-ago summer. He could not take in that Juliet was the little girl who had lived there then. Company seemed to oppress him, and he shambled off to burrow in his room for the afternoon siesta.

Ellen held the four glasses upside down to drain, wrapped them neatly in a newspaper and laid them in the basket beside the empty wine-flask. Taking off her sun spectacles, she rubbed her eyes, for the brilliant afternoon light assaulted them, shimmering back from every green blade and silver leaf. The valley below scorched in the heat. A cloud of dust that hid a travelling car moved along the road to Antella. Ellen leaned back against the twisted trunk of the olive-tree and closed her eyes.

She did not hear footsteps in the long grass, and only raised her eyelids when Juliet's voice above her said "Fenny!" Her glance shifted lazily up the bright cotton skirt of Juliet's sun-dress to her bare arm and shoulder, her face under the wide straw brim. Juliet, she reflected with satisfaction, looked very different from the pale, strained girl who had arrived a month ago.

"Fenny, do you know where Shand is?"

"I think he went to have a look round from the Tower."

"I've found the grotto we made together that first summer . . . all the stones still where we put them, and the channel still there that he dug to dam the stream! I must show him!"

"Well, I think you'll find him up there."

"Oh, good! I'll go up. I'm so sorry I woke you. Go to sleep again!"

Ellen again closed her eyes and relaxed into a delicious drowsiness. The cicadas in the cypresses were making the same creaking din that had so astonished her that first summer, and had seemed then, like so many other things, a miracle of strangeness. That feeling, which she had never quite lost, had merged, since the years in the internment camp, into another feeling: that to be alive, and free to come and go, able to eat with pleasure, and sleep comfortably, was in itself a miracle. Ordinary life, even the ticket-of-leave ordinary life of Europe half-way through this century, had never become ordinary for her again.

She opened her eyes and stretched out a lazy hand to take a cigarette from the open American packet lying beside the basket. Even this was something which for four years she had not been able to do, and she still did such things with gratitude. She drew in a mouthful of smoke, stretched her bare legs luxuriously in the long grass, and closed her eyes again.

"Fenny!"

She blinked at the pale linen of Shand's trousers.

"Fenny, have you seen Juliet?"

"She went to look for you. I told her you had gone up the Tower."

"Sorry to have disturbed your siesta!"

His long legs were moving off, but she roused herself.

"Has Dino been with you?"

"No, I don't know where he is. Asleep somewhere about, I should think."

She sighed.

"He's in one of his moods."

"He'll come out of it if he's left alone." Shand sounded authoritative and impatient. "Don't worry about the kid, Fenny. He's spoilt. He'll be O.K. Go to sleep again. I'll go look for Juliet."

She felt too lazy to argue with him. She closed her eyes, but did not at once drop off. Anxiety about Dino had been the one flaw in the happiness of the last few weeks. A line out of the prayer-book, "more than either we desire or deserve", was running constantly through her mind. It was more than she would have dared to desire or hoped to deserve that Juliet and Shand should be here with her together, both so fond of her and obviously becoming fond of each other. Ellen hugged herself with delight every time she saw them turn to each other to share a new or a remembered experience, every time she came in from work and found on her table one of Juliet's scribbled notes, "Out with Shand."

Only Dino's moody jealousy troubled her. She felt that she must have failed him, since he was still so unsure of her love. He had come more or less to accept Juliet, he admired her beauty, and responded to her friendliness; but he would not come with them if he could help it when the party included Shand. He preferred to take himself off to the Lucchesi. Ellen thought that he had a real affection for Anna, and she could not forbid his company to the old woman who had always been kind to him, but Giuseppe, with his wild discontent, his unknown ways of getting money without visible work, was not a good companion for him. Dino would come swaggering back from him with a black-market cigarette sticking out of the corner of his mouth, would speak rudely to Ellen, and probably absent himself from school next day and hang about the square. It was a bad influence, but she did not know how to break it. She worried for some time, until in the warmth and stillness anxiety seeped out of her and she fell asleep.

When she awoke Dino was sitting near her in the long grass. The shadow of the olive leaves moved in patterns over his white shirt, over the warmly coloured skin of his neck and over his bent, dark head. He was a handsome child, exceedingly like his mother, though he always preferred to think that he must be like his nameless father. He refused to believe Anna's story of the commercial traveller who had stayed for one week at the hotel where Margherita worked as a chambermaid. He had evolved a theory that he had really been fathered by some distinguished man who did not wish to be known. Ellen was never sure how

248

far he really believed this or how far it was a façade erected to save his pride.

He was absorbed now in something which he held in his hand. Seeing that she was awake, he moved nearer and showed her a young bird, starling barely old enough to fly.

"*Ecco*, Fenni." She had taught him to call her Fenny, like her other children. "*Poverino!*" With one finger he tenderly touched the brown head.

"Where did you find it, Dino?"

"On the lawn, under the cypresses. It must have fallen out of the nest, perhaps."

"Is it hurt?"

"I don't think so. It flapped its wings once."

"Poor little thing! it's too terrified to move. I expect it was learning to fly."

"What shall I do with it?"

"I think I should put it gently back on the grass where you found it. The mother will come for it."

"Yes, I'll do that."

He walked away, speaking softly to the fledgling, his head bent over it.

His gentleness to animals and birds, rare in boys of his nation, was a reassurance and delight to Ellen, and seemed to compensate for the violence in him that she found so difficult to deal with. She watched him as he strolled back to her across the grass. When Shand had been a broody boy she had always known what to do with him; but, fond as she was of him, she had watched his moods with a degree of detachment which her anxious heart found impossible with Dino, so entirely her child.

He came back and sat down beside her in the grass.

"They are very rich, the people who own this villa?"

"They were, but they aren't now. They have had to pay two lots of death duties—taxes that have to be paid in England when somebody dies and the heir inherits his estate, just as they have to be paid here. The owner of the villa is now a child."

"They will sell it?"

"I think they would probably like to, if they could find anyone

249

to buy it; but it is so big and would want such a lot doing to it."

"I should like to buy it! I would have it repaired and we would live there. I do not like small houses."

Ellen laughed.

"If you want a big one you'll have to make a lot of money to buy it with and keep it up."

"Giuseppe says that it is quite easy to make money if you only have a little to start with."

"In honest ways, Dino?"

Dino shrugged his shoulders. Ellen did not feel in the mood for lecturing. She decided to let it go for this afternoon.

Dino rolled over and took a cigarette out of the American packet that Shand had left lying by the picnic basket. As he lit it, he shot a defiant glance at Ellen. She thought him too young to smoke, but she could not be always nagging, and at the moment she was not going to bother. She smiled lazily at him, and he suddenly grinned back at her.

"But of course if I go on the films! Giuseppe says that he could get me a film test in Rome. Film stars become very rich. Then I would buy this villa, and while I am away making films you would live here and take care of it for me. You would no longer have to teach."

"I like teaching."

He brushed that away.

"I should not leave you here alone all the time. When I go to America to make a film I would take you with me."

"In the meantime I thought that perhaps next Saturday we might go to San Gimignano. Shand says he can hire a car. Juliet hardly remembers it; she would like to see it again, and you've never been there."

"Shand Warner is very rich?"

"His father was, and I think Shand has plenty of money."

"Why, then, does he work?"

"I suppose he wants to do something useful."

Dino looked bored.

"When will he go back to America?"

"In a few weeks. He has to see the Signora Jackson, the widow of his friend who died."

"They say"—Dino always knew the gossip of Florence long before Ellen did—"they say that Bernardo Moldini wishes to marry the Signora Jackson. She is beautiful?"

"I never saw her. Harry only met her after he left Florence and was stationed in Rome."

"I think that she must be beautiful. Bernardo Moldini is very rich. He comes from Milano, but he has an *appartamento* in Rome and a *palazzo* in Venice."

"Dino, you are always thinking about whether people are rich! It isn't the only thing that matters."

"It is the most important."

"It's not as important as being well, or happy, or good."

"Without money it is not possible to be well, or happy, or good."

"Well, not without any money at all, probably. But you and I live very comfortably on quite a small income."

"When I am a man it will not be sufficient for me to live comfortably on a small income. It was not enough for Lorenzo il Magnifico."

"No, but that was a long time ago, and he was one of the rulers of Florence."

"Well, I shall be a film star, and because my name will be above the cinema, everyone will come and see me, and so I shall rule over Florence!"

"All right, Dino! I shall be delighted to come and see you!"

"No one," Dino said viciously, "will ever come to see the Signor Shand Warner."

"Perhaps he doesn't want them to."

Dino made a contemptuous face, and helped himself to another cigarette out of Shand's packet. Ellen dropped the packet into the picnic-basket and closed the lid.

"Dino, you don't need to be jealous of Shand. You and I are a family. Shand is only a friend. He will soon go back to America." She added, half despising herself for doing so, "If you want to go to America someday, as you always say you do, you are very foolish not to be nice to him. He might help you to get a job there."

"Yes, that is true," Dino agreed.

She looked at him with half-amused despair. There were

times when his steady eye on the main chance revolted her, other times when he made her wonder whether the civilization in which she had been brought up was half-hypocrisy.

"If I am very good during the visit of the Signorina Juliet and Shand Warner, will you give me the money to go and have a film test in Rome?"

"You know very well that I would always help you with any real opportunity. But I shan't give you money to go and play about in Rome just because Giuseppe says he thinks he can get you a film test. If you get a definite appointment I would take you myself, perhaps. But," she added, driven by conscience, "that's not a very good reason for behaving well to my guests!"

"Then I will be good to them because you ask me, *carissima*!"

He touched her hand. His infrequent demonstrations of affection never failed to move her, even though she sometimes knew that there was an element of calculation in them. She experienced a rare moment of exquisite happiness. Her three children—Juliet, Shand, Dino—all here with her in the perfect summer weather, all in harmony with her and with each other. What more could she want?

.　　.　　.　　.　　.

They got off the tram in Florence and walked along the Lung'arno, Juliet and Shand in front, each holding a handle of the picnic basket. She thought of telling Dino to take Juliet's handle, but decided not to strain his good resolution too far, and she was unwilling to interrupt the absorbed conversation of Juliet and Shand. At the doorway of the flat they stopped and waited for the others to come up.

"We don't have to let a day like this finish early," Shand said. "Why don't you and Juliet have dinner with me, Fenny, at Doney's?"

"I think I won't, thank you, Shand. I've got rather a lot of work to correct for tomorrow. You two go. Dino and I will have supper together."

"You have dinner with me, then, Juliet?"

Their obvious satisfaction in the arrangement gave Ellen a mixture of pleasure and pain. She looked apprehensively at Dino, but he only said amiably, "I shall make a *sformagata* while you correct the exercises." He was an excellent if temperamental

252

cook, and was willing to exercise his talents quite often so long as he was sufficiently praised for them.

"I was thinking, Shand, that if you could get a car for next Saturday we might all go to San Gimignano?"

"Why, certainly, I'd like that. Oh, but I can't on Saturday. Erina's arriving on the afternoon train. I had a postcard from her in this morning's mail, asking me to meet her at the station. You know how it is, Fenny. I can't let her arrive and find no one there."

"No, of course you can't."

"Maybe if you could square your pupils we could go the Saturday after, and take Erina? I want to have her know you all."

Juliet said, "Yes, let's wait till she can come too. We must do everything we can to make it nice for her."

"Anyhow, she won't be here for a week." Ellen spoke with a briskness she did not intend. "You two go off and have dinner together. Dino and I will eat the *sformagata* at home."

## CHAPTER IV

ELLEN FINISHED correcting two batches of translations, and began to tidy her desk. Juliet had been writing letters there, and had made havoc of all Ellen's precise arrangements, drawing cats on the clean blotting-paper, filling the pen-tray with cigarette ash, upsetting a box of paper-clips. Oh, dear, Ellen thought, I wish she'd write at the table. Then she rebuked herself: I must be getting what they call set in my ways. As she crossed the room to throw a handful of torn-up envelopes in the waste-paper basket, she caught sight of herself in the mirror. With her dark blue cotton dress, her neat grey hair, her face, which now that the colour and roundness of youth had left it looked bony and long. She was the very picture of a middle-aged school teacher. The happiness of the afternoon had faded out of her. The mirror brought her face to face with what life had done to her, or what she had done with it. A wild rebellion and longing shook her. Was this all? She went back to the window-seat, and sat looking at the lights of the Ponte Vecchio reflected in the thin, sluggish

stream of the Arno. The warmth of the summer night, the voices
and footsteps of lovers and friends strolling on the Lung'arno,
increased her pain. When younger she had always pushed unhappiness away from her, if only with those undefined hopes of
the future which all the young have as the distant landscape of the
heart. Tonight she felt that there was nowhere else to look. She
allowed her unhappiness to go through her. But there was still
something in her which clamoured to fight against it, in other
lives if not in her own. She was glad when she heard Juliet's
footsteps on the stairs.

Juliet switched on the light, and they blinked at each other
across the room. The girl was radiant with the glow of one who
had all day been absorbing light and air and happiness.

"Still up, Fenny? I thought I was very late."

"I had rather a lot of work to do; I left it last night, you know.
And then I was just too lazy to start going to bed."

"Wouldn't you like a cup of tea? I'll make some."

"Have you had a nice evening?"

"Absolutely lovely."

Juliet went through into the kitchen.

"Good Lord, Fenny! you've been washing the floor, and you
said you were tired!"

"No, Dino did that before he went to bed. He was in a fit of
penitence for his sulks, poor boy!"

"Won't hurt him!"

Above the familiar kitchen noises—water pouring, the creak of
the opening cupboard door, the chink of cup on saucer—Ellen
heard Juliet singing softly and happily to herself, one of the
dance-tunes of the year. She came to the door with a lemon in her
hand.

"This is the only one; all right to use it? I'll get some more in
the morning. I arranged to meet Shand early and take him to the
market. He's never been, and I think it's such fun."

She came back with the tea-tray, and established herself with it
on the floor by Ellen's knee.

"You've never been to America, have you, Fenny?"

"No. Shand and his aunts have very kindly asked me several
times, but I've never been able to manage it."

"It must be wonderful to be in a new country that's beginning to make its history, and not in one that's old and tired. Don't you long to go?"

Ellen that evening felt old and tired, too.

"I think I should always feel more at home in Europe."

"I think I should like it over there. I should love to go."

"I hope you will go one day."

"Yes, I hope I shall!"

Some young people going home on the far side of the river were singing a Neapolitan love-song. Their voices rose and fell in the summer darkness.

"Shand has been telling me how you rescued him from Lucrezia! She was a bitch, wasn't she? I remember her quite well. She was always calling me 'darling', and I knew she didn't mean it. She *would* kiss me every time we went there, and I hated her scent. I used to go down the garden and rub her off. It was a horrid house. I don't wonder Shand was miserable there. It was wonderful of you to get him out of it! And then you lost your job. I never heard, really, what happened to you after that. Why didn't you come home before the war? How did you get into the camp?"

The months of precarious joy and searing anguish came back to Ellen.

"Oh, I stayed on in Italy too long because I had friends in difficulties."

Juliet accepted the casual explanation with the readiness of the very young for whom only the affairs of their own generation are quite real.

"We went up to the Piazzale Michelangelo this evening and sat and talked for a long time. Have you ever noticed, Fenny, when you are just getting to know a new person very well, how it seems to make everything new? It's almost like being born again. You feel as if you wanted to look at everything together, and it's as if everything you look at had been dipped in a bath and come out with the colours fresh and unfaded."

"Yes, I have noticed that."

Juliet glanced at her for a second. Ellen saw in her eyes the fleeting questions, When? With whom?

"What I like so much about Shand is that he is so positive and uninhibited. He always knows what he wants to do, and it

255

seems to him the obvious thing to try to do it. For instance, he knows that later on he wants to go into politics. He doesn't just laugh and say that politics are a dirty game and there's nothing to choose between either side, as people so often do in England. He says that in this century the world has become America's responsibility, and he'd like to have a hand in it. I respect him for that!"

And for anything else he does or says at the moment, Ellen thought. She reflected that Shand at sixteen had not been sure of what he wanted to do or uninhibited about doing it. Had he outgrown his difficulties, or only succeeded in avoiding situations that caused them?

"Life is so extraordinarily inconsequent, don't you think, Fenny? It takes you on to the next thing by pure chance."

"Perhaps it only seems inconsequent."

"How do you mean?"

"I mean I think there's a very deep pattern in our lives, often a repeating pattern so deep that we only see it occasionally, and what we do or what happens to us often seems like pure chance, but it's really all very closely knit. It's just that we don't see the pattern."

"It does seem to me the most extraordinary chance that I should have come out to Florence to see you at the same time as Shand."

"Our lives are a network of currents, I think, really. We don't understand yet how or where they pick up the currents of other people's lives."

Yours and mine, she thought, joined before you were born, when I sat at the schoolroom table at Hawton Towers chewing my pencil and learning the dates of the Wars of the Roses, and making up tales to myself about those bad water-colours of the Villa Meridiana. And Grant Warner, then a rising man, making money on Wall Street, and perhaps then he had not met Shand's mother. And here, she thought drowsily, we all are.

"So unusually blue?"

Ellen roused herself.

"What, my dear?"

"I was saying did you know anybody else except Shand who had such unusually blue eyes?"

256

# CHAPTER V

SITTING OUTSIDE one of the cafés in the Piazza della Repubblica on Saturday evening, Ellen realized that the tiredness that had oppressed her when she woke in the morning, and had increased as she cleaned the flat and prepared for the week-end, had only been halted by the siesta. Even the short walk from her flat to the square had brought back the ache at the top of her spine and the dragging heaviness of her limbs. She felt the café intolerably crowded and noisy. She looked away from it at the chattering, milling crowd under the colonnade, at the line of cars following one another past the white-coated policeman on his pedestal in the middle of the square. He seemed to recede from her in the rich evening light; he and the cars and the opposite buildings began to reel over backwards. With an effort she brought them again into focus. In spite of the heat, she felt a wave of chill. Sweat poured down her sides from under her armpits, her forehead was covered by trickling drops springing from under her hair. I suppose I was faint for a minute, she thought; I must be a bit run down. She wiped her face and ordered a campari soda. The tonic bitterness of the drink revived her. She lit a cigarette, astonished to find her hands shaking.

She caught sight of Juliet on the other side of the square. She watched her with pride as she threaded her leisurely way through the crowd. Juliet has something that Madeleine never had; Madeleine was very pretty, but Juliet is beautiful. Beauty was in her fluid grace of movement, in her long limbs and the carriage of her head. She looked very young and clean and fresh, in a crisp white cotton dress with a pattern of black and yellow. Ellen saw several heads turned to look at her, but she was unconscious of them, sauntering as if her thoughts were very much occupied. She looked solitary to Ellen, who realized that it was a long time since she had seen her in the town without Shand. He must, she supposed, have been meeting Erina. There was no doubt that from Ellen's point of view Erina, with her tragic claim to every consideration and with all Shand's affection for Harry to back it, was going to be a nuisance! Still, poor woman, she couldn't help it. She had a claim to

257

sympathy, if anybody had. Ellen reproached herself for unkindness.

Juliet saw her, and came across to her table.

"Hello, Fenny! I didn't see you. Isn't it hot?"

"Have you seen Shand?"

"Not since lunch. He was going to meet Erina at the station. He asked me to come, but I wouldn't. I thought probably she'd rather see him at first without a stranger there. I went round to her *pension* and left some flowers to welcome her. Then I sat in one of the cloisters. What are you drinking? Campari? Oh no, I'd rather have something sweeter."

"Do you know how long Erina is going to be here?"

"I've no idea. I suppose as long as Shand is. In a way it must be awful for her seeing him again. Not only because it must remind her of the time when they were all happy together after the war. But she must wonder if he blames her. He doesn't, of course; but you would blame yourself, wouldn't you? You couldn't help it. You'd think you ought to have seen it coming. You'd wonder even if something you'd done or said might have pushed it on, and you'd feel if only you'd been more sympathetic or understood better you could have prevented it. That must be almost the worst part of it. I do feel awfully sorry for her."

Juliet paused, sipped her drink and added:

"But I must say I rather hope she doesn't want to come everywhere with us. It's been such fun."

Ellen said with some asperity:

"She has an old aunt here, hasn't she? I should think she'll have to spend some time with her."

"Of course we must include her in things. I know very well when you've lost anybody that one of the things you want is for everyone to treat you naturally. So many of them go shy and leave a kind of space round you. Or perhaps that's only in England. Oh, there's Shand coming along now, and I suppose that's Erina with him."

Juliet stood up and waved.

Shand came towards them, weaving his way between the tables, with a young woman in a dark red cotton dress at his heels. Ellen had a fleeting impression of somebody hostile and wary. Then it faded as Shand introduced Erina with proprietary pride, as if he were bringing his sister to his friends, and Erina smiled and responded gracefully to their greetings.

She took Juliet's hand in both hers.

"It is you, Signorina, that I have to thank for those lovely flowers! I cannot tell you what it meant to me to find such a welcome! Not only because they were so beautiful, but that you should have such a thought for me! When those flowers were brought up to my room, I said 'Those cannot be for me, because I have seen Shand, and there is no one else in Firenze who would think of sending them to me.' And then I read the card, and I feel that already I have a friend."

Ellen was observing her. She was of medium height, compact rather than slim, with neat hands and feet. Her face was square, browned by the sun, but otherwise without colour; her eyes large, of a hazel so light as to be almost yellow; her hair, a shade darker, was pushed behind her ears, and hung in a rather lank bob to her shoulders. Everything about her was unremarkable, but the impact was not. Ellen listened to her cordial exchanges with Juliet, who looked open, candid and eager to make friends.

"And you have come out here for a holiday, Shand tells me, because you were here once as a little girl. Well, that is very nice. I hope that you can make a long visit."

"I'm hoping to stay till the beginning of August, if Fenny can put up with me."

"It would be a pity that you should go away while Shand is here. It is so charming that you should have met again, after all these years."

"I'm so glad that you were able to come up while I am here. Will you be staying with your aunt?"

"No, she is very old, and her flat is very small; it is better that I stay in my room at the *pension*."

"I do wish that I spoke Italian as well as you speak English!"

"I am sure that you speak it beautifully, as Shand does."

"No, I don't. I was only here for a few months when I was eight years old."

"Well, that is always something. One does not entirely forget."

"I practise in the shops and with Dino, Fenny's adopted child."

"You shall practise with me; we will speak it together."

259

Shand was looking on at these exchanges with an air of satisfaction which Ellen suddenly found rather fatuous.

"Juliet, I called for our photographs." He took a cardboard wallet out of his pocket. "They aren't all good. I reckon I haven't got the exposure right yet, but there's one of you sitting on the garden wall at Meridiana that's cute, and one of Fenny and Dino in the *orto*."

He spread the photographs on the table, between himself and Juliet. Juliet's face, turned towards him, lit up with an unguarded happiness, their two heads bent over the photograph. Erina watched them for a minute smiling with her mouth but not with her eyes. Then she turned to Ellen.

"Signorina Fenny, I have for so long wanted to meet you because I have heard so much about you from Harry, and I have wanted to thank you for all your kindness to him. He has said how you made your flat a home for him and for Shand when they were stationed here at the end of the war."

"It was I who had reason to be grateful to Shand and Harry! Dino and I were nearly starving when they found me. They helped me to get my flat back and to get it repaired, and settled me in again and found me some work with the Allied Control Commission until I could start earning my living by teaching. . . ."

"Yes, but for them all that was easy. What you did for them was much more difficult: to make a home where they could come at any time. Harry was very homesick, always. I think perhaps it would have been better if we had gone away—right away from everything that reminded him of the war. But do not let us talk of that now. I hope so much that you will let me come and see you, and that we may have many talks together while Juliet and Shand are amusing themselves. I have always made friends among Englishwomen, more easily than with my own countrymen. They seem to me to have a very deep and true quality that makes for real friendship. I hope so much that you and I will be friends."

"Do come and see me whenever you like," Ellen replied. "I'm generally free after six."

She felt that they had some way to go before they could talk of being friends, but she was not impervious to the charm of the genial approach, even while something held her back from a fuller response. She was prepared to take on the Signora Jackson to almost any extent to prevent her from being an encumbrance to Juliet and Shand.

Shand turned round to her now and said:

"Fenny, I was telling Erina that we planned to go to San Gimignano next Saturday. I'll fix a car. I suppose we take Dino too?"

"He'd like to come, I'm sure."

"Where is Dino?"

"At the cinema. I told him to join us here at half-past seven."

"It's after that now."

"He gets quite bemused when he's watching a film and forgets all about the time. But he said the big picture finished at seven-thirty, so I expect he'll be here in a minute."

"I want so much to see him," Erina said eagerly. "Shand has told me how you have taken him when his mother died in the camp. That, I think, is very good! To make a home for a child, that is something that I admire!"

"Here he is."

Dino, his eyes full of cinema dreams, was strolling at his leisure across the square. He came up to their table and stood by Ellen's chair, acknowledging the introduction to Erina with a formal bow. The look that passed between the two Italians was like one of recognition.

"Now we can go," Shand said. "I booked a table for eight at that restaurant by the river."

"*Carissimo*, it was not necessary to book for so early. No one will be there until nine."

"Well, Erina, I'm hungry, and some of you folks are too, I daresay. Come along."

"I have not had a drink," Dino expostulated.

"You'll have to have it there, son!"

"I am very hot and thirsty from the cinema."

"Dino!" Ellen said gently.

He hesitated, but decided to abandon his evident intention of making a scene. He walked with Ellen and Juliet. Erina and Shand went on ahead.

"She's awfully nice, Fenny, don't you think?" Juliet said. "So brave! It must be very difficult seeing Shand again, and meeting

261

strangers who know all about it. And she's so friendly. I shouldn't call her pretty, would you? But there's something very attractive about her face. I think she'll be easy to get on with."

"Yes, she seems ready to make friends."

Shand turned his head and called to Juliet. She ran forward to join them. They showed her something in a shop window. Shand walked on between Erina and Juliet. Ellen saw Erina slip her hand lightly through the crook of his arm.

"*Ecco la* Signora Jackson!" Dino said.

"Yes. Do you like her?"

Ellen was always interested in Dino's opinion of people: he had flashes of natural shrewdness that far outran her own.

He shrugged his shoulders and said in Italian:

"The Signorina Juliet had better look out."

## CHAPTER VI

On a seat in a garden high above the miraculous towers of San Gimignano, Ellen sat resting in the shade. They had come up here for the view, but the midday sun had beaten them off the highest point. The others were exploring the garden which shelved steeply down from Ellen's seat to a low wall. It belonged to an empty villa, whose caretakers made a supplementary income by allowing visitors to come in and look down upon the town and over the spreading Tuscan landscape beyond.

A little way below her, Juliet and Shand emerged together from behind an uncut box hedge and sat down on a stone seat beside a broken fountain. Juliet pulled off her big hat and let it fall on to the weedy gravel of the path. Their voices came up so clearly that Ellen could with an effort have heard what they were saying. They were very much absorbed. The others were not in sight, but in a few minutes Erina's high-pitched voice came in a long wail from behind the hedge:

"Shand!"

He did not at once turn his head.

"Shand! I have broken the strap of my sandal! I cannot walk!"

Shand got up, spoke to Juliet, shrugged his shoulders and moved off towards the hidden voice. He disappeared behind the hedge. Juliet remained on the seat, leaning forward, kicking at a large weed in the gravel with the toe of her sandal. Presently she picked up her hat and climbed the steps to Ellen's seat.

"Ouf! It really is almost too hot!"

She dropped down beside Ellen. Below them Erina and Shand emerged from behind the box hedge. He was carrying the sandal, she was hopping on one foot, holding on to his arm and chattering. She sat down on the seat, and he sat beside her, his hands busy with the strap. Her rattling laugh came up to them.

"Shand goes back a month today," Juliet said.

"Do you know how long Erina is staying in Florence?"

"No. She says that her aunt is failing and needs her."

"Her aunt doesn't see much of her!"

"Erina says it means so much to her if anyone needs her now."

Below them Shand knelt on the gravel adjusting the strap over Erina's instep. Her foot was on his knee, her hand on his shoulder.

"Fenny, why do you think Harry Jackson committed suicide?"

"To get away from his wife."

"Fenny!" Juliet grinned with delight, "that's the only really spiteful thing I ever heard you say!"

Erina and Shand got up from the seat, and sauntered along the path until the box hedge hid them from sight.

"She still talks about killing herself; she says that whenever she is lonely or depressed, it seems to her the only thing to do. That's why Shand says we must take her everywhere with us."

"Shand is very soft-hearted."

"I know. It's one of the nice things about him."

"And of course he was so devoted to Harry. What was Harry like?"

"Oh, a pleasant, gentle, shy boy. I never saw as much in him as Shand saw."

But, then, she thought, one can't expect to see what the young see in each other. Their particular illumination does not shine for our eyes.

"Do you think that Erina is the kind of person to commit suicide?"

"I do not."

"Neither do I. When I said that to Shand he said perhaps not, because she has so much vitality and courage, but he said he should never forgive himself if he didn't help her over this difficult patch. He came out to do it."

"Perhaps he won't have to. Dino says that there's a rich Italian somewhere in the background who wants to marry her."

"Oh, does he?" Juliet's voice sounded livelier. "That would be much the best thing, wouldn't it?"

"Much, except possibly for the rich Italian."

"You don't like her, do you, Fenny?"

"Not really," Ellen produced her final condemnation, "I don't think she's genuine. And I get exasperated by the fuss she makes about everything."

"I don't altogether dislike her. I wish I did. Sometimes when we're alone together I enjoy talking to her. She's often very nice to me, and she's interesting, and I feel that we have a lot in common. She can be rather fascinating. But directly there are other people there she changes and starts forcing herself on everybody's attention all the time." Everybody, thought Ellen, being Shand. "And it makes me feel closed up in myself, and I can't join in. And she will keep on talking about the times when she and Shand and Harry were together in Rome before Shand went back, and of course he likes remembering about Harry, and I didn't know him."

"Shand can't spend his life remembering Harry . . . I doubt very much if Erina will."

"Do you think she loved him?"

"As an appendage to herself, probably. I think she's too much in love with herself to be really able to love anybody else."

"I hope you don't say those things to Shand?"

"I've never discussed her with him."

Juliet looked disappointed.

"But I may, Juliet. I think it's quite time we had lunch. Let's call the others and go to the hotel.

.    .    .    .    .

As they drove along the Porta Romana towards the Arno, Shand said:

"And now let's all have tea at Doney's and finish a good party."

Erina, who was sitting next to him in the front seat because she always felt sick in the back of a car, protested:

"Oh, no, Shand, I do not feel like tea at Doney's! Everyone is so smart, and we are so hot and dusty; and it is so noisy and so full of people. No, I think much better you all come to my room at the *pension*. I have a bottle of cinzano and some lemons; I shall give you all a drink."

"Wait a minute," Shand said irritably. He was busy trying to park the car in a narrow space. Having achieved this, he sat back, pulled out a cigarette and said with some decision, "No, thank you, Erina; I want tea. Juliet likes tea at Doney's . . ."

"That for me is to spoil a nice day—that we should go and sit in that hot place with a lot of dressed-up people! Much better we all have a little party in my quiet room."

Nobody really liked parties in Erina's quiet room, where her laugh seemed to rattle back at them from the walls and there were not enough chairs. Ellen was glad to see that Shand looked mutinous.

"I have a terrible headache," Erina said, passing her hand over her forehead. "I would prefer to go home."

Dino immediately asked Ellen for some money for the cinema. Abstractedly she handed him a note, and he slid out of the car and disappeared.

"Shand, please, I do not feel in the mood for Doney's."

"Well, I'm ready to do what everyone wants, but I'd like a cup of tea right now, and I daresay Fenny and Juliet would."

It was clear that not to have tea at Doney's had become for Erina an assertion of power. The note of hysteria in her voice suddenly reminded Ellen of Lucrezia.

"Shand, I think you are very selfish! You can see that Fenni is tired; she has had a long, hot day. And I am sure that what she would like would be to sit quietly in my room. She does not want to be crowded up in a hot café."

"What do you say, Juliet?"

"I should like tea, really." To Ellen's regret, Juliet added, "but not if you don't feel up to it, Erina."

"Most certainly I do not feel up to it. I shall go to the *pension*."

Shand, who obviously did not want to decide, assumed the air of a man beset by a pack of unreasonable women, and began:

265

"Well . . ."

Ellen struck in:

"I think you are right, Erina. I am rather tired, and if you have a headache you had much better go home. I should like to go back to your room with you, and we'll leave Juliet and Shand to have tea at Doney's."

She saw Juliet's brightening face. Erina opened her mouth for a further protest, but perhaps Shand had had enough of the insistent voice in his ear, for he said promptly:

"That fixes us all, then. Come on, Juliet!"

Joyfully, two young people escaping from their elders, they ran across the pavement and into the café.

Ellen glanced at Erina and saw her face distorted with frustration. She thought, she's mad! Then Erina pulled her face straight and hooked her hand through Ellen's elbow.

"Let us go, then, quietly and sit down in my room. There are always too many people about; I am so tired of them. It is only with someone like you that I can be myself. Let us go and have a little talk."

.    .    .    .    .

Slicing a curl of lemon-peel into a glass of vermouth, Erina said:

"You know, Fenni, I always feel that there is a special bond between you and me because we have both suffered."

"I don't know that I have suffered any more than anyone expects to by the time they get to my age."

"But yes, I read it in your face. I am one of those who can read faces. Directly I saw you I said to myself: The Signorina Fenni is one of those who have been enriched by suffering. For some people, such as my poor Harry, suffering has been a wall that closes them in, but with you it has made your sympathies very wide. I am sure that you have been through some tragedy. Perhaps, like me, you have thought of taking your own life?"

"Certainly not."

"Never?"

"Never. I should think it was wrong, even if I wanted to do it."

"You are a Catholic?"

"No."

"But your own Church forbids it?"

"I suppose so—at least, it wouldn't approve of it, I should think."

"But that does not mean very much to you? Why, then, should you think it wrong? To die this year or in ten years time, how is it so different?"

"I think it makes all the difference."

"But I am curious to know why you should think so? Especially when you remember all those who in one way or another have so lately died in Europe. Thousands driven into gas-chambers, and crushed under bombed houses. Can it really seem to you that your own life is of so much importance?"

"Yes, it does, in a way. I think I feel what Dickens said. You have read the works of Dickens?"

"Certainly, with my English governess."

"He said, 'I don't know what life is, but I feel that it is something to defend at all costs.' "

"How strange! But, then, he was not writing in this century."

"I don't think one century is so very different from another."

"I hope that you will prove to be right. A little more vermouth?"

"No, thank you."

"You see, I do not think that anything matters very much."

Ellen was tempted to say, I suppose that's why you had to make such a fuss about whether we should or should not have tea at Doney's. How boring it is sometimes when there is such a gap between how people feel and how they say they feel! It really makes a conversation like this not worth going on with! She put down her empty glass and thought how much she would like a cup of tea—a good strong cup. The room, dim behind the closed shutters, seemed to her very hot and close. She felt Erina's personality pressing against hers, and her own rising to resist it; there was a kind of excitement in the struggle which she both liked and disliked.

"I will tell you," Erina said, "what has made it seem worth while to me to take up my life again. It is because since I have come here you have all shown me so much kindness, and especially because Shand has troubled to come here from the States to help me. That is something that I cannot forget, that I should mean so much to him!"

267

"Shand is very kind-hearted."

"When we were all in Rome together, you know, after they had been stationed up here, those boys were both so much in love with me! But it was Harry that I loved then. I thought it was so sweet that they remained always good friends and never quarrelled."

Yes, Ellen reflected, that was probably true. In that time just after the war, when they had been stationed in Florence, Shand had been in love with a different Italian girl every week, almost, and she and Harry had laughed at him about them. But he had not cared as much about any of them as about Harry. Probably he had had a fancy for Erina, and later, when she married Harry, he would have been very much more jealous of her. Which would account for the remorse that seemed now to be part of his feeling for her. There was something tangled and dark in it; he never looked happy with her, as he did with Juliet. Remembering that he and Juliet were alone together again almost for the first time since Erina's arrival, Ellen picked up her glass:

"Erina, may I change my mind and have a little more vermouth?"

"But of course! You know, Fenni, I must say that I am so very fond of Juliet! I think that she is a most charming young girl, so fresh, so unspoilt. She is to become an actress?"

"Yes, she has been trained for that. It is in her family. She is going back to join an English repertory company in September."

"She is very talented?"

"I really don't know. She says that she is only passable. I don't think it is a passion with her. I think that she will marry."

"There is someone in England?"

"Not that I know of," Ellen replied shortly.

"I am sure there must be."

"Whether the man who will marry her is in England or anywhere else, he will be very lucky. Juliet is loving and generous, as well as beautiful."

"That is just what I have been saying," Erina replied blandly.

A silence charged with hostility fell between them.

"I must be going back to the flat, Erina. I have to get supper ready."

"You are always doing something for others! I am so glad that we have had this little talk. And you would advise me to take up my life again?"

"Of course I should. Perhaps you could find some useful work that would help you."

"Ah, that is like you, who are always practical. I am afraid that I am a dreamer. I am sorry that you must go!"

"I am sure that as you have a headache you must want to lie down."

"It is very much better now, thank you, since we have had this quiet rest. I think that perhaps in a little while I shall go round to the square and have a drink with Shand."

.   .   .   .   .

On her way back to the flat Ellen stopped to buy some fruit, but found that she had nothing in her bag except some small change. She searched for the five-thousand-lire note that she knew had been there that morning. She must have lost it! Then she remembered. Absorbed in the argument about tea, she had hastily thrust what she thought was a five-hundred-lire note into Dino's hand. She must have given him the larger one. He would not have looked at it, she supposed, until he got to the cinema, and he would never turn back on the doorstep of his Heaven. He would bring the change later. She explained, promised to pay on Monday and went on home.

She opened the shutters and let in the cooling air. The flat seemed very pleasant and peaceful. Relaxing in solitude, Ellen sat down at the kitchen table and began to slice liver and onions. She was pleased that Juliet's tea with Shand had apparently outlasted her visit to Erina and her walk home.

Dino was the first of her household to return. She heard his footsteps on the stairs, and turned from the pan to see him standing in the doorway of the kitchen. He had an air, at once jaunty and hostile, which she had learned to recognize. He had probaby been with Giuseppe, and Giuseppe had stood him a *negroni* or two. She suspected that he often did, for lately Dino had shown signs of boredom with the *arangata* or ice-cream soda that she thought suitable to his years.

"Well, my dear, was it a good film?"

He shrugged his shoulders.

"It was rather stupid." With an air he presented her with a gardenia wrapped in cellophane. "I bought this for you to wear, Fenni. I will fetch a pin."

"Thank you very much! How pretty! But it will only die if I wear it now while I am cooking. Will you bring me a little vase and we'll put it in the other room, where it's cooler."

He had his back to her, reaching down the vase out of the cupboard, when she said:

"Oh, will you let me have the change? It was so silly, I gave you the wrong note. I couldn't pay for the fruit."

"Change! But you gave me only a five-hundred-lire note!"

"No, my dear, I didn't. I gave you five thousand lire by mistake."

He was inserting the flower in the vase with delicate fingers.

"No, really it was five hundred lire."

Her heart stopped for a second and then raced on. Something like this had happened once or twice before.

"Dino, dear, I had only the one big note and some small ones in my bag. I meant to give you five hundred lire, but I gave you the other one by mistake. You must give me the change."

He went off as if she had touched an electric switch.

"You do not trust me!" he screamed. "You would suggest that I have taken the money? You call me a liar! You would not say such a thing to Shand Warner! It is because I am a beggar living on your charity, because I have no father, no mother! Of course you hate me because you have to work to keep me! Always this fuss about money, so little money! If you loved me you would believe my word. You do not call Shand Warner a thief!"

Tired as she was, she felt her knees shaking, but she had learnt that the best way to deal with these passions was to show no signs of disturbance.

"Dino, the change, please!"

His face contorted with fury, he thrust his hand into his trouser pocket, pulled out a crumpled wad of notes, threw them on the floor at her feet, rushed out of the flat and slammed the door. She heard him flinging himself down the stairs. She picked up the notes and smoothed them out. He had spent nearly two thousand lire; probably had met Giuseppe and stood him a drink or two after the cinema. She felt achingly sorry for him because he felt so frustrated in the life in which they had to be careful, because the love which she freely gave him had not been enough to make up for early deprivations. Long before he came into the camp he must have felt himself an unwanted child, and for his bruised self-esteem she had found no cure. What would become of him if ever anything happened to her? Again, as in the café, she had the sensation of the world receding from her behind falling black veils. Steadying herself to lift the pan off the ring, she stumbled into a chair by the table and pressed the palms of her hands over her eyes.

She was still sitting there, although beginning to feel better, when Juliet came in. She had again that glow of happiness that made her look as though light was shining through her skin. She exclaimed at once:

"Fenny, you look quite done in! Did Erina wear you out? Sit still and let me finish that. Are you all right?"

"I'm only tired. I've been feeling a bit run down lately. It's the heat. Yes, will you finish the sauce? You remember how? Tell me what you've been doing."

"We had tea at Doney's, and then we went to the straw market and chose some presents for Shand's aunts, and he bought me . . . look, Fenny, this red-and-white bag to match my dress."

"How pretty!"

"He's got the most lovely plan for my birthday. He's going to get the car and take me for a day to the sea. He said we'd find a quiet beach and bathe, and then have lunch at Viareggio, and perhaps bathe again and come back by Pisa and Lucca. Just ourselves, he said—no one else at all. I mean"—colour swept up under Juliet's clear skin to her hair—"we knew you'd be working."

"Of course. I'm delighted about it. Thursday's one of my very busy days, so I'm so glad you've got something fixed up. You and Shand can come back here and have a late birthday supper at any time you like."

"Just ourselves?"

"Just ourselves. I'll give Dino some money to go to the pictures."

"Oh, I don't mind Dino, of course! I wouldn't want to shut him out of a supper-party in your flat. I wondered just that once, need we have Erina? It would be nice to have the whole day without her. But of course I don't want to be too unkind. I expect she'll come round. And you can't give *her* money to go to the pictures!"

"There may be other ways."

"You don't think, do you, Fenny, that she'll try to come with us for the day?"

"Shand wants you to have the day to yourselves, doesn't he?"

"Yes, he does. But . . . she'll probably make a fuss. She never minds making a fuss about what she wants. She's so shameless!"

"You must try to be more shameless, Juliet."

"Fenny, what advice from you!"

"I mean it. You must make a stand for what you want. Otherwise, with somebody like Erina about, you won't get it. I shall probably invite Erina to lunch with me on your birthday, and tell her we're all going to be out in the evening."

"Oh, Fenny, do," and, as long ago at the Villa Meridina, when Ellen proposed some treat, Juliet exclaimed, "You do have such very good ideas!"

. . . . .

Juliet had gone to bed, and Ellen was sitting in the window-seat reading, when she heard Dino's cautious step on the stairs. No doubt he had been round to Giuseppe with his wrongs. She knew that his mind would retain an impression that she had insulted him, but that any recollection of having helped himself to the money would have vanished from his consciousness. Tomorrow he would stay away from school, and for two or three days she would see nothing of him but an occasional glimpse of his sulky face early in the morning or late at night. But at the moment she had other preoccupations. Dino opened the door quietly and scowled when he saw her still up, stiffening himself to meet rebuke.

She only said:

"Dino, do you know where Bernardo Moldini is now?"

Surprised, he allowed his scowl to slip and replied:

"No, but he will probably be at Milan or Turin. He has a big *commercio* at both places."

"I should rather like to know. Do you think you could find out for me?"

272

"Certainly!"

"I wish you would!"

"I shall make inquiries tomorrow."

"Yes, my dear, do, will you? And now it's very late. We'd better go to bed."

He stood looking at her doubtfully, as if half relieved, half disappointed not to meet with the reception he had expected. She saw him make a movement towards her with the beginnings of a gesture that might have introduced an apology, but he only said with vicious intensity:

"Have I not always said that Shand Warner is very stupid?"

Making a face, he crossed the room and the door of his bedroom shut behind him.

## CHAPTER VII

ON MONDAY evening, when Ellen joined them in the square for a drink before supper, the birthday had already become an issue. As she approached, she saw their three heads round the café table. Erina's light brown, shoulder-length hair had been cut and curled since she came to Florence. She had bought two new dresses, and was much more carefully made up. Beside Juliet, Ellen thought, her looks were nothing; but confidence, experience, and Juliet's reluctance to shout her down often enabled her to dominate the scene.

Ellen was glad to see, as she came up, that Juliet looked particularly happy, while Erina's face drooped peevishly. She knew that Erina had an appointment that afternoon with the dentist, and that Juliet and Shand were going swimming together at the Golf Club—their damp bathing bundles were stacked on an empty chair. Juliet had lost the ribbon from her hair, which hung loosely round her face; she looked relaxed and gay, as though she had been enjoying herself; but Shand seemed uneasy. Erina stretched out a hand to Ellen.

"Fenni, I am so glad that you have come! I am very depressed this evening!"

"What's the matter?"

"I am disappointed because I have arranged a little party for Juliet's birthday—a party for lunch at my special restaurant. I have invited my friends, Roberto and Lucia, and I have spoken with the *padrone*, Ettore, who has known me from a child, that the lunch should be very good, and that there should be a special *dolce* with candles such as you have for a children's *fiesta*. It has been a great pleasure for me to do this, and now I find that Shand will take Juliet all day driving in this heat! The roads will be so dusty and it will be so crowded on the beach at Viareggio, I am sure that she will not enjoy it at all; she will be quite worn out."

"We shan't stop at Viareggio. We reckon to find a quiet beach somewhere up the coast, and maybe we'll take a picnic. It won't be so hot driving there if we start early in the morning."

"And so now I must tell Ettore that you do not want my party, and Roberto and Lucia that they should not come!"

"Sorry, Erina, it's a date."

Shand sounded firm, but looked uncomfortable.

"It was very sweet of you to think of it, Erina," Juliet said, with a touch of remorse. "Only we made this plan days ago, didn't we, Shand?"

"Maybe we could have your party some other day, Erina?"

"To have a birthday party on the wrong day, that is something that I do not like at all."

There was a silence. Erina got up and stood leaning on the back of her chair with her hand to her forehead.

"I am very sorry, but I must go back to the *pension*. I have had this terrible neuralgia in my face all night. I was not able to sleep for a moment, and just now, although the dentist has stopped my tooth, the pain has begun again. He says that there is nothing that he can do: it is because of the bad shock to my nerves, and it will no doubt get better in time, when I recover my spirits. But I said to him that that is not always so easy at first, after a great loss. But I shall not come to have supper at your flat this evening, Fenni, because I shall not be good company and I do not wish to spoil the party. When I suffer like this it is better that I am alone, so I will go back to my room."

"Erina!" Shand caught hold of her skirt. "Don't go! We

can get you some aspirin. I'll go round now to the drug-store. You'll feel better when you've had something to eat!"

"No, I feel that you will all be much better without me. I should prefer to be alone."

As she walked away across the square, her slumped shoulders, her dragging feet and bent head expressed extreme dejection.

"Juliet! Wait here for me! I'll be back in a few minutes!"

Shand sprang up and hurried after Erina. The two left behind exchanged glances.

"You see, Fenny!"

"Tiresome woman! There's nothing the matter with her except temper!"

"I do hate it!" Juliet broke out. "I do hate seeing Shand come to heel like that! Fenny, *why* does he? He doesn't really like her. He says she's maddening! They keep on quarrelling, and he shouts at her in a way he never shouts at anyone else. It makes him sound like an Italian! But then in a sort of way he does like her, too. She flatters him all the time. She keeps on saying that he's brought her back to life."

"What a pity!"

Juliet smiled faintly, but said:

"Never mind about being angry with her. Tell me *why* she's got this queer hold over him."

"I think it's all mixed up with his feeling for Harry."

"I suppose he was rather in love with Harry."

Startled by her matter-of-fact acceptance of something that would never have entered her own head at Juliet's age, Ellen said:

"It was a very romantic young men's friendship: they'd been through everything together. I think he must have been jealous of her when Harry married her. Perhaps he felt she took Harry away from him, and I dare say he blames her for Harry's death without knowing he does so and that he doesn't want to examine his own feelings about her."

"Perhaps. He seems tied to her in some way I don't understand." Juliet sighed. "It was so lovely when we were up at the Golf Club this afternoon. It was like it used to be before she came. He *was* happy—I know he was—and so was I. When we're alone together we seem almost to fuse into one another. We hardly seem like two separate people. What I can't bear"—Juliet's voice trembled—"is that when he's like that with her it makes me want to be angry with *him*. He's always seemed to me so confident and single-minded and sure of what he wanted! I can't bear seeing him whipped in like a little boy with a bad-tempered mother! It gives me a different idea of him."

"Nobody is made all of a piece, Juliet. There are certain stresses that find out the weak places in all of us. Perhaps it's no use being fond of anyone unless you're fond of the whole person."

Juliet said softly:

"I am fond of the whole person. I think it's mostly because he can't bear to be unkind. That's not a bad weakness."

Ellen was not sure that in some cases it might not be, but Juliet was beginning to look happier, as if she had found a solution. And after all, Ellen thought, they must settle it among themselves. She got up.

"I'm going round to the flat to get supper ready. Shand will be back in a minute, I expect. You stay here and have a drink with him in peace."

"Unless you want me to help you?"

"No, thank you; Dino is there, and said he would start cooking."

Looking back from the other side of the square, she saw Juliet searching with her eyes the corner where Shand had disappeared after Erina. With the dark hair falling back from her young face, a hand moving the cigarette to and from her lips, she looked solitary, anxious and touching.

. . . . .

Ellen found Dino in the kitchen breaking eggs into a bowl. She stood watching the skilful movements of his brown hands, then noticed with some dismay the size of the heap of broken egg-shells.

"Oh, Dino, have you used all those! How extravagant!"

He at once looked injured, as he always did at any suggestion of economy.

"I cannot make good *zabaione* for five people with less. I will get some more from Giuseppe tomorrow."

"And he'll get them out of somebody's hen-roost, I suppose! Well, never mind, now you've started on them. It will be only

276

four of us. The Signora Jackson is not coming. She has gone home feeling ill."

"*Bene!*"

Erina often gave Dino cigarettes and sweets, which he accepted, but he had decided that he did not like her.

Picking up a fork, he began to beat the eggs. As the yellow froth mounted in the bowl, he said:

"Bernardo Moldini was in Milan, but he has gone to Holland for an industrial conference."

"Oh, dear!"

"But many letters come with a Dutch stamp for the Signora Jackson: almost every day they come, and she answers them all."

"How on earth do you know?"

"Giuseppe and I took the *portière* at the *pension* out to have a *negroni*."

"Dino! That's going too far! I never meant you to spy on the Signora's correspondence."

"Well, you wished to know about Bernardo Moldini! I had forgotten, of course, that the English are so noble they do not spy. They only employ spies."

"Oh, don't waste time being silly about the English now! Have you made the sauce?"

"Yes,"—he lifted the lid off a pan—"taste!"

"Delicious! You really are a first-rate chef, Dino!"

Absurdly exalted, as always, by praise, he said graciously:

"I will tell you something else. Giuseppe has a cousin whose brother is at the block of flats in Rome, where the Jacksons lived. He says that Bernardo Moldini came often to their flat, and that he was there all the evening alone with the Signora Jackson the day before the Signor Jackson died."


## CHAPTER VIII

AFTER A supper-party which was gay—though, Ellen thought, with reservations—Juliet and Shand made a perfunctory offer to wash up, accepted Ellen's refusal with obvious satisfaction, and went out together. Dino helped her with the dishes, and then said he was going to have a coffee with Giuseppe.

"I do wish," Ellen observed, "that you sometimes went to meet the boys in your class at school—boys of your own age!"

Dino shrugged.

"They are *bambini, poco interessanti*."

Ellen let him go. Of course they were *poco interessanti* compared to Giuseppe, with his drinks and cigarettes, his Partisan record, his swagger, his careless generosity when his pockets were full, his devil-may-care poverty when they were empty! Many of Giuseppe's friends were Communists, but Giuseppe was an individualist who would never submit to party discipline and who wanted easily earned money for himself more than he wanted any political order. Ellen sometimes wondered uneasily why he wanted so much of the company of a boy as young as Dino, but she thought that it was only that he was good-natured and enjoyed admiration. Dino probably had a certain cachet; no doubt he passed himself off as the adopted son of a rich Englishwoman who taught from eccentricity, and who would bequeath him all her estates in England. Even Shand, to whom Dino was barely civil, probably figured in his café conversation as his wealthy and important American friend.

Giuseppe must have been doing well lately on the Black Market; he had been lavish with entertainment. One day, Ellen thought, he will be caught and arrested by the police—he is too vain and careless to cover his tracks—and probably Dino will be involved. Perhaps I ought to go back to live at Ainley, and send Dino to the grammar school. She tried but failed to envisage Dino with a grammar-school cap on his black head swinging down the steep streets of a Yorkshire town with his bag of school books or, in a striped jersey, running on a football field in the November mist. Perhaps I could get Shand to take him back to America and find a job for him! Shand would be reluctant, but would probably do it if she asked it as a favour. Oh, but how I should miss him! I should have to go to America, too. I must just do what I can, and keep an eye on him. I'll talk to old Anna and see if she can persuade Giuseppe not to give him so many *negroni*.

She corrected a batch of translations, prepared some work for next day, and sat down in the window-seat. She felt too tired to read. She switched off the light and sat looking across the Arno at the lit windows of the houses on the opposite bank and the uneven frieze of their roofs against the lighter sky. She had, as so often lately, the sensation of everything receding from her. The voices and footsteps of the people on the pavement below became distant and then very loud, assailing her ears with an intolerable din and dying away again. She thought of getting a glass of water, but did not feel as though her legs had strength to cross the room. The moment of tension broke as sweat sprang out on her body, and she relaxed. I wonder what is the matter with me—if there is something going wrong with my brain, if some illness is creeping up on me, and I am going to die? Lately she had dreamed once or twice of dying, she had a feeling of approaching an end. This feeling, which had been no more than a disregarded background to her busy days, suddenly flooded her mind. It is absurd, she thought; I am not old. I feel old at the moment, but perhaps it is because the younger generation are now grown up. I am watching the children, Juliet and Shand, in this post-war world, and my world in which I grew up seems like an historical novel. Perhaps it is because of the people who have been in my life and gone out of it, Daniel I don't know where. Graziella and Arturo, both dead. They were my family, my generation, and though I may live another thirty years, those are the people who felt as I do, those years before the war I shall always belong to in some special way whatever happens to me in the rest of my life.

Yet in another way how long ago it seems! She tried to recreate in the dim room Arturo's figure, sitting as he had so often sat by the fire, leaning forward with the light of the flames on his thin face. But it was a picture, and not a living presence. She could remember, but she could not recover that living sweetness in the heart that had always been evoked by his presence or even by the thought of him, by the sight of a pair of gloves that he had left behind, or a book that he had returned. She came nearest to that feeling now when she looked at Juliet, sometimes when, after they had been late the night before, she took her coffee to her in bed in the morning and saw her dark head burrowed into the pillows, waited for her waking smile. But that was a different tenderness, though also touched with longing. I cannot understand, she

279

thought, how Madeleine, whatever preoccupations she has, can reject such a child.

Juliet ought to be mine! She is not like her mother at all; in some ways she is like me. Too much like me. She was daunted young—in that summer at Meridiana, I suppose—by the shock of her mother leaving her, though even then she was never a selfish child. There are times when the young need to be selfish, to save their lives. Daniel saw at the beginning what was coming to me; he said that I did not make claims for myself. He was teaching me then, though I suppose he didn't know it, how to be ready when he needed me to be selfish, and I didn't learn, and so I let Madeleine take him and throw him away. I failed him and myself. It was different with Arturo and Graziella—I still do not see what else I could have done—but in a way the pattern was the same. And now for Juliet. All her strength gathered into a resolve. I will not let it be the same for Juliet. How can I give her the confidence that was taken away from her? I tried in that summer after her mother left her. I truly loved her, but it was not enough. There are some things that only a mother can do for a child.

She was half asleep when Juliet came in. She roused herself, feeling some tension in the girl and knowing that she wanted to talk. Juliet sat down on the opposite end of the window-seat.

"Fenny"—she sounded very solemn—"I'm not quite sure. I've been trying to make up my mind, but I think I'm going to let Erina do what she wants on my birthday. We can go to the sea another day."

Ellen was instantly alert.

"Was that Shand's idea?"

"No. Shand says that he told Erina he was going to stick to his promise. He had rather a time with her. She cried and cried, and begged him to change the plan. I don't know how she *can*, do you, Fenny? It's so undignified! And apparently she went on for a long time saying nobody wanted her. Then he said she calmed down and apologized; she said that she was like somebody bruised all over and the least little thing hurt her, and she was very silly, and so on. She kept on telling him she was so very fond of me, and that was why she had been so disappointed, because she had been thinking and thinking how to arrange a treat for me. Shand said he soothed her as best he could, and said we'd talk about it all tomorrow and see if we could have her party, too—the evening before or something. He said she was upset after the dentist, and . . . I don't know what he said, really; but when he came to join me in the square he was quite definite that he'd told her we would stick to our plan. But . . . he was a bit hostile to me for a few minutes." Juliet's voice shook. "I can't bear him to think me selfish and unkind!"

"I don't suppose he does for a minute."

"Well, you know, she does do something to him! And yet I think he knows what she's like, really. . . . But about the birthday. You see, Fenny, what I've been thinking is that it isn't important! I'm not eight now! I can't bear all these fusses about nothing that Erina makes. And I've been thinking that however annoying she is, you can't get away from the fact that she has had this real tragedy, and that compared to that, whether we go to the sea on one day or another is a very small thing. I don't want to hurt somebody who's had such a terrible blow for the sake of a bit of amusement. It doesn't matter really."

"Don't deceive yourself, Juliet! It does matter."

"What, having a picnic one day or another? How can it?"

"It isn't a question of having a picnic one day or another; it's letting Erina exercise power over Shand . . . and over you. The more people use that kind of power the more they want to, and the harder it is to stop them."

"I would stop her if it was anything important."

"It is, Juliet—you know it is, really."

There was a silence.

"I feel it is. I've felt that all the time; but when I look at it reasonably . . ."

"That's not looking at it reasonably. It's looking at it superficially. You feel it matters, and there are times when you have to trust your feeling. My whole life would have been different if I'd once had the courage to trust mine."

"How do you mean?"

"It was that first summer in Italy. I was in love with someone who was beginning to be in love with me. We were having very happy times together, just as you and Shand have, but another woman saw us and set out to break it up. She didn't want him herself, but—well, she was very unhappy at the time, and I suppose that made her want to destroy happiness, and she had a lot of unsatisfied vanity. She didn't want him, but she took him from me. And I let her."

"Why?"

"I suppose because I hadn't enough courage to trust my feeling. And I was fond of her and . . . oh, there were other reasons. I don't quite know . . . but I said to myself that I was imagining and mustn't exaggerate trifles; it couldn't really be happening."

"I know! I know! I do that with Erina!"

"But I was deceiving myself. It was happening. And then I saw them together at the place where I often met him and I started out to tell her what she was doing, and stop her. I could have done it. She wasn't altogether cruel, and she wasn't very brave. And in her way she was fond of me. I think she might have been glad if I'd stopped her. But I let the chance slip. And it was the last chance. Afterwards it was too late."

Juliet said in a small, cold voice:

"Fenny, was it my mother?"

"It doesn't matter who it was. It's all over long ago."

"What happened?"

"He went back to England when he discovered that he didn't mean anything to her; he was humiliated and ashamed, and rushed off without seeing me. I never heard from him again."

"Oh, poor Fenny!"

"It was my own fault. I wouldn't see in time. But I told you so that you should."

There was a long pause.

"I don't want to make Shand come with me against his will. But I know he does want to come. Sometimes I think he wants me to break her spell for him. She has got a kind of spell over him, Fenny! He's a bit frightened of her. I am myself sometimes. I don't know why, because I must say she's always very nice to me and easy to get on with, but I feel something sinister about her. I think she's a destroyer. I have a feeling that in some way she destroyed Harry. . . . I don't mean killed him, but if it's true what you say that there's this other man in the background, she may have wished Harry dead. When I think of that, I can't bear to see her near Shand."

"She can't destroy you or Shand unless you let her. Destroyers can never destroy anybody who isn't willing to be destroyed. And she's not a witch in a fairy-tale!"

"I suppose not. I almost feel as if she was!"

"I've sometimes thought since that in my own crisis Daniel must have felt that I didn't love him enough to make a fight for him. And the worst part of all has been that I've sometimes thought it must be true."

"I do love Shand, Fenny. I couldn't tell you how much."

"I know you do. And I think he loves you. Let's go to bed now, Juliet; you can sleep on it, and talk to Shand again in the morning."

Juliet said slowly:

"There's something else I might do."

She put her arms round Ellen and kissed her cheek.

"I wish you had all the things you deserve, Fenny!"

"I should have them if I deserved them. Don't worry too much, my dear. I think it will all work out. You're a much more sensible girl than I ever was. Good-night."


## CHAPTER IX

IN THE morning Ellen found Dino industriously sweeping the sitting-room. This was evidently one of his good days, for the kitchen had been cleaned and the coffee was made. Dino brought Ellen hers to the window-seat.

"The Signorina Juliet has gone out early, and left you a note. I did not read it!" he added virtuously.

He knew that Ellen attached great importance to such things. He snatched up a vase of red carnations that Shand had brought, made a face at them unseen, and carried them off to the kitchen.

Ellen unfolded the slip of paper.

"Gone to see Erina about my birthday. Juliet."

Gone to make a fight for herself or a gesture of renunciation? People woke in the morning with such different feelings from their midnight resolutions!

Dino came back, carrying the carnations in a vase full of fresh water, and shining with cleanliness.

"I have been up since six studying my lessons before I cleaned the flat."

Ellen looked at him suspiciously. His face was as bright as the vase, full of innocence and zeal.

"You would like some more coffee, Fenni?"

He went into the kitchen for the pot. Ellen looked out of the window at the brilliant morning and saw Shand lounging out of the doorway of the American Express with some letters in his hand. He sat down on the low parapet above the Arno, slit open an envelope and began to read. He glanced up from the letter at the window of the flat, and waved, but did not move. It was understood that he did not come to the flat in the morning before Ellen started for her day's work. At that hour getting herself and Dino off was enough.

"Dino, isn't it time you were starting?"

"*Subito!*" Dino began to collect his books.

"When you go out, will you ask Shand to come up for a minute or two before I go to Santa Barbara?"

"Certainly."

He came and stood beside her, looking out over her shoulder. Preoccupied as she was with Juliet and Shand, she realised that something was up.

"What is it, Dino?"

"*Carissima*, I have a little thing to ask you."

"Well?"

"Next month the film tests are to be held in Rome. Giuseppe has done some small service, for Ravini, and if we go there, we shall both have one."

"I told you, I won't let you go with Giuseppe to Rome."

"I know. But you and I could go there together for a little holiday? You have always told me that Rome is very beautiful and that you love it, and I have never seen it. I think that I should see it! There are many art treasures and historical buildings there!"

"The only art treasures you would see with Giuseppe would be the bottles behind a bar!"

"But I am not asking to go with Giuseppe! I should so much prefer to go with you!"

284

Ellen wanted to believe that.

"I don't know yet whether we could afford it. I should have to go into that and see."

"We could borrow some money from Signor Shand Warner."

"No, no, we don't want to start borrowing! We want to pay our own way."

Ellen saw from the expression that flitted over his face that this seemed to him a ridiculous thing to want, but that he was not going to say so at the moment.

"I can perhaps earn some money."

"I don't think you can earn enough for a trip to Rome! But as soon as I have time I'll look into it and see if I can manage for us to go for a few days. That is, if this film test is really coming off. I must talk to Giuseppe and hear all about it. But you ought to see Rome, certainly, and I should like to see it again. I was thinking that we might have a few days' holiday after the term ends. I had thought of a week at the sea."

"What should we do at the sea? If I am given a part in a film I should make a great deal of money."

"You might not be chosen. There will be a lot of other people having film tests."

"They will not be such as I."

Although never willing to discourage the young, she often felt that she ought to break the romantic dream of his own importance in which Dino lived, but this did not seem to be the moment.

"I'll think about it, and see if we can manage it. Run along to school now, dear, and ask Shand to come up."

She had sent for Shand on an impulse; she did not really know what she was going to say to him. His long figure in the doorway always made the room seem smaller.

"I wasn't going to disturb you, Fenny, but Dino said it would be O.K. to come up, and I'm glad, because I wanted to have a word with you."

"I needn't start for a few minutes."

"Dino didn't scowl at me as much as usual. He's off to school punctually today, I see."

"Yes, he wants me to take him to Rome in August for a film test."

"Film test! A jerk like that! They'd never take him!"

"Probably not, but he may settle down better to something else when he's tried."

"Maybe."

Shand obviously had not much attention to spare for Dino. He strolled to the fireplace and stood with his back to Ellen, lighting a cigarette. Over his shoulder he said:

"Fenny, is Juliet very set on her birthday ride?"

"She's been looking forward to it very much. Don't you want to take her?"

"Of course I do. I've been looking forward to it as much as she has. Juliet's sweet. Not like any other girl I know."

"Well, then!"

"Well, you saw how it was last night. When I went round after Erina, I've never seen her so worked up about everything. You see, she feels that you and Juliet have been pretty good to her, and she'd got her mind fixed on this as a kind of return. And then, having it thrown back in her face . . ."

"Nonsense, Shand! She exaggerates! Nobody threw anything back in her face! Juliet has been very much concerned about her."

"Well, Fenny, you know how it is. Harry was the best friend I ever had, and this is the only thing I can do for him."

"Yes, I know; but can't you be kind to Erina without letting her have her own way all the time?"

"You see, the thing is, having had a shock like that, it's made her terribly sensitive. She's like somebody bruised all over, so that she feels the least thing—I mean a little disappointment that doesn't matter to any of us, it makes her feel she's not wanted and she's got nothing to live for."

How tired I am, Ellen thought, of hearing about Erina's sensibility! It's like an article of faith that they both believe in.

"You know, Shand, I'm not at all sure that Erina's got nothing to live for."

With an expression that Ellen thought complacent, he said:

"Well, of course, she does say that my having come over like this to see her is the one thing that's made all the difference and brought her back to life again. That makes me feel responsible for her. It's up to me to make her feel it's worth going on with it . . ."

286

"I wasn't thinking about anybody here. You know she has an admirer in the background—a rich Italian industrialist called Bernardo Moldini, with businesses in Milan and Turin and houses all over the place."

He looked startled and incredulous.

"I didn't know anything about that. She's never said a word to me about any Bernardo Moldini. I don't suppose he means a thing to her."

Feeling thoroughly ashamed of Dino and of herself, Ellen replied:

"Well, she gets letters from him almost every other day, and she replies to them."

"Maybe he's just some old friend of her family's."

"You don't write to old friends of your family three or four times a week."

He looked extremely disconcerted, but he did not ask her how she knew, nor appear to doubt her. Shand, she reflected, was unconscious in most of the workings of his mind. She had always been a person whom he trusted, and she still had some of her old authority for him.

"It's only a year. She told me she'd been living all that time as if she was made of stone—couldn't think, couldn't feel before I came. I don't see how she can have made a new friend."

"I don't think he is a new friend. I know he used to go a lot to their flat in Rome before Harry died."

She saw him absorbing that, pushing away a speculation that he hardly allowed to enter his mind—saw that she had shaken a beautiful romantic image, of himself as the sole rescuer, the only friend, who could bring a distraught woman back to life. Presently he said huffily:

"It doesn't mean a thing to me whether I'm her only friend or not. I came here to see her because I owed it to Harry to do what I could for her. It's Harry I've been thinking of. If she's got other friends to look after her, that suits me."

He sounded as though it did not suit him at all: he looked furious. He turned his back on Ellen and picked up the snapshot of Juliet on the garden wall at Meridiana which she had propped against the clock.

"I must go now, Shand; I shall be late."

287

Ellen put on her big black straw hat in front of the mirror. Between its wide brim and the collar of her dark blue linen dress, her face looked pale, the grey smudges under her eyes came down on to her cheek-bones. The mirror reflected an unwillingness to begin the day's work which was very unusual with her and surprised her. She thought with a sigh, I'd really rather go to the sea than to Rome. I should like to go to the sea in England! She was suddenly thirsty for the seaside places of her youth— the wide, Northern sands, the great waves leaping in like lions, and the cool, salty air.

"Fenny, don't go for a minute. Must you?"

"Will you close the shutters for me, Shand, when I've gone? I ought to have done it much earlier. This room gets like an oven."

"Yeh, I'll do that. You know, Fenny"—it came out with a rush —"I don't *like* Erina. I'm very sorry for her. I felt if she was depending on me I couldn't do too much for her, but I get mad when she pulls at me all the time and when everything has to be done just her way." Weightily he pronounced, "I think she's selfish. We're always quarrelling, and we don't seem able to stop, and all the time I want to go off alone with Juliet and be happy as we were before Erina came; but I don't know how it is, she's like something I can't get away from. She kind of fills the place, she always seems to be *there*. . . ."

"Shand!"

"Yes?"

"That's just what you used to say to me about Lucrezia when we were at Bronciliano!"

"Lucrezia? Did I?"

"Yes, you had just the same feeling of her being all over the place and of not being able to get away from her."

"Yes, I suppose I did. Yes, I remember I was always quarrelling with her and screaming at her. Maybe I do have the same set-up with Erina. There is a kind of likeness . . ."

"I can't wait any longer, my dear."

Methodically, as she did every morning before setting out, she checked over the things in her bag—money, keys, passport, pen, compact, lipstick. Behind her she heard Shand give a deep sigh, as if shedding a load.

288

"Where's Juliet?"

"She went out early to see Erina."

"I think I'll find her and get her to come swimming with me. We might have lunch up there."

"Yes, do; she'll like that."

"Be seeing you, Fenny!"

"Yes, of course—sometime this evening."

But as she hurried downstairs, she thought, I really wouldn't mind not seeing any of you for a day or two! There seemed to be so many of them, making so many plans and changing them! She was deeply interested in the clamorous urgencies of their young lives, but this morning they exhausted her. I should like someone to think about *me* for a bit! I should like a little peace!

.        .        .        .

It was the day when she lunched at Santa Barbara and went straight on to her classes at the other school. She came back to the flat at the end of the afternoon and found no one there, only one of Juliet's hastily scribbled notes on the table:

"Gone swimming with Shand, meet in the Square for drinks at seven."

Ellen made herself a cup of tea, and spread a biscuit with American peach jam. Shand's aunts had redoubled their parcels under the impression that he must be eating Ellen out of house and home, instead of taking them all out to meals more often than she thought it decent to let him. And would Dino, who loved eating in restaurants, ever settle down again to their quiet routine? It might give him ideas beyond Giuseppe's low haunts, but, on the other hand, it was certainly giving him expensive tastes that she would not afterwards be able to gratify. But Dino had been born with expensive tastes. Perhaps everybody was really born with expensive tastes, and only painfully educated themselves out of them! It had certainly been a pleasant change!

Her thoughts hovering round Juliet and the issue of her talk with Erina, she went into the girl's bedroom. It was, as usual, fairly untidy. The cotton skirt that she had been wearing yesterday billowed as if she had just stepped out of it on the floor. The bed was made, but a nightgown festooned the bedpost, one drawer was open, showing a tangle of scarves and handkerchiefs, a broken string of artificial pearls lay on the dressing-table in spilt powder. There was a snapshot of Shand in the garden at Meridiana stuck into the side of the mirror.

Ellen folded the nightgown, hung up the skirt, dusted the dressing-table, collected the straying pearls into an envelope.

Only a little while longer that I shall have her here to do these things for her. This room will not smell of her scent any more, or be strewn with her bright clothes. I shall not find her illegible notes on the table, nor see her face opposite to me at supper, nor hear her calling, "See you later", as she runs down the stairs. I have had for a month or two the illusion of having a daughter, and, like all illusions, it is coming to an end.

Except to me, that doesn't matter, of course. What matters is how the summer ends for her. She came here feeling unloved. I don't want her to crystallize a pattern of diffidence and failure. Her growing up, since her mother left her, has been a hotch-potch between two families. It would be good for her to start again in the new world. Shand is slow in maturing but there is plenty in him that will mature. And anyhow she loves him. Perhaps I should have seen Erina myself. An interfering old governess? Yes, it is better that they should work it out for themselves.

Unable to read or rest until she had seen Juliet again, she began to wash some underclothes. Her hands were plunged in the warm soapy water, the pale silk billowing up between her fingers, when she heard Dino come in. She knew his mood by his step. He came noisily into the sitting-room, slammed the door and crashed his books on the floor. She called to him, and he opened the bathroom door and stood in the doorway, a cigarette in the corner of his mouth. She thought from the mixture of defiance, swagger and guilt in his bearing that he must have been having drinks with Giuseppe.

"*Ecco!*" he said. "We shall go to Rome!"

He held out to her a wad of notes.

"What is that? I can't take it now, my hands are wet."

"It is money for our visit. Forty thousand lire. Giuseppe has paid me for the help I have given him with his work."

He turned back into the sitting-room whistling an aria from *Tosca*. Ellen knew that he was not at ease.

"Wait a minute!"

Hastily she rinsed the petticoat, threw the bundle of wet silk into the bath, dried her hands and joined him.

"What work have you been helping Giuseppe with, Dino?"

"With his carpentering. Lately I have often helped him in the evenings."

She stared at him incredulously. Giuseppe had a lathe and a few tools, all the property of his father, in a rickety shed behind the Lucchesi *appartamento*. He sometimes tinkered up a repair for a neighbour. He had been known to knock a bench together or to fix wheels on a box for a makeshift perambulator, but that he had earned forty thousand lire in the last six months, let alone paying that to Dino for help even more spasmodic and occasional than the work, she did not believe! She looked at Dino, and Dino, still humming his tune, looked back at her with an unnatural smile:

"That will be enough for our visit?"

"I haven't worked out yet what we should want, but Giuseppe didn't give you all this for helping with his carpentering. What did he give it to you for?"

"I have told you."

"No, I don't think you have!"

"You do not believe me! You think that I am a liar."

He was beginning to work himself up into one of those passions in which he always lost sight of the original cause, but she stopped him.

"Wait a minute, Dino; don't fly up into the air. I know perfectly well that Giuseppe would never give you as much money as this unless you had given him a lot of help with some pretty big black-market deal. I should be rather surprised if he did then. I think you got this money in some other way, and I *must* know what it was."

Seeing him obstinately determined not to speak, she added:

"If you don't tell me, I shall ask Giuseppe whether he gave you the money and what for."

Flinging away from her he muttered:

"Well then, he didn't give it to me. I found it."

"Found it? Where?"

"In a bag."

"What bag? Where was it?"

"It was a handbag belonging to a Signora. I picked it up in the gutter in a little street off the Via Carozza."

"But you should have taken it to the police, or returned it to the Signora. There must have been other things in the bag, some address? A passport or notebook, letters?"

"There was nothing at all."

"Nothing? No powder-case, purse, handkerchief?"

"Nothing. Just this money."

"Even so, it will have to go to the police."

"Why should they have it? They did not find it."

His eyelashes fluttered, he shifted under her hard stare and tried to start his tune again. She summoned up all her reserves of strength to beat down his resistance.

"You didn't find it, did you, Dino? You've told me two stories about this money, and neither of them is true. Now tell me the truth?"

Suddenly collapsing into childishness, he burst into tears. He gulped and sobbed, rubbing his eyes with the back of his hand.

"I wanted to help you," he wailed. "I did it for you!"

Bit by bit she got the story out of him. He had been sitting outside a café, eating an ice. The Signora, an American, was sitting at the table near. She saw a friend passing in the street; she called and waved, but the friend did not notice. She jumped up and ran after the friend, leaving the bag on her chair. Before he knew what he was doing, he had the bag inside his school case of books and was round the corner. He had run until he came to a quiet place, and then opened the bag, slipped the wad of notes into his pocket and thrown the bag over the high wall of a garden. There were some other things in the bag—such things as a Signora would have—but he had not stopped to look at them. Yes, he said, when Ellen pressed him, he could remember the place; it was, as he had said, in a side street off the Via Carozza, and near where he threw the bag there was a branch of wisteria beginning to climb down over the wall.

Frightened, half resentful, he gulped and sniffed and knuckled his eyes. Ellen looked at him with despair.

"Oh, Dino! What am I to do with you? Did you learn this trick from Giuseppe?"

"No. Giuseppe says that it is too risky and often not worth while. Many quite rich people do not carry much money."

He was crying, she knew, not from repentance, but because he had been found out. Only that childish part of him which lived in fantasy could ever have supposed he would not be. He was crying, too, because the money would be taken away from him. He was perhaps a little ashamed, but not very much. Her standards had not really taken root in this haphazard alien soil. Between two gulps, he muttered:

"One has to fend for oneself nowadays!"

That cry of the displaced children of insecurity in the post-war world wrung her heart, but she blamed herself that he should still feel like one of them.

"Dino, do you want to go on living with me?"

He was really startled—so startled that he stopped his noisy crying and stared at her. She had managed to give him at least one kind of confidence: he had never doubted that, whatever he did, she would forgive him.

"If the police had caught you they might have taken you away from me and put you in an institution."

"Of course I should have got out and come back to you!"

But his voice shook, the bravado was thin. He looked genuinely aghast.

"You must come with me to the *Questura*. We will take the money and tell the police you found it lying in the gutter, and you must describe the exact place, so that they may search the garden and find the bag and return it to the Signora. We must hope that they will think that some other boy, some ignorant boy, stole it. They will ask you questions, but you must say nothing else, only that you found the money on your way back from school and brought it to me because you didn't know what to do with it."

"Perhaps," Dino murmured, "if it is returned to the Signora Americana, she will leave some of it at the *Questura* as a reward for me. It is customary."

"If she does, you will give it to the Fathers at San Marco for the poor. Now go and wash your face."

When he came back from the bathroom, spruced and clean in a fresh shirt, with his hair brushed flat, he looked at her hopefully, as if the worst was over; but if she had felt like relenting, she would not have allowed herself to show it. She marched him off in silence through the streets, and she hoped as they approached the police-station that he was feeling nervous.

The *carabiniere* who received the money and Ellen's statement was an amiable, dull-witted man, who showed no sign of suspicion, only a faint surprise that Dino should have brought the money in at all. At the conclusion of the interview he patted the boy's shoulder and spoke approvingly to him. Ellen looked on with disgust as Dino shrugged, smiled modestly and spread out his hands.

"It was not mine!"

As they stepped out into the sunshine, Dino, now moving briskly, heaved a sigh, as though a tiresome business was over and shot a glance at Ellen.

"*Carissima*, it was the impulse of a moment. *Piu forte di me!* I shall never do such a thing again. I am very sorry!"

"I hope you are!"

He sighed again lightly, like one prepared to put up with misunderstanding.

"I thought only that it would save you from working harder to make more money."

"I am quite able to earn all that you and I need. Anything that we can't afford we must go without."

He turned tactfully to a pleasanter subject.

"We shall go now to meet the others in the square?"

"I am going there. You had better go home and start getting supper ready."

"I will do as you wish," he said in a subdued voice.

He turned and walked away from her, back towards the Lung'arno. She looked after his retreating figure, which eloquently conveyed repentance, dejection and a hint of reproach. Absurdly her own heart reproached her. She had always allowed an apology to wipe out his naughtiness. But this was more than naughtiness! She must make him feel it; or what would become of him? She waited to see if he would turn at the corner and wave to her. When he disappeared round the bend without looking back, she felt irrationally disappointed. She glanced at her watch and saw that it was after seven. Juliet's crisis, banished for an hour, rushed back into her mind, and she hurried towards the square. But she knew that she was not as indissolubly linked with Juliet as with the unregenerate creature who had drifted into her life and lodged there like a missing part of it. She turned into the square, pushed her way through the crowd milling in the colonnade and saw Juliet sitting alone at the café table.

. . . . .

"It's all right, Fenny!" Juliet said.

"Where are the others?"

"Shand's gone round to the American Express. I don't know where Erina is. Sit down, Fenny. I want to tell you. It's all right. We're going for our day at the sea.

"I lay awake for a long time last night thinking about what you'd been saying. I still kept on trying to say to myself that all this about my birthday was simply stupid, a fuss about nothing. But I knew you were right, really; I felt it was a cross-roads. It was only the cowardly and self-conscious part of me that thought it wasn't. Once you let a thing slip, it so often runs downhill like mad. I made up my mind to go round and see Erina early this morning.

"I'd forgotten that she sleeps badly and gets up much later than we do. When I got there, they said she was still in bed. I said I'd wait. I'd screwed my courage to the sticking point, and I was going to keep it there. I suppose they went down and told Erina I was there; anyhow, I got a message asking me to go up to her room.

"I went up. She was in bed, looking rather frowsty and yellow, with rings round her eyes. She said she'd hardly slept all night, and she looked as if it was true. I nearly decided not to do anything.

"Especially as she began by being very nice to me. She said how pretty my dress was, and how sorry she was that she had been obliged to leave the party last night. She loved being with us all. I don't believe all the things she says, but I get half hypnotized by them, especially when I'm alone with her. She's so different when Shand's not there. She was drinking her coffee, and she began to tell me a lot of amusing things about when she was in Rome during the Occupation. I sat and

295

listened, and thought, we're all good friends, really. Shall I let it go?

"I didn't because I happened to look round and saw that she had stuck in her mirror that same snapshot of Shand at the villa that I've got in my room. Thinking about it now, I see it is rather funny. But then I was suddenly angry. She saw what I was looking at, and for a second she smiled—just a flick of a complacent smile. She went on talking. But I had become unhypnotized. When she had finished telling me a story, I said, 'Erina, I've come round to thank you so much for planning a birthday party for me. It was very sweet of you to think of it, and I am so sorry we had made this other plan first.'

"I saw her face go different. Have you ever noticed that when she's angry her chin sinks back into her neck and her eyes pop out? She always looks rather frightening like that. Honestly, although she's never been angry with me, I am sometimes rather frightened of her. At least, I was before this morning.

"She only looked like that for a minute. Then she said that she had planned this party because I was so nice to her. She felt as if I was her younger sister. I was one of her very greatest friends. I murmured all the stupid things one does, like, 'It's very kind of you to say so'. When she'd finished I said:

"'You do understand about the party, don't you? I'm very grateful; it's just that we'd made the other plan first.'

"Then she started about it's being too hot for a long day like that, the roads would be so dusty and the beach so glaring. Young men do not think of these things; it was rather selfish of Shand. I wasn't going to have that, so I said, 'Oh, no, Shand knows that I should like it; we planned it together.' She didn't like that "

"I don't suppose she did!" Ellen felt a queer flash of sympathy for Erina. "Go on!"

"She was going to say something very angry, but she stopped herself. She leaned back on her pillows, and laughed and said, as if she was jollying a child along:

"'Well, my little Juliet, it is not, after all, so important! What matters is that on your birthday you should do what you like best. Let us go to the sea, then!'

"Fenny, I nearly let her get away with it! It came so quickly.

It seemed so easy just to let that slide over and ask Shand afterwards not to take her. But that didn't seem fair to him. I had a feeling Now or Never. And I said, 'I'm afraid just that day Shand and I are going by ourselves.'

"Then she went off the deep end, and shouted at me. I hadn't expected it. I thought she'd cover her tracks more. But she let fly. She said that nobody wanted her, that I had always resented her coming. She said that both Shand and Harry had been in love with her in Rome, and that she had married Harry because he was so much more *simpatico* than Shand. She said that she had been so fond of me, and always thought I was her friend, and now she saw that I hated her. I was so astonished at first I couldn't speak. She said a lot more things. She said I was spoilt and selfish, and always wanted my own way. She said I was possessive. I'd been listening without saying anything, just hoping for it to stop, but then suddenly I couldn't stand any more of it. I didn't know what I was going to say, but I shouted back at her. I shouted 'You're not my mother! Be quiet!'

"I don't know why, but after that I felt different. Suddenly it wasn't like a nightmare any more; she was just a hysterical woman in a temper. I felt I could cope. And I felt sorry for her. I got up and said:

" 'Erina, I'm very sorry I came round so early and upset you after you'd had a bad night. I'm going to stick to the plan we made for my birthday, so let's leave it at that. We'll be seeing you later in the day, I expect.' And I walked out. I saw her flop back on to her pillows, with her mouth open, looking more surprised than anything else. She didn't shout at me again, she just stared. I shut the door, and went downstairs.

"I found Shand outside. He'd been round to you and heard where I was, and I must say he looked a bit uneasy. I wasn't going to tell him all that had happened. I just said that I had been to thank Erina for planning my birthday, but to say that we were sticking to our original plan. He said, 'Was she sore about it?' I said 'Yes, she was rather, but she'll get over it.' He said, 'Do you think maybe I'd better run in and see that she's all right?' I wasn't going to tell him not to. I wanted him to decide.

"But I felt as if things had shifted and he wouldn't. I just stood

297

and waited for him to make up his mind. He looked at me and he looked at the door of the *pension*, and then he said, 'Oh, to Hell with it! Let's go and swim at the Golf Club!' And we've been there all the rest of the day. And it's been a lovely day, Fenny—the best we've had."

.　　　.　　　.　　　.　　　.

Shand had joined them, and the three of them were sitting at the café table, when they saw Erina coming towards them across the square. She was wearing a new dark red dress with a pattern of white flowers. Her hair had been curled and dressed on top of her head. They all welcomed her with a readiness that had a touch of remorse in it, pulled back her chair, asked after her neuralgia and offered her a drink, but she refused to sit down.

"I have come to say good-bye. I leave for Milano tomorrow morning. I have had a telegram from a very dear friend, who has been out of the country and has now returned, so that he is anxious to see me. It is rather unexpected, so I have many things to arrange, and I have to spend the evening with my aunt. So I have only just time to say good-bye and to thank you all for your great kindness, which has made so much difference to me. I do not know, Shand, if I shall see you again before you go to America, or you, Juliet, before you go home. But you, Fenni, will be here in Florence, and I hope that I shall often see you again and talk of our happy times together."

They watched her, jaunty and undefeated, walking away from them across the square. Ellen was surprised to find herself thinking, perhaps when the others have gone I shall be glad to see her again; there are things I like about her. She felt a sense of loss, not at Erina's departure, but at coming to the end of a simplified emotion. There was a certain rest for the mind in unqualified love or unqualified hatred, but it was only for a very short time that either was possible in the closely woven texture of feeling.

# CHAPTER X

A week later, early in the evening of Juliet's birthday, Ellen stepped from the doorway of her doctor's house into the glare of the street.

"There is nothing the matter with you," he repeated, shaking hands with her. "You are a healthy woman. It is perfectly natural. Rest when you can and take the pills. In a year, in a few months, these sensations will pass."

She thanked him and walked away. There was a small *rattoria* at the end of the street, with a few tables on the pavement, partly screened by leggy oleanders in wooden tubs. At this hour the tables were empty. The waiter was asleep on a chair just inside the door. He roused himself, as she sat down at one of the tables. She ordered a *cappuccino* and lit a cigarette.

So that is all, she thought; I'm not ill, I'm not dying—I am just getting older. How strange that I didn't realize it! The hot colour of the oleander flowers swam before her eyes in a dazzle of tears. Shakily she lifted the thick china cup, and from a distance felt the coffee burn the back of her throat. She blew her nose, pulled hard at her cigarette and in a minute felt the tears dry under her smarting lids.

The street opened on to a shabby square where in the rich amber light three or four small boys wers scuffling and shouting round a broken fountain. The youngest of them, so small that he was still unsteady on his feet, slipped and fell, banging his head against the stone. His howl brought a woman out of one of the houses; she came running with a hand to the fastening of her dress as she had just got up from the siesta. She snatched up the baby, indiscriminately cuffed one or two of the others, a mechanical gesture which did not interrupt their scuffling play, and carried him into the house. The other boys went on trying to push one another down on to the stones, their naked shoulders shining in the sun like chestnuts.

The instinct which all her life had made Ellen scramble up out of unhappiness deserted her for the moment. The full realization went through her that you do not know how much you have always carried certain things about with you as your future

299

until you discover that they are not even your past. She thought, I shall never have a child.

She paid for her coffee, and walked home. There was no one in the flat. The table on which Juliet had opened her birthday presents that morning was littered with paper and string. Ellen folded the paper and rolled up the string, putting both away in a drawer. Her movements dragged with fatigue; the flat, even though the shutters had been closed since six o'clock that morning, was oppressively hot. She had had no siesta. She went into her bedroom, kicked off her shoes, lay down on her bed and fell into a heavy sleep.

Her dreams were of her old home. The doctor's consulting-room that she had just left seemed to be her father's. She saw from the window the view that she remembered, a colliery head stock rising beyond hedgerows and green fields. She was imprisoned in the room and wanted to get out but could not. The dream was permeated by a deep sadness that remained like a taste in the mouth as she started awake. Voices and footsteps in the next room had disturbed her. She realised that it was much later, she must have slept for several hours.

There was a knock on her door. She sat up and called, "Come in." Juliet stood in the doorway, her hair blown about her neck from the drive, her face radiant. Ellen saw Shand grinning behind her.

"Fenny! Fenny! Are you awake? Listen, Fenny; we've got some wonderful news to tell you! We're going to be married!"

.    .    .    .    .

They pressed her to go out to dinner with them, but she sent them off alone. She knew that they were glad, and it was right that they should be. They ran downstairs, leaving the residue of their joy in the flat like an echo of music.

She had a bath and put on a cotton house-coat. On the kitchen dresser were flowers and candles, a cake and a bottle of Orvieto, which she had bought to make a late supper-party for Juliet's birthday. Well, all those could be used for a celebration party tomorrow. Some cold meat and salad would do for herself that evening and for Dino if he came home. Since the day when he had stolen the money he had been subdued and virtuous, regular at school, sitting down industriously to his home-work in the evening. She had kept to her resolution, and given him no money for the cinema, or for ices. She had often seen him looking at her with tentative inquiry in his eyes.

She felt refreshed and cool, but not hungry. She thought that she would wait and see if Dino came in. She sat down on the window-seat with a book that she did not read. She smiled, seeing again Juliet's face, incandescent with happiness. That fulfilment partly assuaged her gnawing emptiness. It broke a recurring pattern of defeat. Thank Heaven that there were always other lives. In this moment she knew that there was no separation. Lord now lettest Thou thy servant depart in peace. But the remembered words meant for her only something accomplished. She had no wish to depart. It would have been a far worse blow if the doctor had told her that she was beginning to suffer, as she had sometimes nervously imagined, from some incurable disease. Life in itself was worth having. And always unpredictable. It was a question of living what there was of it on a different basis of expectation. One could, she had learned, get used to things.

There was a quick footstep on the stairs; Dino opened the door, switched on the light, and stood blinking at Ellen.

"There you are, my dear. You haven't had anything to eat? I waited to have supper until you came."

He gave her a swift, curious glance, threw down his books and came over to the window. Diffidently he touched her cheek.

"You are sad, Fenni? Of what are you thinking?"

"I am thinking that I am getting older and that I shall have no children except you."

"*Bene!* There would be no room for them in this flat!"

She burst out laughing.

"I dare say you are right! But I am very happy too. I have some exciting news for you. Juliet and Shand arrived back, and they are engaged to be married."

Dino shrugged his shoulders.

"Well, if she likes him! But I am glad that you are pleased, *carissima!*"

"I'm very pleased. Tomorrow you must help me to make a party here, a celebration!"

"And then they will go to America?"

"To England first. They are going to England on Monday to see her father. They want to get married at once so that he can take her back with him."

"And perhaps after they have gone . . . and the term is ended . . ."

"Well?"

"Perhaps then you and I may go together to Rome?"

She could have said that he had not deserved it. She did not know if it was wise. But she looked at his imploring face, she felt like a change and committed herself:

"All right, Dino! We'll go to Rome!"